About the author

I am a former broadcast journalist, now writer, and live in Deptford, London, UK.

When I worked for News & Current affairs at the BBC I travelled widely. I was standing on a hillside in Tunisia one day, looking out over the bay of Tunis. Embedded in the landscape before me was a shining doughnut of water. It turned out to be the remnants of the ancient harbour of Carthage. From that moment I began to imagine what it must have been like to live in those times and travel the seas.

The two books in The Delphis Series followed. *By the Horn of the South* is the first to be published. Its prequel, *By the Pillars of Herakles*, will follow.

First published in the UK in 2023 by SueDaviesPublishing
www.thedelphisnovels.co.uk

Design by Luke Pajak
Copy Editing by Esther Chilton

A CIP record for this book is available from the British Library

ISBN: 9781739422493
eBook ISBN: 9781739422486

BY THE HORN

— OF —

THE SOUTH

SUE DAVIES

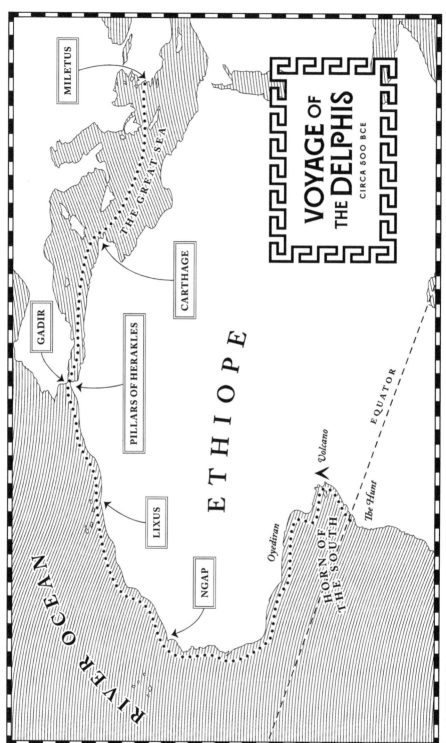

VOYAGE OF THE DELPHIS
CIRCA 500 BCE

MILETUS

THE GREAT SEA

CARTHAGE

GADIR

PILLARS OF HERAKLES

LIXUS

NGAP

ETHIOPE

RIVER OCEAN

Oyediran

HORN OF THE SOUTH

Volcano

The Hunt

EQUATOR

Star Map

It is made of fine animal skin and the marks the navigator has laid out on it have smeared at the centre, the constellations fuzzy, and the ink blobbed. 'All I had to do was lift my wrist as I marked them down,' Dubb grumbles at himself, as he runs his finger across the document, his nail cracked and hand bony. 'Instead, I've made a mess.'

On the side of the page, Orion drops down the sky like a shower of comets and the stars below have melted into dark grey water lines. Even so, he thinks, a frown gouged above bloodshot eyes, I can recognise them, those black dots on the skin; I can still see where they're supposed to be. He licks his thumb to rub at the corner of the hide and see whether the water line can be removed. It cannot. His eyes slide to the writing at the top of the map: "Days since leaving the Strait of Calpe: Season 6, 9th moon, day 12". Fortunately, that has not smudged. A heavy sigh pushes through his lips and his hair puffs about his cheeks. He looks up and along his battered vessel, The Delphis, then skywards, to the upturned bowl of blue above them. Heat haze, pale as ducks' eggs, undulates above the vessel. Low clouds cream the horizon and judder in the heavy air. An inconsistent breeze pushes them homewards and what is left of his crew keeps time to Berek's rowing tune, thrrrummmm, beat, beat, beat. The oars slice the grey-green tide beneath them, and an onshore bird swoops low over their foaming wake.

'You'll be leaving us soon,' he murmurs, as his eyes follow it. In the far back reaches of his mind, his voice adds, If it please you, Mighty Melqart, if it please you, we're going home.

As though to pray, he kneels beside the tiller platform and hunches forward to lay this star map on top of the rest. The records lie one below the other in a pile, displaying how the stars looked in the sky above The Delphis at every different stage of their journey since they first set out. The bottom one, of what might be six seasons ago, is the night they left the strait behind and Melqart was overhead as usual. He runs his finger down the edge of the pile and stops at one where the skin juts out. He raises the rest, heavy on his wrist, and peers at it. This time, Orion is a quarter of the way across, at the place where Hanno became commander and things began to go wrong. He flicks fast through the others. There's a series of blanks, which are relentless in their emptiness. This is the part of the journey where the clouds lay thick above all day and all night, where the night sky vanished and no stars could be seen. This is where the lightning began. His mind goes heavy with memory and fear. And here, with wet splodges at the bottom, is where Nyptan…. His thoughts freeze and the frown on his brow deepens as his heart races off on its own. He flaps a hand across his face. Stop looking at them, he thinks. Stop dwelling on it. He pulls his hands away and lets them all slap back into place. With his teeth clenched and mouth in a straight line, he uses both palms to smooth the top one down. He puts his thumbs at the bottom of the pile and starts to shove them all into a large roll. They overlap each other, curl in like seashells, and he lifts and juggles them under an arm while his other hand searches for the leather cylinder at his side. These are his written records, his evidence for his master, Hekataios of Miletus, of his journey with Hanno, the Carthaginian, beyond the Pillars of Herakles. He promised he would make records of everything he saw in the sky above and sea below and, blank as some are, smudged or imperfect the rest, these are them, his, the navigator's account of every day that's passed, or night sky observed, since the expedition began.

He finds their container and raises it to his nose. It is beaten about in places with long, thin scratches scored down the sides where it's caught the timbers beneath the tiller platform. Even so, the leather container holds its shape, a strong case for this precious store of goods. Each time he opens it, he sniffs inside, convinced that, despite all its time at sea, the smell of the Academy in Miletus lingers in the musty air.

A wave of longing sweeps through him, to pace the familiar docks with Hekataios, to discuss the seasons, eat Miletian food and drink Miletian wine.

His bottom lands, without warning, on the edge of the tiller platform. His knees have given way, too weak to hold him up. Yet his mind races onwards. What if we were sailing through the Pillars right now, the sun on our starboard, the tuna alongside, ploughing through the familiar waters of the Great Sea? Heat flushes through his body and infuses his head. I know these winds, the certain swell, the flights of the birds and the balm of the hillsides. He puts a hand to his forehead and it comes back to him drenched in sweat. Oh, it's the fever again. The shakes start. His heart sinks and his eyes close in resignation. It's turning my mind, making me soft, weak, cowardly. I cannot allow myself to think of home. Another thing which must just stop.

It takes all the strength he has in his torso to reach for the roll under his arm and slot it into the cylinder. The records chock into place. He clamps the lid on top, lifts them over his head by their strap and then slumps forward, elbows on his knees, head bowed as a donkey's. I must be strong. I must not give up hope. The crew needs leadership, Nyptan needs strength and oh, by the gods, I need to find my courage. I will get us back to the Great Sea safely. I will hand over my records to Hekataios, my master. I will do these things or I will die in the trying. His shoulders shake, his throat longs for water, the day's heat rises and makes his blood boil.

The Enquiry – Day 1

The sky maps are under the navigator's arm when The Delphis docks in Gadir at the entrance to the Great Sea. Months, years, a lifetime, it seems, have passed. He tries to stand upright, a commander before his army. Part of the leather cylinder is green with mould; the top is flattened and it's lost its shape. It leaves a residue of brown muck on his calloused hands, where the leather disintegrates, and it feels slimy to the touch. Many moons have come and gone since he last opened it. He has had it across his back, slept on it, lent against it, used it as a head rest, a baton even, yet here it sits, in the crook of his elbow as Chares, the first mate, throws the hawser across the short gap of water between The Delphis and the wharf to pull the vessel in. Dubb's fuddled brain can scarcely credit what's happening to them. We're nearly home!

He swaps the cylinder to his other arm and drags at the gangway with his right hand. It doesn't move, so weak has he become. A mariner, one of the ones lent to them by the Governor of Lixus to get them home, gives it a heave. He and the rest of his temporary crewmen cheer as the gangway goes down. Oars clatter in the rowlocks and the men spring up, ready to move. The old crew, too ill to stand, let alone cheer, now begin the struggle to disembark.

Dubb turns to look for Nyptan. She is coming from their quarters behind the tiller platform, head shielded by a mantle, body stooped. Tanu, their budding daughter, holds her up on one side and Qart, the ship's boy, on the other. His wife's eyes are hollowed out beneath that cloth, he knows, and her hands tremble. By the gods! Look kindly on us, Melqart, he thinks. Save us, get us home. He takes the weight of her body at the top of the gangway, her on one side, the star maps on the other. They move at a sea slug's pace down the wooden frets and, at the bottom, he stops and turns to look behind. He wants to see every last one of his crew off the floating wreck, which is his vessel, The Delphis.

The Lixitanians descend smartly. They skip off through the cargo and loading bays and into the town without a backward look. They'll be back off down the coast again to Lixus on the tide, and all the bars and whorehouses of Gadir are open and waiting.

Next, comes the gang of boys from Libya, the ones they took with them. At some point in their unforgiving journey, they switched from supporting the young lordling to supporting Dubb and his crew. Almost all of them are plagued with fever and one has a hand missing. Shadra, their unofficial leader, falls to the stones on the quayside to kiss them.

Of this own dear gang, the last to leave because most disabled, there are very few. Qart, his ship's boy, the wild-haired, wavy-browed boy, who is more a son to him than his own, comes off first. He carries Nyptan's remedy bag and his own few things wrapped in a cloth. Berek, who lost his precious aulis at the Horn of the South, and yet made fresh pipes from reed, comes next. He limps, his ankle the size of a melon, the sticks and drums he has collected along the way threaten to scatter. Chares, first mate, laid low with fever, though you'd never know it, has his arms full too. He carries his own possessions and, slung around his waist, Rabs's small bundle. And Rabs - Rabs the expert seaman, Rabs the wit, Rabs who could always see a funny side even in the worst circumstances - Rabs is a wraith. Dubb's belly twists and he bites his lip, the small man's absence a yawning hole. He should be here with us, skipping down the gangway and cracking a joke. Wherever you are, Rabs, we wish you well, Dubb thinks, and squeezes Nyptan's arm. Gone to the land of the water spirits at the Delta? Gone to the women who admired you? Nyptan replies with a broken sigh. We miss you, Rabs, we all do.

There are other absences too, people Dubb cared for and many he didn't: the interpreters, Kama and his friends, left behind in their own land; the Etruscan diviners - he doesn't miss them and their persistent droning; but most of all, he's glad to be rid of Lord Hanno, the young Carthaginian prince, who took command of The Delphis as they sailed to the Horn of the South and then abandoned them to their fate. Well, good riddance to you, thinks Dubb, and squeezes the star maps under his arm. You didn't get these, you self-serving lordling.

The braying voice of an aristocrat from Carthage cuts through the weight of his exhaustion. It slips around the crates and slithers across the pallets to pin him to this very spot where, years ago, he heard it for the first time. Oh no, he thinks. It's not him, is it? It can't be, after all these years.

'Where are they?' it says. 'Find them!'

In an instant, the difficulties of the voyage vanish from his mind. Into their place snaps an image of the most supercilious bureaucrat in all the Western Sea, the face of Apsan Azrupal Nimiran, the Commissioner for the Carthage Board of Trade in Gadir. This is a man for whom no murder is too small, no action too vicious, if it is done in the name of the wonderful city of Carthage.

Panic floods the pit of the navigator's stomach. Why is he here? How does he know we've arrived? He's not coming for us, is he?

Before he can decide what to do next, or even raise an alarm, around from behind a stack of cargo comes a tall, spindly man with thin, greying hair and a glossy, young one with jewels in his hair, at their service, a group of heavily armed guards.

'That's them! Take them!' says his lordship. With a flurry of clanking weapons and thudding feet, the navigator's arms are wrenched behind his back, his ankles manacled.

The strong arms, which drag their wasted bodies across the square towards the Customs House, are not gentle. Dubb twists and turns, and is thwacked across the back of his head with something heavy. Chares, Berek and Nyptan cry out for help as they, too, are detained. They are hauled, heads shoved towards the ground, across the crowded docks. Behind him, he hears Apsan's voice, 'Impound this vessel.' In a burst of violence and speed, all the people Dubb holds dear in his life are yanked, carried or thrown into custody, dragged down the stairs of a great building, through heavy doors, into a large undercroft.

Dubb is hurled into soft sand. Nyptan, Tanu and Qart all follow, skeletal wrecks, piling in heaps against the walls. The door slams shut. Its clang ricochets off the stone. Weak shafts of light bear down from the outside, distant cries of the dockside seep in through the sky-lights and silence falls.

What is this? thinks Dubb, head pounding. Why this welcome without the welcome? Why are we being detained? Nyptan's cries wash round the chamber and Tanu's voice murmurs in comfort. He squeezes his arms to his torso to feel for the star maps. Not there. He lifts his shoulders up. No, no straps across his back. Not lying beside him on the sand. He rolls over to search the cellar. With heavy lids, his eyes trail across the sand. His throat is dry; he cannot swallow and tears fizz behind his lids. They've taken my star maps, he thinks. Ripped from my arms, just as I'm home. They've stolen my most precious record of the voyage. Cold dread seeps into his bones. All that work I've done for Hekataios - the whole grim story of our voyage with Hanno, the Carthaginian, to the Horn of the South, gone. Is it really so?

He blinks, his eyelids a means of resetting what he sees in the world. His head expands to rival the sun and his tongue feels huge for want of water. He crawls on his elbows towards Nyptan at the cellar wall, puts a hand out to her. His head drops heavily against the stones. They cool him and his arm remains crooked, as though the star cylinder remains nestled in it, as he falls into oblivion.

* * *

The cylinder lies, rancid, on a work table in the upstairs room of Lord Apsan's official residence in Gadir. Its slimy end shimmers green amongst wax tablets and it has a whiff of dead sea snake about it. The Commissioner for Trade wrinkles his nose.

'Cover that thing, Tasii?' he says, and flaps a hand at it. 'It's worse than a garum factory.' The ageing lord is Head of the Board of Trade, the most senior representative of the State of Carthage on the Western Sea. Prince-like, he presides over all traffic of silver and tin, in and out of Gadir, a frontier town perched on the edge of a shallow bay just beyond the Strait of Calpe. Or the Pillars of Herakles as the Hellenes like to call the place, so given to romance their poets are. Tasiioonos of Knutes, his secretary and confidante in the trying task of bringing order to anarchy, is beautiful, glossy and his slave.

Tasii puts down his writing tablet with a sigh. His hips swing as he weaves his way through the cluttered work tables to the reeking object. With well-toned arms, he lifts his mantle over his head and casts it, cape-like, over the cylinder to smother it completely. Wooden boxes and packing crates litter Lord Apsan's upstairs workroom, a jumble of parchment, velum, tablets, records going back decades of tax years, all the business of running a trading emporium at the edge of the known world. A shipment of terracottas has just arrived, strewn across official documents or stacked in boxes against the wall.

His lordship sits by the window in the sunshine and pops the last of a bunch of grapes into his mouth to suck. The plump fruit flattens to a pulp at pressure from his tongue and his eyes flick to the plate beside him, empty now except for a carcass of stems. If only Tasiioonos, my lovely boy, was not quite so determined to fix my gut problem, he thinks, and shifts in his seat, I could be sliding a lamprey through my lips right now. His legs splay out in front of him like a stick insect and the almond trees beyond the window rustle in the rising heat. The bay beyond gleams in the morning light.

At that moment, Adyat, his lordship's house girl, arrives at the top of the stairs carrying a large beaker of liquid from the kitchen below. It, too, has a whiff of animal about it. Oh, Baal's balls, time for that, thinks Lord Apsan, and his eyes flick to Tasii, who returns the look, severe. If only I wasn't such a slave to my slave. He closes his eyes and pretends to doze.

'My lord,' he hears Tasii say. 'My lord, I know you are awake.' His slave's stiff finger prods him on the shoulder.

Lord Apsan winces and opens his eyes. 'Well, I certainly am now, Tasiioonos. Can't a sick man take a restorative snooze in the sunshine without being woken?' He takes the beaker from his slave's hand.

Another hefty sigh comes from deep inside Tasiioonos's chest. The young man's fine head is crowned with a richly jewelled wrap and in the sculpted hollow of his neck hangs a pendant of beaten silver in the shape of a horse's head with garnets for eyes.

'Please forgive me, my lord, if I am mistaken, but you did say, didn't you, that you wanted me to supervise you in this regime however inconvenient or bad tempered you became?' His slave's voice has taken on an unwelcome edge, one Lord Apsan has heard before.

'Quite right, I did,' says Lord Apsan, and swills the concoction round and round in its terracotta. No point in getting Tasii worked up so early in the day. 'That doesn't mean I wish to be disturbed at every hour of the day or night, whenever it suits you.'

'That's what being on a course of treatment means, your lordship,' says his slave, his voice sharper still. 'Your body doesn't stop because you've fallen asleep.'

The commissioner clamps his jaws together. He's going to get a lecture. He can feel it coming on. As indeed it does.

'If you wish to be treated at the Temple of Melqart, for instance, that's a different story,' says Tasiioonos. 'In their hands, liquid medicine may not be required. The high priest might shove you into a sacred pool to be worked on by one of his lackeys. Or he could charge you a fortune for one of his remedies. Or he could paw and poke you personally. It's your choice.' Tasii shrugs and stands right in front of his lord to wait. 'In that event, you just need to remember that I will not be held responsible for anything which happens to you.'

Lord Apsan puts his nose to the smelly vessel and his head jerks back in shock. 'Should you, however, wish to avoid the temple and all its works,' continues Tasii, tone abrasive as he eyes his lordship's antics with irritation, 'you will drink what has been prescribed for you by the healers of Tartessos. Our holy men are at least as good as yours.' Here, his tone changes. 'And please, Oh Great Hipolito, bring health and happiness to his lordship and wealth to his house.' He bends his head, steps backwards as if in oblation and lifts the horse pendant from his neck to kiss it.

'Oh alright, alright,' says Lord Apsan, and lifts the liquid to his lips without drinking. 'No need to get sanctimonious.'

'Well, I can't go through this every time you need a purgative.'

Lord Apsan gives the beaker several short sniffs. His mouth goes down at the corners and his eyes bulge.

'Now sip it, my lord. Slowly. And when you have done, can I suggest we get on to the main business of the day?' Tasiioonos turns to the worktable and reaches for his writing tablet.

Lord Apsan does not sip. Instead, he runs at the drink like a stallion facing a mare. He knocks the purgative back and brings the beaker down on the table with a crash. The liquid is thick in his lordship's mouth. It tastes, and smells, of mule piss. A grimace the size of Gadir bay spreads across his face and, as the liquid reaches his stomach, he convulses, throwing his head back at first and then forward between his knees.

'Yughhhh, yughhhh,' he gags. 'Yugghhhhhh.' The brown concoction, together with all the grapes and his breakfast, lands on the tiles in front of them, splattering their sandals.

'Errrrhhhhg,' yelps Tasii, and leaps out of the way. 'My lord, I told you to sip it! Sip! Not swill like a dying sailor with his last drink.' His neck goes stiff and his lovely mouth forms wrinkles in disgust. 'Adyat!' he shouts downstairs, 'Adyat!' A female voice responds from below. 'A bucket, cloths and mop. Up here now, please. His lordship's been sick!'

Lord Apsan sits back in his chair, eyes streaming, and wipes the back of his hand across his mouth. Adyat clunks up the stairs, wooden pail bumping against her shins. The handle of a too tall mop pokes around at the air above her head. She does not lift her eyes from the floor and gets to work on the watery mess.

His lordship arcs forward, takes a cloth from the table and flicks at his splattered sandals from a seated position. Flecks of masticated grape fly all over the room, to its crates and writing tablets.

'Here, leave it!' Tasii drags his lordship's arm out of the way. He gets down on his knees and dabs at his lord's sandals with a wet cloth. Then he leans back on his haunches and points. 'Now, stand over there,' he orders, 'and let Adyat get on with her job.'

His lordship pushes his chair back and moves away. The girl works on the vomit without complaint. Surprising to Lord Apsan, his insides feel much better now. He gives his stomach a little pat and glances absent-mindedly out the window. Far on the other side of the bay, company vessels laden with tin and silver from mines up country move in rows, ant-like, along the shoreline of the peninsula. The sun is getting up and the water shimmers. Sploshes from Adyat's mop punctuate the silence of the workroom.

'We have today's records in, Tasiioonos, don't we?' he asks, mind toying with official duties. 'No trader's tried to defraud us overnight? No company theft?' He turns and cocks his head to look at his slave.

His secretary squats on the gleaming tiles, head down, cleaning his own sandals. 'The tallies add up,' says Tasii, voice muffled, and he uncurls to chuck the soiled cloth into Adyat's bucket. 'The figures show all loads, vessels, incomings and outgoings are correct.' He flexes his thighs and stands.

Adyat picks up the bucket and clumps downstairs.

Such well-formed limbs, thinks his lordship, and steps over to Tasiioonos, just as his slave stretches to full height. Tasiioonos's face arrives at Lord Apsan's chest, and his lordship reaches down and cups a hand under his chin.

Tasii looks up and smiles, lashes long. He leans up to give his lordship a quick kiss on the lips.

'I hope you are feeling better now, my lord,' he says. 'Stomach settled?' His eyes are deep brown with flecks of gold.

Lord Apsan's heart leaps. Perhaps we can have a day off. Perhaps we can go to the bathhouse and enjoy ourselves. A broad smile cracks his aged face, and he reaches his arms around Tasii's waist and bends to kiss him. Tasii pushes him off with a hand and steps back to the worktable.

'Why not look at the tallies yourself, my lord?' says his slave, voice too bright, head shaking "no" as he does so. 'They're just there.' He points to them and turns on his heel to walk towards the wooden boxes, packing crates and the smelly cylinder. He lifts the edge of its covering to peek beneath.

His lordship's mouth collapses in on itself. 'No,' says Lord Apsan, 'I don't want to work. I want time with you!' The skin at his chin vibrates in irritation and his eyes pinch together. Why is Tasiioonos always so hard to woo? Why must I want him above all the rest? Others have come to me much more willingly. 'Can't we leave work for today and spend time on our own?' He tries hard to remove the pleading tone from his voice.

'We are always on our own,' says Tasii, voice flat. 'There are no others.'

Lord Apsan nods and his jaw goes slack. That's certainly true, he thinks, and the sunshine turns from bright to brittle. Here we are, cut adrift from Carthage, the greatest city in the world, flung to the furthest reaches of its power, abandoned. Egypt, the Hellenes, even the Parses, are more advanced than this dump. Gadir remains little more than a grubby bazaar however hard I work to improve the place. He listens as a donkey brays at the back of his residence and a rooster marks the time of day. How cut off we are from the rich and powerful, the great clusters of state departments on Byrsa Hill, the temples, markets, the influential people with whom I might mix on the shores of the Bay of Tunis.

'Can we now, perhaps, get on with today's work?' says Tasii, still at the boxes. He lifts the mantle completely from the cylinder and bends to look at it closely. 'We're falling behind.'

'What work?' says Lord Apsan, voice thin. 'I thought you just said all the tallies were in and nothing was amiss.' His eyes drift to the packing cases. 'Unless you mean all these new terracottas from the factory.'

He steps, tentative, over to a work table to lift one of many unpacked boxes. Straw spills out as he removes it and floats to the floor. 'Is this where the good stuff is?' he asks, and looks up at Tasiioonos, eyes hopeful. The artefacts from down the coast, packed in the newly arrived crates, need to get to market as soon as possible. They could do it today.

'No, my lord, not the boxes, keen on them as you are. The enquiry, remember? You have an enquiry to conduct?'

'Of course I remember,' says Lord Apsan, close enough to Tasii now to smell his sweat. 'There's always that kind of work to do. But why should we be in a rush to start it?' His eyes flick through the straw. Amulets nestle amongst it. *If he won't come to the bathhouse, at least we might find something new and amusing amongst this lot.*

'Then you'll also recall you were given three moons to reply,' says his secretary, voice mild, finger poised to poke at the cylinder. 'You know how fussy they are back on Byrsa Hill about speed.' It lands on the rotting leather and comes away sticky with residue. He rubs it down his thigh.

'Well, Byrsa Hill need give me no lessons in response time,' says Lord Apsan, voice resigned and imperious. He returns to the work table by the window and picks up a toothpick. 'The time it takes to get an answer back from them is enough to send a man grey before his time, as you can see.' He smooths back the long strands of hair, which cover his bald patch, then puts the ivory to his mouth to have good old dig.

'I only relay that they want a summary of Lord Hanno's expedition from you by the next new moon and the full report soon after.' His slave lifts the cylinder and tries to turn the contents out. They do not budge.

'Can't you leave that thing alone and join me?'

Tasii is not listening. He has got hold of his writing stick and is poking it into the hole.

Lord Apsan was pleased at first, flattered even, to be invited by the Senate Committee in Carthage to make a report on one of the city's rising sons. *Me, here in faraway Gadir,* he had thought. *I am known to them on Byrsa Hill. The great aristocrats, be they from the Senate or the Supreme Council, have selected me above others.* And he had put a hand to his chest and inclined his head as if presenting his findings in person on the capitol floor. *I am to pass judgement on a Magonid, a scion son of the great city, to investigate how his expedition went, whether he is fit to lead at war.* He had breathed deep of the aroma of success. He would wear a linen kilt made specially for the purpose, with a mauve band running down the side, not too showy, just a nod to reflect his status as the representative of Carthage in the Western Sea. He would be feted, banqueted and retire to the capital in style.

Now, however, things appear rather different. Hanno, the Magonid, has returned from his adventures after years at sea and, instead of paying him any respects, has absconded from Gadir without reporting to him even once. What will Byrsa Hill say about that?! Next, the remainder of his expedition turns up half-dead, unable to speak at all it seems. Getting to the bottom of all this is going to be like wringing purple from the shell. Such hard work.

'Tasii, put that filthy thing outside!' he says testily, and puts a cloth to his nose. 'We will examine it later.'

'I've just about got it now,' says his slave, and bangs one end of the cylinder on the work table. The items inside thud, his tablets jump and Tasii's neck goes long to look. 'They're really solid.' He takes the other end of the cylinder, and his arms fly up and down like a hammer. Out the contents slide to land heavily on his mantle. 'Oh, they're vellum,' he mutters, as he scans them, brows down.

Lord Apsan cannot help himself. He gets up, crosses the room and looks over Tasii's shoulder. 'Why did that navigator have them?' says his lordship, mouth pruned. 'Alright, let's get on with the day.' He reaches to full height to yawn and stretch, then turns away from the smelly mystery and begins to pace up and down in front of the work benches to dictate a response to Carthage.

'So let's start with what we know for certain.'

Tasii gives a small nod and a look of satisfaction crosses his face. He removes his hands from the sodden mess, swipes them down his tunic and moves at once to the work table to write.

'More than three seasons ago, Lord Hanno, with sixty penteconters, supply vessels and thousands of settlers sets off from Carthage to find new markets outside the Great Sea. Agreed?'

'Must we really go that far back now, my lord?' asks his slave. 'Can't we start with the latest events first? Here? Now?'

His lordship's brows rise and he stops to look at Tasiioonos. 'Very well, if you wish, we can begin with the present, though eventually we'll have to write it all down in sequence. More recently then…' The commissioner resumes his pacing. 'Six sailing seasons after leaving Gadir as head of a great and glorious expedition, he, Hanno, the Magonid son from

Carthage, returns to Gadir with one penteconter, scarcely enough men to row it and no support vessels. He fails to report to me, Commissioner for the Board of Trade, as per instructions…' Lord Apsan stops in his tracks. 'No, no, don't say that. Leave a big blank. We'll come back to it. Security is still looking for him, aren't they, and they might still get him.'

Tasii's stylus stops and a look of weariness crosses his face. 'Agreed, we are still looking. Surely the critical question for the moment must be, mustn't it, why has this Hellenic vessel, The Delphis, with its famous navigator and experienced crew, turned up apparently abandoned by Lord Hanno along the way? Isn't that what we should focus on for the moment? You have a cellar full of emaciated and ill people and, aside from attending to their needs, you should take their first-hand accounts as testimony.'

'It's a bit more complicated than that,' says Lord Apsan, a frown on his face. 'In writing the report there'll need to be at least three strands: what each person says happened, whether it actually happened and what was the outcome. Beyond all that is what did the expedition accomplish? And was Hanno responsible for it? What a ridiculously broad remit Carthage has given me!' His lordship's eyes flash. 'It'll take weeks!'

'All the more reason to start soon, my lord.'

A great sigh extrudes itself from Lord Apsan's lips and he slumps forward to pace. 'Yesterday, a vessel named The Delphis, one of Hanno's supporting craft, and most unusual because it's Hellenic, arrives back in Gadir. Its crew is half-dead and the vessel itself is a wreck containing nothing of value. Shame about that,' he interrupts himself. 'I wish there'd been gold stashed in it somewhere.'

'My lord,' says Tasii testily, and stamps his foot.

Lord Apsan's nostrils flare and he glares at his slave. 'On the contrary, it looks like it has been through a real battering. The famed navigator, Dubb of Miletus, does carry one thing, which might be valuable, though it is not treasure. Documents…' Here, his lordship pauses and then explodes with irritation. 'How can I describe them? We haven't even looked at them yet. Leave another blank space!' His eyes sweep across to the cylinder in fury as if it is responsible for the size of his task.

'Security told me they had to threaten to dislocate the man's arm before he would hand over the cylinder. They nearly did it!' Tasii says, eyes wide.

Lord Apsan shrugs. 'I imprisoned the crew of The Delphis in case they, too, should decide to leave without trace and the only question remaining thereafter is, what happened to the treasure?'

'Assuming there was any,' says Tasiioonos, continuing to write.

'Well, of course there would have been treasure!' says his lordship, and stops his pacing. 'For Melqart's sake, you can't travel all that way past Lixus and come back with nothing!'

Tasii's brows lift, head to one side. 'The vessel is wrecked.'

'Just so. A further matter is why was the expedition so demanding? And why didn't Lord Hanno stay at the head of it until the very end? Is he the type of commander who sees his commission through when things get difficult, or one who abandons his post and saves his own skin? If so, he is not good material to lead Carthage into war.'

The cicadas raise their level a notch or two in the almond trees outside and, in the distance, seagulls cry.

'Gatit,' roars Lord Apsan, and the tablets and rolls of papyrus in his lordship's workroom quiver at the sound of his voice.

'Yes, my lord,' replies a voice, at once, from outside the door of the workroom. A head pops round the lintel. It is Lord Apsan's bodyguard, round and hairless, with a mild expression on his face. The man himself follows, large, with big biceps adorned by a leather thong. He walks uncertainly on the balls of his feet.

'Tell security to bring the prisoners here.'

'Yes, sir. Do you want them all up together, sir? Or one at a time?'

Lord Apsan sighs. 'Oh, bring them up all at once. Let's get this wretched enquiry underway as soon as possible.'

* * *

They trail in, the crew of The Delphis, clutching at one another as if being out of touch, even for a moment, will bring certain death. First, comes the woman, a faded thing, ill and stooped, a torn mantle partly covering her face and her tunic with holes. Obviously beautiful once, she is gaunt with exhaustion, lips cracked, hands bone thin. She uses them to cover her face more securely and to keep hold of a girl who follows her. The girl is about Adyat's age, body at the dawn of womanhood, hair tied back tight and with deep circles under her eyes.

The men come next. One is bald and a Hellene, with a foreign garment slung around his shoulders. Another hops on a stick, an ankle the size of a melon.

Then there is a very skinny lad with thick curls haloing his head. His eyes fly all around the room and his eyebrows wave, it seems, at his every passing thought.

Last in the line is the navigator, Dubb of Miletus, a man who Lord Apsan knows only too well. In the course of his many years as Commissioner for Trade at Gadir, they've crossed paths before, though it's true that, this time, the man's much changed. Lord Apsan didn't recognise him at first on the dock yesterday. Thin as a pole, a husk of an individual, hair chopped back to the scalp, bloodshot eyes and shaking with fever. All of them are the same, attacked by wind, sun and tide, each at the rough end of the sea. The navigator can scarcely put one foot in front of the other without teetering.

They settle in a line against the wall. 'You are the original crew of The Delphis?' he says, voice harsh. He doesn't wait for a reply. 'Where's the rest of the expedition? Are you all that's left?' His head tips to one side. The group sits silent in front of him. No one, it appears, has the strength to reply. The window casts morning light across the floor and the cursed rooster is at it again. He's going to have to put the fear of the gods into the prisoners it seems. 'Answer me!' he shouts, and moves closer to the windows to be sure his face remains obscure. Despite their ragged state, you cannot afford to show sympathy to witnesses like this and this navigator is a clever man who can easily cause trouble. 'Do you know why you are here?' he asks, voice ringing around the dusty shelves, crates and stacked tablets. 'I have been asked by the powers that be in Carthage to report on the great expedition of Lord Hanno, the Magonid princeling of Byrsa Hill, to the lands beyond Lixus at the extremities of the known world. Do you know what happened there?'

The woman, it seems, cannot take even this simple question. Deep, croaking, clamouring wails pour from her without warning. Lord Apsan's head goes back in disgust. Tears gouge the filth of her cheeks in rivers and the daughter puts her arms around her. They clutch at each other's hands, heads down and weep together. The prisoners' heads turn, all along the line and their eyes seek out the women. None of them says a word. Baal's balls, thinks Lord Apsan. Is she a witch?

'What is it?' he snaps at the woman.

She glances up at him, eyes big, before her chin drops and she is silent. Lord Apsan turns to look at Tasii, brows high.

His secretary rises from his work table, gets a beaker of water from the jug by the door and offers it to the woman, who takes it and leaves it in her hands without touching it.

Tasii also brings his lordship a beaker of his own, which he places beside him on the table. 'Sip,' he says under his breath. 'Slowly.'

Lord Apsan lifts the beaker to his mouth, takes a tiny glug and pulls a face before he carries on. 'When we are ready,' he blurts, and eyes the woman with irritation. He rubs his stomach. What's she doing on such a voyage in any case? he thinks. No wonder it went wrong. 'I repeat, this investigation is being carried out on behalf of the principal powers in Carthage. It is the Senate and Supreme Council that have asked me, their representative in the West, to uncover the circumstances, details and outcome of the journey you have just returned from. Do you understand?' he asks, as if speaking to dogs.

'He wasn't up to the job,' comes the navigator's voice from the end of the row. His voice is cracked, loud. 'He's a fraud.'

Lord Apsan's head whips round to look at the navigator with narrowed eyes. This man has always been a nuisance. It was him, this very man, who almost ended Apsan's career as Trade Commissioner in Gadir seasons ago. 'By the mighty milk of Melqart's mother, I'll take no disruption from you, Navigator,' he spits. 'You'll speak when you are spoken to and not before.'

'I thought you wanted to know...' the man protests. But then the puff goes out of him and he falls back against the wall, eyes closed.

Lord Apsan runs his eyes along the whole miserable lot of them. What with the women snivelling, this man sleeping, the rest of them stinking and half-dead, if they think they're going to get around me, get control of this investigation, then they have another thing coming. 'I am the one in charge here!' he says. 'Can you hear me?' His eyes go from one to the next in search of life. 'I am Lord Apsan, Trade Commissioner for Carthage in the port of Gadir.' His voice rises. 'I will ask the questions, you will answer them. That's the way we will proceed. Do you understand?' He sits back.

The silence grows sullen and Lord Apsan is at the point of ordering security up to whip a rapid response from the lot of them, when he sees the navigator sliding sideways along the wall and onto the floor. Foam bubbles from the corner of his mouth. His forehead runs with sweat and one elbow lifts and lowers as though he wants to fly.

'My lord, you've got to help him, you must!' says the boy with the wavy hair, and staggers to his feet. 'He's going to die otherwise.

Please, sir,' he says, 'give him some water.' The lad is halfway across the room, arms out to the water amphora, which stands by the door.

'Stay exactly where you are!' commands Lord Apsan, and Tasiioonos catches the boy by the arm and swings him round to stand directly in front of his lordship, hands held tight behind his back. 'Where do you think you're going?'

The boy, unsteady on his feet, starts to slip to the floor. Tasii holds him up. 'To help Dubb, sir,' he says. 'Otherwise, he'll die of fever like the others.' A sob convulses his chest and he looks, with resentment, at his lordship.

'Who are you? What's your name?'

'I'm Qart, from Carthage, sir, the ship's boy from The Delphis. Please, sir, help the navigator,' he says, and a sob leaks from his mouth unbidden.

'Oh, throw some water over the navigator, Tasii?' he says, and his secretary lets Qart go. The boy's knees give way, and he staggers back to the wall and slips down it until he hits the floor. 'We're never going to get anywhere with the witnesses in this state.'

'They need time to recover, my lord,' says Tasiioonos, and upends a whole amphora of water across the navigator's foaming head. 'They need food and water.'

His lordship sucks at his front teeth and the line deepens between his brows. 'Well, we'd better give them something or we'll get nowhere with this examination. Just take their names and ranks for now. And by the mighty milk of Melqart's mother, get them out of here before I lose my patience completely.'

Particulars handed over to Tasiioonos, the men gather Dubb to them and carry him down the stairs, the boy leading the way, the woman and girl following behind.

'And make no mistake about it,' he calls after them, 'you will be back here first thing tomorrow morning to answer my questions. I am not being kind, or giving you a reprieve. I follow protocols from Carthage that state witnesses must be well enough to give testimony. Nothing about this voyage will escape my notice, do you hear?! Nothing!'

* * *

Yet Lord Apsan's investigation begins nearly a moon later, the witnesses taking their time, it seems, to eat, sleep, bathe and recover. By then, his lordship, impatient to get his hideous job over with, declares them fit enough to speak. In a hearing, which takes far longer than he ever could have imagined was possible, the Commissioner for Trade in Gadir questions the crew of The Delphis. With the help of his secretary, Tasiioonos of Knutes, a story gradually emerges, a version of events which they said took place when Hanno, the Magonid prince from Carthage, was in charge of a great flotilla of people and vessels searching for treasure and glory at the edge of the Earth.

Landing in Lixus

Great shards of water form high in the air and drop to pummel Qart's face and body like blows from the sky. The boy doubles over to protect himself and feels the contents of his stomach rising towards his mouth. He rushes for the topside and thrusts his head over the rail. At his feet, the deck bucks and slews and he bends his knees to ride it. He grabs a cable to stop himself from being pitched overboard. In front of him, there is only the mottled sea, rolling, heaving, lashing towards him in uneven waves. What emerges from his lips are long strands of bile and spit. No sooner have they left his mouth than the wind catches them. They undulate low, skimming the water like skinny petrels, before dropping to pulverise in the spume. He closes his eyes and retches until his whole body aches. The Delphis lifts, sail squeaks, beams crack and ballast shifts in the hull. He turns to look back towards the stern. Crew, diviners and healers are all at the mercy of the swell. Only Dubb driving at the tiller, he sees, through half-closed eyes, has a smile on his face.

Land. Surely there must be land soon, he thinks, and his eyes sweep forward, past the bow. But the wind roars in his ears, flattens his hair against the back of his head and whips his curls forwards into his eyes, to blind him. He pushes them out of the way. Across the tops of the brine, the vessel leaps and pivots, and he grips the topside and stares, as before, into grey-green swathes of salt water and their sprawling meadows of foam. How I hate River Ocean, he thinks, how I hate this.

The thin voice of a priest pierces his ears, the rest lost in the air. 'Where is that boy...? ...never here when he's wanted...' A heavy hand comes down on his shoulder and he is dragged away from the topside in the muscular arms of the chicken keeper. The man smells foul.

'Did you bring the birds? Where are they?' asks the voice.

Qart looks up to find himself at the prow, surrounded by diviners. The priest talking to him is tall and wears a pointed hat tied under his chin. He has one elbow hooked around a hawser to steady himself as the vessel rolls. In his other hand, he brandishes an axe.

'I couldn't do it, my lords,' he shouts, and shakes his head. They do not hear him and continue to glare. His hands reach for a cable and his feet splay wide. 'Water floods the hull if I open the hatch.' Do they speak Punic or must he explain all this again in a foreign language? 'Like this, see!' The Delphis does a swoop and a dive, and water mounts the topside and sheets across the deck. 'The chickens will drown.'

The diviners jump for safety and jostle out of the way.

'Errrrh!'

'Not again!'

'Great Tages, save me!' a young one shrieks, as slate-grey swill swirls beneath his feet, upends him and carries him forward on his bum towards a port hole. He is hoisted to his feet by the older men and soothed by his young companion in muttered words, which Qart cannot hear.

'Then we should do stones instead,' says another man, who steps forward towards the diviners to be heard better. He wears a cloak attached at the shoulder by a silver clasp. 'I'm sure there's a precedent.'

The priests nod and cluck, and rearrange themselves into a shallow curve at the prow of The Delphis. One by one, their eyes find Qart, who perches out of the wet on a coil of hawser.

'Well, what's your problem?' says the chicken man beside him. 'Go and get the altar, you stupid boy. They're waiting.' He lurches over to push at Qart's shoulder with his finger.

Baal's balls, thinks Qart. Do these diviners never stop praying, even in the middle of a gale?

'And bring the cup,' says the man with the clasp. 'The leather one.'

Knees bent against the swell, Qart clutches his way through the holy men to the storage space beneath the prow. The Delphis's figurehead nods and plunges into the foam before him, its crudely carved dolphin much loved by its original crew. It has protected them through high seas and low days for seasons beyond the boy's memory, and he touches his finger to its fin before descending beneath the wooden struts to the space beneath. He squeezes himself in between oiled beams. The spot reeks of rats' shit and hangs with cobwebs. An ornate wooden altar is hooked over a nail on the inside of the decking timber and he turns himself around, trying not to hit his head on the swell. At least I'll not get washed overboard from this space, he thinks, and lifts his arms to unhook it. He wriggles round to shove it past his torso and into the open with his feet. Someone snatches it away. Ranged above and beside him in the tiny space, tied to beams or jammed between timbers, are a variety of containers, round, flat-bottomed, of iron, leather, rattan, terracotta, with writing on them, numbers, scrawls he can't understand. He grabs what he thinks is the right leather cup from a hook above his head and doubles over to pass it out along his legs.

By the time he has backed into the open air, the diviners have pinned their altar to the deck and range around it chanting. One of the priests is making a bad job of the aulis. 'Nee roh, kee roh, shumbaleth rah,' or something like that, Qart thinks, as he tries to understand the words they intone. The priests latch on tight to cables and thwarts, and stamp their feet in time as best they can on The Delphis's sliding boards. As well as the ones with the pointy hat and the tall one with the silver clasp, there are two young priests who seem exactly alike to Qart, both smooth-chinned and competitive. There's another one, too, with no neck to speak of, his head set so low on his shoulders that he may be the same size from groin to pate.

Qart scowls at them and sighs. I suppose I'm going to get to know exactly who you all are and what you are saying, whether I like it or not, he thinks. He braces himself and closes his eyes. Nausea has returned and he works at keeping his stomach calm. There's no point in trying to slip away, he thinks, between bouts of bile. The minute I leave, they'll call me back to do something else inane. Despite the wildness of the deck, his mind focusses entirely on his insides. So much for being the navigator's boy, he thinks. So much for helping Dubb with his charts. Chicken keeper's slave is more like it. The priests drone on.

Over the roar of the wind, the dirge intensifies and Qart opens his eyes to see the tall priest make a stab at choosing a few coloured stones from a collection held out for him in a leather case. It swings sideways several times and, when he eventually gets hold of a few, he slips them, as best he can, into the leather cup. 'Nee roh, kee roh, shumbaleth rah,' he says. His voice rises, the chanting swells, and the priests link arms and stamp their feet.

The one with the thick neck kneels down to hold out a large, wide bowl and the tall one whirls his cup above his head. 'Great Tinia, I call on you,' he says, and shuffles his feet. 'Nethuns, tell us when we should land.' He hurls the stones downwards at the bowl.

The Delphis hits a wave as they are in transit. The vessel jerks to starboard and rolls to port. Everything and everyone: priests, stones, bowl, crew and Qart are thrown sideways. The stones ricochet in all directions, tumble along the boards, fly on the wind and are swilled into the hawsers.

Oh no, thinks Qart, and jumps up to grab at them and stop them being washed overboard. He pounces on two and traps another between his foot and a beam. Several more are heading for the port hole.

'Hey you, stop that!' Someone grabs his arm and yanks him out of the way. He falls backwards onto the deck.

'But they're being washed overboard!' he says, and he looks up to see the faces of the diviners all gathered round him, mouths open in protest.

'What have you done? You mustn't touch them!' one of the young ones says, and kicks at him.

'You've desecrated the holy stones!' says the other, and bends to snatch them out of his hand.

'I was told by your master that you know about stones,' says the man with the thick neck. 'You don't. Return them to us at once and remove yourself from this sacred space.'

Qart crawls away from them. What does he care about their stupid rituals? With leaden eyes, he sees Nyptan and Tanu hugging the starboard rail at stern. They, too, are suffering. He lifts a hand to them, which they fail to see. Rabs and Chares lean against cargo and laugh at midships, both of them content to swing in wide arcs up and down as The Delphis rides the waves. Likewise, the crew of Lepcitanians. Oars securely stowed, they almost slouch against the top rail and watch the slapping sea over the side. Dubb, the Navigator, his master, the man he most admires in all the world, continues to guide The Delphis, hair lashed in a pony tail against the wind, arms and feet braced, exhalation on his face, riding the waves like a Great Sea god.

Qart's face crumples. It's all very well for him, he thinks. He can afford to be happy. He's in charge; he likes the waves. He's not a slave to the Etruscans and their antics. He doesn't have to go up and down to the hull all day, feed the wretched chickens, clean their cages below deck, put up with the stink. He's up here in the fresh air.

Resentment replaces sea sickness in the pit of the boy's belly. The navigator promised me, promised me, he thinks, as bitterness rises, that I would be his boy. He told me that if I came on this voyage, I would learn about the winds, the stars and how to sail. He said I would help him with his charts. And he's broken his promise again. Just like before, when I thought I was going to help him. That time, I ended up at the mercy of someone cursed. Now, it's the same. These priests, too, are cursed by the divine. The boy hauls himself up to the topside and pokes his head over the side. Air roars in his ears and bites against his skin, spray douses him and he keeps his lips tight shut to keep the salt water out. Baal's balls, how I hate this.

'The letter C is on top!' comes the shout from behind.

'No, it's not. It's an E,' says another.

'Look, here's a golden stone and that takes precedence!'

'Great Tinia,' says bull neck. 'How is it possible to get accurate readings when we are on the move like this? We need calm waters and dry land to truly understand what the gods are telling us.'

'But we're on a voyage on the sea, my lord,' says silver clasp. 'We must learn to find the will of the gods out here.'

'And ignore hundreds of years of precedent on the land?' says bull neck. 'Is that wise?'

And so they squabble. Qart cannot be bothered with their problems. Nausea sits coiled inside him like a snake waiting to strike. Mighty Melqart, he implores, help me. He focuses his whole being on that moment, which he knows must come soon, the instant when The Delphis hits calm waters, when his gut stops throbbing and the vessel comes to rest.

* * *

Dubb feels the sea change beneath his feet. One minute The Delphis thunders along, sail bursting from the wind at their back, land a thin, far-off line against a grey-white sky. Next, come corkscrew motions, enough to send Nyptan and Tanu dashing for the topside, followed by a strong pull to port and a gentle settling back as the vessel's prow slowly comes level with her stern. The hull sinks down and she slips into calmer water as if sliding into a bath. Brilliant, true, strong Delphis, he thinks, and lifts a hand from the tiller handle to lean down and stroke its oiled boards. He feels like he should step down from the platform and kiss her deck. Old she may be, and a tub, but she responds with style to every hint and nuance of the sea, every gasp of wind or blow of gale. His glance flicks over the side at an increasingly docile swell.

'Well done, captain,' says Chares, first mate, who steps up onto the tiller platform to clap the navigator on the back. 'Wind over tide,' he says, and gives a short laugh.

Dubb snorts in agreement and lifts one hand from the handle to roll his neck and shoulder round. 'Take over for a bit, can you? I've had enough.' He hands Chares the wooden bar and moves away. 'She was only ever s'posed to take on the Great Sea, this Delphis of ours,' he says, and stretches tall enough to see the rough-hewn dolphin at the prow. 'She certainly wasn't built to ride the enormous swells of River Ocean.' The diviners are gathered at their altar just below the figurehead and it looks like Qart is in a sulk at midships. He yawns. So Hekataios will be relieved, he thinks, that our vessel is up to the task, though not as relieved as me. He plonks himself down at the edge of the platform and rubs his eyes. 'Anyway, Hanno'll be with us soon and thanks be to Mighty Melqart for that! I'm sick of doing two jobs at once.'

'You'll get your star plots done, don't worry,' says the first mate as if reading his mind. 'Once that young lordling gets on board, you'll have nothing to do but map the heavens day and night. I give you two weeks before you're bored.'

'Most unlikely,' says the navigator. 'You wouldn't credit the list of things the Academy in Miletus wants us to record.' He rubs at the back of his neck and his eyes feel heavy. Wonderful, kind, steady Chares. Always calm even in the worst conditions. He rolls backwards on the platform, feet on the deck, legs crooked at the knees, to doze. In the distance, the diviners drone. The crew: Rabs, Berek and the new boys settle down for a long haul. The cards and dice come out. For a moment, time is suspended, and his mind floats above his body. Then a worry seeps into the back of it. He opens his eyes and turns his head to search for sight of Nyptan and Tanu. He lifts himself onto an elbow and looks around. There at the back, shoulder to shoulder, his wife and daughter lean over the stern rail and watch the wake. At least they are smiling, he thinks, and blows a big sigh out through his lips. They must be feeling better. Good. He drops onto his back again, closes his eyes and begins to chew a lip. His tiredness has evaporated and he wonders, not for the first time, if this journey really is a good idea for his wife and their child. If only I could persuade them to stay here at the next port, he thinks. I can collect them on the way back. His stomach churns. I'll ask her again, he thinks. He knows already what her answer will be.

'Harbour, harbour,' comes a shout.

'We're here!' Rabs yells back from midships. Dubb sits up. The small, crinkled Carthaginian sailor wears his red hat squashed on the back of his head and his open mouth reveals the number of teeth he lost in recent brawls on the dockside. He bounds back to them at the tiller platform. 'Will we row or do it by sail?'

The navigator gets to his feet and lifts his eyes to the horizon. A cluster of fishing vessels gathers ahead.

'We are going in, Dubb? Sir?' says Berek, drum in his arms. 'Or do you want to pass them?'

'We certainly are going in,' says Dubb, 'after all that. And yes, by oar. So standby, and get ready.' He steps up to the tiller handle.

'Standby to bring down the sail. Prepare the oars,' shouts Rabs, a ball of energy as he tears down the deck, getting the crew onto their benches and oars into line.

Dubb takes the tiller from Chares, who turns to the leads behind and chooses a few to carry towards the prow. 'It's probably an estuary, so we'll need to double lead it,' Dubb says to the first mate over his shoulder.

The first mate loops two sets of cables round his shoulders and unhooks the bucket of tallow with his free hand.

The Delphis approaches the flotilla of fishing vessels with caution. They drop the sail some way away from the group and start to row. Berek marks the tune, thrummmmm, beat, beat, beat, and Chares stands at the prow, ready with the leads, and lifts his hand in greeting to the fishing fleet as they draw near.

The local boats are high pointed at the bow with a low-slung stern and are crammed to the gunnels with today's catch. One of them separates itself from the rest and rows over to greet them. It has a kind of scaffold rigged up for a sail, which is empty now. Otherwise, it is powered by oar.

'Lixus here,' shouts its skipper in broken Punic, and smiles and nods. Silver carcasses mound in a trough along the centre of his vessel and his shipmates look over with curiosity at the newcomers. 'River.' He gestures with his hand. 'You follow. Come.' The skipper turns them towards a break in the line of the land, his fleet following in formation. They must wait for the tide to turn.

The first foreigners Dubb had seen were far out to sea. He had raised an arm to them in greeting, but they were too intent on hauling nets to reply. Now, at the mouth of an estuary, a whole flotilla gathers. On The Delphis, the crew sits, oars at the ready, and chats. The holy men intone at the bow.

Nyptan slips in beside him at the tiller and puts her arms around his waist. 'Hello, my darling man,' she says, and nestles her head into his shoulder and looks up at him to smile.

'Hello, my lovely wife,' he replies, and relishes the feel of her body leaning against his. He muzzles the top of her head. She is warm and smells of incense. Her hair, plaited and circled round her head like a crown, shines in the morning light. She is, and always will be, a very beautiful woman. The gods have smiled on me. Thank you, Great Melqart, he mutters to himself. Aloud, he says, 'How have you two managed in these big seas? Alright?'

'Glad to be in calm waters,' says his wife, 'at last!' A big sigh bubbles out of her lips. 'I thought my stomach was going to burst through my mouth.' She smiles. 'Didn't we all, darling?' She turns to her daughter, Tanu, to include her in this unexpected moment of tenderness on board The Delphis. Tanu is a fresh skinned girl with burgeoning breasts and her mother's beautiful eyes. These three, whose love was forged on the Great Sea in tragic circumstances many years ago, are rarely separated. 'At last, we're getting somewhere. She squeezes Dubb's waist and reaches up to kiss him. 'Though I could do without all that droning.' She looks ahead at the diviners.

'It must be so dull to have to dance like that all the time,' says Tanu, and together they examine the diviners as they circle the altar in a kind of jig.

'I suppose that's why there are the two young ones,' says Dubb, 'to keep it going.' He pulls a face.

Nyptan laughs.

'I'd much rather serve Lady Gula than their gods, wouldn't you, Mummy?' says Tanu, and kisses the feathered amulet attached to her wrist by a leather thong.

'Tanu, no criticising other people's gods,' says Nyptan. 'How many times must I tell you!' She points. 'Say sorry to Great Laughing Dog.' She pulls at a strap around her neck. A brightly coloured amulet in the form of a dog's head with zigzagged teeth rides up from between her breasts and lands in the palm of her hand. 'You know he doesn't like it. Here, make amends and kiss.' Tanu bends to do so and Dubb, too, drops his head to kiss Nyptan's wrist, Great Laughing Dog on her palm, and then stands tall to kiss her on the mouth.

'Yes, let's all make amends,' he says, and grabs at Tanu to land a kiss on her hand too. They scramble at each other's limbs and giggle together.

The tide takes its time to turn. Each time Dubb looks at the lead vessel in the flotilla, its captain shakes his head and tells him to wait.

'Noooooo,' groan the crew.

'It's going to be dinner time by the time we get in,' sighs Chares.

'Play us a tune, Berek, can you?' says Dubb. 'Let's drown them out.'

The drummer nods, puts down his sticks and picks up his aulis. He starts with a few chords. 'I dream of a girl in golden fields,' he sings. He throws his voice out along the deck so that all the crew can hear him.

'In golden fields, in golden fields,' respond the nearest to him at once. They scramble to join him at midships, and most of the rest follow suit and begin to sway to the rhythm.

'Her eyes were dark and her hair was wild,' goes Berek, strong notes, strong voice.

'…hair was wild, was wild, was wild,' roar the men and link arms, the diviners' drones at the prow overwhelmed.

Dubb grabs his moment, a chance to speak to Nyptan alone. He steps over to her, takes her by the elbow and steers her towards the stern. She looks at him, puzzled, and follows willingly. He stands at the rail and peers into the olive-green water below. I've got to be careful how I put this, he thinks, or she will say "no" straight away.

Nyptan stands beside him and waits for him to speak. When no words come from him, she looks at him sideways and her brows go up. 'Well?' she says. 'What's on your mind?'

Dubb starts slowly, his voice soft. 'You've seen the big seas out here in River Ocean, haven't you? Far bigger than you've ever experienced before I think?' His eyes search for hers and wait for confirmation. She nods. 'The ocean here has a mind of its own, even more than the Great Sea. The winds are strong, The Delphis is weak,' he lies. 'You two are precious to me. You are all that matters in the world.' Nyptan takes a deep breath and starts to fiddle with the edge of her mantle. She does not look at him. Even so, he must continue. 'Are you sure... Are you absolutely sure you want to come with me on this journey?' He lifts her chin to face him and smooths the hair out of her eyes, and feels scared for what might become of her, their child, their love. His breath is shallow, tone uncertain. She looks fed up. He hurries on. 'I know how brave you are. I know how good you are as a healer, that you want to come for your own reasons as well as for mine. But The Delphis can get by without you. We did before.' He reaches down and takes her hands in both of his. He kisses them and cups them in his own. 'No one on this Earth can love your healing hands as much as I do.' He presses them in his own palms. 'No one can need you so much, every day, in good times and bad.' She starts to pull them away, out of his grip. He won't let go. He holds them tighter and his voice grows stronger, more insistent. 'We will find other healers, local ones. They won't be as good as you, we won't love them as much. Even so, we will get by. I have lived most of my life without you, my darling, I can do so again for a time. So, please, my dearest Nyptan, stay in port!' He drops her hands. Nyptan's mouth sets and her lids flick. She is getting cross; he knows it.

'Can I remind you,' she says, tone stretched, not looking at him, 'that you would be dead by now without my healing powers?' Dubb nods and tries not to think about how close he came to joining the army of the dead all those years ago in Sexi when they first met. 'Who would look after you if the sail rips and lashes you all? Who would quell your fever? You said I was to be the ship's healer. I am a very good healer.' He is mute before her anger. What more can he say to convince her to stay? She finds another tack. 'And you promised me, didn't you, after that day, that dreadful moment long ago...' her voice trembles. '...that we would never part. Never part.' Her eyes look up at him, challenging. He bites his lip. 'Isn't that so?' She is furious now, and plucks at his arm. 'Do you remember?' She pulls at it again. He nods, dumb, full of dread. 'And it so happens that I want to know how healing is done out here. I, me, Nyptan the Healer, wants to know, for myself, what remedies and cures there are beyond the Pillars of Herakles.

And I will make my own decisions for my own reasons.' She looks up towards the horizon and waves her hand towards the land. 'I want to see who the gods of healing are, what I can learn from them, how they can add to my knowledge of Lady Gula, Eshmon and Aesclyps. Would you deny me that, Dubb of Miletus? Would you, really?' Her fury seems to suddenly abate and her tone become more playful. 'Mr Navigator, sir, would you stop me from doing my life's work?' Her eyes flash and her mouth closes tight.

He is beaten. He swallows, shuffles his feet and shakes his head. There is nothing to be said to her.

'So, no, Dubb, I will not stay behind and nor will Tanu. It is an opportunity, which will never come our way again. Anyway, it has taken us so long to find you, do you really think that a bit of rough water can put us off? You cannot get rid of us so easily. We are with you until the final days.' She is smiling now and he feels his anxiety dissipate along with her fury. 'What trouble can there be? We're just travelling along the coast as usual, aren't we?' He groans despite himself. Oh, if only that were so, he thinks. If only it was so simple.

'Dubb, we're off!' shouts Rabs from the bow, and the deck breaks into a flurry of action. Berek's sticks fly with the rowing tune, diviners dance and the women disappear. The Delphis, with its hundred rowers, is on the move. As the distant gap in the landscape mutates into a real opening, cliffs and headlands emerge and the boom of a huge surf rises in their ears.

* * *

A wide channel of writhing tide drives The Delphis onwards. Rivulets of foam scour her sides and the roiling sea behind pushes her towards the river's mouth. Spray lashes Dubb's face, drenching his beard and chest. The roar of breakers on the beach beside is deafening. Silent gulls swoop in crazy patterns above their heads as first one and then others of the fishing fleet pass across the sand bars or through the narrow channel of the river estuary to the harbour beyond.

'Three fathoms,' shouts Chares from the leads. 'Two.'

Will we scrape bottom? wonders Dubb, and signals to Rabs to raise the oars. At once, the drumming stops and a hundred blades rise skywards to pause, combatants on the battle field, and await the order to engage, which will follow next. Smaller vessels beside them, part of the flotilla, surf the sand bars fluidly. They skim like birds across the thinnest sheets of brine. Dubb keeps his eyes fixed on the vessel before them and grips the tiller handle hard. I hope they know what they're doing, he thinks, as he leans into it and The Delphis swings in behind, directly in its wake. On either side of them, within touching distance to both port and starboard, sandbanks lie like golden leviathans waiting to pounce. Even a fully laden fishing vessel like the one ahead is nowhere near as heavy as a merchant man from the Great Sea. Dubb's jaws clench. He waits to hear the scrape of the sand on the hull and feel The Delphis lurch as she sticks. But it doesn't happen. By the time they get past the bars and arrive at the deep green water of the bay beyond, the navigator's brow is wet with sweat and his shoulders tight with strain. Chares hails him from the bow, Rabs calls to the crew to lower the oars, the drum changes rhythm and The Delphis slips around a high point to settle in the clean, clear water of a river estuary. Across from them a heavily wooded escarpment curves around in a wide arc, at its base a sandy landing place with a welcoming party. Even the diviners are silent for once.

This is where the trip really begins, thinks Dubb, as he chooses a place to lower the anchor, neither too close to the sandbanks nor the shoreline. It starts when we meet Hanno, the Magonid princeling from Carthage, who should be here! He glances at the shore and excitement worms its way around his insides. He tightens the hawsers, locks the tiller handle into its socket and the vessel is at rest at last.

Three penteconters lie, high hauled, on sand at the landing place. They must be Hanno's, he thinks, and his eyes search the beach for sign of the young aristocrat. He left Carthage with sixty war ships, a supply fleet in support and thousands of settlers. Is this all that's left? Dubb looks around the bay. Several aged hippoi are moored in a line on the other side of the estuary and many hundreds of smaller vessels, the settlement's fishing fleet, bob in between, in shallows or lie sidewards on the beach and sandbars. The town proper must be at the top of the hill, he thinks, and his eyes run up the escarpment, past stumpy box trees, to a rocky peninsula. Wooden buildings straggle along its ridge and behind he can just see one built of stone.

'Right, off you go,' says Dubb to the crew, men loitering, keen for the order to disembark. They do not wait. Over the topside, like a school of fish, they slip to swim, wade or paddle into Lixus, the last trading outpost of the great city of Carthage beyond the Pillars of Herakles.

The Enquiry - Day 2

'So, are you about to describe the first time you met Hanno of Carthage or not?' asks Lord Apsan, butting in, voice cutting through the navigator's account like a blade. Dubb looks up at him, startled. 'Come to the point! It's all good fun, I'm sure, for you to remember your journey in this sort of detail, but tell me about Lord Hanno! Why wasn't he with you? What was he doing? And hurry it along! The report has to be with Carthage urgently.'

Lord Apsan, his secretary and the witnesses are in the upstairs room of the official residence in Gadir and the enquiry has been in session for hours. The crew of The Delphis range before him, more or less fit, more or less coherent. They appear to have perfected the art of answering him without saying anything and giving answers to questions he didn't ask. His voice rings around his work room and makes the dust motes jump. 'When did you first meet Lord Hanno? You do know this enquiry is about him, don't you?' he adds, and scowls at each of them. 'It's not about you.' His head goes back, his mouth pinches at the corners and he lets out a loud and liquid belch.

'Here, my lord,' says Tasiioonos, and leans across the pile of straw to hand his master a cloth. 'Try these. They should help.' He passes across a plate of biscuits.

Lord Apsan looks at them. They're coal black and, once between his teeth, make him think he's eating sand. The crunching noise in his head piles pressure on his headache. His mouthful lands on the table in front of him, dark and granulated. He grabs at the beaker of water, downs it, then leans back in his chair to suppress more burps. And I'm doing all this in front of witnesses, he thinks. A wave of nausea rises up to overwhelm the humiliation.

Tasii is at the table, wiping up his mess.

'Whatever this is, it isn't working,' he hisses, as he shoves the biscuits and liquid medicine away from him. 'I need something better.' He stands, unsteady, and moves to the window for a breath of air. Sweat congregates around his temples and he clutches at the sill to breath deep.

When he turns back into the room, the woman is gazing at him intensely. He returns the look, brows furled. What business of it is hers if I'm a bit ill?

'Lord Apsan…' she starts.

'Quiet!' he says, and swallows hard. It is as much as he can do to get his voice to work. The woman purses her mouth. With one eyebrow raised, she shrugs, glances along the line of witnesses and then leans back against the wall to close her eyes. Thank the gods, he thinks, and slides onto his chair. I don't need her interfering. Anyway, I'll be alright in a minute. He looks down at the wax tablet, which lists the names of all the crew and their place of origin. "Nyptan the Healer", it says of the female, "formerly of Miletus, now of The Delphis". "A healer" she calls herself, and a short burst of air comes from his nose in derision. A likely story. Well, fortunately for me, and unfortunately for her, women are not permitted to speak at enquiries. They cry, lose the thread and are unpredictable under pressure. He lifts his head, raises his brows and looks from under them at the faces lined up along the wall opposite him. 'Well?' he says, and cocks his head to one side. 'Who is going to be the first to tell me about Lord Hanno?'

'I thought you wanted to know how it all began,' says Dubb. The man sounds aggrieved, sulky. Lord Apsan's eyes lock on to the navigator's. This troublesome man has recovered sufficiently to be insolent it seems. 'I thought this enquiry was about what happened when Hanno, the Magonid princeling, went to the ends of the Earth and back again?'

His lordship looks away, reaches for a beaker and clears his throat. 'Only the part of the story that's relevant to Lord Hanno,' he says.

'I am not here to learn how the surf roared or what the sky was like. We need to get to the relevant bits.'

'All the bits are relevant,' says the navigator. 'Everything that happened from the time we arrived in Lixus until this moment, here, now, tells you the story of Hanno, the Magonid. Every one of us can give you information, including the woman.' He puts his hand out to her arm and caresses it. 'She might even be able to help you feel better.' The crew murmur agreement.

What? A woman healer! A witch for certain, he thinks. His brows are down. Or deluded. She's certainly got all these men in the palm of her hand.

'It's quite simple, my lord,' says the navigator, his voice insistent. 'It was Hanno's job to guide our actions, take charge of men, routes, sailings, supplies. It was his task to think ahead and strategise. All these things he failed to do. He carried out such duties as suited him and when it suited him. He and his cronies kept as much to themselves as possible and left us to do everything else. So don't start telling us what's relevant to this report and what's not!'

Lord Apsan's eyes grow wide, his mouth opens and his head lurches backwards on his neck. He feels like he's been kicked in the head. 'I am the one who leads round here,' he roars. 'I decide the topics, I set the tone.' His voice breaks with the effort of it. 'I ask, you answer. That's the pattern. And you must answer me truthfully or, by Melqart's mother, I'll end your days here at the lash of a whip.' He clears his throat. The power in his voice seems to have evaporated and his dominance of the room is further sabotaged by a set of hiccups, humiliating punctuation marks.

The witnesses stir and exchange glances.

He gets to his feet and begins to pace around the room. 'Ghar ghar ghar...' He clears his throat. 'La la la la laaaaa,' he intones. I knew this would happen, he thinks, as he takes another turn. The minute I saw this navigator, I knew there would be unwelcome complexities, suppositions, speculations. When any Hellene is involved, let alone a Miletian, confusion always follows. He sighs, rolls his head around on his shoulders and sits down again in front of the witnesses. He gives what he considers to be a smile of great reasonableness, an adult's smile for naughty children. 'So, let's start all over again, shall we? Who is going to answer the simple question of when you first saw Lord Hanno?' He lifts his hand to point at the first person in the line. 'You, there. Speak!' he says to a man Tasii's tablet tells him is called Chares.

'Me?' says Chares, and looks startled. 'I'm not...'

'Yes, you!' snaps Lord Apsan. Oh, Melqart's mother, he thinks, why did I pick such a donkey?

The man sits up straight, his back away from the wall, and scratches behind his ear. He takes a deep breath. 'Right. Well, when we get to Lixus, we come to this harbour. Now, it's got such a wide mouth that a...'

'I don't want to know about the harbour. I want to know about Hanno!' his lordship says and slams his fist on the table.

'Sorry, my lord,' says Chares. 'Of course, of course,' He wipes his forehead with the back of his hand. 'Well, when we get to shore, there he is to greet us!'

'He's a tall bastard,' says the next man in line. Berek of Utica, is it? thinks his lordship, and his eyes swivel to the wax tablet. This witness has a light voice, big hands, floppy hair and one foot wrapped in a large bandage. 'He was very well turned out, embroidered garments, groomed beard, jewellery.'

'Yes,' the youngest of the witnesses breaks in, Qart, the one with the swirling hair. Ha, thinks Lord Apsan, I've got them going now.

'Hanno wore earrings so long they hit his shoulders! Full of red stones, do you remember?' The boy turns to address the other witnesses, ignoring Lord Apsan. Weak smiles rise in response. 'Fortunately, they went by the wayside before we got too far down the coast,' he adds, to knowing looks.

'As did the smiles of the rest of them,' adds the Hellene.

They're a coterie, this group, thinks Lord Apsan, a cabal, tight as a monkey's arse. I'll not get a single independent thought from any one of them.

'You have seen him, my lord, haven't you?' asks the woman, her voice rising clear above the hubbub. Time appears to stop.

'What?' he says. 'Who was that who spoke just now?' He runs his eyes along the witnesses. Can it really have been her?

'Hanno,' repeats the woman, and everyone in the room looks at her.

'Oh, you,' he says, and attempts to blot her from his sight by turning his shoulder to the window.

'The Magonid prince from Carthage. You have spoken to him, haven't you? He must have come through Gadir by now.'

His mouth is pruned, his eyes feel heavy and he busies himself with Tasii's beaker. Such an obvious question, he thinks, yet so difficult to answer. It's enough to make anyone sick.

'Yes,' says the boy, 'you must have seen him. He was ahead of us.'

'By a long time. He'll have been here for several weeks,' says the navigator. 'Seeing as the sailing season's ended and he can't get anywhere.'

'But, in any case, you have spoken to him, haven't you?'

They stare at his lordship as though he were a criminal.

'Speak when you're spoken to,' says the commissioner. But his strength has gone.

'My lord, a break?' says Tasiioonos at his elbow.

'Yes, yes, Tasiioonos, I agree. We will stop early,' he says to no one in particular, and gets to his feet to walk, arse tight, across the room to his private quarters.

'This enquiry is adjourned for the day,' says Tasii. 'Gatit, return the witnesses to the basement.'

The office empties of people and the heavy aroma of stewing peppers adds to his sense of impending disaster as it wafts up the stairwell to suffuse the room.

* * *

'The thing is, how could we have stopped him?' says Lord Apsan, propped up on pillows after a snooze. The weather is on the turn: the wind has picked up and the temperature dropped. 'To be frank, it didn't even occur to me he would do a runner. He comes from an aristocratic family. He should know how to behave!'

They are in the atrium of the official residence, the place where his lordship lives and keeps his treasures. An ancient and beautiful alabaster vase from Egypt, which Lord Apsan has had specially brought from Memphis, stands in an alcove ready to take his ashes when the time comes for him to greet the gods. Scattered around are other adornments of wealth: a bronze horse, glazed vitrum goblets, an ivory mirror.

Tasii is at a table nearby, beakers, oils and remedies laid out before him. 'The instructions say you are to take this several times a day in liquid form,' he says. He puts two lumps of charcoal into a mortar and begins to break them down with his pestle. The minerals crack and snap, and his slave's shoulders flex as he puts his weight into it.

'Can't you do that somewhere else?' says Lord Apsan. 'It's doing nothing for my head.'

'I've nearly finished, won't be long.'

'And throw the cover back from the window a bit. The lunch peppers are making me queasy.'

'It looked like very good at lunch,' says his slave, taking no notice of the instruction to air the room.

'Where can Hanno have got to?' says his lordship, peeved. He snuggles down into his pallet and the woollen geometric rug settles around his shoulders. 'Is he holed up in the temple, do you think? Is Arish, the high priest, hiding him, just to spite me?'

'I don't know,' says Tasii, and slides the black granules into a small beaker. He adds water, then swishes it around. 'I wouldn't put it past him. Ordinarily though, it'd be a big risk for him to stick his neck out to protect someone being investigated by the Senate. Half his priests are the sons of senators and the news could leak back to Byrsa Hill. Take this now; the next one is in six hours. In between, you'll keep going on the cakes.'

'But it's black. It's the same stuff I had from you earlier only in liquid form. You can see it's not working! Get me something better!'

Tasii gives a big sigh. 'It's not the same as the biscuits you've been eating. We've been through this already this morning, my lord. This remedy is better than the cook's. And it's because of Cook's cooking that you are in this position in the first place.'

'What do you mean?! She's the best there is around.'

'There are rats in the dry store as you well know. She can't stop them. That's why you keep getting sick.'

'Well, why aren't you getting sick, if that's the case? You eat the same food as me.'

'Not always, my lord. In fact, quite often those of us who serve in your household eat very differently from you.'

A frown crosses Lord Apsan's brow. 'That's the first I've heard of it!'

'Well, let's not go on about that now. What you need to do is drink this and find Lord Hanno. Do you agree?'

Lord Apsan nods and sips.' At least this doesn't taste as foul as the last concoction.'

Tasii turns to his worktable, stacked with slates. He starts to sort them into piles, making Lord Apsan's head throb.

'These are the latest reports we have received from the security people. They cover the area from up country where the mines are-'

'Well, he's surely not going to hide up there, is he?' he snaps. 'He'll want to get back to Carthage.'

Tasii looks impatient and continues '…to along the coast towards Sexi. There's been nothing from our people in Tartessos itself, though it's difficult to find informers there. They don't like working for us, makes them feel disloyal to Byrsa Hill.'

'But we are Byrsa Hill,' he says, 'or at least we are out here. What's their problem? Must I speak to Arganthonios again? Do I have to refresh the security network yet again?'

'You do go through security advisors rather quickly,' says Tasii. 'Here, my lord, put this on.' He hands him his oldest embroidered garment.

By now, his lordship is off his pallet and wandering about, tunic flapping over his lean shanks. 'Well, can I help it if one died and the other one left the service within a week?' he says, as he swivels his hips into the garment. 'These younger people don't seem to have what it takes to be a spy these days.'

Tasii puts his hand to the tablets. 'It seems that, so far, not a single informer in your extensive security network has caught a glimpse of Lord Hanno. These come from Malaka, Sexi and Abdera. Short of him being stuck down a mine or locked in a vault with Arish, I can't think where he can be.' Tasii moves over to put another mantle across the old man's shoulders. Lord Apsan lifts the mirror to his face to smooth back his hair.

'Get that new man up from Malaka then. The one who says he's run security networks since he first sucked on his mother's teat. And drag them over from Tartessos if you must. We cannot go on like this, conducting an enquiry with wily witnesses when we do not know where the lordling has got to.' He steps over to the door, sticks his head out and shouts, 'Gatit, get the witnesses up! And a bowl of that pepper stew. I'm feeling better already.'

* * *

'So, did Lord Hanno behave in a manner appropriate to a young princeling from Carthage?' he says, and wipes his mouth with the corner of a cloth. The enquiry has resumed, and the crew is lined up against the wall as before. A bowl of stew sits before him with hunks of bread to dip. He's been slurping at it, suddenly hungry.

'Well, I was prepared to like him,' says Chares, and nods into his chest. 'He greeted us on the shore, came to each of us in turn, clasped arms...'

'And, later on, he laid on a few barrels, that sort of thing. Very hospitable,' says the light-voiced one.

'You might even say he treated us royally,' says Chares.

'It was a bit much,' says someone else.

Tasii scratches on his tablet. Ah, thinks Lord Apsan, something to latch on to. 'Extravagant,' he says to Tasii. Bad mark! 'Byrsa Hill should check the expedition's hospitality, expenses and sundries.'

The witnesses look from one to the other, confused.

'And then...?' he says. 'Well, go on one of you.'

The woman sits up, adjusts her mantle and takes a breath.

'Oh, for Melqart's sake, does she have to take part?' says Lord Apsan sharply. 'Is she really the best one of you to take this enquiry forward right now?'

'If you wish to know what happened on this expedition, you must let the woman take part!' says the navigator. The effort of speaking with such force has given the man the shakes it seems. He clutches his right hand with his left and his head wobbles on his neck. 'Nyptan is an entirely credible witness, often the only one of us present with Lord Hanno. You can speak to her and know what happened on our voyage, or not and remain ignorant. It's your choice.' His eyes close and exhaustion takes over.

The witnesses turn irritable. 'That's right!'

'She knows what she's talking about.'

'Let her speak!'

'One person at a time,' says Lord Apsan, and he sighs. 'If you must speak, start!' he says, and points a finger at the woman. 'But you'd better stick to the point, my girl, or I won't let you attend this enquiry again!'

Nyptan swallows. Her chin sets. She sits forward, looks Lord Apsan straight in the eye and her lips open.

Lixus Town

'Careful with that, my darling,' Nyptan says to her daughter, as Tanu uses both hands to clasp their ebony incense holder around its rim and manoeuvre it towards the door of their quarters. It is a highly decorated tripod with curled lotus flowers up the side and three shiny worshippers to hold it up from below. She steps across and tries herself to shove it. 'It's too heavy,' she says, as her lips bubble and twist.

They are on the deck of The Delphis, packing up for a welcome stint on shore. Her concoctions are ready to go. Tanu has their personal possessions wrapped in bundles. All that's left is the altar. Her darling looks frustrated and sticky around the temples. 'Here, drink water. We must drink lots of water.'

Now the bluster and roar of the surf have dropped away, the midday sun beats on them like an iron rod. She drags her mantle from her shoulders to feel the air on her neck. The settlement of Lixus lies above them on a hill and it looks to her like that's where their lodgings will be. There's a lot to carry up that slope.

Her daughter stands back from the burner and looks at her mother, brows raised. 'Really? No incense?'

'Let's take the vials, just not the rest of it,' she says. 'I'd love to have it with us, but I think we'd better not. I couldn't bear for it to be broken or left behind and there's a lot to transport.'

Given to her by Dubb when they last travelled through Carthage, this holy object has something of Egypt about it and something of the East. It reminds her of her years at the Temple of Eshmun in Sidon when she was a girl. It is also the centrepiece of their worship of Lady Gula, their goddess of healing. The amulets which grace both Nyptan and Tanu are proof, if it ever be needed, that Lady Gula is with them wherever they go. Great Laughing Dog, a bright-eyed animal with zigzagged teeth, lives on a leather string between Nyptan's breasts. Tanu has a tiny bead with a zigzag pattern and feather attached to her wrist. When she becomes a full healer, like her mother, she, too, will wear Great Laughing Dog between her breasts.

'We'll find something to make into a temporary altar when we get ashore,' she says, and Tanu nods, 'though it will never be as beautiful as this.' She strokes its ebony sheen.

They turn to gather the last of their healing things. Drying cloths, mixing bowls, their fire stone, pestle and mortar, herbs and essential oils all go into an altar cloth. They tie the ends in large knots. 'It's quite a climb up there,' she says, and lifts her chin over her shoulder to the prow of the hill.

Tanu pulls a heavy embroidery from their store, places it over the incense holder and weights it down. 'To keep the gulls from wrecking it,' she says, and begins to gather the bundles on her shoulder. 'Ready.' She turns to look at her mother.

The crew and diviners have gone ashore already, making them almost the last to leave. Only Dubb and Rabs have stayed on, to check The Delphis one last time before Hanno comes on board.

'All set, missus?' says Rabs from the other side of the curtain drawn across their quarters. 'The dinghy's below.'

Nyptan pushes the cloth aside with her shoulder and backs out, dragging their kit behind her. 'There's a lot of it.'

'Coming,' says Dubb from midships, and he walks towards them, a look of satisfaction on his face. His lean frame, sculpted face and grey eyes still make her stomach turn after all these years. You are a very beautiful man, she thinks, and smiles, her dimple breaking out across her cheek. He grins. What are you so pleased about? she wonders, as he takes their goods from them and passes them over the side to Rabs in the dingy below.

'Happy man?' she says.

'The trip is starting!' he says, excitement creasing his face. 'Finally. And we're about to meet the commander. I hope he's a good man.'

Nyptan's eyes dwell on him. She loves him more than ever when he's like this. Keyed up, boyish, glad to be sailing off to the ends of the world, only his wits to tell him where he's going. 'Who knows,' she says, and shrugs.

She puts her foot on the top of the ladder, tunic gathered in one hand, the other grasping the rope. As she descends, an unwelcome thought comes to her, of how badly journeys can go wrong if the commander is not a "good man". Memories of her time with another commander, far from good, rise unbidden in her mind. She dismisses them. That was another time, a different life. This is now. She steps down into the dinghy and settles herself at the stern. Surely, after all we've gone through with commanders, she thinks, and her throat goes dry, Hekataios won't have teamed us up with anyone difficult. She watches Tanu make her way down the ladder to take the seat beside her.

Dubb comes last and Rabs casts off. He rows in total silence. What's wrong with us? she wonders. Are we all anxious?

The dinghy moves across the bay towards the beach. The water beneath is turquoise, deeper than the brittle sky. A light breeze rises from the oars and Rabs bends to the task. Her mantle drifts from the top of her head to her shoulders and she lets it be. In the far-off haze a range of mountains runs parallel to the sea. Immediately in front, the estuary gleams. Gone are the treacherous sandbanks and channels; the whole bay is completely full of water.

There is a jolt and a splash. They arrive at the beach. She lifts her mantle over her head and prepares to stand. Tanu, too, old enough these days to cover her head, raises hers over straggling strands. I do wish she would do her hair properly, thinks Nyptan. I must teach her again. Strong hands help her out. Her square feet splash and cool water washes across her ankles. She looks up. Before her stands a striking man with very dark eyes, muscly frame and expensive jewellery. His feet are wide in the sand, command-ing his place in the world, she thinks. He has a purple seafarer's hat over lustrous black hair, the quality and shape of his headgear a far cry from Rabs's faded specimen. Earrings, long and glinting, and a jewel-encrusted belt, compound the impression of extreme wealth, power and privilege.

Dubb swings Tanu up and over the water to land both feet on dry land, and turns back to the dinghy to grab the rest of their kit.

'And who are these lovely creatures?' says Lord Hanno, and his eyes glisten. It must be Hanno, she thinks. It's the only person he could pos-sibly be, dressed like that.

Dubb deposits their load on the sand, wipes his palm down his thigh and his mouth opens in a broad smile. His arm goes up in greeting. 'You must be Hanno, Magonid of Carthage!' he says, 'excuse my sweaty state.'

The man nods as the two touch forearms. A welcoming grin graces the aristocrat's face, his cheeks crease in lines around his mouth and his teeth shine. A self-assured face, she thinks, and wavers, feet still ankle deep beside the dinghy. An entitled man, used to getting his own way. She steps out of the water towards him. Her feet slosh. Gulls swoop above noisily. They must be offloading fish nearby, she thinks, and turns to look for the fleet.

'Lord Hanno, this is Nyptan of Miletus, my wife,' says Dubb, 'and Tanu, my daughter.' He gathers the women to him, arms at their backs. 'And I, as you already know no doubt, am Dubb of Miletus, your navigator.' He gives a quick nod.

'Your wife and child!' says the aristocrat, and returns the gesture. His head is to one side and brows up as he surveys the two women with amusement. His lids lower and he gives a half-smile. 'I see.'

He thought I was a prostitute, thinks Nyptan. He hoped I was a prostitute! A familiar weariness sweeps across her and she sighs. So it's going to be like this, is it? Not again. She glances at Dubb who doesn't notice.

'It's most unusual to travel with one's wife in my part of the world,' Lord Hanno says, as he tries to catch Nyptan's eye. 'Lovely dimples.' He bites at a thumb nail and his gaze swings on towards Tanu. 'And even more, you have a girl child with you. Lucky man!' He takes his time to survey Tanu from the top of her half-covered head, down her body, to her ankles. 'Hmmm. Very pretty.'

Nyptan's flesh crawls. A blush rises up her cheeks. In panic, she lurches towards Tanu and stands in front of her, between her and his lordship.

'Ooh, let me at least say "hello".' Tanu dodges out of the way to give the young aristocrat a broad smile. 'I'm very pleased to meet you, sir,' she says, and gives him a slight bob, then turns back to Nyptan. 'Why did you do that?'

His lordship laughs and turns to Dubb. 'But I thought you brought a healer with you?' he says, his gaze scanning the bay for more arrivals. 'Is there someone still to come? Or did I get that wrong?'

'No, my lord, you did not,' says Dubb, and raises his hands to the women. 'Here, these are our healers, my wife and daughter.'

'Women healers!' says Lord Hanno, all amusement evaporated.

His eyes flick with disapproval, mouth down at the corners, creases not handsome without the smile. 'Even the young one? Well, that is novel.' His lids droop at Nyptan as he gives her a stare. 'Well, welcome, healers, I suppose. Welcome all.' He raises an arm to include Rabs. 'Refreshments are laid on for you up in the town. Tonight, you should rest and tomorrow the Governor of Lixus will brief us on the route ahead.'

* * *

The meeting with the Governor of Lixus is on the terrace of his residence, perched on the escarpment overlooking the confluence of the bay with River Ocean. Dubb arrives late, slightly flustered because of a problem with the stores. A cool breeze buffets in from the surf. From this stone pavement, to right and left, only rolling breakers can be seen, their passage to land cut short on one side by sharp rock shelves and, on the other, by the outgoing tide. Beyond lies a silent sea. The sun casts a silver sheen across it and, on the horizon, there is a slight haze.

Lord Hanno appears to have been waiting for him. The moment the navigator's foot lands on the stones the lordling greets him. 'There you are! Better late than never. Come, I want you to meet my crew before we eat,' he says, and takes him by the arm.

Lord Hanno is dressed very finely. A heavily embroidered garment, secured at his waist by a jewel-encrusted belt, falls in wide pleats to his knees. Above, he has a short, padded coat overlaid with dazzling neck armour, the whole embellished with the finest stones at his fingers, feet and ears. On his head, the purple cap of a senior sea commander sent from Carthage, and a feather.

Dubb, in contrast, wears very little. He has a fresh linen cloth around his waist, a sailor's shawl across his shoulders and clean sandals. His hair is washed and tied back at his neck. Nyptan put an amulet round his neck and it, too, has a feather.

He is escorted towards a group of young lords drinking at the edge of the terrace. Behind them, the land drops steeply to the sea. The governor, it seems, has not yet shown up.

A small, thickset man peels away from the group and steps forward. He has heavy brows, muscly arms and a large circular earring in one ear.

'This is Lord Bostar, from Utica,' says Hanno. 'One of my closest friends.'
The lordling stands up tall and puts up his elbow in greeting.

'Hello, pleased to meet you,' says Dubb, and reciprocates the gesture.

'Welcome! A navigator! How I do love navigators,' says the man, his
voice deep and eyes smiling. 'Where would we be without you?'

'Exactly where you would want to be, I hope,' Dubb says, and laughs.
But the joke is wasted on the man from Utica who turns back to his
friends. I wonder why being a navigator appears to be such an exceptional
skill for this lordling.

At that moment a slave interrupts them with drinks. As he takes one,
he sees each in the group turn to look at him with curiosity. Surely every
young lord from Carthage knows how to navigate!

'I'm not going to introduce you to them all right now,' says Hanno,
and forces his way into the group. 'Too many for you to remember. You
only need to know that these are some of the finest young commanders
Carthage has ever seen.' The men look pleased with themselves, flattered.
'They'll be coming with us, two at least, to the very end.'

'Yes, you lazy bastards,' says Lord Bostar, voice booming. He punches
at the biceps of a fresh-faced young man beside him. The man has light
skin and long hair, beautifully brushed, with earrings dangling against a
smooth cheek. 'You can just come and go as you please. No need to work!'

'We don't all have to be muscle men,' replies the youth, and pummels
back. 'Some of us are interested in other things. Oh, and I'm Kanmi, by the
way.' He looks over at Dubb and puts up his arm in greeting. 'Lord Kanmi.'

'Yes? Like what?' replies Bostar, and pumps his pelvis at his companion.
So the argument carries on, the navigator forgotten and Hanno smiling
at them, indulgent, from the side.

'These are family friends. We knew each other in Tyre first, then Byrsa
Hill. It's great to travel with friends. I'm so tired of complaining mariners.'

A flicker of a frown lands between Dubb's eyes before he banishes
it. What? This bunch of entitled young things are better than seasoned
sailors? Are we going on an afternoon picnic?

'Hello, welcome, Navigator! Or should I say welcome Dubb from
Miletus, a man whose fame goes before him!' says a middle-aged man
with iron-grey hair, who joins them from inside the building. Here, evidently, is the governor. He is a middle-ranking bureaucrat from Carthage
judging by his yellow hat, which he wears at the back of his head. 'It is
not often in my life that I have had the privilege of meeting someone so

famous for his skills around the world. We tend to get grasping traders here.' He has a frazzled air about him. Well, this lot will be no exception, thinks Dubb, however highborn, and he raises his elbow.

'Trade makes the world go round,' says Lord Hanno. 'Good evening, sir. I hope you are well?'

'Very fine, very fine.' The man bustles them away. 'Let's get down to business. The sooner we get that over, the sooner we can eat! Are you ready to eat, boys?' he shouts back over his shoulder to Hanno's friends who cheer.

He leads Dubb and Hanno around the corner of the building to a quiet place, facing inland. 'Sit yourself here, Navigator,' he says, and pats the seat beside him. Together, they share a bench, Lord Hanno in a separate seat across from them. 'How was the journey here?'

'They're big seas, as you know only too well, I'm sure,' says Dubb. 'But we've got ourselves a good vessel, a sturdy vessel, and she rode them well.'

'Surely no bigger than the waters around the Black Sea?' says their host. 'Or the route from Sidon to Nora for that matter if the winds are against you?' His eyebrows rise.

'Not quite right,' says Dubb. 'It all depends, I guess.' Images of bad voyages flash through his mind. It's difficult to choose which is the worst; they've all been bad for different reasons. He blows a big sigh through bubbling lips.

'Well, you're here safely at any rate,' says the governor after a pause. 'And for that, Great Melqart, be thanked. We will have a praise ceremony for him before you leave. If you could be so gracious, Lord Hanno, you will preside?'

'I will certainly,' says Lord Hanno, inclining his head and placing an open hand to his chest.

Black shapes, difficult to see, pad across behind his lordship's chair to light flares on this, the darker side, of the terrace. Another comes to offer more drinks.

'Do you have any sense of the scale of this land, your lordship?' he asks. 'Or the sea for that matter?' He takes a sip from his beaker and looks over the governor's shoulder to the wide, open sky beyond. Just the thin line of a mountain range catches the falling sun in the distance.

'We don't know much about further down the coast other than this,' says their host. 'We have a tiny settlement at a place called Ngap, which you will pass through. It is said there are rich lands beyond it, though we've never had the manpower to go there.

'Any offshore islands?'

'There's a group of them partway down to Ngap, which someone visited once, I think. I know nothing about them. After that, as far as I have been able to discover, there are no islands and few places to land. Just desert, for days and days. A ripping current will help you on the way there, but prepare for it to be hard on the way back. It's reported to be a killer. As for straight out to sea, we haven't tried. There's enough to do here to take a lifetime. We leave the madness of trying to find new trading routes to the likes of you people. The settlement Ngap, ahead of you by many days, is the last little fingerprint of Carthage in the known world, the end of civilisation as we know it.'

Lord Hanno looks at the governor in silence as if contemplating the expedition for the very first time. Dubb knows how he feels. When Hekataios had suggested the journey, even he had had qualms, dread and excitement in equal measure.

'But there is gold down there, you do know that,' says Lord Hanno, and leans forward. His hands clench and unclench.

'So they say,' says the governor, 'though I'm too busy with the hills behind here to search for it. Now, what do you need from me?' He throws an arm over the back of their bench and looks at them, frank and brisk.

'I want to leave as soon as possible,' says Hanno, and turns towards Dubb, 'if that is acceptable to you of The Delphis, that is.' He raises his brows at the navigator.

'We can do that,' says Dubb. 'Might as well keep going. We need the usual couple of days to check our corking. She had a refit and new sail before we left Gadir so she should be good, despite what we've been through already. Though extra cables would be useful if you have some to spare?'

The governor nods and Hanno looks pleased.

'Our penteconters are ready to go,' says the lordling. 'You sent a few hippoi ahead, Governor, I think, in case we need spare capacity to return?'

'Extra vessels, food, water, dry supplies, grog, all gone ahead to Ngap.'

A tall, black man comes around the corner and stands and waits to speak.

'Yes?' says the governor. 'Food ready?' The man nods and disappears. With darkness about to fall, light from the flares takes hold and the governor's face glows red in their flames.

'Which brings me to something important,' he says. 'Interpreters.'

'Yes,' says Dubb, 'I was going to ask about them.'

'Well, good ones are like gold dust. The peoples beyond here have many languages, all so strange and new that, even if you have a good smattering of different tongues from places all across the Great Sea, you'll need someone to help you here.'

Dubb nods. 'Of course, of course.'

'The person I have found for you is excellent. He comes from nearby Ngap, and is familiar with the speech of peoples from the whole length of this coast. We call him Kama. He will keep you going for a good while and, after he runs out of knowledge, well, you'll just have to do the best you can. May Great Melqart smooth your way.' He pulls a face and shrugs his shoulders. 'You could be back here quite soon of course. Maybe the land runs out after Ngap.' The three men all laugh and shake their heads.

'Who knows?' says Dubb.

'May Mighty Melqart stay with us,' says Lord Hanno.

'So, anything else?' The two travellers shake their heads. 'Right, come on,' says their host, and jumps up. 'Now is the time to live a little. This journey will be full of dangers. It is also a journey which could make your names and give you wealth and prosperity for the rest of your lives. We will celebrate it!' He sweeps around the corner to the front terrace. 'Let's go!' His words are directed to the lordlings who, juggling their cups, jostle behind him into the residence.

Dubb and Hanno linger behind. From the front here River Ocean is a golden sheet, the sun a blistering vermillion. Breakers boom from below.

'So, why are you doing this?' says Dubb, as the fiery ball starts to drop like molten metal into the sea.

'For money. For fame, if I'm honest,' says Hanno beside him. 'My family needs me to make a name for myself, for them, our dependants, to help them get ahead. You? Why have you come?'

'Curiosity, I suppose. I work for a master, Hekataios in Miletus, who is writing treaties about the world. He wants to know what lies out here, beyond the Pillars of Herakles. As do I.'

'Well, let's have a session about all this before we leave Lixus and make a plan. I'll see you in there,' says the lordling, and moves off to dine.

Dubb dawdles. He looks out at the sun setting before him. I wonder if it steams as it hits the water. He narrows his lids to a slit to follow the course it takes to the brine. The colour pulsates and dazzles, though he can see no sign of steam or fizzing. I'm too far away, he thinks. Yet if River Ocean circles the land, and the sun passes across us to sleep behind it every night, why have I never seen any vapour coming from Helios as it sets? Never once.

He takes a last look at the sky as he steps across the stone pavement towards the banqueting hall, then pauses. Right above is a transparent moon. Ahead, towards the mountain range, sprawls Melqart, the tip of his club just rising in the sweeping night. A frown flits between his eyes. But what is this? Why is his foot above his club? Is it lying at an odd angle or are my eyes just adjusting to the light? He hears the roar of a drinking song. Well, I'll worry about it in the morning. Tonight's a night to celebrate.

* * *

The navigator leaves the governor's banquet very late at night. He's had a lot of wine, thinks Qart, as he watches his master weave his way down the hill towards the visitors' quarters. The boy has been waiting for his master to return to his lodgings. He needs to talk, to argue. He's got to remove me from the clutches of the chicken keeper or I won't continue this journey any further.

The navigator seems to be throwing his feet forwards and leaning backwards in an effort to hold himself upright. His shape disappears into a shadow of box brush and emerges again at the bottom of the hill, a saddle of land between the governor's residence and the latrines. It is there that their huts are situated. Perhaps he's afraid of falling in the dark, he thinks, as Dubb emerges into the silvery light. There is so little wind that the stench of excrement slips down the slope towards him.

'Dubb, I need to talk to you,' he says, as he steps out of the shadows at the gateway to the huts. The man looks like a spirit, a thin, colourless shape with long, floating hair.

His master stops dead. 'Oh, you still up, Qart?' he says. 'Very late for you to be roaming around, isn't it? Such a beautiful night!' He swings his arm towards the luminous sky.

Definitely had a lot to drink, thinks Qart. Not an ideal time to try and persuade him to change the arrangements on The Delphis. His heart gives a little pound.

'Not often we seafarers get to see this special starlight on the land, eh?' says his master, and he chuckles as he passes through the gate towards the hut he is sharing with Nyptan and Tanu.

'Dubb, I need to speak to you,' says Qart. It's as much as he can do to get his throat to work. His chest goes tight. My master's not going to like what I'm about to say.

'Later,' mumbles Dubb.

'No, now!' he says, and grabs Dubb by the arm and tries to pull him out onto the path again. Best not to have a row where everyone can hear us.

'Can't it wait until the morning, lad? Let's talk then.' The navigator pats his arm, then tries to prise Qart's hand from his arm.

'No, please, Dubb. Now! I have been waiting for you all night!' Qart's mouth is pinched and a deep frown scours his brow. I must say it now. In the morning I'll be back with the chicken keeper.

'Have you? Well, more fool you,' comes the reply and an edge comes into the voice, one Qart knows only too well. He's about to get shouted at. Dubb shakes Qart off and lurches on.

'Dubb, stop!' he says. 'I must talk to you!' He leaps around to stand directly in his master's path.

'Oh, Baal's balls, what is it then?' says the navigator, impatience breaking through. 'You certainly know how to pick your moments, don't you?' His breath smells as sour as his voice sounds.

'Why do you let them do it to me?' he bursts out. 'Why me? Can't you give them someone else?' Spit pops out of his mouth and his fists are clenched.

'Do what? Who? What are you talking about?'

'You told me I was your ship's boy, your boy,' he adds, with heavy emphasis, and tries to get control of the quiver in his words.

'Well, you are,' says Dubb, voice softening. 'Is that what all this is about? That's exactly what you are. The ship's boy.'

'Well, I don't want to be the ship's boy. I want to be your boy!' says Qart, and the tears start.

'But you are my boy,' says Dubb. 'My boy, the ship's boy, it's all the same!'

'No, it's not!' says Qart. If only Dubb would listen to him, take him seriously. 'It's why I came with you from Gadir. To be your helper. Now all I am is a slave to the chicken keeper.' A light breeze intensifies the stench of excrement.

Dubb's lips curl and he waves a hand across his nose. Master and boy, as one, take a few steps away from the gate, across the clearing, to find fresher air.

'So, you believe there was a choice for you back in Gadir, do you?' says his master. His eyes are weary and he leans sideways. 'You could have decided not to come with us on this journey outside the Pillars, is that what you think?'

Qart clamps his jaw together and swallows. How I hate it when he argues like this. 'Well, I could have left you and gone back to being a street boy like I was before,' he says, voice rising. 'I made a living out of it in the past. Kept myself alive.' Even as he says this, he knows it is not true. He couldn't have decided to stay behind. He would allow nothing on this Earth to separate him from Nyptan and Tanu, Rabs, the people he has come to love on The Delphis. 'But you didn't tell me…'

'Didn't tell you what precisely?' says his master, face obscured in shadow, iron entering his tone. Qart takes a deep breath and his cheeks blow wide in the dark as he waits for what will come next.

Dubb's tone comes heavy and sharp in the night air. It wraps high around his ears and sets his stomach buzzing. 'Didn't tell you what? What a ship's boy is? Do you really not know that by now? That the ship's boy is the lowest of the low in the pecking order on any vessel. Is at the beck and call of everyone, be they aristocrat, priest or healer. That you have to do the dirty jobs, or the difficult ones, or those the rest of the crew doesn't feel like doing. Surely, if I have taught you anything in the time I have known you, it has been the duties of a ship's boy!'

'But when I was working with you before it was easier!' Qart blurts. 'I was looking after horses. I helped with navigation. I marked the mast. I didn't have to do what these priests are asking me to do, stupid stones and stupid chickens.'

'You also had to clean the heads and run around after a crazy captain if you remember,' says Dubb, voice a metal rod scrapping over rock. 'If you wish to be a navigator like I am, you need to know how to do every single task on a vessel: clean the heads, look after the animals, mix with every single person. That's all part of being at sea and knowing the ways of a vessel.'

'But then it was a horse, a lovely horse!' he says, and thinks back to the beautiful, brown eyes of Xanthos and how warm he was and how much he loved him. A lump gathers in his throat. 'These are just filthy chickens. And stones!' Frustration bursts out of him like water from a blow hole. 'It's ridiculous!'

Dubb's head is a solid ball of darkness now against the starry sky; only a shard of starlight catches at his upper lip as it moves in the darkness. 'Reading chicken livers and stones may seem ridiculous to you, Qart, but it is not to these diviners. It is the way their gods speak to them. These are not grasping soothsayers pulled from the backstreets of any old city. They are Etruscans, holy men, known all over the Great Sea for their ability to tell the future, read the omens in stones, livers and even lightning. You need to know about this and the role diviners play, especially at sea. They will not be present on every voyage you ever make yet, when they are, they change the nature of it fundamentally.' Dubb's voice is low, intense and furious. Qart has never known him this angry before. Perhaps it's the drink, he thinks, and takes a step back.

'Now I'm fed up with you,' Dubb finishes, 'your sulks and your complaints, your self-centredness. Get on with your duties. And, when you've had time to ponder it and see the point of what I am saying, you might also condescend to practice your writing and reading. Reading and writing is what you need to focus on now. Because without them, you'll never be a navigator, never be able to take control of a vessel. You'll just be an ordinary boy run away from Carthage, an ordinary seaman, as plain and unadventurous as any old sailor from the backstreets of nowhere land.' Qart's master turns his back on him and walks off into the darkness towards his lodgings.

Rage and frustration rise through Qart's body like a tidal wave, tears spring to his eyes and his knees set him off at speed into the darkness. He sprints his way up the path leading to the headland. His heart pounds as he tears across the darkened landscape, hands in front to protect his face from the box brush. His feet kick up sand and stones, the night air cools his lungs and the scratches and slashes the vegetation heap on him make him feel alive. At least I can feel these wounds, he thinks, and flails at a nearby mimosa.

He reaches the top of the slope and arrives at a rocky outcrop. It tumbles down in rough cliffs and boulders to form a boundary between Lixus town and the forbidding emptiness of a foreign land. It drops away ahead to nothing. Below, the bay spreads out, a glistening palm of channels, rivulets and lagoons, reflecting a thousand stars above. He slides onto a wide stone shelf to rest, sucks at the welds on his arm and savours the familiar sweetness of his blood. Do I really want to spend my life shovelling chicken shit and sorting stones? A breeze picks up, greets him full in the face, tosses his curls about his head and cools his baking face.

Overhead, Orion slants across the sky, a bit low perhaps but unmistakable. He examines the heavens and exhilaration lifts his mood. There's the Big Bear, and the little one. He rolls his head and his eyes around the myriad lights. He must ask Dubb about Orion's position when he can. He feels proud to have a proper question to ask of his master, a question which will demonstrate that he is learning what he's being taught, is paying attention to the sky. His mouth goes down at the corners. He can't imagine even talking to Dubb right now. Perhaps I really should leave The Delphis here. No one would miss me, he thinks, full of self-pity. The trouble is that, by the look of it, the place is very small. So, if I jump ship here, there's nowhere to escape to. I could go off into the countryside, of course, and he thinks of the impenetrable darkness of the land around him and shivers.

He hears a low moan. It comes on the wind, seeps through the mimosa and box brush. His head whips round and his whole body goes rigid. Where's that come from? Nothing follows. A bird, he thinks, shrugs and settles back on the rock shelf. How can it matter to Dubb, for instance, that an L stone is stronger than C, that a golden one takes precedence?

This time, the night air carries the unmistakable timbre of an angry human voice and the snarl of dogs, followed by a series of rising wails. He leaps to his feet, mouth open, eyes wide. He can't quite hear where it's coming from. There are more shouts, and he turns his head from side to side to try and locate them. Children? Then, with a jump, he hears the crack of a whip. He runs forward to peer over the edge of a rock precipice. There they are, down below. Flares light the way for a forced march of young black bodies, men with whips and dogs to marshal them. They are in single file along a narrow coastal path, which looks as if it leads back to Lixus town. Fear creeps up his shoulders and down into his belly. Children. Being taken! Where? The reality of it hits him as he remembers the hippoi sitting in the harbour below. That's what they are for, to take these children back to the Great Sea and sell them! His mouth is dry and the back of his neck stiff as he creeps backwards off the rock onto the path. Tiptoeing along it as quietly as he can in the dark, he waits until he is well out of hearing range of the dogs, and then pelts it back to the latrines and safety of their living quarters.

His feet are sore and head heavy as he passes through the gate to his hut. No, I don't want to be like them, alone in a big world, without anyone to help me. Yes, there are chickens and it's dangerous, but at least I will not die alone.

* * *

Nyptan wakes when Dubb slips in beside her. His legs slide down under the cover, hips and legs snug to hers, arm crossing her waist and face nestled into her neck.

'Hmmmmm,' he says, nearly asleep.

She loves it when he comes to her like this. She turns her head towards him and lifts it in the half-light. Can she see his face? Her hair spreads wide, like rock pools, on their pillow. He smells strongly of drink.

'How did it go?' she asks, voice croaky. 'Alright?' His eyebrows are getting wiry and his hair sticks out, grey and wispy behind his ears.

'Yes,' he says. 'Good. It's going to be good.' He lifts his chin, eyes slits, and gives a lopsided smile before his head drops sideways, dead to the world.

Relief floods her. Thank you, Lady Gula, for that, and her head flops back and air blows warm from her mouth. Her misgivings evaporate. So much depends on Lord Hanno being a decent sailor and a good man. So very much. She listens to Dubb's breathing, feels it deepen on the back of her neck, senses his chest close to hers. She relishes the touch of him, from top to toe, his solid form, his company, his firm support for everything she does and who she is. She tries to follow him, to drift off, to match her breathing to his. She needs to lose herself, slip sideways into dreams, with a smile on her face like he has, with the certainty that everything will be alright.

But her neck is getting hot and his arm lies heavy across her torso. The distant barking of a dog catches her ear and its insistence drags her back to the present. What's going on with it? she wonders. All at once, she is completely awake and staring at the mud wall opposite her. Is that a face she sees in the shadows? Is someone there?

How stupid of me, she sighs, and gives her head a little shake. She turns and slides her way out from under Dubb's arms to peep beyond the curtain, which divides their shack into two. Tanu's form is long and pale, lit by starlight from the door behind her. Her breath is light as she passes on her way to the door. Darling Tanu, she thinks, and bends to give her daughter's brow a kiss. She lifts her mantle from its hook to wrap it round herself, and steps out into the night air.

At once, the stars leap out - brilliant, sharp and cold above her. A silvered path, flanked by the black and gnarled shapes of shrubs, leads away from their hut towards the gate and the latrines. The crew of The Delphis are scattered about in these dwellings, sleeping like logs, she thinks, except me. A few lights glint still from the governor's house up the hill and the nighttime's tick and crackle of insects surround her. She crosses the main route from the town to the harbour and turns off a side path towards the water. An onshore breeze flutes in the trees. It cools her: the back of her neck, under her arms, her roasting feet. Light from the moon takes her forwards, to the cliffs, high above the bay. Not too far from the others, she thinks.

When Nyptan first travelled with Dubb, she was married to another man, the Delphis's skipper. He was talented, ambitious and cursed with the sacred disease. She nearly lost her life trying to cater to his needs. Since Dubb rescued her from him, the two have never been apart.

This trip, this voyage to the ends of the Earth, will be the furthest she has ever been from home. Go and see what you can find is all that Dubb's master, Hekataios, had said to them. And so she's here, with her man, the love of her life, sailing away from her familiar world, losing all trace of its habits, gods and peoples with every passing port. An unwelcome spurt of anxiety rises in her. Be calm, she thinks. Lady Gula will stay with you. She will never abandon you, and she pulls Great Laughing Dog up from between her breasts and holds him close.

A coarse laugh rings out behind her through the night air and a lot of giggling. 'Shhhhh, you'll wake them,' followed by a crash of vegetation.

'Baal's balls!'

'You idiot,' and more laughter.

Her bottom lip slips back between her teeth. Oh, Lady Gula. Hanno and his young men. 'May the gods protect us,' she whispers, and brings Great Laughing Dog to her mouth to kiss him. She clutches her tunic around her and, with careful feet, turns back down the path towards the huts. When she gets to the edge of the road, she bobs into the bushes to watch. There are four of them. Lord Hanno is being helped up by the others from his fall. All are very drunk and, as they move towards her, they reel from one side of the gravel road to the other.

Checking she is not somehow caught in a pool of moonlight, she sinks still lower towards the ground. They stop directly across from her.

'Is this it?' says the thick set one, and points to the gate, which leads to their huts. 'Or is it further along?'

'Erghh, this is by the latrines,' says one, and neighs his displeasure. 'Let's go!'

'Which one do you want?' says the man nearest her. He has a large, shiny earring, which swings at the side of his head like a bat asleep in the moonlight.

'I want the young one,' says Hanno, words very slurred. 'Or the old one.' They all laugh.

'Who says you should always get first choice?' says a slim one, and leaps at Lord Hanno, both fists up.

They crash into the mimosa trees, this time falling sideways onto Nyptan's side of the road. They are so close she can smell the sweat from their bodies.

'You, Lord Prince of the Magonids,' says the attacker, and pummels the prince. 'You're not going to take my woman this time. I want the older one. Those breasts!'

Nyptan realises with a shock that they are talking about her and Tanu. Her head goes faint. Inside her, the shakes start. Her hand goes stiff, clutching at Great Laughing Dog. She is so afraid she can scarcely breathe. Be still, be very still, she thinks, or you will be discovered. The sound of her heart thumps in her head as she lies flat on the ground.

'Oh, come on, you two idiots. Let's go,' says another voice. 'This place absolutely reeks. We can get ourselves some pussy further down the coast.'

Another voice says, 'And anyway, that navigator bloke and his buddies will fight us over their women. Best look for easier pickings.'

'Yeah, come on,' slurs Lord Hanno, as he drags himself from the bushes. 'It's too soon to have a go at them. Besides, I've ruined my clothes now, you idiot.' He attacks his friend again, just as he is climbing his way out of the undergrowth.

With large amounts of noise and furious "shushing", the drunken party collects itself together and turns to make its way back up towards the governor's house.

When Nyptan can hear nothing except the distant roar of the sea, she stands and flies back down her pathway to their hut. Dubb is still stone asleep. In the darkness, she crosses to the makeshift shrine to Lady Gula in the corner, bends her head to peer at the vitrums lined up beside it in the dark and plucks one of them out. She pulls its top off and pours a little of the oil onto the rim of the lamp. Then, as quietly as she can, she strikes the flint and lights it, incense spitting and sparking to catch and flare and fill the room with a ribbon of perfume. This will ease her mind and make her calm again. Lady Gula, she prays, as she drops to her knees beside the glowing pot. Great Laughing Dog, she adds, and grabs at the amulet hanging from her neck. Glory be to you, my healers, my guiding stars, my familiar spirits. The tears roll down her face. Guard us in this foreign land. Keep us safe from our shipmates. Protect Tanu from the ways of men and me, too, your loyal servant, as we travel these strange shores. Bring us safely back home to Miletus in the Great Sea, stronger, wiser and healthier still. Her head rocks forwards as she inhales the incense, her mind flying out beyond the hut to the stars above. Sirius, her healing star, stands clear above her in the heavens, its piercing light striking all on the Earth below.

The Enquiry – Day 3

'So, there were slaves about and you felt lonely?' snaps Lord Apsan. 'Is that what you're telling me? Poor you.'

It is late morning and the enquiry into Lord Hanno's voyage to the Horn of the South has been in session for several hours. Just as he'd thought, the woman had rambled on and this boy is obviously quite out of control. From now on, they'll be refused permission to speak. His mouth is pouched and eyes move from one witness to the next, brows down.

'There were definitely slaves about,' says a young female voice.

Lord Apsan's head whips around and he sees the girl sitting beside her mother as if for the first time. Not another one speaking! They're impossible, these children.

'We saw boatloads of them the next day and Lord Hanno was with them,' she adds, before he can tell her to keep her mouth shut. 'Didn't we, Mummy?' She looks up at the woman for affirmation.

'Yes, he was gathering slaves.'

'Quiet, all of you. Not another word.'

The woman bites her lip and her daughter's eyes tear up.

'He is a slaver,' says the navigator, 'and much else besides.'

Lord Apsan turns to scowl at the man.

'What does "much else besides" mean? Out with it!'

'That he was crude and licentious,' the woman gets out quickly.

'If you are not silent, you women and children, I'll have you thrown out of this enquiry never to return. Do you understand?' he roars.

'He and his fellows did not respect my wife and daughter,' says the navigator. His back is pushed hard against the wall, legs tucked under the bench. 'He did not recognise their immense skills. Not even their power as healers.' He looks at Lord Apsan without blinking.

'What do you expect? Men are away from home; they have their needs.'

'You wanted to know what sort of man Lord Hanno is, my lord,' says the man, matter of fact. 'He is the sort who doesn't respect women.'

'You just finished saying you liked him, that he was a man of sound mind with whom you could do business.'

'That was true. At the very beginning. Yet we never did meet to plan and divide up jobs on The Delphis as we ought to have done. It was from Lixus that things started to go wrong.'

The other witnesses nod their agreement. Lord Apsan sighs. Clearly something or other has gone on with this navigator's wife or child, though it's irrelevant to ask what. He heaves himself to his feet and moves towards the window. His gaze falls on the far promontory where the trading vessels pass. Numbers have dropped off now the sailing season is coming to an end. If the incident, or incidents, had been really bad, if his wife's honour had properly been violated, then this navigator would have taken retribution on Lord Hanno by himself. As he did not, what point are they making? Such scandals are frequent in Carthage, but that's with high-born women, not a common sailor's wife like this woman.

'If you have further questions for the crew of The Delphis, my lord,' says his slave, voice oily, 'now would be a good moment. We have been in session for several hours now.'

A frown flits across his lordship's face. Have I been silent here for so long? He looks up sharply at Tasii. How I hate it when he tells me what to do. 'Of course I've got questions for the witnesses, Tasiioonos,' he says curtly. 'This is an enquiry and I will get on with it in my own time.' He returns to the table, takes a sip from his beaker and, in his mouth, sorts the granules from the liquid with his tongue.

'You were saying,' he says and swallows, turning to the navigator once again, 'that Lord Hanno took slaves. If there were free people hanging around that place not doing anything useful, it would be a dereliction of Hanno's duty as a commander not to take them as slaves.

Slaves are a commodity in our part of the world. Merchants buy and sell them. They are like tin, though not as valuable.'

The navigator's eyes flick to Tasiioonos and away. 'I have never traded in slaves myself,' says the man, 'in spite of a lifetime on the Great Sea.'

'Well, more fool you then, you prig,' says his lordship. 'Other Hellenes do. So do the Etruscans, Egyptians, Nubians and Parses. Some people are unlucky in life. They get taken. Poor them.' Unexpectedly, he thinks of Tasiioonos in a new way, sitting there across from him with his tablets, the joy of his life, and a slave. Tasii, less valuable than a load of tin? What have I said? He looks at his slave from under his brows. He won't mind such a comment, will he? Tasii's hand holds his stylus ready to write at any moment. He looks out the window, hair gleaming in the light. His limbs are lean, brown and beautiful, and the silver Hipolito shines in the hollow of his neck.

I have to finish this session, get back on an even keel at once, he thinks. He takes a gulp from his beaker and gives what he hopes will sound like a troubling cough. Tasii remains absorbed in the trading vessels. Lord Apsan ratchets the cough up to a splutter and develops it further so that his medicine spews out all over the table and onto his lap. Tasii comes to him then.

'Adjourn, adjourn,' the young man says to Gatit. 'Take them away.' He lifts his head to the witnesses and takes hold of his master's arm, lifts him to his feet and steers him to the door of their private quarters.

Inside the atrium, the atmosphere between the men turns frosty. Tasii helps his master to a chair. On a side table there is, as usual, an assortment of snacks and drinks, grapes, pomegranates, water and wine. Absent from it is fresh bread and olive oil. Lord Apsan looks at the collation with displeasure.

'Why doesn't Cook provide something more substantial to eat?' he says by way of breaking the atmosphere. Tasii remains silent. 'Because you've told her not to, is that so?' His eyes swivel towards his slave with a challenge. At least he'll have to speak to me.

'Because you are on a course of treatment for a stomach upset, my lord,' says Tasii, voice tight and controlled. 'Eating bread leaves you open to gastric problems from contaminated flour. I've told you this already.'

'Why doesn't the cook get better flour then?' says his lordship, warming to a fight. 'I pay her enough.'

'It's not the quality of the flour that's the problem, my lord. It's that you won't allow her to manage the rat problem.'

'They can get rid of a few rats, can't they? These servants need to do their jobs.'

'We live on the edge of town, my lord, as you know. There are rats everywhere. If you want to avoid them completely, we should either move away into the countrywide or get cats. And, as you must live in Gadir, and always refuse Cook's request for cats, your gastric problems remain. From time to time, you will get sick, despite everyone's best efforts to keep you well,' he finishes, sounding peeved.

Lord Apsan takes comfort from Tasii's use of the word "we", when he said "We should move away", and the panic he's felt over the last moments abates. Perhaps it's going to be alright with Tasii after all. How could I have been so stupid to compare slaves to tin?

Tasii, who has, by now, finished helping his lordship into a clean robe, is at his side knotting his girdle. Lord Apsan feels the warmth from his body, smells his smell, the oil from his hair, the lotion from his cheeks. His smooth skin and sculpted lips are within easy reach. He puts out an arm and draws Tasii to him to search for his mouth. Tasii does not pull away. Instead, he leans into him, puts his arms around his lordship's waist, nuzzles his head against his chest and reaches up to give his ageing mouth a soft kiss.

'My lord, we need to talk about this.'

'Talk about what?' he says, and the dread in his stomach stirs again.

'About the fact I'm your slave.'

'We know that. There's nothing to say. That's how it is.'

'But it's not how it has to be. It can be different.'

Lord Apsan lifts his teeth to the inside of his mouth and begins to gnaw at the skin. His eyes bulge. 'I will not let you go, Tasii,' he says, his voice caught in a vice. 'I need you. This office needs you. Don't you like being my secretary, with all the responsibilities and freedoms that that gives you?' Lord Apsan can feel the tears rise at the back of his eyes.

'I do.'

'Isn't it exciting to discover new places in the world, different lives, the sorts of things you could never know about if you did not work for me? And don't you appreciate the fine things I buy you, the place we live in, the benefits there are to your family up country and the way I treat you? You could have it a whole lot worse than me,' he says, his final argument clumsily put.

'You know I like these things.' Tasii stands before him, his Hipolito shining in the light, and nods.

Lord Apsan cannot bring himself to ask the last question. His lips move over it, though no words come forth. He cannot bring himself to ask "Do you love me?", for fear of the answer he'll get. His fear is swallowed up by fury, rage that that stupid navigator and his witchy crew introduced the subject of slavery and put wild ideas into Tasii's head.

'We should flog the prisoners,' he says, voice harsh, and he sits down at the side table to attack a pomegranate with a knife. Its juice slips down his wrist and stains his robe red. 'Get it done this afternoon, Tasii. I'll not have them raising irrelevant matters at an enquiry, especially as it affects you.'

Tasii's mouth opens in shock and his eyes go wide. 'My lord, what makes you think that a simple discussion about slavery unsettles me?' he asks. 'I beg you, do not do this to the witnesses. It's true I have been waiting for a moment like this for a long time, an opportunity to speak to you about my future. Without the arrival of The Delphis, the moment may not have come for years. But the fact I am your slave is not as new to me as it seems to be to you.' He looks at him, one eyebrow raised.

'Of course I knew you were my slave,' he says. 'I just didn't think you had a problem with it.'

'No problem with being owned by someone else?' Tasii says, the frigidity returning to his voice. 'Couldn't care about not being able to go where I want, do what I want, take life's chances on my own?' There's a look of incredulity on his face. 'It just shows you, my lord, that though we live together, our lives really are very different.'

Lord Apsan slumps down into the chair.

'Long ago, my lord, years ago, I decided that the best way to achieve the freedom I desire is to get you out of here and back to Carthage. I, too, wish to leave this place. I want to see the world, to know its great cities and their peoples. I want to live somewhere where music, the arts and learning matter. There are many places I dream of going: Carthage, Egypt…'

'We can go together!' says Lord Apsan, eyes alight. 'We will go as soon as this report is done.' He looks at his alabaster vase. 'You know how much I admire the country.'

Tasii shakes his head. 'I want my freedom, my lord, to go alone, to explore without being in your service, at your beck and call. And, when the time is right, I will ask you to release me from your service.'

Lord Apsan feels winded. 'Well, off you go!' he snaps. 'Go! Become a slave to someone else. He picks up a tablet and throws it at Tasii. 'Return to the hills if you want. Cross the water and serve one of those dreadful mining families. Or even, if you must, run to the Temple of Melqart. I'm sure they'd be delighted to have you there!' Even as these words spurt from his mouth, they ring hollow to him. He knows he will never allow Tasii to leave him, not now, not ever. He will put him under lock and key if he must.

A fracture begins to open up in Lord Apsan's well-ordered life. Tiny at first, it grows larger as he thinks of his work, ambitions, their factories and daily routines. What will I do if he leaves me? he thinks, if he runs away, wants to be sold, refuses to work? All I will have is loneliness, my own self, my dried-up, ageing life. A short, sharp sob breaks from him unbidden, one he immediately tries to suppress. His head drops to his chest and his face goes red with the effort of holding back the tears.

Tasii's warm hand is on his arm, his body close. 'We must get back to work, my lord,' he says. 'These things will become clear in due time.'

He swallows and musters his strength to raise his head. He puts out his hand and lays it on top of his slave's. 'Yes, we must,' he says. 'I will be alright in a minute. But I don't need clarity, not me, Tasii. If you go from me, my life will be over.'

The Gods' Blessings

Qart is on his way to a praise ceremony for Melqart, Lord of the Sea. The holy precinct in Lixus is set into a steep incline on the other side of the river estuary from the town. The boy is up to his knees in water. He heaves the chicken crates out of the dinghy and drops them onto the golden sand with a thump. The whole population: Governor, priests, travelling mariners and all their attendants and paraphernalia must cross the bay to take part. Today, Lord Hanno, leader of their expedition, will implore the great god for safe passage. All departing Carthaginians and crews gather with their gift offerings and amulets in preparation. A flotilla of little vessels gathers on the Lixus shore ready to transport them to the shrine.

'And watch you don't get sand in the crates,' says Malavisch, the chicken keeper, to Qart as the boy stacks the last one on top of the others, ready to be moved up the beach to the sanctuary.

Qart looks down at the birds. The majority are white or speckled. The black ones seem special and there are a few with flamed orange collars. Several lie on their sides, pink legs stuck straight out in front of them, panting. One seems dead. 'Shall I give them water, sir?' The boy has learned to call Malavisch "sir", a manner of speech Dubb has just taught him to reduce friction between him and the man who must, for the moment, be his master.

The man scowls down at the wilting animals and a hand goes to a narrow-necked beaker tied round his waist. 'Take them up the beach, put them behind the altar and give them this when you get there.' He opens a pouch, flicks a few drops of liquid from a vial into the beaker, loosens its string and hands it to Qart. 'This'll revive them.'

What's "this"? wonders Qart, as he ties the container round his waist and sets off up the beach, arms wide with the crates. Never mind the chickens. I need water, he thinks, and curses that he didn't bring any. Though early in the day, the sun is already strong, breaking, as it has, over the hill to the east.

When he gets to the top of the incline, he stops to rest. His legs and arms howl from the effort as his eyes scan the site for the altar. The sanctuary's sacred pavement is pricked with sea grass, a half colonnade built at the ocean end has collapsed onto itself and a granite wall, designed to hold back the hillside behind it, has failed to do so. The sacred space is almost wholly submerged in sand. You wouldn't know it was here unless someone told you, he thinks, as he looks for the holy stone of Melqart, a single standing stone, which should, if this is a proper shrine to Melqart, stand proud and alone, a symbol of the strength of their fearsome lord. He brushes the sand from his arms. This is so unlike the shrine to the great Lord of the Sea at the Strait of Calpe.

Labouring up the hill behind him from a dinghy are the two young Etruscan priests, shaved heads gleaming in the sun. Slung between them is a well-polished box of fine wood containing all the apparatus the high priest will need for divination and prognostication.

'Why's the holy place so far from town?' comes the voice of one, high and complaining. Good question, thinks Qart, but doesn't wait for the answer. He stands and gathers the chicken crates into his arms. Do the priests of Melqart in Lixus really have to do all this fetching and carrying every time an expedition sets out? He lumps the birds across the sandy pavement towards the ocean end of the sanctuary. The roar of the surf beyond the headland intensifies and the sea breeze rises, then buffets. It flings his hair from his brow, rushes into his armpits and makes his eyes sting. He rests his load on a broken-down wall. What a relief!

Up here on the hill, he can see why the sanctuary is so placed. The beach beyond it is huge and wide and white. It rolls onwards, far further than his eyes can see, forever it seems, into the unknown. He shields his face from the glare and tries to imagine what it will be like to travel down the coast on the breast of this ocean. How far does it go? It is far bigger than he has ever seen in his life. Extended lines of breakers curl shoreward in broken rhythm. They disappear into a haze. Spume and spray from them drifts across the yellow sand. How long could you live in a white-hot place like this? he wonders, as he picks up his crates and moves on. A second chicken has collapsed onto the slats and he remembers the stoppered beaker at his waist. I must hurry or they'll all be dead.

'Hey, you, boy!' comes a shout from a group of people he now sees gathered in the lee of a dune at the beach end. The voice carries to him on the wind, aggressive, aggrieved. 'Stay away from there with your filthy chickens.' The eyes of all in the group turn to glare at him. 'That's sacred space.' A vigorous-looking man emerges to head towards him. Qart shunts his crates with haste, veers around a stone wall, knees knocking together, and half-jumps, half-falls, over the wreckage of the collapsed colonnade to the side. There, between its sheared off back and the hill-side, he finds a small clearing where he dumps his load. The man's head appears between a set of broken pillars as he searches for Qart, finds him, scowls and goes away again.

Qart lays each crate out side by side. By now, more of the chickens are in a bad way. Melqart, no, he thinks, they can't die on me, not after all this. He slips one hand through the mouth of each crate in turn, cradles a chicken's head in his palm and, with the other, dribbles the contents of the beaker onto the bird's tongue. It had better work miracles this potion, he thinks, or I'm for it.

The priests, with their box, arrive at the centre of the sanctuary. 'Where's that chicken boy gone?' says one, and they start to search for him amidst the ruins. But the cross man arrives again from the beach, this time with all his friends, and he barks orders at the young priests, who shift their box to the side and start to clear the sanctuary of sand and prepare it for the ceremony to come.

* * *

Nyptan and Tanu face each other in a dinghy, crossing the estuary to Melqart's sanctuary on the other side. A local lad rows them from the front, pushing the heavily-laden dinghy directly into the path of the oncoming tide. None of the men can be spared to help them, all taken up with transporting animals. As ever, on their way to such an event, they sing. Their voices rise in turn, before each is overwhelmed by the onshore breeze. 'I am the Lady of Life…' goes Nyptan. Her hair whips from its place in her plait and flies forwards into her mouth. She pulls at it with supple hands and tucks it behind an ear. '…I expel disease.' They have all their precious herbs, incense and healing goods with them, taking them to the gods to be blessed.

'Most powerful in the sanctuary,' adds Tanu, her voice lighter than her mother's, though no less confident, 'I put men at ease.'

Nyptan smiles and puts her hand on her daughter's knee. How her darling loves to sing that line "most powerful in the sanctuary", with its heavy down beat, as if to reassure herself that Lady Gula really is superior to Melqart, Baal Hammon or any of the other gods they worship. She takes a gulp of bracing estuary air. 'I am the Lady of Life,' she carries on, and frowns. Is the boy going to swamp them and all their precious goods with his reckless oaring? she wonders, and glances up at him, a question in her eyes. His back is to them and he does not see.

'So, go on, Mummy,' says Tanu. 'You've stopped!'

'Yes, sorry, darling. My power makes sickness flee.' The vessel slaps and bucks, and sea wash mounts its side and douses her precious herbs and powders with sea water. 'Careful,' she says to the lad sharply. 'Can't we cross more slowly?' She tugs at his cape until he turns to her. 'More slowly.' She points to her precious cargo, now soaked in its hessian beside her. The boy nods and adjusts the tiller. Nyptan shoves her sodden store under her bench.

'Can we finish?' says Tanu, impatient.

Nyptan nods. Now everything will have to be done again. All that rinsing with fresh water, empowering under the starlight of their healing star, Sirius, and drying in the sun. She sighs.

'Don't worry, Mummy,' says Tanu. 'We can do that really quickly.' She sets her body directly in front of Nyptan's, across the centre of the dinghy, and waits.

'I know. It's just that I should have looked after them more carefully. I didn't know the tide would be so fierce.' She faces Tanu. 'I come to you with my healing hands,' she sings, and both of them place their hands upright in front of them, like Egyptian pharaohs travelling in the Far West. Then the finale comes.

'I root out disease,' they go in unison, and touch hands. Power transfers from mother to daughter, the healing arts moving through the generations as they have always done. Then the round starts all over again. They are nearly there.

In a fruit box at Nyptan's side are the ointments, compresses and decoctions she always takes to ceremonies to be blessed. Its wood is still sticky from the plums, which it had, until this morning, been holding. It is not that her lovely Lady Gula needs to ask Melqart to give her power. It is that, in her graciousness, Lady Gula would never refuse him the right to do the blessing. 'Never miss an opportunity for a blessing, whoever the god,' is what Nyptan's mother said to her when she was a child. In addition, in the stern, are two amphorae of her precious incense, specially carried, unopened, all the way from the Tyre, the vessels used by her mother. They have been waiting for this final moment of departure into the unknown. Then there are their amulets, Great Laughing Dog, hanging on a leather strap between Nyptan's breasts, and the feathered bead at Tanu's wrist. These, too, need to be sanctified anew. Most important of all is Lady Gula herself, nestled in her leather pouch in the folds of Nyptan's tunic. Her scalpel is ready in her hand as she waits to hear what the Great Sea God of Carthage has to say in these final days before they set out to the far reaches of River Ocean.

The dinghy bumps onto the bottom. The boy helps them out, and healer and girl start to drag their goods up the incline and prepare them for the rites to come.

'Uppa! Uppa!' she hears men cry from the far shore. She looks back to see that two dinghies, laden to the gunnels with sheep, are taking their chances across the fast-flowing tide. Dubb and The Delphis crew are climbing into one of Hanno's penteconters and a scraggy bull is creating havoc on the strand, refusing to step onto the platform the governor has laid on for the purpose, the one which will float him across the water to his death.

* * *

The roar from the breakers beyond is so deafening Dubb can scarcely think. He stands at the stone of Melqart, a terracotta model of a dolphin in his hand. It is one of many stored in the hull of their vessel to be brought out and used precisely on occasions like these. It is an unimaginative offering, uncontentious, yet shows sufficient respect. Ranged around the sanctuary beside him, the population of Lixus, Hanno and his men, the crew and priests from The Delphis and the governor all stand, whited out in the sunlight.

'You may lay it there,' says Lord Hanno, the turn of his shoulder ensuring his voice is not whipped away in the breeze. 'May the blessing of Melqart Almighty, son of the great and glorious Baal Hammon and his consort, Lady Tanit, go with The Delphis and all her crew.' He lowers his head and opens his palms wide to the sky.

Dubb steps forward and lays his dolphin on its side amongst the other votive offerings. There are oars, helms, horses' heads and anchors all teetering at the periphery of the altar like discarded clams after a night's feast.

'Mighty Melqart,' he mouths under his breath, as he sets his dolphin on top of piles of others, protect and preserve us until we come this way again. A priest at his elbow clashes his cymbals together, each crash marking the arrival of a new offering. Horns, trumpets and bells ring out as the fishermen, acting as temple assistants for the afternoon's ceremony, begin a drone, voices deep and rhythmic, rolling in time with the breakers to their right and instruments before them.

'Most Mighty Melqart,' says Hanno, voice powerful enough to be heard over the din, 'look kindly on our offerings.' The priests, crew, onlookers and aristocrats all clash cupped shells together like chattering gulls and lift their voices to roar in time.

'Great Melqart, we praise you. Praise!'

Lord Hanno, with his offering, a gold veneered image of his pente-conter, walks around the holy stone in front of the altar. He steps onto its circular markings in the sand as only the officiating nobleman can. His footprints smudge the circled lines drawn with precision around it. This stone, simple, unadorned, is the embodiment of Melqart himself.

'Mighty Lord, in whose presence we tremble, please accept these, our offerings to you to beg you for our safe return. We praise you.'

'We praise you!' echoes the company. The bells, cymbals, roar of the sea and howl of the wind, grit of the sand and fear of god all join as one in sanctified cacophony. Next, Lord Hanno turns to the bull. It is tied, head and feet, to posts on a pavement at the side.

Dubb is fearful and excited. Anxiety and curiosity in equal measure turn in his stomach. He faces the bull. He doesn't have to attend these praise ceremonies and, when he does, it is always at the beginning of an adventure. He twists his head to look for Nyptan. Can she see this? Where is she? Where is the rest of The Delphis's crew? As females, they are banned from the sanctuary itself. She and Tanu will have set up their shrine here somewhere nearby, somewhere clever. His eyes run around the sanctuary, through the colonnade, until he spots them squeezed into a corner of the escarpment, a place where its protecting stones will shelter them from the wind. They are curved in prayer. Before them is their incense burner, the image of Lady Gula and their leather bag of healing arts.

'Navigator, Navigator.' A sandal kicks at his foot. 'You're to come forward now!' Dubb whirls around to see Lord Hanno standing beside him. 'Bring the crew. You lead the way! It's time,' says the lordling, impatient.

'Am I?' says Dubb, trying to remember, amidst the din, whether the instructions given to him in advance included anything about the crew.

'Here, this way. Lead them around the holy stone!' says the man, before his face falls. 'Where are the rest of you?'

Dubb looks around. He can see no one from his crew nearby. They are peppered all throughout the crowd, Chares and Rabs at the front, Berek at the side, with other Utica men, and the new men, from Rusadir and Libya, to the right.

Lord Hanno, face like thunder, snaps at him. 'Oh, by Mighty Melqart, you'd better do this by yourself then. Off you go.' He raises his hand and whips it towards the end of the line of processing Etruscans. 'Go on then. You'll have to represent The Delphis by yourself.'

Dubb feels a fool, trudging behind the diviners, head bowed, attempting the tune of the praise song. Since when have crews had to process around the stone of Melqart? he wonders, his face hot with embarrassment. Is this a new thing in Carthage? Have I forgotten when Lord Hanno asked me to gather the crew together to parade like this?

The processants come to a standstill in a semi-circle around the holy pavement. Lord Hanno, roaming around on it, steps up to face the crowd.

'Now, Mighty Melqart, accept this our blood offering,' he declares, voice riding high over the sound of the breakers. He sweeps his hand up towards the bull, which has its head yanked up by two priests, the great neck broad and pulsating. As the knife goes in, it lets out a huge and desperate bellow. It thrashes against its ropes, hurls its head about.

Seamen and locals alike bow before it. Dubb feels a splash to his face, warm and wet. He puts his hand to it and wipes it off.

'Great Melqart, protect us. Lord of the Sea, bring us safely home,' shouts Lord Hanno.

As smoke and fumes rise to engulf the still writhing carcass, Dubb staggers out of the crush. He feels dizzy with the smell, the noise, the heat. Where is Chares? he thinks. Where are the others? He pushes his way to the crowd's edge. Fire takes hold of the carcass and sends flames high into the sky, the priests pour sea water across it. Rising steam adds to the spitting fat. Smoke engulfs the worshipping men.

He spots Chares and Rabs at the edge of the crowd. 'Melqart's mother,' he says, and wipes the sweat from his forehead. 'I haven't been to one of these bull ceremonies for a long time.'

'Almost too much, even for me, a Hellene,' says Chares.

'I usually manage to avoid them,' says Rabs.

'Dubb, you've got to come!' Qart is at his elbow, pulling him back into the crowd.

'Nothing will get me going back in there,' he says, and sees that the boy is desperate.

'Lord Hanno says you're to come. You're all to come,' he adds, and points to the others. 'There's a ceremony by the diviners.'

'Another one!'

'Over here,' the boy says, and takes hold of Dubb's arm to pull him back into the crowd.

Baal's balls. Must I? thinks Dubb, and his teeth clench together, mouth a straight line across his face. You stay here,' he says over his shoulder to Chares and Rabs. 'I'll represent us all.'

When he gets to the lordling, he is surrounded by diviners. Their tall hats, pointy beards and long robes are unlike anything Lixus has seen the likes of before.

'Here he is!' says Hanno, 'at last. Now go!'

The youngest of the holy men holds a chicken out by its neck and the tallest slits its throat, lies it out on the pavement, eviscerates it at speed, and dives in to the still moving animal to pull out its liver. The priests gather round it.

'This is an auspicious time to set sail,' says one.

'Here, this shows there will be a favourable outcome to this venture,' says another, and fingers the liver's lobe.

'Great riches will come of it.'

Dubb finds himself looking over the shoulder of Lord Hanno.

'What did I need to come to this blessing ceremony for?' he asks. 'Surely one praise ceremony is enough?'

'No, no, you misunderstand,' says Lord Hanno, eyes still glued to the priest's bloody hands. 'This is an extra reading of the gods' will. These diviners can tell us in more detail what the will of the gods' is. They say it's a good day to set sail.'

'But we know that already,' says Dubb. 'Why do we need more information?'

Lord Hanno turns to face him. 'Look,' he says. 'I might as well be clear with you. From now on, since we are all going together to a strange land, the diviners will have a say in everything, and that means navigation.'

'What? Even on matters as basic as when we sail?'

'As you know very well, when we sail is not "basic". I'm surprised that you, Dubb of Miletus, thinks it so simple. It is fundamental.'

Dubb's mouth purses and he is about to protest that that's not what he meant but decides against it. No point. He nods and keeps his aggravation under control. 'Of course, you are right, my lord,' he says. 'When a vessel sails is absolutely key to its success, a matter of life and death. It's just that that mystery, like all the arts of the sea, is something which navigators decide. It is my privilege, my responsibility and duty to know the weather, tides, mists and signs. And my job to say when we depart, when we anchor. All that has got nothing whatever to do with chicken livers, or dying bulls for that matter.'

'On the contrary, from now on,' says Lord Hanno, 'when and where we land is up to them. How long we stay ashore, and where we anchor. The spiritual arts of the Etruscans are exceptional as you know. They have precedent on their side. They don't just guess, hope and pray for success but know, from cases recorded in their annals, what the gods want. This is their purpose on our voyage, to bring their wealth of experience and discipline to our venture and show us the way to the gold. With them on board we cannot fail!' He smiles at Dubb, a look of confidence on his face.

'The Etruscans are not a seafaring people,' blurts Dubb. ' In any case, I don't guess at things. The art of a navigator is also based on experience.'

'Well, now there are two founts of knowledge on board. All the better for us!' beams the lordling.

'Are you seriously informing me that the Etruscans are going to lead this expedition, even on matters of navigation?' He tries to keep the panic from his voice. 'What do diviners, even very clever Etruscan ones, know about the sea, the tides, winds and the way vessels negotiate the routes?' he splutters. 'All Etruscan experience is rooted in the land!'

'You're just jealous of them,' says the lordling. 'We are on a course to great success with these special people on board.'

'Do these instructions come from Carthage?' spits the navigator. 'Who decided this, and when?' Lord Hanno does not hear him. The chanting has started up again and Dubb, abandoning the argument for now, pushes his way to the side to think. The shakes have started in the back of his head and his hands feel clammy. Did Hekataios know about this arrangement with the Etruscans? It would be most unlike him to put so much power into the hands of mystics. And, coming from far up in the Italic hills, what can they possibly know of River Ocean?

Feasting from the bull goes on well into the night. Men from The Delphis congregate to one side, near Nyptan's altar. News of the Etruscan's role in their journey has passed from mouth to mouth, and the meal they swallow is done in silence and fear.

The Delphis leaves in the morning on the tide.

The Enquiry - Day 4

'And what am I to deduce from all this?' says Lord Apsan, and ticks things off the list in his head as he speaks. They are in the upstairs workroom, witnesses lined up on benches at the wall. 'That Lord Hanno was experienced in the great occasions of state? That he understood the sacred rites completely? That he'd got it wrong about the diviners? What is your conclusion?' He takes a sip from the concoction beside him. Where is all this heading? I haven't got a clue.

'I was extremely disturbed, from that moment onwards, about the undue respect Lord Hanno gave the diviners.'

'You knew Etruscans were going to be aboard, did you not?'

'I did not. Even if I had, I would not have opposed it. I have been on many voyages where gods of all kinds are worshipped. On this particular journey, the Etruscans turned out to be a problem.'

Lord Apsan pauses, a frown on his face. He wracks his brains, thinks about all his years in Gadir. No, I can think of no other expeditions in which the Etruscans have played a part.

'May I ask you something, my lord?' The navigator's voice is respectful and Lord Apsan's eyebrows rise. Should I let him ask a question?

'If you must,' he says, 'but only one.'

'Lord Hanno came ahead of us back to the Great Sea,' says the man, and looks at him, eyes steady and unyielding. 'Is he here, in Gadir?'

He curses himself. Oh, why didn't I see this coming? Back to that again.

'I assume you are going to question him too?' the man adds.

'That's enough,' says the commissioner. 'I said one question and you've had it.'

'But you haven't answered it, Lord Apsan. Why not?'

'Of course I'm speaking to Lord Hanno. What do you take me for, a complete fool?' His mouth is down at the corners, his neck straight. 'In any case, who I speak to is no concern of yours.'

'But you don't appear to have questioned him yet. Otherwise, you would already have some of the information we are telling you. We might all be dead now because of him.'

'So you said.' The thought crosses his mind that it might be better if the navigator was dead. Yet without the navigator there could be no enquiry. Without an enquiry there would be no report, no route out of this dump back to Carthage. He looks across at Tasii, who lifts his head, and their eyes meet across the room. The navigator catches the glance and the tension in the room congeals.

'Of course we've spoken to him already,' he lies. 'I'm not sure how you got the impression that I have not.' A kind of mutter goes through the witnesses, a growl before a dog barks. His lordship looks back at the faces, then swallows, mouth pruned. He prepares his defence before the tribunal on Byrsa Hill. My lords, I ask you, how could I have tracked down a man who did not wish to found in a place four times larger than the size of Sicily and filled with boulders, goats, slaves and rampant traders? There are mountains, holes, rivers, scheming priests, a swathe of the great unwashed and, he shudders even to think of it, Tartessos city. He could go the land route back to the Great Sea during the winter, skip through the strait on an autumn tide, or stay put and wait for the weather to turn. I posted guards all along the route and paid huge amounts to the security staff to watch the ports. The witnesses to the enquiry, my lords, were uncooperative, ill, deranged, women and children. Tasii coughs.

'Well, who's going to carry on?' he says, voice high, a squeak.

'With what?' says the navigator. 'I asked you a question.'

'I'll carry on with the story,' says Chares, 'if that's what you want.'

Oh, Melqart's milk! he thinks. The Hellene. He rolls his eyes at Tasii, who turns to look at the man, a question mark on his face.

'Well, go on then, Chares,' says his slave, polite. Thank the gods for

Tasii, he thinks. Even this man droning on is preferable to more questions about Lord Hanno.

'Sailing in these parts is entirely unlike being aboard a ship in any part of the Great Sea,' starts the fellow. 'To begin with, the seas are huge, the currents vicious and the weather unpredictable.'

He gives a deep sigh. Alright. I'm in for a lesson in sailing techniques. He looks with longing at a stack of packing cases, which have just come in from the factory.

A Desert Shoreline

'It seems strange to be setting out on a big voyage like this after the peak of the sailing season, doesn't it?' says Chares, and squints at the sky's high cloud. The first mate, face as round as his body, is brown and flaking from long days in the open sea. 'Looking at the height of the sun at this time of the year, I can feel my body expects to head home to Miletus rather than be speeding away from her.'

He and Dubb bump shoulders at the tiller. They have worked together on the same vessels for most of their lives, one always the navigator, the other first mate.

'It's something about how the sunlight slants in the late morning,' says Dubb, and gives his shoulders a shake and stamps his feet. He has been at the helm for hours now and he welcomes the change. 'It must be desert over there.' He lifts his nose to the wind.

Hot gusts bluster at them occasionally from the port side and give The Delphis a wonky skip. The crew, mostly men from Rusadir and a few from Libya, stowed their oars long ago and lounge on hawsers or curl up against their benches to sleep. All of them, including those they took on in Gadir, know how to cope with rising heat and count themselves lucky that, for the moment at least, they don't have to row in it.

'Anything?' says Chares, as he grasps the steering handle, his hands slipping in behind Dubb's as the navigator moves off.

'Not too much. She seems to tug to starboard occasionally. We'll need to move closer to shore at some point.'

Chares nods. 'I'll keep a look out. And for him, of course.'

They stand in companionable silence for a time as the sun beats down. Lord Hanno should make himself known soon. The princeling had gone ahead from Lixus in the penteconters with his aristocratic friends to try and get intelligence about gold perhaps, and to prepare the way for them in Ngap.

'We can't be sure to meet him,' says Chares, reading his mind.

'No,' says Dubb. 'I'll also keep an eye out. We all will.'

Chares lifts his chin in acknowledgement, eyes ahead. 'Why did he insist on using the penteconters?'

'He said because they can hug the shoreline more easily than a merchant man. Which is true. The Delphis is not great in shallow water.'

'Well, he'd better be smart enough to catch us as we pass or our expedition's over,' says the first mate.

'He's smart enough to catch us,' states Dubb, though he is not entirely convinced. Both men know without saying it how disastrous it would be for The Delphis to overtake their leader by mistake in big seas like this.

A clash of cymbals rings out from the prow and the sleepers stir. Dubb looks up. In contrast to the languid forms immediately in front of him, the bow is all activity - young diviners are on their feet and circle each other in a kind of dance, and the older ones sing.

'Oh, Nethuns, Lord of the Deep...' comes the thin voice of their leader. 'Hear us, help us.'

There is more crashing of bronze, followed by a scrambling sound and banging from beneath Dubb's feet. He looks down. The back end of Rabs appears, feet first. Then his head. He is so small he has somehow inserted himself below the tiller platform for a snooze. He sits, crumpled, and looks forward, still half-asleep.

'Oh no, not that racket again.'

'Rabs, that's where you've been! I knew you'd be holed up somewhere. How could you criticise our holy men like that?'

The small mariner staggers up until he stands beside them at the tiller. 'They're jokers, aren't they, this lot?' he states. 'Listen to them.'

'I was shocked to hear what Lord Hanno said to you back there,' adds Chares, eyes on the horizon.

'Unbelievable,' says Rabs. 'Did he really mean it, do you think? That this lot should be given as much power as that?

Dubb pulls a face and shakes his head. 'Who knows what he thinks. Perhaps he was just caught up in the drama of the moment. I hate to think what will happen to us if he really means it. Let's just see how it goes, shall we, before getting too worked up.'

A bell rings. Then a different one. 'I, the magician, am thy slave,' comes the chorus of voices.

'They're no more than common soothsayers,' snorts Rabs. 'I don't care what Lord Hanno says. They're going to be trouble, this lot, I put my share of the booty on it.' He stamps his foot to confirm the pledge.

'They do seem to take things to an extreme,' says Chares. 'Even worse than us Hellenes.' A look of anxiety crosses his face.

'At least the vestal virgins of Memphis are of more use!' says Dubb, with a short bark of derision. They all laugh.

The priest with the pointed hat jigs in a circle, and stops and points with his finger at the mouth of a bowl. The one with the silver clasp follows him, ready to catch whatever he might throw. Before long all the Etruscans are obsessing over the stones.

Rabs steps down to the deck and starts to mimic them. He is joined by Berek, up from midships. The women come from their quarters to see what all the fuss is about and Tanu joins in. Berek pulls out his flute and begins a different tune. The Delphis scuds along on its hot wind, two sets of people dancing to different tunes.

***

Most unusually, Nyptan has started to feel sick. The seas have been rough it's true, though such dramas have not troubled her before. Perhaps it's the bigger current, she ponders, as she leaves the topside and takes a step across to the curtain behind which their private quarters lie. She leans forwards and pulls her leather healing bag from under a hessian cloth to open it. Her eyes run along the remedies laid out in it in rows. So, something for a rolling sea, she thinks, a new remedy for a new time. A decoction, which slows things down, to counteract the speed with which The Delphis is being dragged along the coast? Or something for her stomach directly? In her bag, her remedies conform to her own systematic categories of oils, compresses and ointments, from sharp antiseptics through to soothing balms. What should she choose? The vitrums gleam in the sun, the bag itself a bit clogged with fine sand. She brushes it out. Perhaps she should try cloves in case she is catching something? Rosemary to ward off feeling low? What feels like an ancient pain rises from below her belly. Perhaps it's my monthlies early. She frowns. Tanu is at midships, laughing with Rabs and the others as the small Carthaginian tries to balance an oar across his forehead. I hope I'm just late this month, she thinks, and peers into her leather case to see if she can spot Lady Gula amongst her things. There, beneath them, she spies the golden stone head with its slash of red at the top. It nestles amongst the straw and hessian, calming, consistent, faithful. I couldn't be pregnant, could I? she wonders. After all these years? All is silent in the bag.

* * *

The current, that little tug to starboard, which began hours ago, has become a sea snake, a living animal in danger of dragging them to their deaths. The tiller handle is rigid in Dubb's hands, the rudders it controls working at odds with one another at the sides of the vessel. One, on the starboard side, wants The Delphis to slip away to the wide-open ocean. The other, he must hold rigidly parallel with the land. He leans his whole weight against the bar, his muscles straining. Chares dozes beside him, worn out from similar exertions. Unless we come to rest soon, we could be in trouble.

'Time to check how fast we're travelling, Rabs,' he says. The man nods, elbows Chares awake and the pair go to collect the ropes and leads they use to measure speed. They butt their way through the swaying diviners, throw their leads to count the knots and repeat the process three times before returning to him.

'Six knots,' says Chares.

'I make it five and a bit,' adds Rabs.

They both say together, 'Fast, very fast.'

'Faster than I've ever been before, except when we were hauled through the Strait of Bosphorus that time,' says Chares.

'Right, let's try and get her closer to land,' he says. 'You'd better get the boys up and rowing. We've got to work against the current and haul her over to port.'

Berek beats a complex rowing tune as the rowers on the port side drag their oars in the water. Those to starboard pull in unison to shove their vessel towards the shore. Chares, Rabs and a bristly-headed man from Libya play ropes so that the sail catches what little wind there is to help them on their way.

As Dubb keeps his eyes ahead and his weight on the tiller handle, a worry sets up in his head. However straightforward this trip is along the coast, how will we get back? We'll have to battle this current all the way. Or perhaps it changes at a different time of the year? In which case, what time of year is that? He feels excited at the thought of finding out.

By late in the afternoon, it seems, to Dubb's nose, like there is vegetation of some sort on the land. He gets a whiff of its fruitiness, though there are no distinguishing features on it. They have eased themselves out of the current and moved closer to the coast. Orange shards of light from a setting sun criss-cross the silver sea. Then, ahead of them, he sees a row of black dots, a clear sign of a flotilla of local craft. They range out from the land in a straight line like an arrow. It's a clear signal. Lord Hanno is here. Relief shoots through him from toe to scalp. A great smile emerges from his face.

There are shouts from the foredeck, 'We're landing!'

His lips, cracked from the sun, form a silent prayer. Thank you, most Mighty Melqart, for that.

Yet Lord Hanno is not with the welcoming party. When they come alongside the lead craft there is, instead, another man, dark brown, with his arm up against the sea's bright light.

'Hello. Lord Hanno, Prince of Carthage, sent me. I am here to guide you into the settlement.' He speaks good Punic.

Dubb hangs over the topside to wave, Chares at the tiller. 'How glad we are to see you!'

* * *

This river is blessed by the gods, thinks Nyptan, as The Delphis slips from the open ocean through a deep fissure in the land to the interior. They glide past box brush, palms and lush green on both sides at its mouth. The tall heads of acacia trees poke above the olives and the brown roots of mangroves sink deep into briny mud at the river's edge. Their passage narrows and twists towards what looks like, to her at least, a fine anchorage. She and Tanu hug the topside, curtain looped up, so they can see what's happening on deck. It's not only her who finds the landscape entrancing. Dubb, Chares and Rabs all gape over the side and only the insistent thwack of Berek's drum keeps the rest of the men from rushing to starboard too. They move under stately trees, branches spreading, bower-like, out across the water. Beyond the greenery, there's a dappled plain. Golden grassland, goat herds, bells from distant flocks, air as thick with haze as the river is with swarming fish. Children run along the bank, shouting and waving, women washing in inlets stop to stare and egg-shaped humpies cluster together in what look like villages.

Tanu is open mouthed in wonder. 'Wave, wave at the little girls,' she says.

'Who would have thought that after all that desert, we'd come to this!' she says, eyes alive.

'Hear the bells!' says Tanu, and jumps up and down, excited.

'Never seen anything like it,' says Rabs, as he joins them. 'Even in sacred Hellas.'

Dubb, at the tiller, follows the pilot to the mouth of a small water-way tucked to the side of a main river channel. It is here they will stay. There is a wide beach and a village further off. Her husband's eyes are crinkled with excitement, his long hair looped behind his ears. As he stands and waits for the ladder to be fixed, she goes to him and puts her arms around his waist.

'Time for a quick moment? Just a minute with me?' She leans her cheek against his muscly arm. He turns to her and smiles. 'So much for the horror of the great unknown!' she says, and pokes him in the ribs.

'Yes,' he says, and pulls a face. 'This, I agree, is a very fine introduction for you to the pleasures of long-distance sailing.' He leans his back against the tiller handle, and puts both arms around her to hold her close. His body feels familiar, comforting and strong; the smell of dried sweat and salt mingle together in the fabric of his tunic. She nuzzles into him and his jaw caresses the top of her head before coming to rest on the top of it. She knows his eyes roam the scene, however. Not a thing passes in this process which he misses. Might she speak to him now about her woman's issue? she wonders. No, now is not the right time. Her breasts are squashed between him and her rib cage. They're certainly tender. There is definitely a child on the way.

His voice booms in his chest below her ear. 'Over there! Can you see?' he shouts, and unhooks himself from her arms, a hand trailing behind, and steps over to the topside.

A few small shanties sag together on the shoreline and beyond them, the plain opens out in a late afternoon haze.

Lady Gula, thank you, she thinks, and pulls Great Laughing Dog up into her hand and kisses him. We've made it this far, to this lovely place. The bay of his oil fills her nostrils and her heart with hope. Whatever the future, in this moment, all is well.

'Oye! Oye! Oye!' come shouts from the shore. A swarm of small craft is on the move to greet them, buzzing around the moored up hippoi.

Lord Hanno is on the shore, bent sidewards. He's holding a sheep around the neck by a rope, the aristocrats with him. 'We're coming!' he yells.

There is the familiar rumble of the chain hawser as the anchor shoots out of its porthole, followed by a splash as the stone lands in the water.

Frantic action breaks out at the bow as the diviners launch into a frenzy of chanting.

'Oh no!' says Tanu. 'Are we going to have another sacrifice?'

'It looks like it,' says Nyptan. She takes her daughter's hand and they return to their quarters. She closes the curtains. 'Best be out of the way.'

'But I wanted to go ashore,' says Tanu, a whine in her voice for once. 'Why do we have to wait? Can't Rabs drop us off in the dingy now and come back for the ceremony?'

'No, darling. We can't ask him to break off his work. We must wait our turn.'

'But it would only take him a minute and then he could get on with other things.'

'Tanu dear,' she says, voice firm, 'you need to understand that we are very low on the list of priorities when it comes to getting ashore.'

So they sit behind their curtain and do their best to ignore the thundering feet, clacking ladder, cursing and clamouring, which follows.

* * *

Dubb helps Lord Hanno and his hopeless aristocrats on to the deck with the distressed sheep, and the enormous amount of kit, which comes with it.

'Good morning, my lord. I hope you had an uneventful journey here?' he says, as pleasantly as he can. He hasn't, after all, seen him since they left Lixus many weeks ago.

'Yes, hello to you, Navigator,' says the man crossly. 'Can you just help us get this animal on board?'

'If you must have it on board,' Dubb says. 'Wouldn't it be easier on shore?'

'Well, we're all moving onto The Delphis from here on. Too many biting things on the land.' The sweat pours off him as he lifts more boxes towards the bow. 'For Melqart's sake, give us a hand, can't you!'

Dubb bites back his irritation. More clobber on board, just as we are about to give the whole vessel a final check over before the big journey. 'You mean that all six of you are coming to live here?'

'Only for a few days. It's just three of us coming all the way. So no need to fret, old man.'

As he heaves goods around The Delphis and endures the next round of Etruscan sacrifice, he endeavours to keep the impatience from his face and frustration from his voice. It is midway through the afternoon when he turns to stern and sees that Nyptan is on the tiller platform, and talks to a new man on board. It's the one who met them out at sea, the pilot who guided them in to the estuary. He is smooth shaven with shiny, dark skin, curly hair and a wide smile. A multicoloured shawl lies over one shoulder and a bundle wrapped in woven material sits between his feet. It looks like he has just arrived on board.

'Dubb, over here,' calls Nyptan across the deck, and she beckons. Her voice is cheerful, excited. 'There's someone who wants to meet you.' She smiles. Dubb's heart skips. His beautiful woman, in this beautiful place. She is so clearly pleased to meet the stranger, he almost skips to her side. 'His name is Kama.' His wife opens her hand to the man beside her.

'You brought us in safely,' says Dubb, and grasps the man's arm. Thank you. How many days had you been waiting out there for us?'

'Many, it is true, but we are used to that,' says the man, and turns to sweep his arm across a couple of other men, who sit on their haunches, Dubb now sees, at the side of the platform. 'We didn't want to miss you.'

'We didn't want to be missed.' They all laugh. 'In case you don't know it already, I am Dubb of Miletus, the navigator on this expedition. This is my wife, Nyptan, and daughter, Tanu. They are the healers on this voyage.'

The man bows. 'I am called Kama.' He turns to his companions. 'This is Pa and Tala, my brothers. They know the currents and at least as many languages as me. Welcome to Ngap, our home.'

'You're our interpreters! Well, welcome. Make yourselves at home here on board,' he says, 'if you can find any space. I've been looking forward to meeting you' and he claps the man on the back.

Kama is a handsome man, middle-aged and strong. The others are a stringy, tall fellow and a shorter man wearing woven fabric across his shoulders. All of their goods seem to be stowed in gourds. We've met them, our helpers! Dubb thinks, and his heart skips at the thought. In all the stink of the sacrifice and antics of the diviners, these are people who know the tides, the landscape, fresh water sources, the locals. We are not alone. Thank you, Mighty Melqart! Kama looks up from beyond midships and catches his eye. They raise fists at each other and smile.

The Enquiry – Day 5

There is a knock at the door. Lord Apsan rolls over on his pallet and tries to ignore the urgency of its tone.

'Lord Apsan,' says Gatit, in a grating whisper from the other side of the door. 'Your lordship, there's a message.'

'No need to whisper, you fool. I'm awake now! Get Tasiioonos to deal with it,' he squawks, and turns over.

'Mr Tasii is out, sir. It seems urgent.'

Mother of Melqart, he thinks, and heaves his body out from under the covers. 'Alright, alright, I'm coming,' he grumbles, wraps a shawl around his shanks and goes to the door to open it a crack.

Gatit looks agitated. 'Your lordship, sorry to trouble. It's just there's a young lad downstairs, says he is from Tartessos, with a message for you. He says you have to see it at once.'

Tartessos, he thinks. That filthy place! 'Send him up and tell him to wait outside this door til I call him in.' What can Tasii be doing out so early in the morning?

The boy is young, voice croaky, scantily dressed, with tightly cropped hair, poor teeth and a dazed expression. The great unwashed, he thinks, as he opens the door.

'Beg pardon, your worship,' says the boy, and attempts to take hold of his hand to kiss it. Lord Apsan pulls it back. The boy drops to his knees, head bowed. He stinks to high heaven. A boy like this, from the street, thinks his lordship, nose wrinkled. In my house! It had better be a good message.

'Stay there,' he orders. 'Don't touch anything. Say what you have come to say and go.'

The lad swallows, mumbles and his forearms start working at his chest as he pulls something from a pouch at his neck.

'Oh, stand up, you idiot. And speak up. I can't hear you.'

'My father sends you this,' says the lad. He pulls a scrunched rag forward and holds it out. It is in a ball, faded red and reeks of sweat. 'He says you will know what to do.'

Lord Apsan dare not touch it. He takes a step back, opens the door wide and points to the table.

'Over there. Put it there,' he says, 'and go.'

The boy lingers.

'So leave! Gatit,' he roars over his shoulder at the stairwell. 'Come and get this hideous specimen of the local population.'

The boys drops to his knees again. 'So sorry, your worshipful,' he says, face upwards, hands out, 'my father said I've got to wait for you to read it.' His lips work across his teeth with anxiety, and his eyes dart between the cloth and Lord Apsan.

Lord Apsan skirts around him as he goes to the table. Rolled up as it is, the message reveals no sign of any writing, or of any marks at all. 'There, I've read it,' he says. 'Now go.'

'Beg pardon, your worshipful, but you haven't,' says the lad, and his head hangs down.

Lord Apsan's eyebrows go up and his mouth opens. 'What? You dare to contradict me? How do you know?'

'I can read, your worshipful,' says the lad, 'and it's inside out.' His voice quavers and his head, hinged on his shoulders, goes up and down. 'Very sorry to disagree.'

'You? Read?!' His mouth curls with disgust.

The boy continues to nod like a deranged monkey.

Oh, Melqart's mother, he thinks. Just deal with it and get rid of him. He steps forward to the table, and his eyes narrow. He leans forward to pull one of Tasii's stylus sticks over to raise the rag at one corner. There seem to be big, white blobs on a frayed geometric shape with strokes along a line.

When it unravels he is left with rows of large, white marks on a red background and a message he cannot understand.

'What is this?' he says, and turns on the boy. 'Is it a joke? If so, it's not funny.'

'I don't know, your worship,' stutters the lad. 'I've not read it, just carried it, your worshipful.'

Lord Apsan's jaws feel locked together. This place. How can I stand it, to live here, year in, year out? 'So, where did your father get it from?' he says through clenched teeth.

The boy gives a series of short head shakes and Lord Apsan feels his fist ball, ready to hit him, when he hears the downstairs door slam and Tasii's footsteps in the stairwell. Thank the gods. He turns to face the window. A moment later, his secretary arrives in the room, windswept and damp. Supplies are in his hands and a small amphora under his arm. He looks surprised to see a visitor so early in the morning and in their private quarters.

'Oh,' he says, and puts his armful down on the table. At once, he sees the fabric. 'What's this? What's happened here?' His mouth is open, eyes puzzled.

'How do I know, Tasii?' he says. 'This boy just brought it to me, says it is urgent. He's been told to stay here until I've read it. Despite the fact I am well educated and have at least five languages from around the Great Sea, this is not a script I understand. Do you?'

'What? This young boy has come over the water so very early in the morning, in this weather? With a message like this?' Tasii seems flabbergasted.

'Yes, Tasiioonos, the boy has just arrived in this weather,' he says, voice getting thin. 'Yes, this is the message. Yes, it's urgent. So, can you read it?'

'Of course I can,' says his slave. 'It's in Tartessic.' Astonishment is written all over his face. 'Why is someone sending you a message in Tartessic?'

Lord Apsan glowers.

His slave bends over the cloth and his nose wrinkles. 'Usually, this form of message is only used way up in the hills, between family groups. It uses up old rags,' he says, as his eyes run across the letters.

'Security,' it says. 'Secret-'

'Stop,' says Lord Apsan. 'Boy, leave. This message is not for you. You have done your duty and can see that it is being read.'

'Worshipful lord,' says the boy, and bolts out the door.

'The nub of it is,' says Tasii, as he rearranges the fabric several times with his forefinger, '"a strange lordling with heavy jewellery and a weird accent passed along the road the day before yesterday".'

'What? A message like this, coming from a family group up country, in a language I have never seen before? How is it possible?!'

Tasii looks sour. 'Yes, clearly the message has come from up country, my lord, and is clearly in a script you cannot understand!'

'Oh alright, alright,' he says, his brows down. He's too smart by half, my slave, he thinks, and gives his head a little shake. 'It's got to be Hanno, hasn't it? They've found him.'

'Could be.'

'Well, what direction was he going in?'

'It doesn't say, my lord,' says Tasii, eyes knowing. 'It says nothing about that.'

'What? Nothing?!' he explodes. 'Oh, piss in Melqart's milk!' he roars. 'What is the point of sending a message like that if it doesn't say where the stranger was coming from or going to? Get the boy back! He must tell us more.'

When the boy returns, he is very frightened. He huddles by the door ready to dart out at any minute.

'Move into the room. No, stop. Back a bit. There. Stay there!' he says. 'Gatit, stand guard.'

His lordship's bodyguard moves into place, the friendly hulk of the man between the filthy lad and the stairs.

'On what road was this stranger to be found?' he spits.

'Please don't hurt me, your worshipful. I'm only young, my whole life ahead of me.'

'Answer the question. Where was this stranger going?'

The boy starts to wail. The intensity of his voice rakes the quiet of the residence's domestic rooms until the furniture shakes.

'Shall I take him out, sir?' says the bodyguard.

'You'd better,' says Lord Apsan, and swings away to look out of the window. 'Or I'll strangle the boy.'

'No, no, don't remove him,' says Tasii. 'Get him food. Bring up bread, Gatit, and grapes and cheese. Because I'm sure this boy would like breakfast, wouldn't you, son?' he says, as he takes him by the elbow and leads him to a chair. 'Now calm down.' The boy's eyes are awash with water and he wipes a stream of snot from his nose along his wrist. 'Look, we're getting you something to eat. You'd like that, wouldn't you?'

The boy does not answer and Tasii waves a hand in the air around his nose. Lord Apsan leans against the window frame at the other side of the room.

'You see, we're not going to hurt you, are we, Gatit?' he says when the bodyguard returns with a pile of bread, cheese and a beaker of water. 'Here's something to fill you up. Then you should feel better.'

The lad's eyes light up and he consumes everything at speed.

'Now that you've had a bit of nosh, his lordship would like to ask you a few questions. Are you ready for that?' The boy looks up, full of dread. 'You can have lunch straight afterwards.'

'I don't know nothing about the message, your worshipful. It's mi dad who knows who's who and all.'

'When did it first arrive with your father?' asks his lordship. 'Were you there when it came?'

The boy's head starts to shake 'I weren't there…' he says, fear beginning to take over again.

'Hush, hush, hush. Did someone come and visit you in Tartessos, for example?'

'Mi uncle come from the country, but I was out.'

'Did he bring this message with him? Was he there long?'

The boy can find no words and Lord Apsan heaves a sigh.

'Hold out your hands,' says Tasii, and the boy's skinny arms turn over to reveal a tattoo on one of his wrists. It is in the shape of a horse's head and is about the size of a baby's palm.

'Where did you get this?' Lord Apsan asks. It is the same shape as the Hipolito at his slave's neck.

The boy puts his hand behind his back. He shakes his head. 'I didn't do it. I was a baby. I didn't know…'

'We are not going to hurt you. What is the name of the region where you come from?'

Not a word more can they get from the boy's mouth. He sits at the side and snivels.

'Someone, not you, needs to go with this boy back to Tartessos and persuade his father to come and see me,' says his lordship.

'If not me, then who?' says Tasii. 'There is no one else.'

Lord Apsan ignores him. 'And I thought I asked several days ago that the security man from Malaka come and see me. Why hasn't he arrived yet? Send to him again. Get the whole network in, all five of them - plus that old boy from the temple gate, the company secretary from the Tartessos office and the man from the dockyard in Sexi. They should be here by the day after next,' he snaps. 'And, Gatit, remove him.' He points at the boy.

'The temple gate man died,' says Tasii, 'and the dockyard man hasn't been seen in weeks. Maybe he, too, has gone to Melqart.'

'Well, get whoever's left,' he pouts.

The boy's protests shake the furniture as he leaves. 'I've got my whole life ahead of me. I done nothing wrong. I'm going to tell my da about this.'

* * *

His lordship is seated at the table, looking over Tasii's work tablets, when his slave returns from sending off the runners. 'This security network is completely useless,' he says. 'Look at this report, from the mother's teat man at Malaka. He shoves the tablet at Tasii as he joins him. '"Saw a sail today. Followed it until Sexi, where it put in for the night". And then nothing more. No follow up. No investigation, no going ashore to ask questions. Is that really what we're paying for, this level of incompetence? The whole vessel could have been loaded with bullion without this fellow spotting a thing.'

'Well, spotting an unauthorised vessel in an established sea lane and finding someone who does not want to be found are different things, my lord,' says Tasii.

'I grant you that. But this oh so clever person doesn't even appear to have asked a single question about his unauthorised vessel, let alone done a house-to-house search for an individual.' He flaps his hand at the rest of the tablets. 'Generalities and lies, rubbish to bluff us while taking our money. And yet a message like this rag here is sent to me by person, or persons, unknown, completely out of the blue. How does the sender even know we have an alert out? It's supposed to be top secret! Then they write a reply in a language I don't understand and with no useable information in it. Though they appear to be a rough and ignorant sort of people, top marks for initiative!' he finishes, and shakes his head in disbelief.

'People from our part of the world are neither rough nor ignorant' says Tasii, voice prim.

'At least it's a sighting, which is more than has been delivered by the extensive members of our professional security team. We send them urgent instructions and they go straight to sleep! Otherwise, how can Lord Hanno have gotten away from us?'

Tasii shakes his head and a long sigh comes from between his lips.

'And anyway, how come you know this language and I don't?' he asks. 'I've been here in Gadir for more than twenty sailing seasons and I've never come across it.'

'It's usually only used between families,' says Tasii, 'for private purposes. There's nothing official about it. I doubt that even King Arganthonios and his ruling families know about it. It's mostly used by people from up country who venerate the horse.'

'Don't all you people follow the horse? I've seen statues and demonstrations at banquets,' he says, and knows, the minute he said it, that he should not have used the words "you people". It gets Tasii worked up. He doesn't like to be reminded that natives of the area, like him, are different from true Carthaginians.

'The horse is a source of great comfort and inspiration to those of us who come from our region,' says his slave, voice tight. 'On the coast here, it is different because of the king, though even here there are devotees of the Hipolito, as you well know.' He smooths down the silver pendant at his neck, resentful.

Don't say another word, he thinks, and drums the fingers of one hand on the back of his other. Don't speak. His neck feels stiff.

'And the horse is a source of healing too,' Tasii adds. 'The temples up country are known for producing remedies and regimes to cure people of all kinds of ills. Your charcoal comes from there.' He points to the fresh supply lying on the table.

'What? Is that the one you've been giving me for my stomach problems?'

'It's the charcoal of a horse,' says Tasii, still angry. 'The remains of a burnt offering to the gods, which the priests of Hipolito have blessed.'

'What?' Lord Apsan's mouth opens in shock. 'Excuse me, Tasiioonos. May I be clear. Do I understand it that I have been swilling back, or crunching between my teeth, the blackened remains of a horse?!' He senses his voice has gone up in range.

His slave nods. 'Exactly, my lord. A holy animal, one which has lived a blessed and sacred life, been served by priests, prayed over by the knowledgeable and then ritually slaughtered in a temple to the great Hipolito.'

'Have you completely lost your senses, Tasiioonos?' he explodes, and jumps up to swipe the supplies off the table onto the floor. 'Are you trying to poison me slowly, so that I don't notice, to contaminate me with the weird ways of this region and its people?' He stands in front of his slave now, fury in his eyes. 'I will not take one bite more of your biscuits or sip of your concoctions. I instruct you to get Cook to provide me with standard remedies from our kitchen, which will keep me healthy and safe. In future, you should keep all your horse stuff within the bounds of your own space.'

'What space, my Lord?' says Tasii, sour, lips thin. 'I have no private space as you know. In any case, you cannot deny that you have been better since you have been using the charcoal.'

He can think of nothing to say in response. It's true that his gastric problems have settled in the last days. He has even eaten peppers. But a horse!

'There, I told you. It is working, which is a good deal more than can be said for anything you might get from the Temple of Melqart.'

Lord Apsan is silent. He sits on the edge of his pallet and shakes his head. 'What can possess you, you native peoples, to eat a horse like that?'

'We are not native people. We live in this region rather than exploit it for its minerals. In any case, we do not eat horse, my lord. We use the blessed remains of ritually sacrificed gods for the sake of human health. And anyway, we "natives", as you call us, do not kill our children in sacrifice,' he spits, triumphant, 'just to keep yourself safe in war.'

'Oh, that's unfair,' groans his lordship. 'Do we have to go over all this again, Tasii? How many times do we have to talk about it?'

'Well, you raised the issue of how uncivilised we natives were, not me,' says Tasii. 'If we are a bit excessive in the horse department, at least we draw the line at ritually slaughtering human beings!'

'But we don't go on to eat our children, even at a time of war' his lordship counters. 'We honour them!'

Both men look at each other, exasperated. It is a row they have had so many times in the past, it has exhausted itself.

'So I'll not have any more of your charcoal, thank you. If you think charcoal works, find another type for me to consume.'

'As long as it's not that of a dead child,' says Tasii, I'll do my best.'

The two turn away from each other, Tasii to hover over the message, Lord Apsan at the window, biting his nails.

* * *

In an out-of-character fit of efficiency Lord Apsan decides to call the witnesses up to his workroom again later that day.

'The boy should carry on the story,' says Dubb, and sits back with a shrug.

'I'm not a boy,' says Qart. 'You know I'm a man now.' His eyes flash at the navigator, who sighs.

'Why him?' says Lord Apsan. 'Why have you chosen him?' It is so irritating that, although he often says very little, the navigator still attempts to direct this enquiry.

'Because he was the only one of us who was with Lord Hanno at the time. Because he is good at remembering things. Because he knows what went on.' With each thought, the mariner seems to sink lower into his seat. By the end, his head leans back on the brick wall behind and his face is grey with exhaustion.

The boy looks pleased to be praised. He sits up straight and his eyes swing to the commissioner, mouth open.

'Well, go on then,' says his lordship, voice settled again, 'since you seem to have been chosen this time. Get on with it.' He glowers at the boy, face as crumpled as his mantle.

'We came to this river estuary,' says the boy, 'a very beautiful place with large trees and forests along the banks.'

'Yes, yes, I know all that,' he says, 'get on with it.'

'Well, we set out to land, Lord Hanno and me…'

'What, by yourself? You, a ship's boy, with an aristocrat from one of the most senior families in the whole of Carthage? I don't believe you.'

Pastoral Paradise

Qart's bum lands on the bench at the prow of the dinghy. Lord Hanno
and the other lordlings are with him, The Delphis high above them
as they row ashore.

'Boy, you can write, can't you?' says Lord Hanno to Qart, and his
heart skips a beat.

'Yes,' he says without thinking. He's noticed me, he thinks. Perhaps
he likes me. Perhaps he can give me something other than chicken shit
to look after. Then his heart sinks. 'Well, a bit.' He bites his lip. 'No, I
cannot write,' and his head goes down onto his chest.

'Well, which is it, fowl boy?' says one of Hanno's lordlings, a man
with light skin and long, brushed hair. 'Yes or no?' The rest of them titter.

'And it's "Lord Hanno" to you, boy,' says the man just in front. He is
heavy, muscular, with one earring.

The vessel wobbles on the glassy inlet. 'Hold still,' barks his lordship at his comrades. 'By Melqart's mother, I've told you before.
If you make sudden movements when you are in a vessel, you can
end up in the water.' He turns, incredulity in his eyes, back towards
Qart. 'You cannot write?'

The dinghy is full, too full, of lordlings, dressed for a picnic on Tunis
Bay rather than a voyage in the land of who knows where. Most still

sport their embroideries and jewels, though a few have donned something new and foreign to them, perfectly formed mariner hats, all of which are red except for Lord Hanno's, which is blue to indicate his higher status. Qart's headpiece, so battered it could no longer even be called a hat, had been mud-coloured and disintegrated long ago. None of the original crew from The Delphis bother with them any more.

Qart's fingers clutch tight to the wooden topside. A blush moves from his neck to his cheeks. Dubb had been telling him for months that he must concentrate on his writing. 'I can count, though,' he blurts.

'So much for the expertise of the crew of The Delphis then,' says Lord Hanno. The whole vessel is in danger of overtipping as the men laugh at Qart's shortcomings.

The boy's shame deepens as he hears the crew of The Delphis being castigated because of him. I really do need to get on to the writing, he thinks, and his eyes flick up towards the Carthaginian aristocrats. 'I did numbers for my mother on the docks at Carthage,' he says, almost at a shout. 'I can calculate into the hundreds and...other things.' He wishes he could remember the name of the system Dubb taught him when they marked the masts. 'I can mark masts and read the stars.' It's an afterthought; he hopes they don't go on to ask too much about the stars.

'Alright, alright, boy, don't shout,' says Lord Hanno, and puts a hand up to calm his men. The boy's head jerks backwards and his eyes flick wide. What's this? He's not taking my side, is he? From the corner of his eye, he watches as the lordlings settle back with knowing smiles and decide to let the boy be. They approach the beach without further comment and, as they land, a small glow of satisfaction ripples through him. He purses his lips together to hide a smile. I'm the only one on The Delphis that Lord Hanno wants to come ashore. Of all of them, I'm the one he's asked to come with him. Perhaps there'll be some special task he wants me to fulfil, one that only a special boy like me can do.

He follows the lordlings out of the vessel and along a narrow path, which skirts the river's edge. Thank you, Mighty Melqart, he thinks, as he skips along behind the commander. Tall grasses hem them in, in single file, between what looks to be a broad wooded area and the mangroves at the river's edge. I'm out of the clutches of the diviners at least, doing something other than dragging chickens around all day. And Lord Hanno needs me! He hears the first of many shouts from a crowd somewhere off up ahead. He peers forward over the grasses and sees nothing other than cattle grazing on plentiful grass, their horns far longer than any he's ever seen before. In the near distance smoke from many fires curls up through the trees.

The shouting gets louder as they approach a village. It has egg-shaped huts, rooves covered with grass, hay stacks and clothes hung to dry on bushes, though not one human being is to be seen.

They stop when they get to the edge of the settlement and spread out in a ragged group. 'They're expecting us,' says Lord Hanno to his lordlings, though it doesn't seem very much like that to Qart, who cranes his neck around the buildings to see what's happening up ahead.

A crowd has gathered in front of an enormous tree and, from their midst, arms and legs project above their heads as people roar. No one is looking out for them despite the arrival of their vessels on the river. It's a wrestling match! thinks Qart. It must be a party! He thinks of his Lady, his spinning top, which lies safe amongst his things back on The Delphis. Perhaps Lord Hanno will let me run back and get her, and I can join in the fun! He imagines the clink of small coins in his palm, as in the old days, and the treats that having a bit of cash might bring. With a smile on his face, he turns back to Lord Hanno. I'll persuade him to let me go back. I'll only take a minute. He's just in time to see the bald-headed diviner step towards the lord.

The man says, 'Oh good, you brought the boy.'

Qart's face falls. Him! Here? I thought he was back on The Delphis.

'That'll make it easier,' says the young man and, with a thud, Qart realises this has been Lord Hanno's intention all along. He had no plans for Qart to join him, to do something special, interesting and different. He brought him ashore to make it possible for him to continue to work with the diviners, that's all.

'He says he can count,' says Lord Hanno with a chuckle. They are speaking about him as though he wasn't there. 'It's worth a try, anyway.' The lordling turns and, together with his friends, makes for the bellowing crowd.

The muscly man nods and Qart's head droops. 'What, you thought Lord Hanno had brought you along to be friends with us, did you? You! The son of a whore from the docks in Carthage?'

Qart's face burns. 'My mother isn't a whore. She's an embroiderer,' he says, though no one hears him.

'Right, you, you're to follow me,' says the one without the neck, and he sets off back down the narrow path along the river. His body rocks from side to side as he walks. He must be drunk, thinks Qart, as they veer off down a dirt track towards the water, push through the grass and step onto a small cove with a foreshore covered by smooth white stones. There is box scrub in places and the river is muddy with silt. A few collapsed dug outs lie sprawled at the water's edge and, on either side, mangroves hem the place in.

Puffing up behind them come the two youngest diviners, linked together with large baskets, which they hold by the handles. They drop them onto the stones in front of him and head off back up towards the village.

'Right, you are to collect and number these stones,' says baldy. 'You do know how to count it seems.' He waits for Qart's head to give a nod. He feels as though he's gifting his life away. 'Here's chalk.' He hands the boy a small clutch of unevenly-shaped balls. 'You mark each stone with a number, your standard number like this.' The man lifts one of them from the beach and makes a single line on it with his chalk. 'This is one. This is two.' He draws two single lines together. 'Right?'

What do you think I am? A complete fool? thinks Qart, and, again, must nod his head and be silent.

'And so on, up to as much as you can mark. You must put the num-bered stones into one of these baskets and give us the total in each basket at the end, plus an addition of how many there are altogether. Do you understand?' the man finishes, didactic, patronising. 'If you don't do it right the first time, you will have to do it again. So you'd best pay attention. We must know exactly how many stones are in each basket and each one must be numbered. If it's too small to mark, it's too small to use, so don't put it in the basket.'

Bitterness rises in Qart's throat at the work he has to do. These obsessive diviners, utterly convinced of their own specific interpretation of the world, determined to find patterns of meaning in everything, whether it be the drop of a stone or the mark of a chicken's peck. How can he stand to work for them any more? And behind them there is Hanno. He supports them and gives them their authority. And, in turn, giving credence to Lord Hanno, is the greatest culprit of them all: his master, Dubb, the Navigator. Why must he stick with these religious men, whatever the work they ask him to do and however senseless it is?

The boy's jaw juts forward over his top lip as he drops to his haunches and starts to count stones. The bald one disappears up the bank through the reeds and he is left alone in the cove with the empty baskets and pieces of chalk.

* * *

Dubb lurches to the topside. A dinghy is departing The Delphis. Two dinghies, he now sees, rowing their way side by side across the silver cove, the plash of their oars reverberating across the viscous water. He scratches the back of his head and stretches into a great yawn. He's had a good night's sleep despite the humidity. The air is thick with vegetal smells, bark, mimosa greens, mud. Reflections from acacia trees dapple the water and a heat rises from the land. He rolls his head round on his neck and opens his eyes wide to crack the gummy crust settled at their edges. Ripples flecked with blue fracture the dinghies' images and, he realises, mouth snapping shut, that he is in fact looking at one vessel, not two after all. Furthermore, one is overladen with lordlings and Lord Hanno is at its stern. Bejewelled aristocrats giggle and glint in the morning light and, another surprise, there is Qart at the prow, straight backed and proud, taking his place in Lord Hanno's party.

What are they doing? he thinks, and frowns. Hanno only just came aboard last night. Now he's off for the day by, the look of it. I thought he was going to be with us today to clean The Delphis out.

'These blighters had me up before light,' says Rabs, sauntering up from midships. He cocks his head towards the dinghy. 'They wanted to get to shore before they'd even woken up and, as most of them don't know their blades from their bums, I've had to set it all up for them. What they don't know about sailing I dread to think!' He shakes his head.

'Infuriating.'

'None of them can have even been to Utica by sea, let alone any further,' adds the small Carthaginian.

'They'll learn quick enough,' says Chares, and appears from below the tiller platform. 'We have to hope. The sea has a way of teaching hard lessons in double quick time.' He, too, is bleary eyed.

The three men stand transfixed as the vessel lurches towards the shore.

'Don't let Nyptan hear you say that,' says Dubb. 'She hates predictions. Thinks they give the gods ideas.'

'Yes, well some of us are blessed by the gods, as she surely is,' says the first mate, 'and the rest of us get by as best we can.' He shrugs. 'Not that I'm giving you permission to laugh at the gods mind.' The mood is anxious as their eyes stay fixed on the wallowing dinghy.

'Imagine what a fuss they'll make if their clothes get wet,' says Rabs. He raises his eyes to heaven and opens his hands out wide. 'Please, Mighty Melqart, let them get to shore! Greatest Lord, I'll even stop visiting the whore house if you'll get them to land without tipping up.'

A distant shriek tells them the lordlings have landed.

'Speaking of the gods, where are our friends from Etrusca this morning? I haven't seen them either. Or should I say, heard them,' says Dubb.

'They went off at day break with the interpreters,' says Chares. 'Said something about needing stones.'

'I'm liking how this day is turning out,' says Rabs, and turns to lean his back against the top rail to survey The Delphis with an experienced eye. 'Just us, the old gang, in charge of The Delphis! We're going to turn her out this morning, skipper, right?'

'That's the task. As soon as we've had some grub.'

'And by the way, Lord Hanno sends you a message,' says Rabs. 'He informs you that he'll be back later to help with the work.' The small man gives Dubb a meaningful look.

'What? Does his lordship really mean that he's taking the day off?' says the navigator, his good cheer vanished.

'I give you his message, that's all.'

Dubb is annoyed. He leans across the topside, arms stiff and shoulders powerful, and watches while the aristocrats haul their dinghy up out of the river.

'You'd imagine a new commander would welcome the chance to get to know his vessel in detail, wouldn't you? To learn her every corner, quirk and weakness. Not this one it seems. He knows her by instinct. No need for even a peek.' His shoulders are tense and he presses back his aggravation to take a deep breath. No point in getting worked up about it, he thinks, and tries to smile. 'He'll be back again any minute though, won't he, eager and willing to lend a hand.' He slaps his hand down on the topside with force. Rabs and Chares exchange glances.

'So, where shall we start, skipper?' says Chares, as Rabs sets off down midships, kicking the remaining men awake as he passes.

'Right, work to be done, you tossers,' he blares. 'Not the time to lie around on your backsides all day.'

For the next hours the crew examines rowlocks, sails, mast, cross bar, cables, tallow, leads, buckets and benches.

'This is the very last stop for supplies,' says Dubb. 'So everything must be scrutinised and we'll get a list to shore.'

'While you're at it, men, we can have new supplies too,' says Nyptan, as Dubb lifts the hatch from the hull to peer inside. His heart leaps.

'Nyptan,' he says, 'you're up. I thought you'd have taken the chance of a calm morning to have a lie in.' He abandons his work to look at her. 'What are you doing this far towards the bow, stranger? You rarely move further forward than the heads.' He reaches forward to kiss her.

'Too many people occupy this space already. The last thing the Etruscans would welcome in their space is a healer from Tyre. But I thought I heard someone mention going ashore and decided, before you all get too engrossed in that hull, I should tell you what we need. Barrels of fresh water, for instance. Is that possible?' she says, and smiles, the dimple on her cheek the glory of her face.

'Of course, missus, of course,' says Chares, and wipes his hands down his tunic as if preparing to give her jewels. 'Tell me everything you need and I'll add it to the list.'

'And while you go about cleaning, are there any plans to do the sick bay? If so, can we rearrange it?' She glances over her shoulder at Tanu, who watches from their quarters at the stern. 'And it would be good if we ourselves could go ashore, just for a visit?'

Dubb nods. 'Of course. Take over here Chares. I'll be back soon.'

* * *

By the time Dubb returns to the hull, Rabs and Chares are deep in its darkness. The stench from the birds hits him like a solid wall. In the half-light and penned in wicker baskets piled high on top of each other, the fowls slump against the sides of the cages or lie flattened at their centres. Most of them look completely dead. Bird shit coats every surface, its grey and white crusts forming stalactite-like shapes, which run from the top cage through to the lowest. Precious little grain appears around the cages and almost no water lies in the drinking bowls. Qart has got to give these animals more food and water, he thinks, with a frown. I don't care how busy he says he is.

'Mother of Melqart, what's going on here?!' comes Rabs's voice ahead. Dubb's irritation turns to dread. What now? He hunches forward to see. The seaman has a lamp lit at the underside of the mast deep in the centre of The Delphis and pokes upwards at it with a metal rod. This is the place where the mast is cradled into place below deck, a square of timbers, which secures their fir mast to the vessel. And there, poking down from the hull with its finely-shaped mast, is a thick coating of green mould.

'Holy Poseidon,' says Chares, and his mouth falls open.

'Baal's balls!' says Dubb, eyes wide, neck craned. He reaches up to shove a finger across the slime. Green and white algae comes off with the scratch. Of all the places in The Delphis, there should be no sign of rot or weakness here, the strong heart of the vessel, its inmost core, where the roominess of the hull locks onto the power of the sail, the place where their mast nestles, and from which it is raised and lowered at times of need. To move, to traverse the sea, relies on the strength of this connection, the one right here before them draped in green.

'Something's been eating away at our mast for weeks,' says Chares, brows across his forehead like a plummeting seagull.

'It's condensation from the chickens, those flaming chickens,' whispers Rabs, and, together, the three men turn their heads towards the birds as though locked in step by the gods themselves. 'They are breathing, after all!'

'I knew we should've stopped those Etruscans from storing their birds down here!' says Dubb. Remorse and self-censure rise in his gullet. 'Why did I let them do it, all those weeks ago? Breathing, farting, cackling; it's created such a fug that worm has found a place to root. And in our mast! By the gods, I hope this is the only place the mould has taken hold!' He jumps down from the ropes and the three of them scatter across the space. The light of their lamps, almost entirely engulfed in darkness, flits to and fro beneath the beams as they examine every timber in their beloved vessel. How strong is she now to ride the big seas of River Ocean? Will she have the power to get them away and home again?

* * *

Mother and daughter screen themselves from onlookers in a clump of acacia trees beside a fresh water stream. It is a stone's throw from The Delphis yet completely private. A short waterfall drops, in a gleaming strand, through a series of rock pools down to the river. They are graced by white, sandy banks. Beyond the waterfall the terrain steps up in sandy terraces to a drier plain above.

'That man is always complaining!' says Tanu, long strands of wet hair spreading out across her shoulders to dry in the sun.

'Who? Oh, that one!' says her mother, as another curse reaches them through the trees from The Delphis. She bends to look through the black and green tangles at their vessel, just as a man drops like a stone from the side of it into the water with a noisy splash. 'Perhaps it's not so easy to swing like a spider on a rope across the side of the hull.' She suppresses a giggle. 'Mustn't laugh.' They both laugh loudly.

Today is an easy day, and she lifts her face to the sunshine, unpins her plait from behind an ear and combs at it with outspread fingers. She shakes her head and her hair, thick with sea salt and dust, tumbles round her shoulders and down to her waist.

'What a glorious place!' She breathes out deeply and plonks herself down on the bank beside her daughter.

'Well, come on,' says Tanu, and eyes her mother's hair. 'Let's get going. I'm ready.' She lifts her chin towards the waterfall, a small vitrum of lotion in her hand.

Nyptan bends sideways and, with a forearm, swings her hair from behind her to the side. She puts a towel around her neck, chooses a place to drop onto her knees and sticks her head under the spouting water. 'At last!' she says, voice muffled. 'I've been longing for this for weeks!'

Tanu steps her feet wide, ankles in the water, and launches into her mother's hair with both hands. Water spurts across the top of Nyptan's head and down her back as suds rise and are rinsed. Her hair floats like weed along its length and curls around Tanu's feet as the stream makes its way towards the river.

'How to get out of this now! Help!' says Tanu. 'I'm trapped like a fish!'

Nyptan lifts her head and the strands retreat like fronds of an anemone only to rise as a gleaming rope alongside her shoulders. Water pours into the towel around her neck and downwards onto her tunic, along her legs and runs in rivulets into the pool again. The two of them laugh and stamp in the water, splashing and cupping and chucking it until they are both completely drenched.

They wash not only themselves, their hair and clothes but also all the cloths, implements, vitrums, amphorae and bedding they have used so far on the voyage. At the very least, all their Lady Gula equipment needs to be freed of salt. All are laid out to dry on stones and branches. Their whole space looks like a laundry, steaming in the day's heat.

As she slips a clean tunic down over her head, Nyptan glimpses for the first time the slight bulge of the baby. Peeping out beyond the amulet of Great Laughing Dog, there it is, plumping up between her breasts in the mellow light. Her nipples, she sees, are darker than usual. Her belly button is extending. She stops and stands completely still to stare at all the promise it holds until she starts to stifle in the humid air. When am I going to tell Dubb? she thinks. When, if ever, is there going to be a right time? She bends her arms and lets the tunic drop. Her head pops out into the open. When am I going to tell Tanu? She looks at her daughter, already dressed, cross-legged, starting to work.

'I've begun on the staunch weed,' she says. 'The sun's good.'

Nyptan nods and turns out the wicker box of weed, which they brought with them from the sick bay. A burst of laughter rolls across the water, through the sunken mangrove trunks, followed by a snatch of song. The crew is enjoying themselves at last, she thinks. And they set to it, to sort, split and crush in the shade of the acacia trees.

But she can't settle. The thought of this secret baby nestling in her belly, a new and fragile human being, demands more than quiet reflection. 'I'm going for a wander,' she says and, before her daughter can protest, she adds, 'I won't go far. You'll be able to see me the whole time.' Without waiting, she steps up the grassy slope towards a higher level. 'I've got the scalpel,' she adds over her shoulder, and brandishes it. 'You never know, I might find something exciting to bring back!'

'Do you need me to come?' asks her daughter, half-heartedly. 'I just want to get this finished.'

Nyptan leaves her behind with a large quantity of staunch weed flowers and stems still to be separated. As she steps onto the hillside, she wonders what Dubb is doing now. From up here, it's easier to see The Delphis. Its sail is going up and down lopsidedly, with much shouting and giving of instructions. Oiling it, she thinks. Her husband is in the thick of it, as usual. Her eyes turn to scan the surrounding ground and trees. Are there healing herbs here? Or grasses? Or birthwort, she adds to her list. I'll need it, lots of it. She takes a few steps across the clearing.

Even this little hill makes me feel tired. She searches for somewhere to sit and drops down onto a fallen log with relief.

I've got to get clear what to do about this baby, she frets. I've got to either find a way of telling Dubb, or I've got to get rid of it and pretend it never happened. She feels depressed at the thought. Sounds from the river tell her that the different sized anchors are being tested, dropped into the water and hauled up at various rates, the buckets flying. So, if I'm going to do this deed, I need to do it quickly. The hair on the back of her neck prickles in realisation. Today or tomorrow at the latest. And better to do it on land than at sea, she decides, as she ticks off her options. Then I could leave it all behind and start afresh. The Delphis will not stay here for long, three days at most. Now is the best time.

The day grows ever stickier. The hazy atmosphere comes down in a blanket and she lifts her heavy hair over her shoulder and starts to plait it. The tide is going out. Salt flats emerge on its other side.

Can I really raise a child on The Delphis? It's a question which, once she's thought of it, goes round and round in her head unresolved. She pulls at the string from around her neck and Great Laughing Dog comes up into her palm. His zigzags gleam in the sun and she can't tell whether he's chuckling at her or grimacing. She lifts him to her nose, smells his bay and calm creeps into her. So far away we are here from the Temple of Eshmun in Sidon. The great tradition of her mother's medicines and gods don't seem relevant in this environment. What gods do they worship in these parts? What are their names? Can they help the likes of me, in my position? She raises handfuls of the sand beside her and lets the grains slip through her fingers. Still, she thinks, despite the distance, Lady Gula is with me. I must have faith that everything will work out. She gets up from her seat, kneels down on the sand and bows her head to the earth. What would you have me do Lady Gula? she asks. Should I keep this child of ours, despite the difficulties, or should I be brave and let him go? On this subject, Lady Gula, her lovely goddess has, so far, remained silent. Tucked into the leather bag in their private quarters, she has been mute. I need to offer incense, she thinks. I should call her up, please her. Nyptan's mind turns to her mother and her mother's mother, and all the generations before them, who worshiped Lady Gula and her healing hands. What would they do?

'What are you doing, Mummy?!' comes Tanu's voice, alarmed. First, her daughter's head appears, coming up to the higher ground, followed by her whole self. 'Why are you kneeling in the middle of a field?'

Nyptan's heart jolts even as her body feels as heavy as lead. You, my lovely daughter, are the best thing I have ever done with my life. How can I deny this world another human like you? She stands quickly, brushes the sand from her tunic and opens her arms out wide. 'Of course I'm alright. Just having a quiet moment, that's all.'

Tanu joins her and gathers her into a tight embrace. 'I thought you were going to see what you could find,' says Tanu, and points to the scalpel tied at her waist.

'And so I am, darling. A bit weary, that's all.'

Her daughter looks at her hard, eyes sceptical. 'Oh? Really.'

Nyptan sighs. Time to be frank with my dear one, she thinks, and turns to look for a spot big enough for two. 'Come, sit with me a minute,' she says, and leads her over to a fallen box bush.

She tells Tanu there is a baby on the way, that there has been for some time, but she has not wanted to say anything about it because she has not known what to do.

'What do you mean, you don't know what to do? You have no choice, do you?' says Tanu, her eyes fixed on her mother's, anxious, worried.

'My sweet girl, there is always a choice when it comes to having children. We have spoken before, haven't we, about what happens when you get your menses.' Tanu nods and she takes hold of her hand. 'Well, when you miss a few monthlies, and you can feel your body change, you know that a child grows inside you.'

'Yes, yes, I know all this,' says Tanu, impatient. 'You've told me before about how a baby comes. What I don't know is how to stop a baby once it's started.'

Nyptan's voice drops so low that Tanu moves her head in closer. 'Well, it would be possible, even up until the last days before birth, to force a child out of the womb. Before it's ready to come. To make it sick if you like.' A frown appears on Tanu's face. She stares at the ground. 'One of the things Lady Gula teaches us, as healers, is how to do this. How to make a child come out of the womb before time.'

'But I thought Lady Gula only did happy things, things which made life better. Not things which made it worse,' says Tanu. She sounds indignant.

Nyptan's stomach clenches and she purses her lips. So clear-headed, my child. So sure of the value of her healing hands.

'Or even destroy life,' her daughter adds. 'Because isn't that what it amounts to, taking a baby out before its time?'

Nyptan wonders how it has come to this. How can it be that now, before her maturity, she must to explain to her daughter, little more than a child herself, what aborting means? She takes her darling's hands in her own. They are rough with work, clean from the stream. 'Sometimes, my dear one, life is made worse when a baby arrives, not better. When the circumstances in which a child is to be born are bad, or when the mother is sick or dying, perhaps it is better for the baby to come out before time.'

Tanu's eyes snap to hers. 'But you are not sick or dying, are you?' she says, panic on the rise. 'You said you are well.'

'And so I am, dear one. What is troubling about this baby is the circumstances into which it will be born. Think of it. Life on board The Delphis is difficult enough, as you know. And we are on a voyage to the gods know where. How can we bring up a child in these times?'

'But I will help you. You are not on your own. We can manage this together.' Tanu's voice goes up a tone and she pulls her hands away. 'Why do you think we cannot manage?' she says, and her eyes begin to fill. 'I am here, I will not leave you. It will be lovely to have a baby brother or sister.' The tears begin to fall in great drops down her chin.

Nyptan wraps her arms around her skinny shoulders. 'My darling Tanu, this is not about whether you can help. You always help. I don't doubt that for a second.' Tanu looks up to search her mother's face, to search for falsehood. 'It is whether or not The Delphis is the right place to raise a child. A small, confined space like that. Full of men and shouting and swearing. We don't know where we'll end up, or whether we'll ever get home again. And how safe is life at sea for a child, even a child as old and beautiful as you?'

Tanu takes a small gulp, her lips purse and she is silent. The croak of cicadas reverberates around them. The Delphis has gone quiet. A bull lows in the distance. It's as if the land holds its breath as it waits to hear what Nyptan decides to do next.

'Did we bring our Lady Gula lamp with us?' she says, voice too bright. Tanu nods glumly. 'Well, why don't we go back to the waterfall and light it?' says Nyptan. 'Let's bring out some incense, call her up. She will enjoy this lovely spot. And we can see if, after we've been with her, a baby will seem more welcome on this Earth than it does at the moment.'

So mother and daughter return to their washing place, set aside their essential oils, decoctions, book of magic words and vitrums and pull the embroidered cloth from their bag to set up a makeshift altar. They pour precious incense into the lamp, strike a flint and prostrate themselves.

'Deliver us from evil, lovely Lady Gula,' says Nyptan.

'Cleanse and protect us, sweet one,' says Tanu.

Water from the stream courses through their sanctuary; the waning day glows. Nyptan and Tanu, drenched in the incense of their Beloved, crouch on their haunches in obeisance as they wait to hear Lady Gula's voice.

* * *

Lord Hanno had still not returned to The Delphis by late afternoon. As soon as they had found the mould, Dubb had sent for him. 'Tell him to come at once. It's urgent,' he had told Berek, and hustled him off to shore to locate the commander.

Berek returned later, alone. 'He says he's getting information about gold,' he reported. 'He says he'll come soon.'

That was at the beginning of the day. By the early afternoon, Lord Hanno is still nowhere to be seen.

Dubb's mouth forms a straight line across his face and his eyes are hard as he lifts his chin to Berek, and again beckons the young musician to him. 'I need you to go ashore one more time, Berek, to find our commander and insist that he returns with you,' he says, and tries to keep the fury from his voice. 'Are you up to this?' The young man nods, eyes low. This is normally the type of task he tries to avoid. 'I know you don't like to do this sort of thing. You are a drums and music man. It's just that I need someone I can trust to do this job and the others are all taken up with repairs. Are you happy to try?'

'I'll do my best, Mr Navigator,' says the musician, addressing Dubb formally under the circumstances.

'I won't hold it against you if you come back without him, you know. It's just that I need him here, now.'

Berek nods, puts his instruments away and tips over the side into the coracle to find his lordship for a second time.

It's becoming clear what he's like now, thinks Dubb, and turns back to the mast, though I didn't realise it yesterday. Yesterday, I believed he'd do what he said he'd do, that he'd be with us when needed. How could I have been so gullible? All that business back in Lixus with the diviners ought to have alerted me. The Etruscans are much more important to him than us. And the day's work continues long into the evening.

The Enquiry - Day 6

The boy's father arrives two days later. Like his son, he is an ill-kept individual, who appears without warning, very early in the morning. Fortunately, this time, Tasii has not yet gone out. Lord Apsan staggers off his pallet, into his clothes and Gatit ushers him into the atrium at the same time as his breakfast. Bread and milk are what the kitchen is telling him to eat these days.

'Why did you send that message?' he asks the visitor. Thin and wiry, with a bristle of hair and scars all up his arms, the man does not present himself as a very reliable source of information. Rather the reverse. He's more like a crook than a snitch, and he prepares himself for a tussle to get to the bottom of the mysterious message written in Tartessic on rags.

'I thought it would be useful to you,' says the man in broken Punic. 'I'd heard you were looking for special… information.' He pauses to see what reaction his use of the word "information" produced. 'I want to help.'

'Help with what? What do you think you are "helping" with?' he asks.

The man hesitates. 'With the mining and that,' he says. 'Getting you rich and all.' His eyes flick sideways.

'That's very noble of you. Out of the goodness of your heart, you want to help me to get rich,' he scoffs.

Tasii looks at the man, puzzled.

'As long as, like, I can get my share too, for a return on my information, if you know what I mean,' he says, and gives a long sniff.

Lord Apsan chokes back revulsion. This is exactly the kind of man who makes me want to leave this place, he thinks, and watches Tasii become ever more careful with where he puts his hands and how he holds his head. He's feeling it too, a rejection of the ways of the world beyond this immediate enclave, this residence on its hill overlooking the bay. Whatever Tasii says about him being a native, these two men are as different as night and day. His mind flicks to himself and Tasii in the bathhouse tonight, washing all this filth off.

The man seems to change tack, to decide to be frank. He bursts out, 'I just want to get in on all this.' He waves a hand around the room. 'I seen it all. Them slaves working, heaving loads along the road, worse than donkeys, on barges on the creeks. How it's the drivers and middle men who get rich. And you lot, who live here, in a place like this.' His eyes fill with resentment. 'What I can't see is any benefit to me. Why should me and my family go outside? Why can't we have something for ourselves? I heard you wanted that Carthage fellow, and I put the word out up and down the route between here and the temple. And that's how it come about, the message.'

Finally, it is clear, thinks Lord Apsan, why it came and why it is so imprecise.

'But I want something back off of it,' the man carries on. 'My family took their own lives in their hands gettin' them words down here. Now I've passed 'em on and we need our reward.' He looks between Lord Apsan and Tasiioonos, clearly not knowing who is who.

'How do you know if we are looking for a Carthage person, as you put it? Who told you anything about what we want?' he asks.

'I have my know-how, I hear things,' says the man, 'and I certainly 'ain't goin' to tell you.'

'What if we aren't looking for anyone?' asks Tasii. 'You could be wrong.'

'Ah, don't waste my time,' says the man, and stands to leave. 'If you're not goin' to give me nothin', I'm off.'

Lord Apsan puts out his hand. 'Stay a moment, my man. Not so fast.' Tasii looks over at him, brows up. A plan is unfurling in his lordship's head. Their eyes exchange information silently, across the room.

'Well, what?' the man says, and sticks his chin forward.

'Please, Mr…Mr…What is your name?'

The man's brows go down. 'None of your business. I ain't havin' my name doin' the rounds in a place like this.' He spits on the floor.

'Gatit!' he shouts down the stairs. 'Call Adyat up with a bucket and mop.' He turns to the man. 'You do realise, don't you, sir, that despite all your supposed efforts with this message, it is worthless?'

'My arse it is,' says the man, and jumps up to hit him, fists clenched. The table stops his progress.

'The message has no value,' says Lord Apsan, voice soft and reasonable, 'because it lacks the information necessary for us to act on it.'

A frown falls on the father's face and his eyes flash. 'What's wrong with it? It was writ out specially for you.'

'It didn't state the destination of the stranger with the jewels, the road he was taking and in which direction.'

The man swings around and smashes his fist against the wall. 'Oh, I knew they'd balls it up! I guessed it. The stupid fools! We done all that for nothin'!' He pummels the whitewash until it begins to flake.

'Calm down, sir,' says Lord Apsan. 'Gatit, get the gentleman a drink and some food. Sit yourself down.'

The man plonks himself into a chair, elbows on his knees, head in hands. 'After all I done, after all my boy went through, comin' across the water at this time of the year, puttin' his life at risk to get it to you.' His head swings from side to side and he blows long, hard breaths out of his mouth in a broken stream.

Lord Apsan examines him. Unkept, filthy, wiry, strong - someone like this, with his background, his knowledge of a language, which very few know, with a network, which reaches well up into the hills, along the mining settlements, who is scarcely above the status of a slave himself - how very useful it could be if he became one of us, our ears and eyes.

The man devours the food Tasii offers from the side table and eats it with much slurping and smacking of lips.

Lord Apsan lifts his brows to Tasii and indicates the window with his eyes. Together they move to it and stand private in the sunshine. 'This family group of his, his network, could be very useful for us, couldn't it?' he says under his breath.

His slave shrugs. 'I don't know. I haven't been up there in years, as you know. He won't tell us his family name and he clearly doesn't live there any more. Ask more questions,' he whispers, as the man looks over at them under lowered brows.

Together, they return to sit at the table, Lord Apsan behind it, Tasii at the side. The man watches, eyes alert. He's getting the measure of us, thinks Lord Apsan, a sharp man.

'So, let's start again, shall we? What's your name?'

'Gargoris Street Cleaner and my son is Gry, Gry son of Gargoris Street Cleaner.'

'Very good. How is it that you can read and write in your family?'

'We can all do it up there.'

'Where is "there"? Is it near Cacho Roan?'

The man shakes his head and says nothing.

'Even your son says he can read. How is that?'

'I learned him to, as he should.'

'Who taught you?'

'The priest, at the temple.' Tasii's chin lifts just a little and his lids flicker.

'Unusual, isn't it, for a man…' he hesitates, '…man of your sort to be able to do such a thing?'

The man doesn't even seem to notice the slur. 'Everyone knows how to do it up there, even the women.'

'What's it for? For helping the priests at the temple, or something else?'

'For rituals and that, to do with the sacred animals. And other animals, to get 'em to market. And for counting.'

'You do counting too?' he says, surprised. This man really is going to be useful, he thinks.

'Sort of. It ain't the kind of countin' and writin' you got here,' he says, and his eyes swivel around the shelves. 'I don't know nuthin' like this.'

'But now you've left the hills and you live here on the coast?'

'At the edge of Tartessos,' he says. 'Me and my boys, we look after the streets outside the palace. Look, what's all this about? I'm fed up with answerin' your questions.'

'Well, as it turns out, despite the fact that this message was not very useful, there are other messages you might deliver,' says his lordship.

The man's mouth goes wide in a grimace, his smile. 'An' you'll give us something for it, in return, like?' His eyes light up, a look of intense satisfaction crossing his filthy face.

Men will be Men

By late afternoon, Qart has five baskets around him. The diviners brought him more and the stones have piled up. Each is filled with one hundred and fifty, his workings laid out on top of each on a thin slate marker. The master workings are on a larger one, set beside him, and they show signs of much rubbings out and recalculation, the pattern of four strokes and a diagonal becoming smaller as he worked down the rock. If only I had a Carthaginian counting board with me, he thinks, with the beads and the basins, I could go much faster. Every now and again, the roar of the wrestlers and the village fete drifts towards him on the breeze. There is precious little companionship for him. Only an occasional fish jumps from the water. Everyone else, it seems, is either having fun at the village or tied up on the vessels.

I could, of course, leave The Delphis here, he thinks. There are more people here than at Lixus and more scope for making a living with my Lady. He wonders if the boys have tops here in this culture. He imagines the scene. The priests would come for him at the end of the day and find the baskets lying on their side, stones scattered, counting undone and no boy. He thinks of their faces, the horror of the bald one, the aggravation of Lord Hanno, the shock of the lordlings. Then he thinks of the pain on Nyptan's beautiful face, the dismay on Dubb's, Tanu's tears and the sorrow and worry of Rabs and Chares. He dismisses the idea of absconding. Same old problem, he thinks. I can't take life on The Delphis, yet I can't bring myself to leave. He marks the five hundred and eleventh stone and puts it into the final basket. He can prise no more stones from the shore to collect. No one comes near him with water. No one brings food. The river at its edge is brackish; he's tried to drink it. He has to concentrate or he risks having to do the whole task again. And when, finally, all the baskets are done and his stone is covered with workings, he slumps down at the water's edge and splashes to make the most of whatever cooling breeze there is. The sun starts its afternoon fall towards the sea.

* * *

Chares hauls their bundles out of the dinghy first, and mother and daughter follow next up the side of The Delphis. The ladder is awkward in a tunic, keeps catching under Nyptan's feet. Tanu is light and fast despite it. The wooden frame bangs and bounces on the side of the hull as she races, making holding tight a matter of priority. When her daughter gets to the top, she goes straight to their precious leather healer's bag, to claim it before it can go astray.

'You've arrived just in time,' Dubb says to Nyptan the moment her feet land aboard. 'One of his lordship's favourite friends, Lord Kanmi, is in the sick bay - the one with all the jewellery.' Dubb seems grumpy.

'Oh,' she says, and a frown flits between her brows. 'How long has he been there? Why didn't you send for me?'

'He's only just arrived,' says Dubb, quick, defensive. He shoves his hair behind his ear. His forearms are caked with large blotches of golden sap, and there are blobs of it stuck to his chin and forehead.

'Does this hurt?' she asks, and pulls at one of the blobs with a nail. The hair on his arm comes up with it and the skin rises as she tugs.

He looks down. 'No, of course not,' he says, and rips it from his skin, irritated.

She remains silent, eyes on him. 'Well?'

'Filling gaps in the mast cradle. They use it as a glue in this part of the world,' he adds, and nods. 'Innovative.'

'Thank you,' she says. 'That's good to know.'

He lifts their bundles in one arm and carries them across the deck to the healing space.

Nyptan follows him. 'Bad day then?' she says, their leather box under her arm, Tanu ahead of them already.

'Terrible,' he says, and his head stays down. 'The mast turns out to be rotten at its foot and Lord Hanno hasn't been here since dawn. I've had to make major decisions on my own.' He dumps their bundles, looks up, eyes full of resentment.

'I am sure you are up to that, dear man,' she says, and grabs at his hand to kiss it. He pulls back. Oh, things are bad here on The Delphis, she thinks. There will be no conversation with him tonight about our baby. She bites her lip.

'That's not the point.' He turns his back to the man lying prone on a pallet on the other side of the healing space. 'It's the principle of the thing. Hanno is the leader of this expedition,' he spits. 'So he should be making the decisions, not be off with his friends on shore.' He glances over his shoulder at the restive man.

Their space has been swabbed, the altar, packing cases, boxes and personal goods all cleared and jumbled together in a pile outside the curtain. The sick man has a high colour and moans softly. His long hair is matted with sweat and his earrings are tangled.

Nyptan's eyes fly to him. 'He's in a bad way.' She drops her bundle. 'Very high fever,' she adds, and her face creases in concern. 'Tanu, the essential oils, here, now, please. Dubb, I need the altar back in as soon as possible.'

Tanu grabs their bag, pulls the bay from it and hands it to her, then she and Dubb step outside to find where the altar is amidst their piled up goods.

The healer follows them, a large beaker in her hands. 'When you've got the altar up,' she says to the two of them, their backs to her as they sort through the paraphernalia to find the incense burner, 'Tanu, you must light a drop or two of bay to sanctify our space temporarily, and Dubb, I need all the fresh water back in into the sick bay immediately. As you know, we need a lot of it.'

'Rabs!' calls Dubb down to midships. 'Up here! We've got to get this space up and running again. This minute!'

Nyptan notes the sound of running feet as she kneels down beside the sweating lord to start to bath him. His clothes are saturated, breath short, smooth hands sweaty and legs trembling. She drenches a cloth in water, folds it and places it on his forehead. Water drips down the side of his face and pools on the pallet. She leans over to pull her embroidered scorpion cloth from the back to place it under his head and looks over her shoulder as the men, at Tanu's direction, manoeuvre their altar into position and place their black incense holder on top. She keeps bathing him until Tanu strikes a flint to get the incense going and fans the smoke towards her mother with the edge of her mantle.

Nyptan kneels up on her haunches and closes her eyes. 'Lady Gula,' she mouths, words scarcely audible, 'we call on you. Lady Gula, come to us.' She squeezes her daughter's hand as she feels her slip down beside her on her knees. Together they perform, voices rising alternately, a hymn to Lady Gula, their Lady of Life, their holy one.

'You are the physician, you know how to heal,' comes Tanu, her voice high, chin on chest.

'We bring along all healing plants, you expel disease,' adds Nyptan, and leans forward to place her hands, feather light, on the sick man before them.

The lordling's lids open and his eyes roll forward from the back of his head. He gives a start and a scowl slides across his face. 'What's this?' he asks, mouth flecked with spume at the corners. His hands go to the side of the pallet and he tries to get up.

'Lie still, my lord,' says Nyptan, and nudges him back. She leans to place a new cloth across his head. 'You have a bad fever but are in good hands now. We can heal you. Lie back, be comfortable.' She takes the essential oil, which Tanu hands to her, a finger's length stick with cloth on the top, dipped in bay.

Instead of lying back, the man starts to thrash his head in wild arcs. 'No, no. Not here! I am Lord Kanmi.' Though his bottom stays fixed to the pallet, his feet lift up from it and his hands search for a grip to pull himself up.

'Hush, hush, my lord,' says Nyptan, and tries to slip the oil beneath his nose to calm him. 'No need to be afraid.'

The man grabs at Tanu, first with one hand, and then the other, to drag his body up. He claws at her with all his strength and levers himself off the pallet, before pushing her onto the deck and staggering forward.

'Aghhhh!' The wind is knocked from her.

He swipes Nyptan's beaker from her hand, sending the water flying and lunges for the dividing curtain to take him onto the main deck.

'Owwww!' cries Tanu, 'arghhhh.' She doubles over, clutching at her hand. 'He stepped on me. He got my fingers!' Her head comes up, eyes fill with tears and she flicks her wrist up and down, mouth wide.

'What is it? What's happened?' comes Dubb's voice, as he bursts at speed through their entrance. He stops dead when he sees both Nyptan and Tanu on their knees beside the empty pallet. With a frown, he helps them to their feet. 'What did he do?' His voice takes on an edge.

'He leapt on Tanu. Used her to get himself up off the pallet and ran out saying, "No, no, not here". That's all I know.'

The lordling is almost at the bow by now, lurching from one set of hawsers to the next. He swings his head around from side to side, addressing anyone he can find along the way.

'I won't be treated by a woman, do you hear!' Crew, old and new, pause what they are doing to see what the fuss is about. 'I won't be touched by a common slut from Tyre.' He collapses. The crewman from Libya, the one with bristly hair, lifts a bucket of sea water from the side to throw it over him. 'A soothsayer. Never!' the lordling mutters. He is left alone to wait for the diviners to return.

'I'm sorry for this,' says Dubb, as they turn again into the healing quarters. 'How can he be so stupid?'

'He'd prefer the diviners to help him is my guess,' says Nyptan, 'though I would have thought that Carthaginian lords prefer the medicine of Tyre and Sidon to new-fangled theories from Etruria.'

Dubb grimaces. 'Who knows with this lot. They're all a mystery.' He pulls at the curtain to drop it down and shield them from the deck.

'Oh, my darling, you poor thing,' says Nyptan, as she sees Tanu's hand. 'Here, this will help.' She slides over on her knees beside Tanu to take her daughter's hurt hand in both of hers to rub it. 'Let me see.' She turns it over to examine it. The first three fingers are bright red. 'Rub it hard and plunge it in sea water alternately. It will help with the bruising. We'll get essential oils onto it. And what a disgrace, that man.'

'He's a rude pig,' says Tanu, and puts her hand up for Dubb to see. 'Look what he did to my hand.' Her mouth is down at the corners, a frown between her brows and tears in her eyes.

'Well, more fool him,' says Dubb, and takes Tanu's hand to stroke and kiss it, 'to run away from healers like you two.' He pauses. 'But as soon as you've got your space back in order, I'm sorry to tell you there's a long line of people who need to see you. We've had a number of prangs today and, in the process, a lot of other medical problems have suddenly emerged.'

'Ah,' says Nyptan, and a look of satisfaction comes over her face. 'Well, that's what we're here for. You know how we work. Tell the men to get themselves into a line and when Tanu has had a bit of a rest, she will bring them in to see me one by one. I'd prefer it if you could give us a short while to get ourselves sorted out first. We're still not back to normal in here.' She opens her leather bag and starts to lay out the oils, bandages, scalpels and herbs. 'Tanu, come here with that hand.'

The injured or sick troop into the healing area one after the other. They come with deep splinters or crushed toes, burns from the sap, bangs on the head. There are also cases of diarrhoea from bad water and grinder's elbow from rowing.

As night draws in, another case of fever shows up. 'When did it first start?' she asks the man, a quiet soul with bushy eyebrows and a head which drops away sharply from the top of his head to the back of his neck. He sits on an upturned box, which is the healers' consulting place, elbows on his knees, head bent low.

'A few days ago,' he says, and struggles to make his voice heard. 'Now I've got the runs.'

'Why didn't you come to me sooner?' she says, and kneels in front of him. 'I could have helped you.' She puts her hand on his forehead.

He shakes his head and his shoulders shrug.

'Lie down please.' She leans forward to shunt another box towards him to form a makeshift bench. Their healing space is wrecked already even though they've not properly moved into it since it was scrubbed out. 'Take this.' She dips a cloth into cold water as the man lifts his legs up to lie down. 'Rest it on your forehead and close your eyes.' She turns into the space to grab the embroidered cloth from the last man who used it and slips it under this patient's head. 'Tanu, grind four cloves of garlic into paste and make an infusion. I'll need to cool him. Chares, Rabs, Dubb, anyone!' she calls, and waits before repeating herself.

Berek pops his head around the corner of the curtain, a question in his eyes. 'Missus? You need something?'

'More fresh water. Still more! As much as we can load up. It looks like we're going to have a spate of high temperatures. And salt water to the heads, barrels of it. From now on, every single time anyone shits, they must dip their hands in brine.'

* * *

When Lord Hanno finally returns to The Delphis, the moon is low in the sky. His lordship's party is drunk, raucous and splashing at the water's edge. The diviners balance baskets of white stones into dugouts and start to paddle them out.

'The prince returns to his kingdom,' says Chares, who stands beside Dubb, 'with his bleedin' holy men.' He spits overboard into the muddy brine.

Dubb's eyebrows rise. Chares is most unlikely to be rude about anyone, let alone an aristocrat. Rabs, on the other hand, is a law unto himself.

'Though, by the gods, look at the state they are in,' adds the first mate, as a neighing laugh crosses the cove. He shakes his head and turns away.

'There you are,' comes his lordship's voice. Dubb looks around to see Lord Hanno's head coming over the topside ahead of the others, ringlets dishevelled and mouth stained in red. 'I thought you must have abandoned ship!' He laughs.

'Where else would I be?' says Dubb, and examines the lord with fury.

'Looks like you've got everything shipshape here,' says Lord Hanno, as he weaves past the benches and renovated oars. He seems to be making for his bundle. The lordlings disburse to the bow and start changing out of their fine clothes, leaving the diviners and crew to struggle with the stones.

'We've discovered something,' says Hanno with scarcely concealed excitement.

'Though it took us a lot of time to wring it out of the natives,' says Bostar.

'We've found what we've been looking for.' Hanno sways at midships.

One of Dubb's brows goes up and he shrugs. He is too angry to answer.

'Well, aren't you going congratulate us?' Hanno says. 'We know where there's gold.'

Dubb is silent.

'Ooooh, no response, Dubb of Miletus? I thought you'd be pleased to hear the news.'

'While you were onshore having fun with your friends today, we found slime, worm…' begins Dubb.

'Oh, you are in a mood,' says his lordship. 'Now is not the time to report on what's happened today on The Delphis.'

'If not now, when? You are never here, even when I specifically called for you, twice! I have ordered expensive mast gum, oil and the servicing charges to local people will be high.'

A deep scowl flits across Lord Hanno's face before his brow lifts and he beams at Dubb. 'But we've got no need at all to worry about costs, my dear sir,' says Hanno. 'The gold will pay for everything.'

'You haven't found it yet!' Dubb replies. He cannot help himself. 'I have been doing work for you all day while you have been cavorting amongst your fools like the privileged boy that you are. I don't care what you've heard, what you might, or might not find. I need you to come when I call for you urgently.'

'Oh, dearie me,' says the man, and slaps his own wrist. 'I've failed to do my duty. Well, I promise to do better in future. After tonight. Tonight is the last night Lord Selvans and the others will be with us, isn't it, men?' He turns to his friends for affirmation, which they duly supply. 'They're returning to Lixus tomorrow.'

'Time to get going. Are you coming with us?' says Lord Bostar to Dubb. He too has stripped his clothing back to plain essentials and has an amphora of wine under his arm.

'Yes, why don't you? After all that hard work today, you could do with a bit of a break. The missus need never know,' Lord Hanno whispers, leaning in to the navigator's ear. He looks over Dubb's shoulder at the curtain behind him and gives a wink.

'Yes, time to go,' says Bostar. 'Off we go a-hunting,' and he sings a jolly tune.

'To see what we can find,' follow the others.

Selvans, the departing lord, thrusts his pelvis out and pumps his hips forward.

'Strong meat,' says another, and pulls his penis from beneath his robe to push it back and forwards in his cupped hand. Selvans follows suit.

Dubb didn't think he could be any more astounded at Lord Hanno's behaviour than he already was, yet here the man is, on the deck of The Delphis, behaving like a fourteen-year-old. I'm going to hit one of these idiots soon, he thinks. He turns to Chares, outraged. The first mate stands by the tiller platform and gapes. The remaining crew gather around to watch the spectacle. Dubb gives his head a vigorous shake, clears his throat and finds some business to do with a hawser. He can't trust himself to say more. Are we really to be saddled with these people for the rest of the journey?

* * *

When Nyptan sees the penises come out, she turns to Tanu, puts her hand across her daughter's eyes and steers her by the elbow back into their healing quarters. At least she won't be subject to the crudeness of the men in this sanctuary.

'Hey, let me go,' says Tanu, and breaks herself free.

Nyptan drops the curtain behind her and says, 'More cloves of garlic, now,' voice as light as she can make it. How hideous these lordlings are, how out of control. Those poor local women. She hopes to the depth of her bones that there's no one to be found out in the creeks and villages tonight. The thought of any woman or girl being caught up by such men fills her with dread. And I won't even know who they are, those victims, so I won't be able to help them. She thinks of the birthwort lying in their stores, the healing balm and staunch weed they might apply to stop the bleeding and sooth the wounds.

'What were they doing, Mummy, those men?' says Tanu, and sits beside her. 'Why did they do that with their hands and laugh so hard? Was it funny? I don't understand.'

'It is not funny,' she says, 'not at all, though it certainly entertains them. It shows you what kind of men they are. They don't like women, or respect them. And you and I, my darling girl, simply must stay out of their reach for the whole journey, do you understand me?'

'But what were they doing with their hands?'

'They were pretending their hands were the private parts of women. As we have talked about before, the private parts of men and women are used to make babies.'

'Pretending? Why would they do that?'

Nyptan feels short of breath. How much longer will she be able to protect Tanu from the world of men? How much does her daughter need to know now?

'Because they are going on a hunt tonight, my darling, not for gold but for women and girls like you, to catch them and hurt them. You will understand it more when you get a bit older. And here,' she says, and bends over to pull Tanu's veil out from under a pile of clothing, 'here is your veil. From now on, out on deck, we are, both of us, always, to cover our faces!'

* * *

As the lordlings, diviners and some of the Rusadirians tip themselves over the side into the dinghies, Dubb moves down through midships to check who's gone and who's stayed. There, hung between a thwart and a cross beam, is the slip of a loin cloth, which Qart calls his "best clothes". And where is the boy? he thinks. Not off with the raiders, thank the gods, or I would have seen him. He peers into every nook and cranny of The Delphis to find him.

'Have you seen Qart since the party returned?' he asks Rabs.

The small Carthaginian's eyes go wide. 'No, I haven't. Not since this morning.' They both rush to the topside to double check whether he has slipped into the dinghies.

'Has anyone seen the boy?' he shouts at the remaining crew. 'The ship's boy, Qart.' Panic rises in him. Another bout of fury at Lord Hanno. At the very least a ship's commander should keep his crew safe.

* * *

The day had ended well for Qart. When he climbs back on board The Delphis in the dark of night, he is full of the stories he will tell Rabs. Just as he finished the stones, two boys paddled by in a dugout. He had waved at them and jumped into the river to splash about. They had followed suit and they'd all ended up down river in a swimming hole. He'd left the baskets fully loaded behind him on the beach.

'Where have you been?' demands Dubb, no smile on his face or friendly greeting, as the boy comes up the ladder and over the topside. His master looks to be in a very bad mood.

'I've been with these boys,' he says, and leans forward to wave over the side and nod his head elaborately. 'Look! Say "hello". They want to come and visit The Delphis tomorrow. Can they?'

Dubb steps to look over at the canoe. An older man stands in the back, paddling with two boys bunched up against each other in the middle. The man waves and Dubb gives a short nod.

'We'll see,' he says, words clipped. 'Where have you been?'

'Tomorrow,' shouts Qart over the side, and makes a circular sign with his finger, head nodding.

Dubb grabs him by the arm and shoves him backwards down onto a bench. 'Where have you been?!' His master is so worked up, the spit from his mouth splatters his face.

'I went off this morning…'

'I know that already, you nuisance boy. Where have you been for the rest of the day?'

Qart sees that a little crowd of the crew has gathered round to hear his news. He's pleased. 'I got taken by the diviners to this cove, over there somewhere,' he says, and raises his hand towards the river mouth. 'I was given a whole load of baskets by the stupid priests and told to fill them with stones and number them individually.' Nyptan and Tanu have joined the crowd. Why is he the centre of attention like this? It's far from normal. 'I was there all day until the sun started to drop. No one came for me or the baskets until those two boys came by. That was their father.' He lifts his chin in the direction of the departed dugout.

'You mean these stones?' says Rabs, and points towards the bow.

Qart turns and peers along from midships. There they are, all six of them, with his numbered workings on top. Oh, I'm glad they didn't get lost, he thinks, or I'd have had to start again.

'The diviners left you all alone for the whole day? Out here, in a foreign land?' says Chares, a Hellene afraid of barbarians even though he works with them all day.

'Where were the priests?' asks Rabs.

'And Hanno?' adds Dubb.

'There was some sort of party going on in the village. I haven't seen them since this morning.' He catches a look, going from Dubb to Chares.

'You poor boy, you must be starving,' says Nyptan.

'And thirsty,' says Tanu.

'There's food soon,' says the healer, and she gives him a quick hug round the shoulders. 'Welcome back to us. We thought we'd lost you.'

The group breaks up.

'What? That I was missing?' says Qart to Dubb, and plucks at his forearm.

'Yes,' says Dubb through tight lips. 'We've sent out a party to search for you. Berek and his friend have gone. Chares, you'd better find someone else to go and get them. I hope they've not got too far.'

Oh, this is the reason everyone gathered round, he thinks. They decided I'd gone missing. But how could they think that when it was perfectly obvious where The Delphis was moored the whole time?

'Were you worried about me?' he asks, and grins as they settle down to eat. It's not often anyone on The Delphis seems to care about him at all.

'We were, my boy,' says Dubb, and gives his arm a little punch. 'We wondered if you'd been taken by a tiger. Before you get too full of yourself though, eat up big because there's an astronomy session for us tonight.'

The Enquiry - Day 7

'So, you didn't put your foot down with Lord Hanno, did you. Despite the fact that you could have? His actions were not so bad after all. Just young blood,' says Lord Apsan.

'No, I didn't, my lord, not just then,' says the navigator. 'I didn't really have the measure of the man quite yet. Yes, he was negligent. And crude. But we were at the beginning of a voyage, a difficult trip, which could take us gods know where. I didn't want to sour relations too early.'

The weather has definitely taken a turn for the worse and they are in the downstairs room of the residence with a fire in the grate. His lordship has been obliged to find warm clothes for the witnesses. He himself is robed in wool, and heavily embroidered hangings cover the windows on the western side to keep the gale out.

'Still, you felt it was your job to let him know, to remind him of his responsibilities?'

'If not me, then who?'

'You didn't think you could let him off, just this one night, until the voyage started proper?'

'As I told you, I walked away from further conflict at that point for precisely that reason.'

Lord Apsan's stomach does an uncomfortable revolution. He puts his hand to it. Oh, not again. He glances over at Tasii for the charcoal drink. 'You'd better bring biscuits,' he says to his slave. 'It's starting again.'

'It turns out the princeling lord from Carthage did not have even a working knowledge of the constellations either, my lord,' the navigator continues, oblivious to his gut problem. 'He knows less than my boy here. He simply wasn't interested in it. So, if Carthage is looking for people who can be lords of the sea, then they'd best look for someone else to recruit.'

Ah. This is the first piece of concrete information the navigator has offered since the beginning of the enquiry. He takes a note and his lips pouch, head feeling light and his temples sweaty.

'He knew enough for the purpose of this expedition, didn't he?' he manages, and coughs at a charcoal granule. 'You were coasting after all, not going across the open sea. And anyway, he had you. You were given to him to be the navigator. What else did he need? Tasii, get me water. Plain water…'

His slave disappears to the side table.

'The point is, my lord, that the sky started to change. And once I had realised, I just had to tell him. It was imperative he understood what was happening. But I failed. He wasn't interested. The thing is that…'

Lord Apsan puts his hand up to the navigator. 'Stop, stop.' The navigator pauses and looks at him, surprised. How I hate to be lectured about the sky.

Then the man carries on. 'They were important changes, my lord. Fundamental to navigation.'

'And you're about to tell them to me,' says Lord Apsan, face ashen. He leans back on his chair, spreads his arms over the back of it. Oh, I've never been good at the sky. Give me numbers, figures, writing, speeches. Don't set me down on a foreign hillside at midnight and expect me to get home.

What the Stars Say

Dubb empties out the hessian bag, which contains his star gazing kit. He and Qart have gone ashore and are tucking into a bend of the river with a good view of the whole sky. Their dinghy is drawn up on the sand, The Delphis a ghost on the rising tide to their left, the feeble light from its brazier making zigzag patterns on the water. Low bushland surrounds them, the ticking of insects and squawks of disgruntled birds. Dark as the land is, the sky above them is brilliant with life.

'I've never seen so many stars in all my days,' the boys says, eyes upwards, mouth open.

A long, straight pole and heavy stones clatter out first. Then there is twine, flints and oil lamps. From a separate bag come writing materials. They thud onto the soft sand.

'Here,' says Dubb, and passes the boy a flint pouch. 'Light us some lamps.' Qart ties it around his waist. 'Make sure they don't go out. Screen them behind something to stop them getting into our eyes, those stones for instance. You need to keep the lights topped up with oil. After you've done that, you can lay out the tablets on the dune there behind us. Keep the grains of sand from the wax. We can't have our records mixed up with more sand than necessary.' His instructions have come out in a rush and he knows Qart will struggle to remember them all. Too bad. He should learn to pay attention.

On easier voyages, when The Delphis is coasting, Dubb's usual practise is to keep an eye on the heavens whilst on the move. Unless you get into serious trouble, run into a storm for instance, or get attacked, all you normally have to do is right yourself, find Kochab in the night sky, and follow it. It always takes you home. Out here though, the sky is less straightforward. "Keeping an eye" whilst on board doesn't seem enough. Practical land-based astronomy is what I need to do, he thinks, regular, methodical, meticulous. I've been so busy fighting off the Etruscans over the last weeks, and doing Lord Hanno's job, that I've let it slip. Which has got to change. From now on I'm going to get to land and watch the heavens closely, whatever the consequences for the skippering.

At the shoulder of the beach, he stands tall to pound the heavy stick directly into the sand. Round and round he takes it with his arms until it is firm. He uses his feet and secures it into position. He smiles. It is good to be back with an open sky above him and a night free to study it. He lifts his eyes to look for Melqart. He twists around. There he is, their Great Sea God, on bended knee, club raised high. But wait, is it high enough? Is he leaning over, left foot too far up, club too low? Something's not quite right. His stomach suddenly convulses. What? Has he lurched to one side, slipped his moorings? Well, what about Kochab, their guiding star, where is it? His head whirls round and panic stirs in the pit of his stomach.

'Finished,' says Qart, voice clear and expectant.

'What do you need to remember about Little Bear?' Dubb blurts. It's the only question he can think of at present, a hard question, one which should keep the boy going for a minute or two while he quells his growing fear. Why isn't Kochab where it should be?

'That the "Little Bear never bathes in ocean deep",' Qart says instantly, as he comes into view from the darkness.

'Good, very good,' says Dubb. It feels to him as if his voice has disconnected itself from his body. It floats free in the night air and might, at any moment, disappear altogether into the crystal light. 'What is the name of the Little Bear constellation in the language of astronomy?' he adds. He grinds the words out, forces them through his teeth. I must get hold of myself, control my speech.

'Ursa Minor,' says Qart. 'What's next?'

'And Ursa Minor is important because...?' he adds, his head pounding. Where is it? Kochab has got to be here somewhere! His eyes flick backwards and forwards along the line of the bush behind them, a deep frown on his face.

'Because Little Bear is the constellation which holds Kochab our guiding star,' says the boy, voice triumphant.

There it is! Just behind that taller clump. Far lower in the sky than it ought to be but visible nonetheless! Relief floods through him and a huge sigh flows from his chest. We are not lost yet.

'Hold this,' he says, gives his head a shake and clears his throat. He hands Qart the top of the stick. 'Keep it straight. Do not let it move,' he adds, peremptory. He stamps his feet on the sand and rolls his head around on his shoulders.

'What's wrong?' asks the boy.

'Nothing,' he replies. He takes a circular shell from his pouch and bends to begin the process of lining their star up to the side of the stick. 'It's just that the night sky seems a bit different here than at the Great Sea. Now that Kochab is so far down the sky, I have to make new markings on the measuring pole, that's all. I just got confused for a minute.' He takes his knife, makes a notch on the stick with it and then ties on the shell.

'From now on, you're not to touch this stick, you understand. Neither the shell nor the stick. They both need to stay exactly where they are until I say so. As still as stones.' The boy nods.

Dubb steps up towards the dune to grab a stylus from their bag. He plonks himself down and pulls a tablet onto his knees. He adjusts the oil lamp. Time to make a record, to mark down how off course Kochab has become. "Fourth season from Gadir. No moon, 3rd quarter", he writes, and his lips bubble and blow. "Kochab very low, only half a hand height from the horizon". He draws an arc onto the tablet and a horizontal line. These two should never cross, he thinks. Little Bear should never bathe in ocean deep. A curlew calls from the brush behind them. Yet how is it that here, along this coast, that doesn't seem impossible. The constellations appear to be sliding around, their usual fixed points untethered? He chews at the end of his stylus.

'Dubb, why do the diviners use the images of stars on a chicken liver?' says the boy, right beside him on the sand now.

'Do they really?' he says, and shoves his precious record deep inside the hessian bag. He is glad to have something else to think about for a minute. 'Have you seen them do it? With a real liver? I've never known that.'

'On a model of a liver. Yes, I've seen it.' Qart's eyes are serious; his brows wave. 'They throw stones onto their model and say they can tell the future by reading it. There's a whole load of constellations written around its edge and they say it's by that means their gods tell them what to do next.'

Dubb looks hard at the boy. He is a pale form lit by the magical light of the heavens above. 'Are you sure?'

'Of course I'm sure. I've been stuck with them for months,' says the boy, irritated.

'Alright, alright. I knew they foretell their future from throwing stones and reading livers. What I didn't know is they divided the heavens into constellations and put them onto models. Can you remember the names of any of them?'

The boy shakes his head. 'They say they can read thunder and lightning from it too.' Qart is so close Dubb can feel the heat rise from his body.

'They're famous for that kind of thing,' says Dubb, 'but I didn't know they were interested in the stars. They certainly know nothing about the sea. They are not a navigating peoples, not now, never have been. So you must keep an ear open for any mention they make of the stars, their names, their constellations or gods. It's an important job eh, to have you there with them, day and night.' He gives the boy a jab in his ribs with an elbow.

'Owww. Why did you do that?'

'Because you finally seem to have understood what your job is with the Etruscans,' he says, and stands. 'To get information about them, learn what they believe, how their laws work? It's essential to have you there, in the middle of them.' The boy scowls. 'Oh, don't get into a temper. Come on, let's get back to work.'

The navigator and boy work through the night. They use the stick and shell to plot the course of Kochab as it swings around, and follow Melqart, their Great Sea Lord. They watch for Orion and wandering stars. A soft breeze nudges at them. Crabs clack in the sand.

When Dubb looks around next, he sees that sandbanks have appeared at the river's edge and dew falls on the brush beside them. The night wanes. 'Time to pack up,' he says, and blows on the wax of a tablet to set it. He swipes his writing stick down his tunic. Qart extinguishes the lamps and they begin the careful task of packing their records away.

'Dubb, Dubb,' comes Chares's voice from across the water. 'Hurry. Return to ship!' He looks up. The first mate's head is at the stern and he beckons elaborately. 'Hanno, Hanno,' Dubb can just hear.

They load the dinghy as fast as they can, haul it through the mud and battle back to The Delphis across a now heavily falling tide.

Even before his feet are firmly on the deck, Lord Hanno stands in front of him, arms crossed, legs astride. His eyes are bloodshot and his handsome features obscured by fury.

'Where have you been?' he demands. 'I've been waiting for you.'

'What?' says Dubb, surprised. 'We've been sorting out the star map, finding out where we are. About time someone got to grips with our location.' He turns his back on Lord Hanno and starts to stow the tablets and astronomy kit.

A younger priest launches himself bodily at Qart and drags him towards the diviners by his hair.

'Owwwwww,' comes the cry, and the boy's arms flail. He topples onto his knees and is hauled, towards the chicken keeper.

'We know perfectly well where we are,' says Lord Hanno. 'We are at Ngap. Your absence from The Delphis just now has cost us the tide.' Beside him, stands Lord Bostar and the one who refused to be treated by Nyptan, Kanmi, recovered apparently after a night's sleep.

Dubb looks over the topside. The current runs out fast. What is his problem? he thinks, and shrugs. 'We can go on the next.'

'Don't you shrug at me, Navigator,' says Lord Hanno. 'I came back to the vessel early this morning with the intention of catching the tide. My fellows from Carthage have said goodbye. The diviners have said the time is propitious. We wanted to leave, yet you weren't here.'

Dubb feels his stomach clench. I really am going to have to have it out with this lordling, he thinks, once and for all, even though we've not properly set off yet. He stands silent before the young aristocrat, the crew quiet all around.

'We can do that sort of stuff later,' adds his lordship. 'We're on the coast. What more do you need by way of information? What does it matter where we are?'

'It matters to me, my lord. Part of the funding of this voyage comes from those who have commissioned me to discover it, to mark it down and note the heavens. The other part is, Lord Hanno, as navigator of this vessel, I need to know where we are at all times. That means I need to be on the land. You may not consider our whereabouts significant. Others do. And whether you realise it now or later, if we get lost, you will be happy to have the information. Thus far, in fact, my lord,' he adds, and takes a deep breath, 'all you have done on this voyage so far is please yourself. You've run off to have a good time with your friends, neglected your duties as a captain and failed to learn about the running of this vessel. And unless you change your ways, I dread to think of the impact you are going to have on the outcome of this voyage.'

'How dare you speak to me like that?!' says the lordling, and goes red in the face.

Before he can say more, Dubb turns away and steps up to the tiller platform. 'Raise the anchor,' he says curtly. Chares and Rabs scuttle to the leads. 'Berek, strike the rowing tune.' The mariners scatter to their benches. The Delphis jerks and shudders its way against the tide from Ngap to the open sea, Dubb of Miletus at the helm.

The Enquiry - Day 8

Lord Apsan has been waiting for the security man from Malaka since first thing. Shipit Eli had sent a runner late yesterday to say that he would be arriving at first light, so his lordship had postponed this morning's witness session and even got up a bit early to work out the most testing questions he could think of to ask his inefficient security chief. "Why should I keep you on the payroll?" and "Why is it that a security network set up by you, with the extensive resources I put at your disposal, has failed to apprehend a Carthaginian lord walking through the land in broad daylight?"

Yet "first thing" has drifted by; it is now mid-morning and the man has still not appeared. Sitting in front of a small fire with hot milk, charcoal biscuits and grapes at his side Lord Apsan is becoming increasingly aggravated.

'I'm not surprised he's late,' says Tasii, as he takes a hot iron from the hearth to the side table, where he is rejuvenating old writing tablets. The hiss from his wax fills the air. 'Maybe he's had to come by land.'

'That's beside the point. An appointment with me was fixed, arrangements made, runners sent. He should be here. If it's blowing a gale, he should have come a day early.' He throws off his mantle. Is it the fire or is it all that astronomy from yesterday, which makes his head ache? 'Tasii, open the door. Let's get a bit of air in here.'

'You wanted it closed a minute ago,' says his slave, and opens it a crack. The wind whistles in.

'Well, I can't help that. It's stuffy in here. Bring me that box.'

'Which one?'

'The top box, of the samples. Which other box could it possibly be?!'

'Oh, you mean the one from the factory? You want to start looking at them!' says his slave, disapproval in his voice. 'What if he arrives any minute?'

'Well, too bad. He'll have to wait. We might as well do something pleasurable for a change.' He moves to the table with a small knife to slit open the wooden box.

It is filled with straw and he rummages through it.

'No, it's not this one,' he says, and slams the lid on again. 'This one's got urns in it. I want the one with figurines.'

'How should I know which box has got the figurines?' says his slave. 'There's twenty boxes here; it could be any one of them.'

'Well, get going then! Don't want to dawdle.'

'You want me to stop what I'm doing and find the individual ones?'

'I do. Please give me the box from the factory with the figurines in it. Is that clear enough?'

Tasii's eyelids flutter, his mouth goes into a straight line and he turns his shoulder on Lord Apsan to thump around in the packing cases.

'I know there's nothing in that group.' His lordship points to a pile at the left of the stack. 'Try there. No, to the right. There, those ones,' he says with heavy emphasis, and points to boxes in the centre at the bottom. 'It's got a different type of label on it. See? Is that makers from Tamuda across the water or down the coast? There'll be something different to look at in there.' He turns to the windows, throws the hangings back and plonks himself at a table near the light.

Tasii brings the first box, takes the lid off and within minutes the whole workroom is covered with straw, the wind outside being as it is. While his lordship rummages, Tasii takes a hessian bag into which he places all the packaging which Lord Apsan is letting loose.

'Stop, stop a minute, will you! Let me catch up. You'll cause a fire unless you're careful,' he says. He seems annoyed.

'Oh, calm down, dearest Tasii,' he says. 'Bring the bag to me. I'll empty the stuff into it straight away. Get a chair and let's sit for a minute and have a bit of fun. If we can't work, why don't we play?' His hand reaches into the box, shoves aside the packaging and there, carefully padded with wadding, is a selection of precious artefacts made by specialist craftsmen from down the coast. His eyes light up. With careful hands, he unrolls the first to reveal a jug. It's in the shape of a monkey, its tail curled in the form of a handle and its mouth the spout. The body of the jug will contain the liquid as it squats on hind legs. It has a long face, scoured by the maker to look like bones and fur, with looped red markings down its side. His heart leaps. How completely beautiful and unique. His mouth is open and he looks over to Tasii, who seems equally transfixed.

'I've never seen a monkey like this before!' he says, 'and there are millions of the blighters all over the Great Sea!'

Tasii shakes his head in wonder. 'Where does it come from?' he says, and shunts the straw out of the way to look for shipping marks. 'It's from a place called…I can't read it. It's in a foreign language.'

Lord Apsan lifts it by the tail and turns it this way and that. His fingers flute over it in the air as his eyes run around the precious objects. 'Monkeys like these could make us a fortune!' he says. 'Can we get more? Places like Nora, Tharros and Motya. For the tombs of the wealthy. We could get them made in batches of twenty and sell them on. How much did we pay for them?' He looks up at Tasii, eyes sharp.

Tasii turns and rattles around in his tablets, moves from table to box and back again. 'Sorry, I can't find the waybill just now. It'll turn up. Meanwhile, there's another box here, from the same source by the look of it. Shall I get that up?'

Lord Apsan nods with enthusiasm and reaches into the box again. There's a child's feeder in the shape of a porcupine and a spoon fashioned to look like a duck. It has a long, arched neck and its beak is the bowl. This is one he rather fancies for himself.

* * *

The enquiry resumes after lunch in the freezing workroom upstairs in the commissioner's residence. Lord Apsan, wrapped in a shawl, stands at the window and looks out at the bay from behind the hangings. There is nothing to be seen but sheeting rain. It obliterates the promontory, almost everything up to the docks below. The wind howls and there's a slow drip, drip in the corner of the room from a leak in the roof.

Tasii has brought up buckets from the storeroom and his lordship moves to a brazier to huddle.

Now, where were we yesterday? he thinks, and looks at the witnesses who are themselves wrapped in shawls, shivering intermittently and bunching together for warmth.

'You say you got back from doing your stargazing and gave Lord Hanno a piece of your mind. That's it, isn't it?'

'No, your lordship,' says the navigator, eyes firm. 'I did not give his lordship "a piece of my mind", as you put it. I simply pointed out to him his responsibility as head of our expedition to stay on top of our location, so that we might, just possibly, be able to get home again.'

Lord Apsan's brows come down at the sarcasm. 'You decided that the officially appointed head of the expedition, one appointed by Carthage itself and from a famous family, should be taught astronomy by you. Is that it?'

'He would certainly have benefited from a lesson or two,' says the man, and straightens his shoulders. 'My lord, where is the star map? You took it from me when we landed here in Gadir. Where did you put it? I want it back.'

A spot of bile pops into Lord Apsan's mouth and he starts to cough.

'Your lordship, more of this please,' says his slave, and pushes a beaker and biscuit across the table.

He's gotten very cocky lately, thinks Lord Apsan, as his eyes stream. He gets his breath back. 'You'll have it back when I'm good and ready to give it to you. It's perfectly safe with us,' he adds, voice strangled. Without thinking, his eyes slide towards the cylinder, now buried under Tasii's paraphernalia on the side table.

Dubb follows his glance to see a pile of tablets, a heap of woven fabric and the rounded end of decaying leather. At once, his elbows go out and he levers himself up off his seat and onto his feet. Tasii leaps forward to stop him. His tablets clatter to the floor and Gatit emerges from the doorway.

'Help, sir?' he says, eyes round with anxiety, hands at the ready.

'Oh no, you don't! says his lordship, as Tasii slips in front of the side table to protect it. Gatit grabs the navigator's arms and pins them behind him. 'That item is confiscated as you well know!'

Dubb collapses in front of Gatit, who takes the man back to his seat. 'Please, my lord,' he says, a note of fear in his voice. 'Please may I see it? Nothing else is of value from that whole wretched voyage.'

'Well, what is it exactly?' he asks. He thinks he knows the answer already but he must get the words from the navigator's lips and down verbatim onto Tasii's tablet if it is going to be at all useful in Byrsa Hill in the future.

'It's our maps of the stars, my lord,' says the man, head down. 'Please, I beg of you. Let me at least look at it, at them, to see they are safe. The velum could be rotting, water bleeding into it…'

'You will do no such thing. Since it is so precious to you, and concerns navigation and the stars, I will look at it later,' Lord Apsan adds with emphasis. Dubb looks up, hopeful.

'And will you tell me, tell us, please, Lord Apsan,' says Dubb, and lifts his head in a circle to indicate the crew, 'how it looks, whether it can be read?' His look goes cloudy.

Ah, I've got you where I want you now, you irritating man, thinks Lord Apsan, and his eyes gleam momentarily. 'Tasii, take it away. Put it in the safe downstairs. I don't want it in harm's way.'

'If I may be so bold as to suggest something, your lordship?' his slave whispers into his ear.

'What?'

'Can I suggest that you allow the witnesses to see their precious object? They might be inclined to tell you more if you do.'

'What?! Give them the star map?' he hisses back. 'Are you mad? It's the only real thing they seem to care about. Why would I give it away?'

'That is true, of course, your lordship. Isn't it also true that harassing people, who have powerful friends and have obviously been through so much, may not yield you the best results? These are intelligent people from whom you might discover more if you could let the man see his map, at least for a short while, under supervision, of course,' he finishes.

Lord Apsan looks at Tasii, unsure whether to be offended or pleased at the help his slave offers. It's true that allowing the navigator to see the map might make him more cooperative. It could also complicate things still further.

'I'll think about it,' he says. He gives a big burp.

Life on Board

'Can't you go any faster, boy?' says the chicken keeper. 'Why are you so slack?!' The man sits across from him at the prow, cages piled high beside him, one of them with its door open. There is a bird on his lap with its wings tied down and a net over its head to protect him from its beak. The animal squawks piteously as his hands press and poke at the stringy body to find and feel the outline of its liver.

Qart looks at him from under his brow and scowls. They are several days' journey out of Ngap, days when the interpreters took their place on board and Qart became the subject of even closer scrutiny from Malavisch. One hand held out in front of him, he clutches the claws of a dead hen. Its head and neck, upside down, are jammed between his knees. The other hand yanks at the feathers. His arms, from finger tips to elbow, are drenched with blood, his knees and thighs too. Plucked feathers are caught on the wind and swoop in circles around the hawsers, and there are eviscerated animal parts all around. Feathers stick to his cheek and are caught in his hair. He turns the carcass the right way up and lays its head on top of a block. Thwack goes his axe as he separates it into three: top, middle and bottom. He throws the head and claws aside, and plunges the torso into a barrel of sea water, before he stands and, without moving his feet, chucks the carcass into a basket with the others in readiness for the ceremony.

'Flaming Melqart, can't you keep your blood and feathers to yourselves,' comes a surly voice from behind him. 'You're disgusting!'

Qart turns his shoulder against the voice and barricades his ears to the complaining crewman. What can he possibly do to stop it? He picks up the next carcass.

'You, boy,' comes the same voice, louder now. 'Stop it, I'm telling you or I'll come up there and personally throw your precious chickens overboard!' Something hard hits him in the middle of his back. He turns to see a bit of broken rowlock lying beside him on the deck and the angry face of a new crewman, from Rusadir by the looks of it, staring at him from a bench.

'Look to your own work,' says Malavisch to the man from across the bow. 'What we do here in this sacred space is no concern of yours!'

'It is our business if we are getting all your blood and feathers,' comes a reply from somewhere else. 'Stop it!'

'Or it'll become your business whether you like it or not,' says the first man. 'I'll come up and sort you out personally.'

No wonder they're complaining, thinks Qart, as he looks down and along the deck. The bloody water and innards from the animals seep in rivulets towards their benches, forming a wide band as it heads towards midships and pools at the men's braced feet. He glances out of the corner of his eye to see the chicken keeper put aside his bird, about to deal with the men. He ignores the ensuing words. There are benefits to being so insignificant that no one cares about what you say. The liver of at least one bird, possibly three, is read morning, noon and evening so he has to keep the supply up. Afterwards, each bird is cooked and eaten.

Lord Hanno and his men amble back from a long discussion with Dubb at the tiller platform.

'He's going on about the sky again,' says Lord Bostar to the diviners. 'Something about entering a rainy season.'

'Lots of clouds, apparently.'

'That man we took on board at Ngap, the interpreter, he's getting him all worked up about no sky.'

'As if it matters all that much,' says bull neck. 'As long as we're on board reading the signs, what's the problem?'

'We're travelling along the coast, anyway,' says Hanno. 'We'll always be able to get back.'

'Well, unfortunately we're stuck with that man for the rest of the journey,' says Bostar. 'Though, why can't we get rid of him, Hanno? Him, his lady friend and the girl.'

'The whole lot of them in fact,' says Hanno.

'You could skipper us yourself, Hanno.'

Qart keeps his head down, his hands working and his ears open.

'It can't be done. You know my uncle in Carthage would have my head. I'm supposed to be in training or something.' He sees Qart dart a quick look at him. 'What's it to you, you snooping boy?' he adds unexpectedly, and Qart looks down again quickly at the chicken's neck, the hairs on the back of his neck suddenly standing on end.

'Look to your own work,' says Bostar, and he and the rest of them turn away and continue their conversation in whispers. Another chicken's head hits the block and gradually his panic subsides. Thank the gods they don't seem to realise Dubb is my master!

Rath, the Chief Diviner, bustles up to Malavisch. His pointy hat has a slight crook in it and, in his right hand, he has his axe. 'Right, now they're back, we're ready to start. Line them up,' he says to Malavisch.

They lay the carcasses on a board on their backs, necks towards the bow, amputated stumps at the sky. 'This one felt promising, my lord,' says the chicken keeper, and he presses a finger on a bird, the third in the row. 'Although, as you know, they are all good quality birds.'

'As you say, Malavisch,' says pointy hat in a superior tone, and his hand hovers over each bird in turn. 'Eli alum shumbaleth rah,' he whispers, backwards and forwards about a thumb's height above the dead animal. 'March through my right hand, assist me on my left.' He stops over one. 'This one, take this.' He settles his hand on the one at the end. 'Truss the rest and prepare them for lunch.'

Qart steps forward to scoop up the remaining birds and gets to work tying twine around the legs and bodies of the discarded animals.

'Please join me in calling the gods,' says Rath in a grand voice to their lordships. Hanno and his men lay down their smokes with reluctance and stand. Diviners straighten their hats, plunge their hands into a barrel of water and wait. 'Eli keili rumba bluff.' The rest start a slow dance around him in a circle. 'Eli alum shumbaleth rah. Give us pure words, Great Tinia, let me be blessed wherever I tread.'

Baal's balls, how sick I am of all this, thinks Qart. Since the night he and Dubb were star gazing at least he understands why Dubb wants him to stay working with the diviners. And, after today's comments, his purpose at the bow seems even clearer. Even so, all this blood and filth!

With expert hands and supple fingers, the high priest stabs the animal and opens it out. He shoves his fingers into the wound and feels around for its liver. As he lifts his hand, the long string of organs and blood gush. He raises it to the sky and the priests start a drone. 'Guide us to your truth, oh Great Tinia,' he says, and peers at the slimy mess in his hands. He turns it this way and that. The chant crescendos and, with a quick nod of his head, Rath deems the specimen good and chops a small, red blob away from the rest of the organs. A young priest pours blessed water over it and, as he does so, out from amidst the bloody clots, comes the shining shape of a bird's liver.

Each priest in turn scrutinises every angle of the organ. They circle their fingers around part of it. 'Grant us, Great Tinia, that this lobe is upright and all the same colour,' he says.

'This, too, is perfect,' adds Ani. 'Light in colour, not too cream, nor too milky. Its base points wholly to the outer circle.'

'Do we all confirm that this is what we can see?' says Rath. His fellows nod their agreement. Then, with the flick of a thumb and forefinger at the central lobe of the liver, he looks to Hanno. 'My Lord Hanno, step forward.' His lordship moves close. 'I am happy to inform you that Great Tinia tells us, via this liver, that here, at this place, is where we need to find land.' He turns and sweeps his arm across the empty horizon. 'This is the place in which we will find shelter, water and fresh food. And gold, of course. Gold!'

Lord Hanno punches the air with his fist. 'Treasure,' he says. 'Excellent!' He and his fellows clap each other on the back, and he turns and bows deeply to Lord Rath.

'Where then, exactly, is the place to land?' he asks, and from bow to stern his eyes roam the side of The Delphis.

The priests all look at him, confused.

Rath says, 'Look here, at the bird. This bulge tells us.' He lifts the liver for Lord Hanno to see. 'This protuberance predicts treasure, right here.'

'But we're at sea,' says Bostar.

The high priest frowns at him. 'You do not understand. Not all livers have this and we know from our holy discipline that, when they do, riches follow. If you want gold, you must make landfall now.' His hand waves around in a general way.

Bells ring and the priests start up a drone. 'The gods have spoken. Nee roh, kee row, shuhumbaleth rah,' he goes. 'I, the magician and thy slave, add thy pure spell to mine.'

'Good, so the gods have spoken,' says Lord Hanno, and shrugs to his fellow aristocrats. 'Come, let's tell the navigator that we must prepare to land.'

Qart lifts his face from emptying the guts of a chicken onto the deck to find Dubb. He doesn't know what's coming, he thinks. He will not be happy.

* * *

'We've got to go in now,' Lord Hanno says to Dubb. They have come up to him at the tiller platform in a little gang, full of importance.

'Oh,' he says, 'who says so?'

'The gods. They have spoken. They have told us here is a place to find gold,' says Ani, at Lord Hanno's side.

Rabs's mouth twists and he rolls his eyes at Dubb. He gets on, filing the battered rowlock in his hand.

'Do as Lord Hanno says, Navigator,' says Lord Bostar. 'He is the commander of this vessel, after all.'

'Oh, that surprises me. Given the amount of work he has done since we left Lixus, I thought I was in charge of it,' he says, voice tight. 'It's difficult to conclude anything else under the circumstances.' He holds the tiller handle steady, chin forward.

Rath arrives at his elbow and sticks a shining liver into his face. 'See here,' he says, and points. 'The direction of this lobe points to that bulge in the liver which predicts boundaries. Here it is, the line between poverty and wealth.' He flicks his finger at the topmost part of the lobe, which he holds just to the side of Dubb's mouth.

The navigator closes his eyes. 'I am forced to inform you, my Lord Rath,' he says, 'that I read the tides, the currents, the sky, not livers.'

'What are you saying?' asks Rath, annoyed. 'I repeat, we must go to land.'

'And I said that although your knowledge of livers may be unparalleled on land, such information is not a useful guide on the sea.' He looks directly into the eyes of the high priest. 'Following land gods on the ocean can be dangerous, so dangerous it could cost our lives. Is that what you want? What you all want? To die?' He waits for the shortest moment before carrying on. 'No, I thought not. So, no, we'll not be going for land at present.'

'Why don't you just do as you're told?' says Hanno, and steps towards Dubb, shoulders squared, chest out.

'Hush, hush, my lord,' says Rath, and takes Hanno by the arm to turn him away. 'This is not the time for violence. Come away. Let's seek guidance from the gods on how to make this navigator see sense.'

Chares is by his elbow, a look of incredulity on his face. 'Did I really just see that? Priests coming up in the middle of a long coast and telling you what you, the skipper, should do? They'll tell us where to cast anchor next, and when to set off! It's a nonsense. Not even Poseidon demands that!' He gives the amulet on his wrist a little rub of affection.

Dubb shakes his head and scratches behind an ear as his eyes follow the men up the deck. They start a slow dance around their sacred space. 'And we've only just begun.'

Some time later, Dubb feels the current beneath them change. The Delphis is being drawn to port, towards the land, of its own accord. Into his vision comes a thin, purple line, growing in size as they cross a grey-green sea.

'Land! Land!' shouts Qart from up front. The boy turns and hails Dubb from the bow.

Lord Hanno is on his feet and already halfway down midships towards the tiller. 'There, we told you.' He points at the land as if Dubb was blind. 'The diviners said there would be land. Now do you believe them? So it's time to go in, and that's an order!' he bleats.

Rabs and Chares are beside Dubb, eyes pressed ahead, frowns on their faces.

'It looks reasonable,' says the Carthaginian under his breath.

Chares lifts his chin slightly in agreement. Hanno stands, arms folded, eyes ablaze, at the side of the tiller platform.

Dubb examines the coastline. He looks for sharp edges in the line, which might indicate a break, an estuary, a bump, which might be a headland. Nothing is spiritual about this, he thinks. Lumps and bumps mean actual channels, rivers and beaches, not signs from the gods. Perhaps they could go in. Nothing he can see or sense indicates the contrary.

'What are you waiting for, you fool?' says Lord Hanno, and leaps up onto the platform to get at the tiller.

Chares blocks his way.

'We will do as you want,' says Dubb to his lordship, voice mild, 'but we will do it slowly, carefully, and to my orders, not yours or the diviners'.' His lordship looks relieved and takes a step back. 'And by the gods, if you don't stop those seers from making that terrible din I will come up there and personally throw them all overboard. I need to be able to hear everything in the next few hours from the cry of a gull to the plop of a fish.'

'Rabs, look to the leads. Chares, take over here. I will speak to the crew.'

The navigator steps forward to the first row of benches. Berek raises an extra roll on the drum and the rowing team looks up. They are young and old, originating in countries or cities located all over the Great Sea and beyond, on benches twenty a side, along the entire length of The Delphis. 'Men, we are going to try to land. We do not know what is ahead of us. When we come close to it, and at my signal, I want all but the first three rows of you to raise your oars.' The men nod. It is a common way of moderating the speed of a vessel in unchartered waters. 'If necessary, I will call on other rows to join or pull back. Is that clear?' Seeing the looks of concentration on their faces, he adds, 'And I promise you good grub if we make landfall and a rest even if we don't.

'Rabs, Chares, soundings!' he shouts, as they come closer to the shore, and the two men collect the leads and head for the bow. They barge in on the diviners and start to feed the knotted ropes over the side. Is that the crashing of breakers he can hear? Are there rocks or is it beach? We might go in now, he thinks. 'Right, men, raise oars!' At once The Delphis slows to a crawl.

Deep silence falls on deck, broken only by the mariners calling measurements. The crew wait, priests kneel and Dubb is on the tiller platform, alert to every clue. A soft rain starts. It falls delicately on the deck, on the men, over Dubb's wrists and arms and soothes his taut nerves. All he can hear in the foreground is the brush of light rain. In the distance, there is nothing dangerous or dramatic. It seems to be safe. He leans on the tiller handle to turn the prow of The Delphis towards the land.

The Enquiry – Day 9

Shipit Eli sits across from Lord Apsan, at the fire, and leans back in his chair. Every visible part of the security man's body is covered with hair: legs, arms and face, from chin to ears. His brows are especially bushy. He has discarded his outer mantle; it lies on the floor beside him. As it begins to dry out, it stinks.

'Very sorry, my lord. I could see Gadir in the distance but couldn't get here. My animal went lame right after I'd sent you the message and, by the time I'd found a place to stay for the night and a replacement for the animal, it was too late to warn you that I wasn't going to arrive in time.'

Lord Apsan grunts and pulls his fine woollen mantle higher around his shoulders.

'Remove that garment, Tasii. Put it outside.'

Shipit Eli's mouth opens in protest, before he sees Lord Apsan's wrinkled nose, and he closes it.

Two days have gone since his security chief was supposed to arrive. His excuse is flimsy, as expected. 'You could have let me know the following day. I have spent half my precious time waiting around for you to appear.'

'Very sorry, your lordship. It's the roads. In winter.'

Lord Apsan decides to let it ride for the moment and see what else the fellow has to say. 'So, why haven't you found this lordling?' he says.

'It seems straightforward enough a job to me. A young Carthaginian aristocrat travels the roads in winter along a well-known land route between Gadir and Malaka. You have men along the route. There is an urgent security alert, yet he's still missing.'

'I have informers at every hamlet and cove along the way, my lord. No stranger has travelled this route. So few people pass in the winter that it is easy for locals to spot someone new. Your missing person will still be here in Gadir,' the man says confidently.

'You fool. Do you think I would have called you all the way from Malaka unless I had done a thorough search of Gadir? Of course he's not here. He absconded from his lodging house weeks ago, without paying for his accommodation, and was last seen heading for the port. Did you go through every vessel as it arrived before the end of the season?'

'As I said, we have a man in every port and stopping place, my lord,' says Shipit. 'There has been no sighting.'

Lord Apsan is suddenly furious. 'Sit up straight when you talk to me. You slouch as though you're sitting in a grog shop. You're not having a conversation with a friend in front of the fire. I am the Commissioner for Trade at the Port of Gadir and the representative of the Senate here in the Western Sea. I can bring the whole weight of Byrsa Hill down on your head.'

The man's expression changes from confidence to defence, and he shuffles back in his seat and lays his hands out flat on his thighs. He bows his head. 'I can say, on the blessed milk of Melqart's mother, that no Carthaginian lord has passed in and out of Malaka since I first received your instructions, my lord.'

'That's not what your task is, you idiot. Your task is to find someone who could be anywhere from here to Carthage by now. What if he changed vessels at sea and slipped past you to Sexi without calling in? Have you spoken to our agents there? And at Abdera? What do they say?'

'You can ask them yourself, my lord,' says the man sulkily. 'I have presumed to convene a meeting of all the representatives of your security network here within the next few days.'

'What? And in order to do that they've left their posts unmanned? Is that really what you've done?'

'No, my lord. There is a strong line of command at all our inform-ant stations. People will fill in behind those meeting us and they have instructions to send runners if there are any developments. As I have mentioned many times before, I have great experience of setting up and maintaining strong security networks, not least along the Sicilian coast.'

'So, we are to expect a troupe of security men to arrive at any minute, are we? When were you going to inform us of that little fact?'

The man is silent, grown sullen. His hairy shoulders flex in the fire's light.

'What about Tartessos? What sort of security arrangements have you made for that side of our operations?' he asks.

The man's eyes flick up to him and then look away.

'Well?'

'I was not aware you required me to cover that area in my work, my lord.' His voice is low. 'Your commission was to concern myself with all aspects of security between the port of Gadir and the Great Sea,' he says, as if quoting verbatim from the official document.

'Oh, for pity's sake,' says his lordship. 'And what do you think we do here at the Port of Gadir? Set up picnic cruises for the local nobility?'

The man's jaw juts out. 'Of course not. I am completely aware this is a mining port, that valuable cargos go out of it to Carthage and beyond, that it is my responsibility to check the shipping companies carry what they claim to. We do all that in the office at Malaka as you know. At no point since you appointed me have you ever mentioned anything about Tartessos.'

Lord Apsan throws his hands in the air. 'Do I need to list every single port, cove and beach out for you? You know the route. You know the minerals come down from the mountains, are transferred to vessels here and then pass through the Strait of Calpe. Who did you think was looking after this end of my operations if not you?' he challenges.

The man gives a quick shake of the head and looks at his hands.

'The upshot of this conversation is that we have had no one looking for Lord Hanno in Tartessos, is that correct? What about the hills behind?' The man does not reply. 'Or the high routes, that go along the mountain peaks? Still silence? So, despite your supposed vast experience in security, there is a huge hole in it when it comes to anything further west than this residence.'

'I know what has been going out of this port, my lord. Along with your slave here, Tasiioonos of Knutes, of course,' he adds slyly.

Tasii's head goes up and his eyes lock on to Lord Apsan's.

'Don't you start shifting the blame onto this office, my man,' says Lord Apsan, and gets up to stand over his security chief. 'If you were ever in doubt about where your jurisdiction ran, you could have asked. Did you enquire? No! Did you never once wonder who was doing security before the goods reached this port?'

'There are one or two informers in the companies, my lord,' the man says, his back pressed hard into his chair.

'One or two, you say, in a port which sends out hundreds of ships every sailing season, loaded with treasure. Tasii, show him the cloth.'

His slave opens a box at his side and lifts the putrid rag out. It hangs limp and blotchy, the colour of dried blood, on the end of his stylus. Lord Apsan takes hold of the stick, goes to Shipit and wafts the filthy thing in front of his eyes.

'What language is that?' snaps Lord Apsan.

A frown comes down between the man's eyes. He drops his head to one side and then the other. 'Is it a language, my lord?' he says. 'It looks like a code to me.'

'It's Tartessic, you idiot!' he says. 'How many languages do you speak? Have you been intercepting runners and searching them for information?' There is a pause. 'Well?'

'We haven't got the resources, my lord, to stop every messenger. I have sometimes pulled someone over in Malaka. Nothing has ever been found that way.'

'So again, to summarise, not only are the roads as open as a whore's legs, you speak no language but Punic and you don't stop runners as a matter of course. What sort of security network was it you said you manage? Let me see if I can remember. Did you say "The most secure arrangement of spies and informers beyond Sicily"? That was it, Tasii, wasn't it?' He looks at his slave in triumph at remembering the exact wording. Tasii's head drops and he fiddles with his stylus. 'Well, that will be all for today,' he says, and lifts his chin to the door. 'You are to stay in Gadir, in your lodgings, until the rest of your leaky network arrives. We will then shake up this world class security system of yours and put new men in place.'

He is very gratified to see the shock this statement brings to Shipit Eli's smug face. That'll teach him not to be so incompetent in future.

* * *

'Despite all the predictions of the diviners about finding gold when we landed, Lord Hanno found none at this stopping point,' says Dubb. The man sits, wrapped in a blanket, against the wall in Lord Apsan's workroom in Gadir. He looks weary and they have been going in detail through everything that happened that day on The Delphis.

'We got in and out of that place on a gentle surf with a local dinghy or two. The locals brought us food, we found fresh water, and Lord Hanno and his mates went off in search of treasure. The place smelt extraordinary, sweet, the land fertile. Rich and promising as that was, gold did not materialise.'

'Why didn't he find gold then?'

'We don't really know, my lord. Something about being chased away by the villagers.'

'Rabs went with them,' says the dithery Hellene. 'He would have known.'

Lord Apsan looks up with mild interest. 'Well, Rabs, where are you? Speak for yourself.' His eyes scan the witnesses, waiting for one of them to open his mouth.

'He was left behind, my lord,' says Dubb, voice low, eyes down.

'Taken,' says the woman, 'by Melqart' and her voice breaks.

Lord Apsan's heart sinks. What, a dead witness? Well, there's an opportunity missed. Might have discovered something useful about Lord Hanno since he seems, by all accounts, to have no clue about the sea.

'There's always a price to pay for riches,' he says briskly. 'Can't be helped. Though, they did find gold eventually, didn't they?'

'I'm not entirely sure,' says the navigator, 'though I understood that this investigation is about Lord Hanno and not the treasure.'

'Look, you fool, the state of Carthage is, of course, interested in treasure. You might even say, only in treasure. Otherwise, why do you think I'd be going to all this trouble to hold an enquiry?'

Tasii's eyes catch his across the workroom. "Don't be so impatient" they seem to say. Oh alright.

'I thought the Senate might be interested to know whether this brave, new commander of theirs could navigate. Whether he's a good leader, knows his vessels,' says the navigator. 'Byrsa Hill would require their leaders to know all this sort of thing, wouldn't it? Carthaginian commanders have been executed by the state for lesser crimes than this.'

Lord Apsan's eyes narrow. Who does this navigator think he is? Overreaching himself, as usual. He's lecturing me, representative of the

State of Carthage in the Western Sea about what would be acceptable on Byrsa Hill. He looks hard into the navigator's eyes and searches them for signs of sedition. How does he know what Carthage wants? Is he a spy? His mouth goes down at the corners. 'Look, Navigator, I don't care why you are all on this voyage, whether it was Hekataios of Miletus, the tyrant Polycrates or Poseidon himself, I am in charge of this enquiry and we will do things my way. Do you understand?'

Tasiioonos clacks his tablets on the other side of the room, rather too loudly it seems to Lord Apsan. What's he doing that for, he thinks and pauses. I'm only doing my job and he scowls as several of them fall to the floor with a clatter.

By the time the enquiry starts again, the woman is sobbing in the corner and the room has started to stink from the fire and too many bodies. 'Let's do one thing at a time, shall we,' he says, voice a hiss, Tasii's words ringing in his ears. He takes a sip of water before standing to start and paces about the room.

'So, what happened the day, any day, pick one at random, on which Lord Hanno did find gold? I don't want to know about the night sky, the smell, how many chickens the diviners had for breakfast or anything else. Just tell me about a day Hanno found gold!'

'But first of all, my lord, you need to hear this,' blurts the woman. 'Lord Kanmi died.'

He pivots on a heel to stare at her. 'What? An aristocrat dead! Why didn't you tell me this before?' How am I going to explain this to Byrsa Hill?

A Thunderstorm

Nyptan is woken by a strike on the cheek so sharp it might have come from a knife. She puts a hand to her face, seeking blood. Water, she notes, bleary, and shoves a finger in her mouth. Not blood. There is a blaze of blinding light. A crack of thunder follows and makes the deck shudder. Ears ringing, she lifts herself up on her elbows, hair dropping around her, and looks down towards midships. In an instant, the whole scene is obscured by torrential rain.

'Tanu, Tanu, get up, we've got to move!' she shouts, and lurches to her feet. She grabs her sleeping things and drags them the two steps it takes to get from one side of their sleeping quarters to the other.

Her daughter's head emerges from under her blanket and she leaps into action. 'Can you save them?' Nyptan yells, and points to batches of staunch weed as they're carried on a channel of water towards a porthole.

Dubb's head appears through the curtain, along with a burst of sheet lightning. 'Help's coming,' he says, and she gets a glimpse of him, grey hair flattened down the side of his face like shit from seagulls, before he disappears again. A moment later, Rabs rushes in, Chares right behind, and they start to rig a shelter over their quarters and sick bay with rolls of canvas and an old sail.

'There's more of this in the hull,' says Chares, rope between his teeth, knife in hand, lashing it. Berek's getting more.' He sets off to do the same in the larger space where the feverish men are. Since they left land, several weeks ago, the numbers of men coming to them for treatment has risen. Consequently, their already cramped private quarters have been divided off by yet another curtain and a bit of space pinched from the leads' area. The ill men lie prone on makeshift pallets, mainly with fever. And, since it's not clear to Nyptan what kind of fever it is, she has been treating them all the same. She has also been insisting that the salt water barrel by the heads is changed every day. The men don't wash their hands nearly enough.

Before their sheet is fully rigged, thunder rolls across the sky again. The heavens, it seems, might collapse under their own weight any minute. Kama and his companions join them to build the cover, move the men to new places and clear a space where the healers can work. They lurch from side to side on a choppy sea as they reposition the poles and canvas.

'Don't be frightened, missus,' says Kama with a smile as, shoulders hunched, he moves a couple of the larger leads out of the way. 'It will be over soon. And anyway, this is good, exciting. Better, we locals think, than day after day of drizzle and grey cloud.' One of his mates nods.

Nyptan, her medicine box in her hands, is astounded at how fast their normally tiny quarters have been transformed into a wide, covered sickbay, men ranged around the side.

'I'm sure you are right, Kama, but it's not good for my patients. Thank you,' she says, 'to all of you, and you too, Rabs and Chares.'

Outside on the deck all is chaos. Men fall over each other as they rush to rig themselves coverings. Rain pounds the deck, jumps as high as their knees and forms pools, lakes in and around all their personal effects.

'Baal's balls!'

'Melqart's mother!'

'By the gods!' they curse.

'Oh no!' Tanu yelps, as a bunch of garlic is caught by the swill, and heads for the side. She grabs and ties it to the underside of the tiller platform. Her eyes are so full of water, she can't see what she's doing and she wipes at them with her wrist.

'You poor love. Thank you, my darling.'

There is another great crash of thunder and the baby inside her kicks. 'Oh,' she says, and puts a hand on her belly to calm it.

Tanu looks at her sharply. 'What is it? What's happened?'

'Feel it,' she whispers to her daughter, and grabs her hand and moves it low over her belly to the spot where the child has protested. I don't blame you for kicking up, she thinks. I'm not happy about this either.

'All well?' comes Dubb's voice, hurried. He appears beside them, to check they're alright. His already strained face drops further into a frown when he sees Tanu's hand on her mother's belly.

'Quite well,' she says, too bright, and he nods and disappears. I do wish I could tell you about this new one of ours, she thinks. It's getting late in the day.

'Oh, blessed rain,' murmurs a man beside her. A compact, intense man, with a dark head and grizzled eyes, he's been hit hard by the sweats. Now he sits, legs wide, on a newly placed pallet just outside their canvas shelter, head back, mouth open, arms out to embrace the weather. Water pours down his forehead, past his nose and mouth, and drains onto his chest.

'Here, come inside out of the rain,' she says, and puts a hand to his forehead. He is on fire and shivery. 'Tanu,' she calls, and looks for her daughter again amidst the restless men. Together, they persuade the man to move inside.

'He needs cool water on his forehead, and a cloth, to get that temperature down.'

The man opens his eyes and tries a smile before sinking back into a stupor.

'We'll bring you something,' Nyptan says, and then, to Tanu, 'we should give them all something. To settle them.'

They go to their shrine and she pulls out her bag of remedies. While she drops spots of lavender into two shallow dishes, Tanu finds the tiny, flat sticks, which act as spatulas. 'We'll go to each man in turn. Give them just a speck, under their noses.'

The rain has lost its violence and turned to a steady thrum. Cave-like shelters have sprung up all across the deck and the men curl up in them, octopus-like, to wait it out.

'I am the Lady of Life,' sings Tanu, as she places her first dab on a man from Rusadir. Her voice cuts through the heavy atmosphere and the sick shift on their pallets; a smile or two breaks out.

She seems to like it when there's an emergency, thinks Nyptan. She enjoys being surrounded by people who need her help.

Next in turn is a Hellene, looking grumpy beside the leads.

'Can't you provide me with bay instead of lavender?' he growls. 'Lavender gives me a headache.'

'It's the fever that gives you a headache,' says Nyptan, and sighs. 'Tanu, see if you can find something else for this man, will you. Thyme perhaps?' She moves off to the others. 'We'll come back to you soon.'

In Nyptan's experience, it is the Hellenes who complain loudest when they are sick and, fortunately, there are not a lot of those on board. The men from around Carthage, Libyans, Rusadirians and so on, and those who came with them from Gadir, are used to fever and know that, after a few days of the sweats, it goes quiet for a while before the cycle begins again.

'And, Tanu, light some incense, can you, on the way back. It will cheer us up.'

As her daughter passes the heavy shrine with its curlicues, she strikes a flint. The vapour rises to fill the space. That should put the men into a doze, she thinks and looks over as Tanu administers thyme to the Hellene.

'I expel disease,' she starts.

'Most powerful in the sanctuary,' Tanu responds.

Their eyes meet across the healing space and they turn their song into a round. 'I put men at ease.'

'Thank you, missus,' says the man. 'I am Shadra from Libya.' He tries a smile before his eyes close and his head slips sideways on his pallet, exhausted. She recognises him now as the man who tried to help the young lordling who escaped from the sick bay back at Ngap. She gives him an extra dab of lavender under this nose.

'Thank you,' says the next man in line, the one with the sloping head, who has come down with fever again. He catches at her hand and kisses it.

'Here, try this,' says Kama, who is, suddenly, at her elbow. He clutches a calabash in his hands. He tips it forward and out tumble small, hard, golden-coloured lozenges. She recognises it immediately as the type of sap she had pulled from Dubb's arm, the type the men had been using to cork The Delphis. 'It's used here for a lot of things. They're from the Acacia tree. You can suck it, like this.' He turns to the slopy-headed man to pop a piece into his mouth. 'It can be used on its own or you can add things to it, like garlic or herbs. It's used for healing, especially fever.'

'Thank you, Kama,' she says. 'Very useful.'

'And there's lots of it!' He gives the gourd a sharp shake, the sap clacking inside like beans, and indicates two other large ones of the same design, swinging from a place near the leads. He hands it over and then steps outside into the rain once again.

The fever the crew is coming down with seems to be of two sorts. There is one, which is a bad dose of malaria: high fever, headaches and shivers, of the kind she has seen many times around the Great Sea. It is partly why there is a sick bay, to give those suffering in this way a place to go and rest. This illness repeatedly comes and goes over a few days, and has the men running to the heads. For them, there is garlic paste and now this sap to chew.

The other fever seems to have the opposite effect. Patients need rest, have a high fever, headaches, a cough and are constipated. For these men, she can do nothing. Are they, too, suffering from the mosquito or from something else?

'Come, Dubb, Nyptan, come,' she hears Qart's voice, urgent, breathless. 'Something's happened!'

Tanu's eyes catch hers across their sick bay, alarmed. What can have brought Qart down here at such speed? Normally, he's tied to the chicken keeper. Nyptan dabs bay under the next nose and then, with a nod to Tanu, says, 'Carry on.' She pulls out her veil from within her robe and peers out from under the canvas. Her eyes search ahead for trouble, lips pruned.

The boy is already halfway back up towards midships, body and legs whirled round, shouting behind him to Dubb, 'It's that lordling.'

The downpour has cleared the air; only a few spits and spots continue. Like her, the crew all crane forward to see what the trouble is. At the bow, a knot of men gather around a figure lying slumped on the deck. She lifts her veil across her face and starts to walk forward.

On the way, she passes Chares, who has taken over from Dubb at the tiller. 'Gods go with you, missus,' he says.

The navigator himself is already partway through midships. As they get closer, Lord Hanno breaks away from the group to come and meet them.

'My Lord, Kanmi has fallen ill,' says his lordship to them both. His face is creased with concern. 'It was impossible to wake him this morning, even in the middle of all this.' He lifts his chin to the water running in streams from the hawsers, cables and canvas of the deck around him. There's a note of panic in his voice. 'Last night, he kept on saying, "Get me to the temple", over and over again.'

'We just thought he'd chewed a bit too much herb,' adds Lord Bostar, shoulders hunched, arms crossed and scratching at his muscly biceps.

Dubb looks at Nyptan, weary. She knows exactly what he's thinking. Spoiled aristocrats, finally forced to face reality.

'What shall we do? We've got to help him,' says Hanno, and squats down to put a hand to the man's head. 'He's my closest friend.'

'Why do you ask us?' Dubb says. 'Why not ask your diviners for help?'

'No no, hush, husband, not now,' she says to him, voice quiet. 'Don't cause trouble.'

He turns his back to the lordlings, to shield his words. 'These men have been working to their own rules ever since they left Ngap. Why should you try and help them now?'

'Because this is what I do. I'm a healer. It's why I'm here.' She puts her hand out and holds his arm.

'The diviners say they don't want to touch him,' Lord Hanno replies, a whine in his voice.

'They say he is too filthy,' adds Lord Bostar, and steps forward to lift the corner of Kanmi's loin cloth. Beneath it, faeces and diarrhoea mix with rain water from the deck.

Her husband shakes her hand away. He can't help himself it seems. 'This is the man who refused to be treated by a woman, do you remember? The one who turned down the services of our healer weeks ago, when she might have done something to prevent this,' he spits, voice hard.

'Well, never mind that,' says Lord Hanno. 'What can we do now?'

Nyptan bends to the man and hovers her hand above his forehead. She puts her fingers to his wrist and peels back the shawl covering his chest. There, on his shapely frame, is a series of red spots, which spread all the way down his torso. Lifting her arm higher, she pulls the whole garment from his body and reveals, in full, the effluent which has poured from his nether end.

'Right, this man needs to be brought to me at the sick bay now!' she says, stands tall, voice commanding. 'His fever must be reduced at once. He must be given a poultice for his diarrhoea, and we must try and find a way to stop his internal bleeding.'

'How do you know he's bleeding internally?' says Lord Hanno, the hint of a challenge in his voice.

Nyptan's shoulders are set. She looks the man directly in the eye, her frame only half the size of the lordling's. 'Because I am a healer, my lord, and I have seen this kind of thing before. Because I have worked all over the Great Sea and beyond. The darkness in his stools shows blood; the hardness of them suggests his inner organs are in spasm. Unless you get him up to the sick bay at once, I will take no further responsibility for him and he will be dead within days. He may well die in any case.' She turns on her heel and walks back towards the stern, mantle billowing behind her.

The men she passes in midships follow her with eyes full of admiration.

'They are idiots, missus,' says one.

'He should have come to you at the beginning.'

'You'd have saved him.'

'So, what are we doing now, my lords?' she hears Dubb ask the men at the bow. There is a triumphant note in his voice. 'Is he coming back to the sick bay or not?'

* * *

They juggle Kanmi's body up the deck towards the sick bay, clearing rowers out of the way as they pass. The navigator holds the legs, the others the rest. When it comes to her healing art, my wife really is fierce, Dubb thinks. His mind flicks back to the fights she had over him, when he was sick years ago, and how she saved him then. The hours she spent looking after him on the Great Sea where they first met. Nothing, no one, has the power of her healing hands. She saved me; she can save this man and many others.

'Hey, chicken keeper. This whole deck needs purifying again,' he hears an Etruscan shout across to the chicken keeper. He sighs, as he thinks of poor Qart. 'Get that boy of yours onto cleaning it up. Right now!'

As the sprawling figure passes, the crew look troubled, kiss their amulets and feel for their lucky charms.

'Melqart have mercy.'

'Eshmon be praised.' And Lady Gula too, thinks Dubb. Because that's who Nyptan is turning to now. He looks down at his wrist; his Great Laughing Dog amulet, with the beaten-up feather, is still fastened there despite the months of wear and tear it has endured. He smells the incense she lights to Lady Gula in the sick bay, all the waiting men lying there to be healed, and the heady aroma of her precious liquid from Tyre.

* * *

When Qart hears the words "get that boy", his mouth sets in a straight line. Any minute, he will be called to do the most disgusting job ever given to him. Even cleaning the heads is easier. He pretends he didn't hear, bends to a bird cage and lifts it off the deck to place it out of the wet. His hair, normally springy and flying all about his head, has been beaten straight by the rain and the grime on his face is streaked with water marks. From a pouch around his waist, he takes a handful of grain, lifts the door of the cages to put his hand through and feeds the flagging animal. This might revive it. On the horizon, sheet lightning flashes.

'You boy, come here,' comes the sneering voice of Malavisch. He turns to look at him. 'It is now your task to clean up the shit left by Lord Kanmi.' His voice is triumphant. 'Before you do it, put a barrier up between yourself and the rest of us. Be quick about it! Lord Rath needs to read the lightning.'

Flaming Melqart, thinks Qart, and slams the cage door as viciously as he dares. How can they possibly do that? He steps to the prow. He bundles chicken coups, hawsers and old canvas into a makeshift barrier, finds a water bucket and hurls it over the topside. Its rope runs through his fingers and he hears the splash as it hits the brine.

'Do you need help?' comes a friendly voice beside him. It is Rabs, up from the stern. 'Dubb thought you could do with some support, so he sent me,' says the man, and gives a short bark. 'If you consider me support that is.' He slaps Qart's forearm.

'Rabs!' he says, and he holds back tears of relief. He looks towards the tiller platform to see Dubb's eyes on him. He lifts his hand to wave. 'I've got to clean up that filthy mess,' he says, and points at the stinking mix of diarrhoea, faeces and rain water, which has formed a small lake and islands where the lordling lay.

'Melqart's arse, you have!' The small Carthaginian's nose wrinkles. 'Is that what's wrong with the poor bastard?' He looks solemn. 'Right,' he shrugs, 'is there another one of these buckets to be had?' He finds another and they winch seawater up to swill the deck.

Together, they collect the excrement into a bucket with shovels and mats. They work messily but quickly and, by the time the thunder threatens again, Qart is down on his knees, giving the whole deck a second scrub over with a brush. Whoosh comes water from Rabs's bucket, and it's finished! Just as the last of the water disappears out of a porthole, there

is a huge crack of thunder from the starboard sky, followed by a barrage
of sheet lightning. The sky explodes with jagged light.

The diviners on the other side of the barrier hurl themselves into a
dance. 'Nee roh, kee row, shumbaleth rah,' they shout, Lord Rath at their
centre, a pair of sticks held high, joined by a silver clasp. 'Oh, Nethuns,
King of the Deep. To see thy face is glorious.' Round and round they go.

'Wait, it's moved!' shouts Ani, the bull-necked one. 'We need to
circle the other way.'

'No, but you must write it down!' says Rath, and dances by him as the
man scribbles. 'We have to know what it looks like as well as where it's
come from and where it's going to. Record it, quickly!' He moves forward
to the apex of the bow.

'Look, it's Grade One, Type Four, elongated.' Ani's stylus whirls.
'Meaning sickness,' he shouts, as he attempts to be heard over the din.
'Disease will infect men, though not many will die.'

'What are they talking about?' says Qart.

Rabs shrugs.

There is another flash. 'Type Two, Multiple Fractured Bolts, frayed
at the end,' he yells.

'That means the women are more astute,' shouts Ani in response.

'Well, at least they are right about that one!' says Rabs.

'What are they quoting from?' asks Qart, and his friend shrugs. 'Why
does it matter where the thunder and flashes come from, as long as it
passes overhead soon!'

A tremendous roll shakes the deck. Even the high priest and his scribe
duck for cover then. They retreat to a shelter on the other side of the
prow and immediately start to consult their sacred tablets.

'The gods are not my department,' says the small man. 'Dubb
will know. Ask him.'

Qart makes a mental note. Another thing to check about the strange
divinations of the Etruscan priests whom he serves.

* * *

The body of Lord Kanmi is buried the next day. The lords Hanno and Bostar have washed and perfumed him, and loaded him with white stones. Dubb calls a halt to rowing and The Delphis glides to a halt on a calm sea. The diviners say a few words before the gathered crew. His body is then tipped over the topside and disappears immediately below the surface. This brief ceremony had been preceded by a lengthy debate between the diviners about whose rite was most appropriate for an aristocrat dead in such circumstances. There is, it seems, no precedent in the sacred texts for what to do when a lord dies at sea. In the end, Lord Hanno settled the dispute. He wanted his friend to go to the gods quickly so, instead of the Etruscan way, they'd followed common practise.

The minute they'd heard the splash, Dubb had said, 'Right men, to oars!'

Nyptan stands, face covered, at the front of the crew. 'I tried my best,' she says, unhappy. 'He died in the storm.'

'You said you could help him,' says Lord Rath, challenging. 'You failed!'

'He was too ill by the time he got to me,' she says, and feels more and more guilty. 'He should have been treated by me all those weeks ago. Then I might have had a chance to save him.'

The diviners and aristocrats alike look at her, lips pursed, eyes hostile, then turn away.

She walks back to their sick bay, looks around at the feverish men and her heart drops. Oh, Lady Gula, do not abandon me now, she thinks, and pulls Great Laughing Dog up into her hands to kiss him. The men need me. Dubb needs me. I cannot lose my courage. 'I am the Lady of Life…' she intones, and her hair whips from its place in her plait and flies forward into her mouth. If only I was. If I was a real healer, I could have done something for Kanmi, not let him die. Tears threaten. I need my husband. Where is he? I must talk to him now. On a whim, she turns back to the deck, sees Dubb at the tiller. She steps up to him.

'Husband, I need to speak to you,' she says. 'Soon, at once?'

His eyes are on the horizon. 'Can we talk later?' he says. 'Got to keep these men going. They can't be allowed to get too gloomy.'

'As soon as you can then.' Her heart roils leaden within her.

For the next days, the men row hard, helped along by a strong current. They wash their hands after using the heads, offer silent prayers to their gods and keep their amulets close. Lords and diviners alike keep themselves to themselves for once. All is silent at the bow.

The Enquiry - Day 10

'How long had you been away from Gadir by then?' asks Lord Apsan. He, the navigator and the healer are in the upstairs room by the fire. He has his back to it and the samples from the factory are stacked all around the walls. The witnesses, only two of them today, perch on stiff chairs, wrapped in blankets. A nearby window has its hanging thrown back to let in light. The effect it has on the room is the opposite. Gloom from the foul weather beyond pervades the place.

'Three sailing seasons, my lord, as if that mattered any more.'

'What?' he says. There is a sudden squall and rain sets up thunderous poundings on the tin roof. 'Speak up!' There is nothing to be seen outside except wind and sheets of water.

He sees the navigator's lips move in reply but can't hear him. Oh, Melqart's mother, he thinks, and a big sigh escapes his lips. He puts down his stylus and shoves his chair back. I knew this would happen if I let Tasii go this morning. Now I've got to get Gatit to move us downstairs. He stands, eyes roaming around all the tablets, styluses, writing sticks and other bits and pieces strewn around in front of the fire. What a mess.

'Gatit!' he shouts.' Gatit!' His body guard appears. 'Take these two below,' he yells into the man's ear and points theatrically. 'Lock the door on them, and then come down and help me move downstairs.' The man disappears. 'Oh, and get a fire lit.' As they leave, he attempts to collect as much of the enquiry paraphernalia as he can into one small packing case. Tasii will have to do the rest when he gets back. It's going to be freezing down there and he trails behind the others, box held in skinny arms, mantle dragging behind.

'There was no such thing as a sailing season,' says the navigator when they begin again.

'Oh, why not?'

'There were rainy seasons instead, of different lengths, at different times of the year in every place we travelled along.'

'And the type of land we passed through changed,' says the female. He looks up at her, cross. She's become an expert on the land now, has she? Her eyes are large upon him. 'It was fertile, rich, full of disease as it turns out.'

'We decided to sleep and live as close to the shore as possible from then on throughout the voyage,' says the man.

'For one thing, the mosquitoes are far worse than anything I have ever seen in the Great Sea. The air was thick with them. Young Kanmi might have died from the bite of one of those,' she says. 'They make you very sick indeed. But I don't think he did.'

Lord Apsan's neck goes back and his eyes snap on to hers. He picks up the stylus and begins to write. 'Why don't you think he died of malaria? What evidence do you have?'

'Lord Kanmi had all the known symptoms of malaria, my lord: a raging head, vomiting, diarrhoea, fatigue. We all got it at some point. However, in Lord Kanmi's case, when he got it, it seemed to go, well, different.'

Lord Apsan looks up. He's just finished writing "vomiting" and his hand aches already. So difficult to do two things at once.

'Different. That's all you can say? His disease was different. Can you be more specific?'

The navigator glances over at the healer and she nods. 'His faeces went black.'

'Ergggh.' His face crumples into a grimace. 'No need to go into the details.'

'I understand, my lord, which is why I hesitated to tell you. You just need to know that I did what I could to save him.'

'Oh, and what was that, exactly?' he says, nose wrinkled. 'Let me see, a bit of hot water here, cold water there, followed by a waft of bay. Is that it?'

'It's complicated, my lord,' she says, mouth set. She seems sulky. 'I was present with my mother once in Tyre when I was a child. There had been an outbreak of some strange disease, something which mimicked the mosquito but which, she realised, in the end, came from dirty water. That's why, when I first realised Lord Kanmi's symptoms were a little different from the others, I asked for salt water to be put at the heads. The men don't wash themselves regularly enough, particularly after defecating. They believe it sucks the strength from them, makes them weak.'

'But doing this simple thing, putting a barrel of salt water there, and insisting that men try and look after their hands, seems to have saved others from contracting the problem,' says the man beside her. 'No more men died of black shit at least, even though we all still suffered with malaria.'

'Even this man could have been saved,' she says, 'if he'd just listened to me. He died before I could treat him properly.'

'He refused to be seen by a woman,' says the navigator.

Ah, well, at least that's something his family in Carthage will understand, he thinks, thankful that no further writing is required on that score. 'Always a good route of escape for a healer. The patient died before I could solve the problem,' he says, voice cutting. 'What did Lord Hanno think about all this?'

'As you already know, he went to the Etruscans for help about everything, even this. And they didn't have a clue. They sacrificed a few chickens and threw their stones.'

Lord Apsan looks down at his own, well-manicured hands. How often do people around here wash their hands? he wonders. Here, in this household? 'Can you catch this disease, this illness Lord Kanmi died of?' he asks, and turns to the woman. Then, he realises with a jolt, that he's treating her as if she really is a healer. He coughs and his lips pouch. 'Don't bother to answer that. You probably don't know, anyway.' He congratulates himself that he and Tasii go to the bathhouse every night. Still, I must get a barrel of salt water and put it in the yard, he thinks. Just to be on the safe side. His lips curl and his nose wrinkles as he thinks of all that black excrement the lordling produced. Rather you than me, he thinks, as he eyes the woman. I wouldn't want to be a healer.

He hears a bang from the outside door, a lot of clumping of feet and voices. Tasii is back! Thank Melqart for that! His heart leaps, a way of getting out of her clutches. He stuffs his half-written records aside amongst the rest of the tablets, puts his arms on the table and heaves himself up. 'Well, that is all for the moment. We will resume later. Gatit! Come and take these two away.'

The King of the Western Sea

There is a shout from the front of the vessel. 'Fire! Fire!' A chill goes down Dubb's spine. What? Are we about to be burnt out now?

He stoops to peer beneath the crossbar and sees his boy jumping, hair in all directions, pointing forward to starboard. The Delphis rocks as those not tethered to oars lunge across deck to see where the blaze is.

There, far ahead, against the deep blue mountain hills, a series of long, thin smoke threads curl skywards. Thank the gods. The land is inhabited.

For many weeks now, The Delphis has been cruising along the coast of the country Kama calls "Ethiopia", in search of provisions, sometimes on the oar, other times on a fitful wind. Every place they have stopped thus far has appeared uninhabited, though they have found fresh water. 'What is it with these waters?' the interpreter had asked at their last stop. 'Does no one even fish here?' Exactly why the land seems so deserted isn't clear. He's a stranger to these parts. Neither he, nor any of his fellow interpreters, have been so far from Ngap before.

'Right, prepare for shore,' Dubb says briskly. 'We might try the wind.'

The first mate sets off towards the sail and Rabs begins to clear sick men out of the way of the leads. He untangles the ropes and checks their knots.

The thought of habitation has put more muscle into the crew than they have had for weeks. Fires mean meat and oh, how sick I am of ship's biscuit, he thinks. Someone even starts to sing.

'I dream of a girl with golden hair...'

'...golden hair, golden hair...' go the rows at the front.

That's the spirit, thinks Dubb, and starts to bellow his own version, a smile breaking out on his face. What I could do with sheep's haunch right now? It's going to turn out well. Fire! This is what I live for, sighting new places, new people . '...of golden hair, of golden hair...'

Nyptan's head pokes out from behind the curtain to their quarters, a look of surprise on her face. He laughs at her, light, like a boy. 'You don't often hear me doing this, do you?!' he says, body leaning on the tiller handle. Her mouth curves into a half-smile, dimple at the corner, as she, too, tries a line or two before shaking her head and turning back into the sick bay. Dubb stands tall. Lord Hanno and those diviners have a lot to answer for, he thinks. They've had too much power over us all. It has to stop.

The bow remains silent, a blessed relief. Since the storm and burial of their friend, the aristocrats and diviners have been subdued. The lordlings have not wanted to even search the river and creek for gold. The diviners have spread their sacred texts all over the deck, arranging, then rearranging them. What guidance are they looking for in those? he wonders.

They approach a low headland marked by a series of jagged bluffs and small islands dropping down into a ruffled sea. An onshore wind is picking up.

'We'll take a wide sweep around this,' he says unnecessarily. 'There'll be rocks.'

The singing trails away, leaving Berek's drum to lead them on. Thrummmm, beat, beat, beat, it goes, in charge of the heft of a hundred oars. The first mate joins Rabs at the bow and together their voices are all that's left in the air, reporting knots.

The Delphis noses around the point into a vast scoop of landscape stretching further than the eye can see. The coastline plunges off inland, away from the open ocean. Water turns to deep forest, forest becomes stands, stands dissolve into individual trees. Dubb wants to take her as close to the surf as he dares.

* * *

The moment Qart sees the fires, he longs, with all his heart, to sit beside one. Not for warmth but to get dry. For days he's been drenched: eyebrows, armpits, groin, even to the marrow in his bones. He's abandoned his loin cloth since working with the diviners, as most of the men have, and his angular shoulders and rounded bum gleam with sweat and drizzle. He stands at the chicken coop in anticipation of the order to pull a bird out for sacrifice.

'Ten, eight, four,' go Rabs and Chares alternately, counting the fathoms. The ropes, as they come up and down over the topside, threaten to tangle.

Qart wonders whether he can slide over to help and takes a quick look at the chicken keeper. The man seems fed up.

'You're not to bother with the birds this time,' he says, tone aggrieved. 'Their Holinesses have decided to use stones instead.' Qart pivots to the prow to see one of the diviners hauling the box from the space beneath the dolphin's head. At least it's calm water, thinks the boy. No chance their precious predictors will get washed overboard today. He nods, stands back against the topside and waits for his moment to escape the clutches of Malavisch.

The Delphis nudges its way forwards to the thickest clump of smoke trails. A thickly wooded plain is broken by creek outlets, swampy areas and wide lagoons. As they move closer, it seems from the growing numbers of fires that the land is very settled.

'Can I do anything?' he says, and stands at the back of the small Carthaginian to help as the ropes pile up at his feet. 'The chicken keeper seems to have forgotten me. Is this any good?' He pulls out the rings of hemp from below the pile to lessen the load.

'Good lad, good lad,' says Rabs over his shoulder. 'Do the same for Chares. We're approaching the point where we have to drop anchor.'

On the other side of the surf, on the sand running parallel to them, a few locals stand to stare. They are very black-skinned people, far darker than Kama even.

* * *

'Right, off you go,' Dubb says to the nearest seaman. 'Watch that surf. And don't be rude to the locals.' Although loud, he's too late to be heard. The vessel rocks sideways as, elated, men leap from her side into the water to make their way, lunging and thrashing, through the breakers to shore.

'We are in a land of the dark-skinned,' says Nyptan, as she steps up to the tiller platform and Dubb's side.

'A wonder to behold,' says Dubb, mouth open, eyes greedy for new things. For a moment, the two stand in silence and watch the men struggle to shore, and gauge the help and welcome they receive from the people there.

'This is promising,' he says, and puts his hand around his wife's waist. 'It looks like we'll get water and food here.' For a moment, she leans into him, her body warm and compact, hair thick with salt. He rests his chin on the top of her head. 'Exciting.'

A deep sigh comes from her mouth and she rubs her cheek on his chest. Then she pushes off him, back to business. 'I need to talk to you. Properly. And once you get to shore, can you send a crew back with coracles to collect the sick men? Before everyone gets too drunk that is. Tanu and I would welcome some time off The Delphis as well. It doesn't have to be immediately,' she adds, swiftly, 'just some time today, if possible.'

'We can certainly do that by late this afternoon,' he says. 'It's not only the sick who need the grub and water. We all do. Kama!' he shouts towards midships. The shiny black man appears from the midst of the benches, bundle slung over his shoulder. 'Once we've made friends here, can you arrange for us to have a big spread of something, preferably meat: sheep, goat, anything red? And after that, we need to get our sick men and our women ashore.'

Kama nods. He and his interpreters take a coracle and glide themselves expertly onto land. Dubb looks out over the side to see if he can spot Qart's head amongst the thrashing bodies. Where has that boy got to?!

He looks towards the bow. The Etruscans have come to conclusions about the meaning of the lightning it seems and the boy has been dragged back into the clutches of the chicken keeper. Sacrifices are to begin again.

'Get him to pluck six birds first,' Lord Rath says, 'and then send him away. We don't want him polluting this space any more than necessary.'

Malavisch yanks Qart's arm and hauls him over to the cages to start his chopping work again.

'Why don't you move all the old cages towards the heads?' says Lord Bostar. 'That would give us more room.'

'And not smell so much,' says Hanno. 'Both lords have made a comfortable space for themselves on an unfurled sail and have been chewing red weed.'

'Come on, boy, you heard what the gentlemen said,' says Malavisch. 'Move it!'

* * *

So, before Qart starts to chop, he must move the whole operation down to midships.

'Boy, what are you doing here?' comes a voice from behind him. It is Dubb's.

'What I'm told,' he replies, voice tight. 'What do you think I'm doing, Mr Navigator?' He keeps his eyes down, picks up several cages to balance them on his hip and staggers towards the heads.

'Why are you bringing them here?'

'Why do you think?' he spits. 'Because I've been told to.' Any minute now, he'll lose his temper and he knows that doing so never goes well.

'The fact the crew has gone ashore does not give the Etruscans licence to take possession of The Delphis,' says Dubb curtly.

'Don't say that to me, master,' he says, before he can stop himself. 'It's not my doing.'

Dubb brushes past him, steps heavy, towards the bow. For the next few moments, there is a furious argument he doesn't want to hear between Lord Hanno, Lord Rath and Dubb. He blocks his ears to it. He examines the birds, shoves the legs of a half-dead one back inside its cage. The shouting is still going on as he heaves the feed sack down to the heads and rolls down a water barrel. It is not clear who is getting the upper hand, Lord Hanno, the diviners or his master. Whatever is happening up there, he's got to do these flaming birds.

A furious Dubb passes him moments later. 'You'll do this relocation for the diviners,' says the man through clenched jaws, 'then you will clean their deck, wash yourself and come ashore. From now on, you are working with me and me alone.'

'Oh,' says Qart, and his heart leaps. 'I'm free!' He jumps up to run after Dubb's retreating back. 'Thank you.'

His master does not stop but goes up to the topside and straight overboard. He turns back to the bow. Malavisch squats on an empty coop and stares at him, knife in hand.

It is well into the night by the time Qart has finished the job of moving all the birds and cleaned the deck. His hands are raw and his arms covered in blood as he leaps over the side of The Delphis, elated, to brave the waves. Gone from them at last, he thinks, as he thrashes in the surf. His jaws ache from smiling, and the salt water stings his cracked and oozing hands.

He buffets forwards to the shore and balances in the shallows to wash himself. He takes handfuls of sand to scour off the blood and grime, which has accumulated since he first began working with chickens, filth so thick he must scrape his fingernail through it to start the process. "Your armour against mosquitoes," Rabs had said to him once when they met up by accident at the heads. "Really?" he'd said. "I thought nothing could protect you from mosquitoes." They had compared forearms. Rabs had shrugged and turned back to the tiller platform, he to the bow. Now that I've become the ship's boy, I must be clean, he thinks, or as much as possible. He rolls himself in the shallows. He dunks his head, scours at his hair, opens his mouth and swills at his teeth. Dubb demands cleanliness. I do too. Here it is, my fresh start. I'll be a new boy, a new man. Foam spreads all over his legs and up the incline of the beach. He scrubs until, head bent over his knees, he hears the squeak of his hand on his skin in every part of his body. He stands, jumps up and down to dry himself and walks over the shoulder of the beach towards the fires.

For once, it's stopped drizzling. The sand runs out and he enters a forest. Water gathers in wide pools on the ground. Palms fringe both sides of a long lagoon, which runs parallel to the ocean. Flames dance at him through the trees and figures move about in firelight on the other side. Smoke from the fires stings his eyes and the rich aroma of roasting fish billows towards him. His stomach turns and visions of biting into fresh flesh flit through his mind. He quickens his pace towards the wide, open space at the end of the lagoon. His feet catch and snap at unexpected roots and branches.

As far as he can make out, a feast is underway: platters of steaming meats are being handed out to guests seated on the ground.

He recognises a few of the crew from The Delphis, the slopy-headed man who has had malaria, a man they picked up at Gadir and someone from Ngap. There is a large man seated at the centre of the festivities, by a bonfire. Men stand beside him with weapons. Dubb, Kama and the other interpreters gather nearby. Various other smaller fires fan out from the centre, all with men huddled around. Nyptan and Tanu are nowhere to be seen, though he knows they vacated the vessel long ago, they and their sick men. Where are Rabs and Chares? It's impossible to pick them out amongst all the heads. He skirts around the side of the party and peers into the crowd. On the way, he passes what looks like the edge of a village, with grass huts and washing lines.

'Qart! Qart!' comes Rabs's voice from nearby. He stops and turns, scanning the crowd, unsure of where the voice has come from. 'Here!' He takes a step into the darkness to find him. 'There you are!' says the small Carthaginian, his mouth evidently full of something. 'We wondered when you were going to be free.' He sees him, in a knot of men right in front of him, beside a small fire. It has its own cooking pot surrounded by lots of discarded fish bones. He lunges into the bodies, plonks himself down beside Rabs and discovers he has joined a small party of The Delphis crew: Chares, Berek and a group of Libyan men, all in various stages of devouring fish, brown cake, boiled porridge and a grain stew. They nod at him in the half-light, part smiling, part chewing. 'This is Shadra,' says Rabs, and lifts his chin from the joint between his teeth long enough to indicate the man to his right.

Qart nods and eyes the food. Is any going to come my way?

'Hello,' says the man. He is the intense-looking man with bristly hair and a wide smile. With him are the two rowers who were so furious with Qart for sending chicken innards their way.

'Why you no with magic men?' says one of the men in broken Punic. His eyes are hostile.

Qart shrugs. He looks at the ground and bites his lip. What can I say? He turns his head to search for the people serving food.

'Where chickens?' says the other, and looks around beside Qart on the ground.

He is suddenly irritated. They think all I do is look after fowl. He's not in the mood to be laughed at.

'This boy is free from all those men now, aren't you, lad?' says Chares fondly, and leans over to nudge him with an elbow. His mouth is covered in grease.

'He's done his time with the diviners,' says Rabs, saving a bone in his hand. 'He's our boy now, aren't you? Free to be the ship's boy at last.'

'If you call that free,' says Berek, and gives a quick bark of a laugh. He rubs his slimy hands clean in the sand. He picks up his aulis and begins to pick out a tune.

'Here, have this fish,' says Rabs, and passes him a black, half-eaten carcass scoured across the middle in criss-crossed lines. 'There'll be more around in a minute.' He lifts his head to look out for another platter. 'Here! Here!' he calls to the nearest bearer and beckons with his hand.

'You aren't with them?' says Shadra. He looks at Qart from under a furrowed brow. 'They say you are a magic boy.'

'With the crazy ones, you mean,' says Rabs. 'Of course he's not. He's one of us!'

'You are not a lord, a diviner boy?' he asks once again.

Qart's face burns. 'I am the ship's boy of The Delphis,' he blurts, jaw tight. 'My master is Dubb of Miletus and I am Qart of ...' He falls silent, unable to think of what to add next. The men laugh.

'You leave this boy alone. He is a good boy. He is a bright boy. He's our boy, aren't you, lad?' Chares says, and clasps Qart around the shoulders. 'He's had a difficult time, cleaning chickens and looking after their lordships, haven't you?'

Qart looks at the ground. Are these new men, the Libyans, friend or foe? He can't decide.

'So, you are old friend, crew from The Delphis long ago,' says Shadra, and makes a circle with his finger around the three of them. 'We hear a lot about The Delphis tonight.'

'He definitely is,' says Chares, nodding his head elaborately.

'Ah,' the men say together, 'you, one of us.' They smile broadly. 'Welcome.'

'Don't take it to heart,' says Rabs to Qart, as they munch, shoulder to shoulder. 'We've all had to do the shit, you know, when we were first at sea. Working at stupid things with crazy people in crazy lands is part of the job. But look here, more food!' A platter arrives. 'This'll cheer you up.' He piles freshly roasted fish, millet and a scoop of porridge high on a large leaf plate lying on the ground in front of him.

'And this,' says Shadra. He pours a quantity of wine into a beaker to hand to the boy and slaps him on the back, his teeth very white in a smile.

'Go careful on that mind,' says the first mate, of the wine. 'It's from palms. Very potent!'

'Oh, go on, Chares, let the boy have his head on this night of all nights,' says Rabs. 'Tonight, Qart returns to us, free!' They all cheer.

Berek's voice joins his aulis and one of the men in an adjacent group pulls out a drum. There is a general rearrangement of the crowd as musicians join from all over the crowd. Long, stringed instruments twang, pipes soar, fingers pluck and there are drums, drums as powerful and expressive as the human voice.

Qart sits by the fire, dry at last and stomach full. He drinks to celebrate until sleep gets the better of him and his head slips down onto Rabs's lap.

* * *

Dubb's eyes focus intensely on Kama's lips as the interpreter tries to make himself understood to the king. The king is a large man, skin very dark, eyes cheerful in the firelight. He sits, knees wide, on an elaborate carved stool, a short distance from the flames. He has a staff in one hand and fly switch in his other, which he uses to flick away ash from the bonfire. Strapped to his torso is a breastplate of magnificent feathers and shells, adorned with what looks to be iron beads. Finely woven cloth is wrapped round his waist. Circulating around him there appears to be, advisors, holy men, security chiefs and slaves. Chares has joined him to try and help. If the navigator understands correctly, what Kama is trying to discover is what, if any, advice his lordship might offer to seamen from far away who want to learn about the sky in these parts. At least that's what he's asked him to ask.

He has been watching for less than a minute when someone pokes him in the arm, invites him to sit and shoves a bowl of palm wine into his hand. Chares gets the same treatment and they exchange glances. It is going to be a long night.

Kama leans across to them. 'I don't know the word for "asterism" in Kwal,' he says, troubled. 'That seems to be the name of the language people speak here.'

'We've tried lots of alternatives, but we can't work it out,' adds Pa, another interpreter from Ngap.

'I tried to draw the pattern of Ursa Minor,' says his fellow, and points to the sand at his feet. 'You need that because of Kochab.'

Good for you, thinks Dubb. You know what's important.

'But the king doesn't recognise it.' In frustration, the man sweeps his foot across it and destroys it.

'It's not helped by the fact it's overcast and we can't see a thing beyond the colour of the clouds,' adds Pa. 'We can't even show him what we're talking about.'

'So I'm sorry, Mr Navigator, we might not be able to help you with interpretation here after all,' says Kama, and shakes his head.

'What?' says Chares, 'every single language round here is completely different from those further up the coast?'

'Your lordship,' says Kama, 'can we pause?' He bows to the king, who has just sent one of his entourage off into the darkness, looks at Dubb, and lifts his hand and flaps it between his own mouth and the navigator's. 'We must speak.'

The king nods. Kama beckons them closer.

'His highness here tells me, I think,' says Kama, his head inclined towards them, 'that he speaks four languages.'

Dubb and Chares both nod, and the navigator turns to the king and bobs his head in deference. The king smiles back and turns to speak to a man at his elbow.

'That gentleman beside him is the king's translator and he speaks another three,' says Kama. 'So, between us all, those of us from Ngap and the people here, we must have about ten different languages. And yet we can't understand one another. Almost none of the words overlap, nor the speech patterns. What they say is mostly incomprehensible to us.' His palms go wide, he grimaces and lifts his shoulders.

Dubb thinks of all the languages he himself knows, and looks at Chares, who himself could add various different ones to the tally.

'The sky is a universal language, surely,' says Dubb, and looks up at the canopy above him. There is not a star to be seen.

'Not with the cloud covering we've had.'

'I did warn you this could happen,' says Kama. 'Unfortunately, you're here at the wrong time of the year. And with every day that passes, we travel further and further away from places we know.'

Dubb's heart sinks as the size of the challenge before them becomes clear. Kama's right. In the absence of the stars, we need local knowledge. If we can't get that, we're going to be really up against it.

'Maybe we can hear about the currents?' says Chares, in an attempt to be positive. 'Fishermen here must know about them.'

'If they fish far out that is,' says Dubb, doubtful. 'Which they haven't done all along this coast so far. Perhaps the seas are too dangerous. It could be our only hope, though.' He turns to Kama. 'Ask the king if there are fishermen here who know the coast.' He points to fish bones from the feast. Kama nods and turns to the king again.

'Your lordship, Sir, fishermen,' he says, and mimes paddling in a dugout. 'Get these?' He bends to lift the remains of a skeleton and holds it up to the king. 'Here?' He runs his finger up and down the line of the beach, head on one side, with a question in his eyes.

The king nods quickly. He puts his hands up before him and presses the air many times. We're being told to be patient, thinks Dubb. For what?

His lordship gets to his feet. He faces the assembled company and waits for silence to fall. When the chatter has stopped he makes a short speech, claps his hands together and immediately there is a roar of approval from a hundred voices. Yoked together by wooden poles, a party of men process from the area around the lagoon. They have the baked bodies of gazelles hanging between them. When the cheers have abated, the king adds something at length to his subjects, and sweeps an arm towards Dubb, Chares and those crewmen within his sight. Dubb gets the strong impression all the generosity is for them. They are being wholeheartedly welcomed. Without being quite sure of what he should do, the navigator stands, puts up a hand to catch the king's eye and his other to his chest. He bows low to his lordship and then to his subjects. His majesty inclines his head and jiggles his switch in return. The drums start up again, joyful. Yes, it's a feast on our behalf!

'What about finding fishing men?' Chares whispers as he sits down again.

'I don't know. Perhaps he didn't understand what we were asking for.' He turns to Kama. 'Do we at least know his lordship's name?'

'It's Oyediran,' says the interpreter, 'Great King of the Western Sea.'

Dubb takes a swig of wine and is wondering what to do next, when a sleek man of medium height and solid build plops down beside him. He has the same feather and shell breastplate as the king's. The navigator exchanges glances with Kama. Who is this?

'Akin,' says the man, and taps his finger on his chest. 'Akin.' He leans over and sweeps their wine bowls away with a forearm. Then, with a stick, he draws the asterism of Orion, Melqart and Ursa Minor in the sand. With each flick of his stick, Dubb's mouth opens wider. Kama and the others yelp with relief and punch the air.

'We're saved! Someone knows about the stars!' shouts the interpreter, and grabs the man round the shoulders to hug him.

So, collectively, the crew of The Delphis and the men of this far-off kingdom begin the task of deciphering each other's languages, sky and coastline as Oyediran's servants and slaves slip amongst them all to fill, and refill, their bowls with wine and plates with food.

The Enquiry - Day 11 – Part One

'After that, things got a bit easier,' says the navigator, wrapped in a blanket from the bench opposite.

The wind still howls outside. Lord Apsan has the fire at his back and Tasii brought them lamps to help lighten the gloom. It is a leaden day. He is alone with the navigator and the Hellene, with only Gatit to protect him if things go wrong.

Tasii has gone again, this time with the other witnesses, to the port to examine what's left of The Delphis. He's got Shipit Eli with him, despite the fact the man seems useless. Everyone but the woman has gone willingly, just to get out of the cellar it seems. It's dry there, and safe, he thinks. What more do they want? Well, it seems they want to find what clues they can from their vessel, something which will help them in their plight, the leads for instance or diviners' stones. Tasii is to take a note of everything they remember and add it to the other evidence, like the layout, size of sail and so forth. He'll add it as an appendix to the report, whenever it's finished. Nice touch that, he thinks. Byrsa Hill should be impressed.

'So, why were you at that king's place for so long? Was Hanno searching for gold?'

'We have no idea what he was doing,' says the Hellene. 'He spent all his time with the diviners on board. He rarely came ashore and had food and water delivered to him.'

'In truth,' says the navigator, 'he seemed to do nothing. I asked Qart, the boy, to find out.' He shakes his head. 'We never got to the bottom of it. He might have been going out every day for all we know.'

'Well, why didn't you make it your business to find out? Using a boy to do your work is insufficient.'

'Because, my lord,' says the navigator, an unwelcome note of impatience entering his voice, 'we had worries of our own.'

Oh no! Not more about the stars, thinks Lord Apsan.

'It's just that the sky was so out of alignment,' says the man. 'The length of the days was different. As were the seasons. And the more we managed to speak to Akin, the more confused we became.'

Lord Apsan nods and tries to take a note. 'But why are you telling me this? What does it matter?' he asks, a general question to give him time to finish scribbling the last point.

'It matters because I began to think there was something wrong with the sky.'

'"Something wrong with the sky"? What are you talking about?!' He puts down his pen and looks hard at the man. Yes, I'm correct, he thinks. Here come the constellations.

'You remember that the last time Qart and I managed to see any of the night sky back in Ngap, Orion was falling onto his side and Melqart's club was further from the zenith?'

'No, I don't remember that,' says Lord Apsan. 'But do go on.'

'It also seemed that new stars were showing up at night, though we didn't get a good enough view.' The navigator fixes him to the spot with his grey eyes. 'You recall that, yes?'

He keeps his mouth shut and concentrates on fixing the end of his stylus.

'So, what with the seasons being so different,' says the navigator, 'and the stars seeming to get themselves out of position, I began to wonder.'

'What? Wonder what? Melqart's mother, you idiot. Spit it out.'

'Well, whether we were sort of slipping sideways off the Earth.'

Lord Apsan stares at the man. Who did he think was slipping? Is he mad?

'Slipping away,' continues the navigator 'because we had unmoored ourselves from the Great Sea, because we had gone into River Ocean.

We'd somehow lost our connection with our guiding stars. It was as if we had lost our place on the Earth completely.'

Lord Apsan, for once, can think of nothing to say. He stares at the man.

'I am a navigator, my lord, as you know. My father was one and his father before him. Never have I heard, in all the stories that have been handed down to me, anything about the gods in the sky or Kochab, our guiding light, moving out of position. The place of heavenly bodies is set according to rules established hundreds of years ago. We Phoenician and Carthaginian navigators rely on them to guide our vessels home. So believe me, it was a shock to find that, after so many moons simply coasting along as usual, we had slipped our bearings. There's absolutely no doubt the heavens are changing. The sky maps you have prove it.'

'And you realised all this at King Oyediran's?'

'Well, no. We got the first clues there about what was happening.'

'And Lord Hanno. What did he think of this idea?'

'I couldn't even discuss it with him, for reasons which must be obvious. I suggest to you that, when you speak to him next, you ask him. My guess is that he has no clear knowledge of the heavens at all. May the gods have mercy on those in his convoy when he tries to flee some battle over the sea,' he adds to finish.

Yes, thinks Lord Apsan. Quite right. He makes a mark on the tablet in front of him. Commanders have been shunted aside, or worse, for being ignorant of the skies.

'All of this, and more, is in that cylinder. I can prove it by observation. You must never destroy it. It's there, all of it: days, moons, where the constellations were on each of them and where we couldn't see anything because of the weather. Those records are of major importance for any future convoy sailing outside the Great Sea.'

Lord Apsan sighs. Perhaps there is something to this astronomy stuff after all.

* * *

'There was very little left of The Delphis,' says Tasiioonos, as his lordship sips warm wine by the fire in the downstairs room of the residence. The witnesses are all back in the basement, blankets provided, and his slave is finally warming up. Safat has brought him a pot of hot lemon to drink, but he'd refused to speak until he'd had time to relax. Now he is feeling better, with his feet up on a stool and his hair drying in the heat, he has begun. 'When we got to the port, we couldn't locate the hulk at first. Turns out it was round the side, near the cattle yards.' He looks over at Lord Apsan in an expectation of acknowledgement.

He has nothing to add, except how wonderful Tasii looks, how he wants to take him, this minute, have him in the bathhouse, massage his back and torso, and do several more very intimate things with him. He says nothing of this. Instead, he lifts his chin for Tasii to continue. Later, he thinks. He'll only get annoyed with me. Maybe tonight, after dinner.

'We climbed across several damaged barges before we could get onto her. The boy and the floppy-haired musician were pretty upset at the state of it. Despite our guards, most of the leads had been looted. The boy scoured for diviners' stones though he found none. There is a lot of evidence of fire on board, especially at the bow. Singed deck, the remains of hawsers and burnt beams. Most of the oars have been heavily repaired, snapped again and again, and the rowlocks were very gappy. Needless to say, there were no remnants of sails to be seen and the hull has sprung a leak. She'll sink soon unless something is done about her.'

'Thank Melqart The Delphis is not our problem,' he says, and wonders when lunch will be ready.

A Baby

Nyptan joins Tanu on the matting in their palm and acacia tree shelter, the air heavy with the night perfume of many unseen blooms. Her daughter's breath is regular, slow, deep. She envies her her ability to just drop off. The baby inside her kicks, heavy and restive, and she rolls onto her side to bring it comfort. Creatures great and small scratch, chirp and rustle in the bush beside them. There is a constant whine of mosquitoes. Her head swims with exhaustion. They have worked all day to bring sick men ashore, and all night to get their healing space arranged. Now all are fed and watered and tiredness has overcome her.

'Lady Gula,' she whispers, and her lids droop. 'Stay with us, keep us safe.' She raises her knees and hugs her arms around them, a wider womb than the one inside. Sleep comes.

Her eyes spring open. The boom of breakers has become a roar. The distant drumming, clash of cymbals and singing, which has accompanied them all day, is stilled. It's over, the feast. Dubb might come to her soon. And suddenly she longs for him, to feel the strength of his body lying beside her own, to rub her face into his skin, to feel his arms surround her and his breath at her side. She throws an arm out and off their sleeping pallet. She needs action, not sleep, has to get up and out, somehow, somewhere, to find Dubb. She untangles her tunic and heaves herself onto her haunches. Tanu stirs and rolls over. Above their clearing, the night sky is a blank, no sign of any star, moon or planet. The embers of the fire cast weird shadows on the trees. She can feel the rains coming early, as they have in the morning for months, and she knows that even when they arrive, there will be no relief from the humidity.

Taking care not to make a sound, she takes a lamp from their shrine and a flint from her bag, and picks her way through the sick men in their shelters ranged around. Some mumble in their sleep; others are dead to the world.

'You alright, missus?' slurs one as she passes, the man with the slopy head.

'Just going for a walk,' she says. 'Sleep now.'

She sets off towards the beach. She comes to the edge of their clearing then stops. No, I'll go and find Dubb first. I'll go up to him, see the surprise on his face when I arrive and bring him back to me. Nothing, no one else, can fill the void inside her. She carries on down the path towards the main encampment. I can be back soon, she thinks, to look after the men, and she hurries along in the trees. Her hands go to her shoulders. But where is her veil? Her mouth twists and a frown appears between her brows. I've left it behind. She imagines searching for Dubb through crowds of drunken men without it, making her way amongst people she doesn't know, who might not speak her language. She pauses, balanced on one foot. Her head moves before the rest of her body. She turns back towards the beach, her mouth a straight line across her face. I can't do it.

Her lamp sets the shadows dancing as she approaches the edge of the forest and the sea breeze hits her the moment she steps out onto the dune. The flame goes out and she stumbles sideways in the soft sand, and finds herself secure in the lee of a great tree. Breakers head towards her on the ocean, ghostly rows, rising and falling. Sheet lightning flashes on the horizon. Spray lashes against her cheek. She lifts her arms and stands with her legs wide to let the fresh air in. It rushes about her body, across her belly, round her private parts. She leans forward, doubles over the baby, to loosen her hair and shake it free. At once, it becomes a gorgon of snakes, snapping, flicking, tangling all around, catching in the branches. She stamps from side to side in a kind of dance, lips curved in a great smile. She rolls her head around on her shoulders and throws her arms about. Lady Gula, be praised, she thinks, mind numb in the roar and relief of water and wind. You are the most magnificent, the greatest one, the liberator. She can't even be bothered to reach for Great Laughing Dog to kiss.

How long she is there, she does not know. When she lifts her head, she sees that the lightning has come closer, the waves ride higher and the sky is darker. She gathers her hair, wild and woolly, into a bun and drops down into the sand. She nestles into its softness and sleep comes.

Dreams take her to the birth of her baby. She is on The Delphis, Tanu with her and Dubb. The baby takes a long time. She is racked with pain. 'You can do it, come on, Mummy,' Tanu is saying. With a last great effort, the baby's head comes out. There is a streak of lightning. Tanu goes silent. Dubb's eyes widen. She looks up. Between her legs, the child has been born. It has two heads, two sets of shoulders and one body. Lady Gula, my lady, where are you?! Do not abandon me to this fate.

She wakes up, her body on fire. Dubb kneels at her side in the gathering light, ashen with tiredness. 'Nyptan, come,' he says, and puts his hands under her shoulders to raise her. 'You must come to camp. The rains are about to start.'

* * *

Dubb raises Nyptan in his arms and carries her back to camp. Her body is heavy and her hair has come loose, a tangled mat. It catches on the undergrowth as they pass. He weaves in and out. The thud of rain on the canopy, heavy blobs at first, becomes a deafening staccato as the encampment appears. Humpies are rigged all around, Chares and Qart stand at the fire with food and sick men are being tended to by Tanu. He lurches over to their own temporary shelter and ducks down. He lays her on the grasses, rolls up her mantle, puts it under her head and smooths down her entangled tunic. It is then that he feels it, the bump. His hands stop dead and his eyes fly to Nyptan's face. Her eyes are closed, face flushed. His mouth opens and he gulps down the air. With both hands, he feels for the swelling, from under her breasts to her private parts. There is a baby there. Definitely a baby there! He looks up to the palm leaf roof to see if there is any curtain to close, which will give him privacy. There is not. He sits down with a thump, dread rising in his belly.

Tanu barges in. 'Where were you! Why did you leave us?' she demands before she realises Nyptan is lost to the fever. 'Oh no!' She turns to the navigator, fear and terror in her eyes. 'She's got it too!' She turns back to Nyptan. Tears flood her face and she crumples in on herself.

He leans forward and puts his arms around her. 'My darling daughter. She will be alright. She is strong. She will come out of this. Now we need to do for her what she has done for us. And you, above all people, know how to manage that.'

While Tanu weeps on his knee, he strokes her hair. He lifts his brow to Qart and mouths 'fresh water' at him.

Chares comes with porridge. His lips go sideways when he hears she has fever and a frown appears between his eyes. 'I'll tell the others,' he says. 'By the gods. Bad news.'

Qart brings the water, Tanu calls on Lady Gula at her shrine and Dubb sits with Nyptan's head on his lap as his world reels.

A baby. Here? Why didn't she tell me?! His hand rests lightly on her shoulder, her forehead too hot to touch. Now, too late, he must stay connected with her, whatever the consequences. Why did she keep something so important secret from me? I thought we didn't keep secrets. I haven't been all that busy, have I? He bites his lip. He takes a cloth, dips it in water, and drips the water over her forehead, around her cheeks, the back of her neck. His mind flicks back to the time, many moons ago, when he saw Nyptan and Tanu huddled up on The Delphis, how they parted, guiltily, when he appeared. Was it then, the first time I missed the signs? Or the time when she wanted to speak to him in Ngap? Or after the lordling died? I kept putting her off until later, didn't I? Shame spreads up his frame, from his belly to the top of his head. Is this what it was about? Oh, Great Melqart. Why didn't I pay attention to my wife? His mouth purses and his shoulders hunch. Have I not learnt by now the wisdom of Nyptan, never to underestimate her, never to ignore her? His head drops down, and hot tears fill his eyes and fall down his cheeks. His shoulders shake and his nose runs. Look what I have done. She is well gone with child, in a place like this, a child I haven't known about. I have expected her to work, ignored her requests and allowed her to push herself to the point of illness.

Rains drops in lashing strands from the sky. The forest drips and seeps, the insects still and the air thick. Those who have the strength, shore up their flimsy shelters. Those who don't pile under someone else's.

Qart darts from each to the next to assist. Tanu is at Lady Gula's shrine; incense clouds out from the holy place. Dubb sits, legs out straight, Nyptan's head on his knee and wishes he was dead.

* * *

She drifts in and out of consciousness. Tanu's face is above her sometimes, Dubb's at others. Dragging her backwards to oblivion is the two-headed baby, born on a lightning bolt. He scratches at her face with sharp nails, bites her nipples, sucks her dry. She protests and weeps, and implores him to stop. He cries incessantly and will not be comforted.

She opens her eyes one day to see that the canopy above her sags. The mat beneath her prickles and the air is tangy from the forest around. She takes a deep breath and puts her hand to her forehead. She knows then that she has been ill. Relief floods her as she passes it across her belly and into the grasses beside her. Yes, the baby is there. Nothing has been born. It's been the fever. She rolls over to find Tanu at her side, eyes wide with anxiety, brow crinkled.

'Darling,' she says, and reaches for her daughter's hand. 'I've been sick.'

'Lady Gula, praise!' says Tanu, and clutches at her hand, kisses her amulet and bursts into tears. 'You are safe! You're safe!' Her wails fill the camp.

Sick men look out from their shelters. Dubb jumps to his feet and runs towards them.

'What's happened! What's going on?'

When he sees that she is awake, relief floods his face. He drops to his knees, hunches over, and joins both hands out before him. 'Thank you, Mighty Melqart! Thank you,' he says, head bowed. 'Thank you for the life of my adored, kind and clever wife.' He scrambles forward to grab hold of her hand. In his other there is a sea shell, tiny, green and iridescent. He looks across at her, his eyes wet, exhausted. 'My darling woman, I thought you had gone to the land of the dead.' He kisses the shell and then leans forward to kiss her. 'Great mother of Melqart be praised.'

When he stretches out beside her, his skin smells of firewood, his hair of salt. He takes her face in his hands and strokes it. He massages her temples and brushes her hands with his lips. 'You have been so ill, my Nyptan. So sick.'

She bites her lip and nods. 'I know it.'

'We thought the spirits had taken you, didn't we, Tanu?' he adds, and reaches for his daughter's hand, to bring her in to a circle.

'We did. We really did.' Her daughter's eyes have dried, her look practical. 'Mummy, do you want food?' she asks. 'You should eat.'

Qart comes with fish and baked cake. He puts it by her side, shy for once. 'You have survived, missus,' he says. 'We are all glad, so glad.' He takes her hand and kisses it. Chares and Rabs are there at the fire, Berek and others from The Delphis.

'I have missed you,' she says, and looks for the sick men, 'missed you all.' They sit and look over at her from under their shelters. She lifts a hand to wave. They raise their fists: Shadra, the slopy-headed man, sick and healthy alike.

'Healer, heal thyself!' shouts one across the crowd.

'She's done it!'

'A worker of miracles.'

'Can I light a bowl of incense perhaps?' asks Tanu, a smile on her face at last. 'I could take it round and we can all celebrate.' Nyptan nods and her daughter goes to the shrine, lights their most precious oil and moves from person-to-person to offer a prayer. 'The breath of Lady Gula be upon you. Lady Gula's breath is with us today.' Men stick their noses over the bowl and mutter incantations. If they have an amulet, they raise it to bathe it in the sacred vapour. The whole clearing is filled with its perfume.

Finally, the bowl comes to Nyptan. She has been longing for this moment ever since she woke, a way of forgetting, of focusing on the future, of renewal. With Dubb's help, she kneels up and over it. She waves her hands into the vapour and sends its sweetness towards her. She lifts her head high and says, voice as firm as she can make it, 'I am the Lady of life, my power make sickness flee. I come to you with my healing hands, I expel disease.' She takes Great Laughing Dog up from between her breasts and kisses him. The men kiss amulets, their lucky stones, their shells or keepsakes and praise the name of the great healing goddess, Gula.

Berek begins a tune. One by one the rest of the men join in. They create a long, low drone as the perfume rolls around inside Nyptan's head. Dubb holds her tight and the two-headed baby comes again. His body divides. He howls. He splits again, each part dividing, mewling, kicking, shrinking until there are only teeth left. Her legs jerk as she kicks at them. They fly off into the bush and are lost.

'Hush,' says Dubb. 'All is well.'

Then, with Dubb's arms around her, she falls asleep, without fever, for the first time in days.

Rain is coming down hard when she wakes. The clearing around them is obscured by it, all sounds muffled. There is a persistent drip close by in their shelter and the grasses beneath her feel damp. Dubb is stretched out beside her, head propped on one elbow, his other hand resting on her belly.

'Good morning, my Nyptan,' he says, and kisses her. 'A calm night's sleep.'

How can she not smile at him, wonderful man that he is. Yet his resting hand might as well be a sign, written large, for her to see. "I know about the baby", it says.

'A good night's sleep,' she says, and bites her lip. She struggles up to sit. He pulls a platter across to her: plain boiled vegetables, fish and a beaker of water.

'I'll get hot water in a minute,' he says, 'when this rain stops.' His grey eyes look at her, sober, serious.

She nibbles at a piece of boiled root, then puts her hand to her hair, a tangled mess around her shoulders.

'Why didn't you tell me there was a baby on the way?' he asks, voice low. 'I didn't think we kept secrets.' He has taken to wearing a shell around his neck. It looks fine against the grey hair and tan of his skin.

She lifts the beaker to her lips to try and think of what to say next. 'I didn't want to bother you,' is what comes out of her mouth. She picks up another sliver of food. How can I explain it? That I tried to tell you many times, that either you were too busy or I was. Or that Lord Hanno had put you in a bad mood, or the current was taking us off course. 'There didn't ever seem to be a right time,' she says, and bites down on the cooked root.

He looks down, face difficult to read. 'Am I always so taken up with The Delphis that you can never find a time to speak to me?' his voice is hoarse. 'Not even when we have been alone in our quarters? You couldn't tell me then?'

'I suppose I only wanted to say something when I thought you would approve, not when you might get upset and want me to…do… something about it.'

'Do what? You mean get rid of it?'

'That you would think The Delphis wasn't the right place to bring up a child. That it was too dangerous, rough, that we needed protecting. And that I, with my womanly arts, would know how to…' Tears come to her eyes.

'To abort it,' he says for her, and takes her hand. 'It's true. I almost certainly would have done that. The Delphis is no place for a baby.'

Anger flashes up through her throat. She snatches her hand back from him, tries to move away. 'I will not get rid of this child. I will have him and raise him on The Delphis. He is yours and mine, an indication of our love. Nothing will induce me to remove him.' Her eyes are alight with fury.

He captures her hand again. 'Hush, hush, my darling,' he says, finding the other hand and kissing them both. 'I am not saying that. What I am saying is that you are right. If you had told me straight after Ngap, I would have asked you to remove our child. I would have found it too much to cope with. I cannot do that now.' He caresses her belly and bends over to nuzzle it. 'This journey, The Delphis, is hard, but we can manage. We will find a way to fit a baby in, amongst the interpreters, the lords, the chickens, the crew and the sick men.' His lips curve a little into a smile.

She looks at him through her tears, and laughs. 'Yes, there are a lot of us. We are crowded. Some of us are sick, more of us are difficult to deal with. A baby is only small though, and Tanu and I shall look after him.'

His arms feel strong as they circle her; the gap in her soul is filled. He is here for me. Dubb is always here for me. He lies down beside her. They touch from head to toe, the baby cocooned between.

* * *

Dubb sits with Kama, Qart and the others on open ground outside the king's compound. Many days have passed, days in which Dubb and Qart have been working on their records. The tablets and sticks lie in piles on a pallet above large puddles of stagnant water. Early this morning, it poured. The mosquitoes have picked up and all of them, newcomers and locals alike, swat and slap. Lord Akin, as they have realised, belatedly, they should call him, has drawn a coast line for them in the wax with a stylus and added small circles on both sides of it, shapes, which they eventually realise are islands and lagoons. There are very many of them, everywhere. And he has marked a large slash across it, which Dubb thinks will turn out to be a river.

A young woman with a baby strapped to her back serves them coconut juice and popping seeds. They have been at it for a long time.

Dubb's back aches from leaning over and his head from concentration. They have placed their tablets in a row before him and his elders, and they all pour over the marks. Dubb notes with admiration how clear Qart has made them in the wax. Good work, boy, he thinks. Now he's released from the Etruscans, he's finally applying himself to navigation. A surge of affection suddenly overtakes him for the young man he has been tutoring these long years. The lad sits at the back, concentrating on how the men move their tablets. 'Come, Qart. Come forward! This is my assistant,' he says to the priests, as he makes his way towards them, and Lord Akin nods his head. 'He has done a lot of the work.' Kama and the others smile, and Qart's eyes flick around the crowd, clearly happy to have his moment of acknowledgement after all these months of being cast out of the centre of things.

'Lap it up, boy,' says Rabs. 'Take your place in the sun while you can. This old boy will be on you like a ton of rocks soon enough, won't you, Dubb?'

Dubb takes the teasing well enough and cuffs Qart on the back of his head with his hand. There is a huge smile on the boy's face.

Akin turns to a young man in their company. He has a shell and iron beads around his neck. He, too, is an apprentice, thinks Dubb.

There is a shout from the other side of the clearing. 'Dubb! Dubb!' comes Tanu's voice. She dashes across the open land towards them.

Oh, what now? he thinks, and looks up at her, anxious. Is it the baby? The girl's hair flies everywhere and her veil has fallen to her shoulders. 'Mummy says you're to come. Once of the men with fever, the slopy-headed man, is going a bit mad. He's biting himself and frothing at the mouth. She's afraid he'll do harm to someone, or himself.'

The Enquiry – Day 11 - Part Two

'That was the first sign of a new kind of malaria,' says the healer, 'one I'd never seen before.' Her eyes focus intensely on Lord Apsan's feet. 'Instead of just the sweats people begin to lose their reason.' Her hands twist together in her lap and he has to bend forwards to hear her. The weather outside the residence in Gadir has relented but, even so, she speaks very softly.

'What sort of sickness was it?' he says. The session started again briskly after lunch. Tasii was not in the mood for anything other than work. Now there is just four of them in the upstairs room, the sky bright and blustery, and the rain gone sufficiently for his lordship to risk sitting by the fire again. We're going to finish with this sickness issue, he thinks, and get on to finding gold. He watches as his slave looks at his notes from this morning with a puzzled face.

'Did you make some notes this morning, my lord? Are there more tablets around?' he says.

'Of course I made notes, Tasii,' he says, 'they're all there.' He points his finger at two gathered at the side of his slave's table. The man looks dissatisfied and Lord Apsan shrugs. How can I take notes and ask questions at the same time? he thinks. Thank the gods he's back.

'Both of these fevers were so vicious,' says the woman. 'Lady Gula knows we tried, we all tried,' she says and, with relief, he sees she is not about to cry. Her eyes focus on a space immediately in front of her, her mantle tight around her shoulders, an amulet in her hands, brightly coloured, with zigzag patterns.

'You say "both". What do you mean by that?' he says briskly, and watches with satisfaction as Tasii takes a note of his question. Back on track, he thinks. They'll know they've got a good investigator with me. He imagines being patted on the back by the Chairman of the Senate.

'The confusion was that the symptoms in all the patients started out the same: high fever, headaches, aches and pains,' she says.

'No need to go through a long list of symptoms or we'll be here all day,' he says testily.

'I am answering the question you asked me, my lord. "What sort of sickness was it?" I am describing to you how two apparently similar sicknesses can have different and unexpected outcomes.' She pauses, looks at him and waits for his reaction.

Is that a note of condescension in her voice? he wonders, and his eyes narrow as he looks at her. She sits grey-faced and without rancour against the wall. He decides not and nods. 'You may carry on.' His mouth forms a straight line across his face.

'Perhaps you think that knowing this kind of thing is simple, my lord. It is not. Each of these illnesses had to run their course in different ways in different men for at least three days before I could find how they differed. By which time it was too late to help many of them. They died before I could start to understand it.'

Lord Apsan is taken back. Here is the kind of measured approach to illness he has only previously come across in the temples of Byrsa Hill. His mind flicks back to his days in the military school in Moyta. Did they say anything about how to analyse sickness like that? Nothing springs to mind. He pats his stomach. At least my little problem is not so bad.

The woman seems to take his silence as licence to carry on. 'If you want simple answers to these questions, my lord, then speak to Lord Hanno or the Etruscans. Their way of keeping men alive is to sing incantations and throw stones into the sea. Even they were not untouched by the sickness. One of their young priests died of the new kind.' There is a tremble in her voice, eyes misted over. The navigator, beside her, takes her hand. 'Altogether, there were two men from around here, Gadir, who went to the gods. They died while we were at the kingdom.'

'Another from Rusadir died later, soon after we left Ngap,' says the navigator. 'Eventually, we gave up having a sick bay because so many of us were ill with the milder form.'

'That was followed by someone from Lixus, who went so crazy he threw himself into the sea one day.'

'We stopped rowing but couldn't find him.' The man seems upset.

'There were many more who died of this fever, Libyans, Rusadirians, others. I'm so sorry, I've lost count,' says the female.

Lord Apsan is stunned. Had it really got to that stage? Even Lord Kanmi's death pales into insignificance in light of such numbers. 'What? So many deaths all in the space of a few moons? How did you manage to row?' he asks, voice sharp. 'Surely Lord Hanno must have decided to call a halt to the expedition at that point.'

The navigator hesitates. 'Well, no, my lord, he didn't. As soon as he got over the death of Lord Kanmi, it seems he became obsessed with gold again.'

'Did he do nothing to prevent the loss of… How many men did you say?'

She shrugs. 'It was always rising, my lord. From then on, through the rest of the voyage. Twenty? Thirty? We got it too.'

'Of course,' he says, and remembers how sick they were when they had first arrived in Gadir. 'And did this problem remain for the whole of the voyage? How did you manage to get back here on The Delphis if you were so sick?'

'We didn't go inland,' says the navigator. 'The mosquitoes are worse there.'

'We kept barrels of sea water by the heads and prayed,' says the woman.

'I hope it's not contagious,' he says, alarmed.

The man shrugs and looks at the woman.

'Perhaps it is, though I think not,' she says.

'And you, personally, did you go searching for gold? Because for gold you have to go up into the rivers and lakes, to take risks. And that's not something which, it seems, you were willing to do.'

'No, not me, my lord. I never left the coast. Lord Hanno sprang back into action, eventually, didn't he Qart,' says the navigator. 'You went looking for gold with him once.' He looks at the boy. 'Ask him. He'll tell you about that.'

What a Fright

Qart is in the ship's boat, a six-benched dinghy tethered to the side of The Delphis. It bobs in the water as men step backwards down the ladder to take their places. The lords Hanno and Bostar are in charge at the stern.

'Go to the bow, Qart,' Lord Hanno orders. 'Sit as far forward as you can and keep a look out. I want to hear about smoke from campfires or any signs of natives in the trees.'

Since he has been freed from working with the diviners, Lord Hanno seems to treat him with more respect. The ladder clacks as one of the Etruscans makes his clumsy way into the dingy. His pale ankles hesitate on the rungs and his mantle flaps; it's too long and, when his foot hits the woodwork, the whole dinghy lurches from side to side.

'Watch it, you fool!' says his lordship, exasperated. 'You'll tip us up!'

Qart snorts and looks away. Shame he didn't step harder, he thinks. Quite a few of us on board could do with being dumped in the water.

'Move up, Qart,' comes Rabs's voice in a whisper. Qart turns to see that the small Carthaginian has somehow found a way to join them in the boat. He has slotted himself into a gap between Qart's knees and the first bench, crammed behind the Libyans. He puts a finger to his lips. Quiet!

'How did you get here?' Qart mouths, and his eyes flick wide towards Lord Hanno. The lordling continues to instruct the Etruscan, who makes heavy weather of stepping across the dinghy.

'Felt like a change. They won't notice until it's too late,' Rabs giggles.

'Get down then!' he says, and pushes at Rabs's head as Bostar stands to survey the empty spaces. He smiles guilessly up at his lordship and gives Rabs's shoulder a squeeze. How good it is to have a friend by his side.

'Didn't want you to be left behind this time,' comes a whisper. 'A bore to have to come and find you.'

Qart pulls his legs in tight underneath him to try and make more space.

Kama is the last to board. His eyes catch Qart's and a finger rises in acknowledgement. He takes his place at the stern beside Lord Hanno.

The vessel casts off and Lord Hanno steers it towards what looks to be a creek. There are many similar openings into the bay, forest and mangrove unevenly clustered at the water's edge, the blue of a mountain behind. Halfway across the bay, rain begins to pimple the flat, grey sea. Soft drops cluster and disburse as it grows heavier. Qart wipes it from his eyes to try and make out what lies ahead. A muted roar sweeps in from behind, the landings of a million raindrops. In an instant, all is obliterated by the downfall. He and Rabs might be the only two people left alive.

'Flaming Melqart,' hisses Rabs, water streaming through his eyebrows and down his chin. 'I'm sick of this wet.' He flattens himself further into the lee of the rowers' backs.

For a while, it is not clear where they are heading or whether they are moving at all. Lord Hanno's voice, muffled in the rain, keeps count. The crew behind him seems to be rowing, though no water creams at the bow.

Rabs gets up from the gully to slip onto the bench beside him. 'What's he up to? Do you know?' he asks.

'Just the usual, I think,' says Qart. 'Did Dubb say anything?'

'Only that I should come with you,' says Rabs.

'Really?' says Qart. 'He sent you specially?'

Rabs nods. 'Got myself into the dinghy before it came round to pick you all up.'

Oh, thinks Qart. My master worries about me after all, and a swell of happiness rises inside him.

By the time the squall has passed and the air cleared, they are near a small opening in the bay. Pushing against a muddy current, the dinghy rounds a bend and heads upstream.

'Halt,' says Lord Hanno. He stands in the stern, a long pole in his hands. The rowers lift their oars and at once the dinghy starts to drift back out to sea. 'From now on, I want quiet, total silence.' His voice drops to a rasp. 'You are to take your timings from Lord Bostar here.' He points at his companion. 'I don't want to hear a single splash or squeak, and you are to say nothing. When it gets narrow, Lord Bostar and I will pole the vessel. We will work like that until we come to somewhere. Right?' He lifts his hand, ready to count. The crew leans forward, oars ready. 'Oh, and, Qart,' he says, at the last minute, 'your eyes are to be peeled for any sign of life, you understand? Anything you see, tell me.'

Does he think I'm dumb? thinks Qart. He's told me that already. The vessel moves off upstream. Qart slips a sideways look at Rabs and lifts his brows. If his lordship had an objection to the older man sitting beside him at the bow, he gave no clue of it. 'You're on board with us, no problem,' he says out of the side of his mouth, and grins. They scan ahead, into the greenery.

'What are we looking for exactly?' says Rabs. 'Did he tell you?'

'Rising smoke, local people, streams, landing places, anything which will help him find gold.'

'So he's not really interested in other things, like iron working, or ivory?'

Qart shrugs. Who knows what Lord Hanno is really interested in. 'He didn't say anything more.'

'Watch out for crocodiles,' says Rabs. 'Keep your hands in.'

Qart nods. 'I'll do port side.'

'And me starboard then.' They both drop to their knees, eyes only above the gunnel, and settle down to watch.

The creek begins to twist, overhanging branches obscuring their route. Ferns and mangroves reach far out into the waterway. When it becomes so narrow that it is impossible to row, the men slip down onto the dinghy's boards and the lords use their poles. They are not expert and progress stalls until men begin to pull the dinghy along by hand, heaving on overhanging branches, ducking and cursing. Rain-laden vegetation drops heavy splodges of water on them and the sky disappears. For some time, Qart sees nothing ahead but branches and the flick of a fish's tail. Then a bright sheet of water glints through the greenery. They nose around a point and in front of him is a wide lagoon.

'Stop!' he gasps, and tries to raise his head and send the message to Lord Hanno. The man is completely obscured in the vegetation. He turns to Rabs and catches his arm. 'Look ahead!'

Rabs turns, eyes alive, and he puts his finger to his lips. They both crane forwards as far as they dare. Around the mangroves, tucked into a wide meander all of its own, is a fleet of dugouts. The vessels float black against a slate-grey creek. Amongst them, in the water, many heads bob and weave. Calls and chants rise and ricochet around the clearing, moving in a relay from forest to water and back again in a haunting rhythm. Nearby, on a beach, a crowd of people mill about. They are adorned with palm leaves, headdresses and elaborate fans. Floating on a raft between the fleet and the land, a large, shark-like creature dances and swings its head in circles. It throws out its arms and leaps from side to side. Swags of seaweed and cloth attached to it in an elaborate style fly and catch in the dripping air. Then, with a yelp, it leaps into the water. It crashes through it and begins to attack and scatter nearby swimmers. Cries of fear replace the chanting and the swimmers rush shoreward. The spirit returns to the raft and a new batch of swimmers enters the water.

'Holy Melqart,' says Lord Bostar startled, as the stern of the dinghy finally catches up with the bow. The whole of their vessel is now exposed for all to see.

'Tinia, Great Lord!' explodes the young Etruscan, alarm all over his face, and begins to drone.

'Shut up!' hisses Lord Hanno, and sits down to cover the diviner's mouth with his hand. He stares, open mouthed, at the scene.

There is an enormous thrashing of water and bodies peel away in every direction. Voices rise high in rage and protest, and the whole ceremony lurches to a halt. They've been spotted. The shark whirls around to look at them. It flings itself into the lagoon and swims, at speed, to shore. As it leaves the water, its headdress topples to the ground and a man appears beneath, running. There is a huge scramble on the beach. People pile into coracles, haul in the dugouts, drag the raft to shore and disappear deep into the forest and waterways. A wail of anguish rises from behind the wall of vegetation. The hills above echo to the sound.

'Kama, where are you?!' barks Lord Hanno, then sees the interpreter right in front of him. 'You're to get out and swim over there. Talk to them.' He points to the still shuddering bushes. 'Find out what the people know about gold.'

His words slur and rush out of his mouth with anxiety. 'Row,' he adds to the others, and the men pick up their oars.

The interpreter's face is calm. 'Certainly, Lord Hanno, I can try to do that. You know we do not speak the same languages.'

'What's the point of having you here if you can't be understood,' the man squawks. 'Try to speak to them, by Melqart's mother, or I'll have your head. And hurry! Can't you see that everyone's run away!'

Kama's eyes are down, lips pursed. With stiff shoulders, he lifts the hat from his head and wraps his loin cloth firmly around his waist. He slips over the side of the dinghy and half-swims, half-wades onto the beach. Qart can't resist. He, too, lifts himself, puts his leg over the side and drops into the water.

'Stop, Qart! Are you mad?' says Rabs, and tries to grab his shoulder. 'You don't know what's in the water.'

I don't care, he thinks, and shrugs Rabs's hand away. Kama has gone in and he knows what he's doing. His legs are heavy as he moves through the muddy shallows. By the time he arrives at the beach, all that's left of the ceremony is the shark's headdress.

Kama is at the shoulder of the beach where it meets the forest. He steps into the greenery and calls down its overgrown tracks into total silence. 'Hello, hello,' he tries, in various languages.

Qart recognises some of the words from campfire conversations he has overheard at King Oyediran's. He runs up the incline to join him. Perhaps I can help?

'This is ridiculous,' Kama says, as he turns his back on the forest and begins to walk down the incline. 'We've given everyone a bad fright and now we come to ask for gold.' He blows a breath out through bubbling lips and shakes his head. The two head back down to the lagoon's edge.

'What is this?' Qart says, as they come to the shark's head. It lies on its side partially covered in grey sand. Large, white shells gleam for eyes and its back is carved, painted and decorated with large feathers. Beneath it, a rolled rush mat is entangled with twine. 'Look at those!' He points to the teeth.

'Don't touch it, you mustn't touch! Step away!' says Kama, voice urgent. 'It is the spirit of these people, most powerful, sacred!'

A frown darts between Qart's eyes, his lip goes back between his teeth and he takes a step backwards. Sacred? From the gods? He examines the eyes, the workings in wood, the oil marks, which run across its teeth and into its mouth, the seaweed and woven cloth. Beautiful feathers, now crushed under its weight, are a big contrast with his own paltry amulet. By comparison, his is laughable. Spirits? What would Nyptan say?

'We peoples here, who live far from the Great Sea, have a different sacred world to yours,' says the interpreter. 'I myself know this spirit, even though I don't know its name. It is born in water, finds its power in the creeks, lagoons and inlets of this land, and leads the people from there. Where I come from the spirits-'

'Kama, what are you doing?' comes Lord Hanno's voice, sharp. The man arrives in their midst in a foul mood, dinghy drawn up behind him on the sand. 'You should be up in the woods asking questions about gold, not down here talking to the chicken boy. He sees the shark's head on the sand. 'Go and find them.' His foot comes out to kick the sacred headdress and catches it on its underside with his sandal. Up it swings and across the beach to land and crack in two. He steps after it and stamps on it. He breaks the polished wood and gouges out the teeth. Its shell eyes fall from their sockets and he grinds its feathers into the sand. Qart jumps out of the way as bits of broken wood and seaweed fly across his feet. Thunder rumbles in the distance.

The boy turns and walks off. Don't get involved, he thinks. Leave the idiot man to himself. Powerful water gods surround us. They must, he thinks, and his eyes begin to search the landing place for other signs of the spirits. Beyond, through the trees, the lagoon shimmers. What gods lie beneath it? he wonders. Will they rear up and attack us? To his right, the meander continues into the forest. He sees signs of worship everywhere: the remains of fires, piles of clam and coconut shells, beakers lying empty on their side, chunks of meat tied to a tree or gathered at the base of stones. This whole place must be alive with spirits, he thinks: the water, trees, stones - different spirits than the ones I'm used to. He glances up to search for Rabs amongst the crew ranged along the landing place to wait.

The man leans back on the side of the dinghy, feet crossed. 'Alright, boy?' he says, as Qart joins him.

Kama's voice rings out at the top of the beach. 'Gold, gold!' he shouts up the forest paths, as Lord Hanno stomps behind.

'What do you make of it all, all this…' Qart says, and his voice trails off. He can't think how to describe how unsettled the place makes him feel.

'Make of what? Lord Hanno? He's a joke! He doesn't have a clue about how to search for metals. He's a monkey amongst concubines.'

The shadow of a smile crosses Qart's lips. 'No, not that. The spirit.' He lifts his chin to the remains of the shark's head. 'What do you make of it?' he asks, voice low. He feels as if he is being watched, judged. He shivers. What should I do? Gather together the pieces of the shark? Worship them? Worship who? Give them my amulet? He fingers it on his wrist and tries to straighten out the feather.

'Oh that!' says Rabs, as he examines the wreckage of the abandoned head from the safety of the dingy. He frowns. 'Well, I'm with Chares on this one. Never annoy the gods, any god, whose ever they are. Every place you sail to has different gods. Do what you can to stay on the right side of them. If you do that, you can't go wrong.' He shakes his head at the lords Hanno and Bostar as their search continues. 'They're complete fools.'

So, if you learn about and follow every god, just to stay on the right side of them, then you spend a lot of time thinking about them. He suddenly realises why Nyptan and Tanu are so taken up with their incense. I don't even know who the gods are here, or maybe they aren't gods, they're spirits. What's the difference? He rubs the amulet at his wrist, hair bouncing round his head.

There is a whack. Then another. Stones hit the dinghy's hull and drop to the sand heavily. 'Hey!' says Rabs, and leaps up to look around.

There is a yelp from Lord Hanno, hands above his head. Further missiles fly from the bush, from the mangroves, the trees by the sacrifices and suddenly they are under attack. What was one or two rocks has become a hailstorm. Missiles rain down on them from all sides.

There is a dash for the dinghy. In an instant, Lord Hanno is back. Qart and Rabs leap for the bow and the Etruscan lumbers into place. The crew step over, on or around him. Bostar pushes the vessel off, Lord Hanno crouched at the stern.

From habit or training, the men begin to row backwards to get away. Disorientated, they go in circles until Lord Hanno, pole held high and sideways to deflect some of the stones, begins the count. The thunder has come closer now, and large spots of rain begin as they lie flat to return through the waterway and pull themselves along. The rain starts to drum on the vegetation as they slip by and when they emerge into the open, at the creek's mouth, both heavy rain and stones fall on them.

'Nee roh, kee roh,' goes the diviner, 'shumbaleth rah.' Qart closes his ears to the sound.

The prow swings around the end of the channel towards the bay and, as it does so, the people on the shore break onto open land and run alongside them. Rocks, sticks, coconuts, brush, all is hurled. A fearful howl starts. Qart looks up to see a very large man about to chuck a log into the dinghy. His mouth is open in fury, his eyes wide. A chill of fear drops down Qart's throat and through the back of his neck. We have made these people very angry. We have insulted them and their spirits. The Etruscan intensifies his chants. They buzz around the vessel like a whirr of mosquitoes. Mighty Melqart, shut up! Blood fills his mouth; he has bitten his lip. He turns to look for Rabs. The Carthaginian's face is screwed up tight, blood coming from a cut on his forehead. Sweat sparkles at his temples. He, too, is afraid. The lords Hanno and Bostar use their long poles to fight back, the dinghy wobbles and soon they are in the clear. Lord Hanno's voice beats the time, the diviner drones and the dinghy sweeps across the water back to The Delphis, the men bailing it out in the pouring rain.

The Enquiry - Day 11 - Part Three

'That's a botched job,' says Lord Apsan. This story has taken up most of the afternoon and he is ankle-deep in straw. Their grey funeral ware must be checked before sale, and he's spent his time doing it and listening to Qart.

'As you know, the locals weren't always like that,' says Dubb. 'We had more problems with Lord Hanno than with them. Oyediran could not have been more helpful.'

'There was just such a difference of perspectives between us all,' says the woman. 'Etruscan, local, Hellene, Carthaginian.'

'He can't have been as incompetent as that all the time,' he says. If so, he thinks, he never should have been appointed a commander. 'What about his settlements? What's happened to them?

'We know nothing about them, my lord. We came straight here from Lixus without stopping.'

'Find out, Tasii,' he says to his secretary, who lifts his brows and notes it down on one of his tablets. His lordship's gut grumbles and he puts a hand to his stomach, round and round. Perhaps too much spice at lunch. Is he going to need a shit any minute?

'After that, he and the diviners retreated more and more into their own world,' says Dubb. 'He began to seem unhinged.'

'It was hot by then, oppressively hot,' says the floppy-haired young one. 'There was a pattern to it. Light drizzle in the morning, then it cleared up, heavy rain again late afternoon.'

'We were passing through well-protected bays, past river heads, into lakes which sheltered us from tide and wave. It was very easy to get lost, even if you thought you knew where you were going, wasn't it?' adds the navigator, addressing the crew. They nod agreement.

'It never broke the weather, never cleared to fresh air and clear skies,' the young one continues. 'Though we did try and keep lists of landmarks.'

Lord Apsan gets the impression this has all been hashed, and rehashed, by them many times before. He might as well not be present.

'In the end, we stayed with The Delphis at the beach fronts. No fear of losing our way then, was there,' says Dubb, looking down the line of faces beside him. Heads go up and down.

'Also less humid,' says the young one.

'We left going ashore to dugouts and coracles,' comes the Hellene.

'To Lord Hanno, in fact,' adds Dubb.

'Every night they took off when we anchored, came back in the morning with nothing as far as we know,' the youth carries on, and shrugs.

'It was us who kept the vessel going. We did all the work,' concludes the first mate.

The eyes of all in the room turn to Lord Apsan to wait for his reaction. Hmmm, he thinks, they appear to be honest, seem to be telling the truth.

A sudden hiccup ejects itself from his throat and his gut gives a great gurgle, so rumbling this time that everyone can hear it.

Tasii's head goes up. 'A little break from proceedings, my lord?' he says.

'I can give you a remedy for that if you'd like,' says the woman and her eyes look bright with hope. 'I know how to treat it.'

'Never you mind,' he says, and frowns. 'And you remained ignorant of your position on the coast.'

'That is correct, my lord,' says the navigator. 'I could get no bearings from the sky. I'd done no practical astronomy for weeks.'

Without warning, Lord Apsan's bowels begin to move. A boulder drags itself from the right side of his stomach to the left, by way of his pelvis. He stands abruptly, the chair tips over behind him and he walks, bottom clenched, to the door. He makes it to the top of the stairs without embarrassment. There is a lot of them to run down.

'Cinnamon!' the woman says. 'Cinnamon oil!' she repeats, insistent.

Her voice rings in his ears as containment becomes catastrophe. He lurches full tilt down the treads, Tasii on his heels. He gets to the outside door too late and squats in the yard where his whole hind quarters explode.

The Enquiry - Day 12 – Part One

The day has leaden skies, a stiff wind and biting air. Even the neighbourhood donkey seems numbed by the storms. Lord Apsan hasn't eaten anything since yesterday lunchtime and feels lightheaded. It is early and not even the kitchen has begun to clatter.

'I'm not in a fit state to be working today,' he says, curled up on his pallet in the warm.

'Of course, my lord. You've had a nasty turn. It is, of course, up to you what you do,' says Tasii, voice oily. He's clearly in one of his obsequious moods. 'If you want to have the day off, I'm sure you'd be able to catch up with the enquiry. It would be a struggle, of course, though once you feel better, naturally you could do it.'

Lord Apsan waits for his next few words. When his slave begins a summary of events like this, there is always a caveat somewhere.

'It's just that the security men will be hard to placate.'

Ah, there it is. 'Placate? What do you mean?'

Tasii sits across the room from him and looks fresh, crisp and shiny despite the chilly air. The amulet at his neck glints and his shoulders flex. He's like a seagull, thinks Lord Apsan, capable of riding any wind, in any weather, and still completely free and true to himself.

'You made an urgent call to them, you may remember. You demanded their presence immediately. Today. These men have taken many days to get here, in winter, across the land route, from ports far away. And Lord Hanno, no need to tell you, is still at large.'

He sighs. Yes, that's the nub of it. Lord Hanno continues to be "whereabouts unknown". The land is vast, the obstacles great.

'Alright,' he says, 'if we must.' He pushes back the covers. 'Let's start with them this morning, get them back patrolling their patches as soon as possible and return to the witnesses in the afternoon if I am up to it.' His slave gives a slight nod as he holds Lord Apsan's tunic up to slip it over his head.

'Meanwhile, tell Cook that after yesterday's episode, I am on a liquid only diet from now and for the next few days: no grain, no stews or vegetables of any kind. Just water. And get that woman to make me up one of her remedies. Cinnamon oil, did she say? I will start it immediately.'

He feels his slave's hands go stiff on his robe. 'Ah. So no more charcoal, is that the plan?' he says, and pulls a face. 'Very well, my lord. If that's what you want. I would just point out that every time you've used a charcoal remedy, your problem has improved.'

Lord Apsan shrugs off his slave's hands and picks up a mirror to smooth his long hair over his pate. 'I will try what she suggested last night,' he says. 'Charcoal has been all well and good. It's had several days to work and nothing has changed. In fact, my complaint has become worse. Why not give the healer a go.'

'I thought you did not like being treated by women, your lordship,' says Tasii.

'Well, that was in the past. It's different now. Get it done.'

'As you wish, your lordship,' says Tasii, and, with a wide swing of his arm, he plucks the amphora of his charcoal drink from the table and sweeps it out of the door. 'I shall tell the healer woman to prepare you her remedy and Cook to put a stop to all your food. Let's see how that goes.'

The security men troop into the upstairs room of his residence looking spick and span. Shipit Eli has on a finely woven mantle. The three others from down the coast are more roughly clothed, hair arranged with Carthaginian mariners' caps. The boy and his father are the exceptions. Gargoris Street Cleaner and Gry arrive last and cause a stir. Bare footed, bodies loosely covered in old cloth, stinking and unkempt, they sit by the door, the boy in particular ready to disappear any minute.

His eyes roam wildly round the room and he fidgets continually. The security men pull back and wrap their cloaks around them as if even being in the same room as the newcomers might contaminate them.

'Stay still, boy,' says his father, and looks up at Lord Apsan from under his brows. 'You're in the presence of a very important man from Carthage and he don't want you to be jumping around like that.' His eyes move from his lordship across to the faces and clothes of the other people in the room. 'Can't you see there's lots of grand gentlemen in here? Don't want to annoy them, do we?'

The men look revolted. They sit in silence in front of him until Tasii arrives and, once he has settled, stylus in hand, the session begins.

'Two moons ago, towards the end of the sailing season, I gave specific instructions that you were to look for a Carthaginian aristocrat who had recently returned from ports down the coast. I do not need to reveal to you who exactly this person is. I simply remind you that you were under strictest orders to find him. He had recently left from Gadir for a destination unknown. You were to report to me the moment you saw him.'

'I can't speak for the others, your lordship, but I have personally investigated every vessel on my patch for weeks,' says Halos, the man from Sexi. His face is deeply lined and he seems worked up. 'There are just so many vessels in transit, it's impossible to be everywhere at once. I have no one to help me in the office. If he did get through, I did my best.' He juts out his chin and his eyes settle on Lord Apsan with resentment.

'And what about you there?' he says, and points his finger at the next man. 'Aris, from Abdera, I believe your name is. Why haven't you spotted the Carthaginian lord? We know he is here in our region somewhere.'

The man speaks quickly. 'As you know, my lord, Abdera is quite far from the Strait. And though it's not impossible, it's most unlikely that this person would travel through our port to get back to Carthage.' He is somewhat better spoken than Halo and more convoluted.

Lord Apsan sits beside the work table. The fingers of one hand tap rhythmically against it as he thinks. They clack across the shelving and hard surfaces. It's true that shipping only occasionally travels up the coast as far as Abdera before heading off into the open sea. Normally, they head out past Sexi. And it is most unlikely that Lord Hanno will have gone to Abdera overland and by choice.

'So, that's three of you. We already know how hopeless you have been, Shipit Eli, in spite of your boasts. And it's clear now that those you put in place are just as incompetent. So, as from today, I am introducing a new security regime,' he says, and looks with spite at the three coastal men who have so plainly failed to do their job. 'For the remainder of the winter, Gargoris, Street Cleaner from Tartessos, will take charge of security matters here in Gadir, Tartessos and all mountain routes between here and Malaka. You three can return to your posts and work out your contracts. They will come up for review before the next sailing season. At that point, unless you find the missing lord, your time working with me, Commissioner for the Board of Trade, will terminate.'

'No, please, my lord,' say Shipit, and he and Aris leap up out of their chairs.

'Most unfair!' says Halo.

'A second chance,' says Aris.

'Gatit, come!' roars Lord Apsan. His bodyguard enters the room, moves towards his security men and they sink back into their seats, heads bowed.

'What you have failed to take into account, you useless men, is the whole network of roads, passes, byways and communities up in the hills. The mines, temples, businesses and factories of the region are all serviced by them, which any lord could easily use. And equally easily be spotted on. There is also a whole other language, Tartessic, which you could use in such situations and of which all of you are clearly ignorant.' Tasii catches his eye across the room and his lips curve momentarily. 'There is a whole civilisation there which you have failed to make use of.' He thinks of the bathhouse tonight, how Tasii will massage his shoulders, his back, his bum. 'This man here,' he points to Gargoris, 'and his scrag of a son know more than you do, have been more alert than you and are more successful than you. They have come to me to report a sighting, despite the fact they are not a part of our network, are not paid for it, and have not been trained in any of the arts of vigilance. They have knowledge of this special language, which they and their community use to communicate amongst themselves, a most valuable tool for security which I'm sure you've not heard about.'

The men from Sexi and Abdera sit open-mouthed. Shipit Eli turns to glower at the two from Tartessos and mutters, 'Street scum.'

Gargoris and Gry beam.

'Oh, my lord, thank you, thank you,' says the father, and gets to his feet. 'Just for the chance.' He moves to take his hand until Gatit intervenes. 'We won't let you down. We'll learn fast how to do what you want. Just say the word and we'll do anything.'

Lord Apsan turns to them, irritated. They fill up the room with their presence; they are too eager. 'Let's just see how it goes, shall we? Hopefully, you can do better than this lot.' They smell: their hair, their teeth, their rotting clothes. And suddenly he is fed up with them all. 'The session has now ended.' He stands to leave. 'You coastal people, I will call each of you here individually for review in the coming months. One way to save yourselves for sure is to find the lordling. And, as for you two from the streets,' he says, turning to Gargoris and Gry, 'clean yourselves up. You stink and will be quite revolting to work with.'

The Sky

For the first time in many moons, Dubb gets a glimpse of the stars. Just as the crew returns from the shore with fresh water, the clouds shift and there, between two great banks of grey, is a triangle of stars.

'Qart, let's go!' he shouts at the boy the minute he sees the glisten. He shoves aside his vegetable stew, bends to grab the astronomy bag from beneath the tiller platform and heads for the ladder.

The boy pushes his bowl of food into Rab's hands. 'Over to you, you lucky bastard,' he says, face cheerful, and heads for the ship's store.

'Mine, all mine?' says the wrinkled Carthaginian, and slurps his lips at the bowl to laugh in the boy's face. 'Off you go, master's favourite.'

'The cloud's broken!' Qart says to the men, as he passes them with ship's biscuit and water.

Shadra and his Libyans stop eating, and twist their necks to locate the gap in the clouds. 'Gods go with you,' he says.

'Great Melqart reveal himself!' says another.

'It's about time we know where we bleedin' are,' mutters a Rusadirian sourly.

Only the bow of The Delphis remains somnolent. There, the lords and diviners have been engaged in a meal of red meat and palm wine. Its aroma has drifted down through midships and made their millet dish seem paltry by comparison.

Dubb looks up at the complaining man sharply. He's that one who seems to be very interested in their location, a part of the group which joined The Delphis in Gadir. Well, I can hardly blame him for wanting to know. It's a worry, and his brow furls. I should draw him in, sweeten him up somehow, he thinks, as his feet find the rungs of the ladder and he starts to descend to the dinghy. Qart follows.

Within minutes, they have begun the long paddle towards a low, dark shadow in the midst of the wide, black bay. It is one of many islands dotted around this place and one which they have used before in their fruitless attempts at plotting their location. Dubb sits in the stern. Qart has the oars and they both crane their necks to search for fresh breaks in the cloud. So far, there's been no more than one.

Far across the bay, birds settle for the night in the forest, their squawks angry and sharp across the water. A wisp of a breeze from Qart's oars brushes his face. Beneath them all is heavy, dark, brooding. He can hear every breath Qart takes. He'll be happy with this task, thinks Dubb, and tries to make out the expression on the face of his near-invisible boy. He has been a joy these last months: willing, inquisitive, obedient. He'll make a fine navigator one day.

'Are we going in the right direction?' says the boy, whose back is to the island. His face is the merest smudge in the darkness. 'Tell me.'

'Of course. And you'll tell me if anything shows up.' He twists his body right and left to scour the sky for signs of light. He drops his hand over the side into the warm, viscous bay. The dregs of the day have turned to black night.

The Rusadirian's sour face still lingers in his mind. 'It's about bleedin' time…' he'd said. How right he is, thinks Dubb. We've been at anchor for days. And since Oyediran, many moons ago, there's been no settlements, villages or kingdoms. There's no treasure, no women, no cities, nothing for the men to discover, no release, nothing to relieve the boredom of tedious coasting. Isn't it time to call a halt to this endless journey? The minute he asks the question, he knows he's right. The time has come. His conviction grows from sprat to whale in the space of an instant. He's completely right, that Rusadirian! he thinks, and his neck lengthens and goes stiff. What on earth are we here for, anyway? We've seen nothing in the heavens, found little on land, the men are sick and we've been away for many seasons. His head gives a slight nod as though he's speaking to Hekataios. Best to cut our losses and return if we can. If we see something tonight, all well and good. He lifts his eyes to search for a clear patch in the clouds again. But time is up on this failed journey. He peers ahead to see if he can locate where the island is. It is calm here, sheltered from the sea. We should use it to refit, fill ourselves up, gather food and start the long, slow slog back to the Pillars. He lurches forward and his chin whacks his knees as the coracle hits the beach with a thump.

'Baal's balls!' Qart says. 'Didn't expect that.'

They disentangle themselves.

'Where's the lamp?' They scramble around in the hull, oars in the way, pulling and shoving at the hessian. Dubb turns back to find the boy's head completely silhouetted against a dazzling sky. His heart lurches. We have stars, we have planets, we can find out where we are! 'Qart, look!' he breathes, and the boy looks up, and they are both bathed in an iridescent glow.

They race as fast as the gloom will allow, up the incline to their observation post at the top of the island. Remnants of past visits litter the place: wood from an old fire, stacked stones, gouges in the sand. Dubb's hands shake as he dashes to fix the stick and shell into the ground, his head all the while lifting and turning as he attempts to locate familiar constellations. We can see! 'Qart, you do it,' he says, as his hands refuse to obey him. 'You set it up!'

He leaves the boy behind with the lamp and bag, and moves beyond him to the edge of the mound. Now, a whole half-sky above has opened up, graced by trillions of points of light, great and small, blue, yellow, white, red. What a marvel. This is the landscape that I know; this the terrain I walk as truly as I walk this Earth. More familiar to me than these islands and peoples, more my home even than The Delphis. How I have longed for you, missed you, found my life the poorer without you. Tears come unbidden. The stars double or triple in size and shape; their colours merge and meld. 'Thank you, Melqart,' he says, voice low. 'Thanks be to you, most severe of the gods, for revealing this to me.' He swipes at his nose with his hand and sinks it into the sea grass beside him. Thank you. At last, I can know where we are.

Qart's hand rests on his shoulders. The boy slides down beside him, legs long and lanky, head a whirl of hair and brows knitted together. 'Are you alright, Mr Navigator?' he asks. 'There's wine and biscuit here if you want it.' He pulls out his supplies, takes the stopper from the beaker and hands it over.

'Thank you, Qart,' he says. 'Thank you, dear boy.' He takes a swig. In silence, they share their snack and, shoulder to shoulder, contemplate the dizzying display of heavens before them.

The first pattern his eyes discern is the constellation of Orion, directly above them. Except he no longer stands, he lies sideways. A frown crosses his brow and his eyes move on. What about Sirius, Nyptan's guiding star? Oh, over there. He chews his bottom lip. And Kochab, where is it? He lowers his gaze. Instead of Ursa Minor at half a hand above the horizon as it was a few weeks ago, Kochab has completely disappeared!

'...little bear, which never bathes in Ocean deep,' he mutters.

'What?' says Qart.

'It's gone. It's not there!'

'What isn't?'

'Think about it, boy. Use your eyes and your mind!' he blurts in irritation. 'Kochab, in Little Bear, our guiding star. It's gone!'

A flutter sets up in his stomach. So it's finally happened. We have broken the golden rule of astronomy and now we are truly lost. Cruel Melqart, he thinks, and feels himself go hot around the ears, true to form, you have shown us a night sky only to snatch away our knowledge of it all in an instant. I have no idea where we are.

'Lie down, lad. We have to examine this,' he says, and stretches out.

There is absolutely no doubt about it. Everything that he has ever known about the night sky has been overturned. It is sideways or upside down. Old constellations have disappeared, new stars emerged. Lying here, he thinks, it feels like we're slipping, sliding away from the plane of the Earth, floating in ether, going where? To be burned in a fireball? Suffocated by gas?

Together they lie there, man and boy, until dawn first blushes the eastern sky. They search for vestiges of sky they thought they knew and clues as to where in the world they might be now.

* * *

The minute they arrive on deck, Qart goes to Lord Hanno and summons him to a crisis meeting.

'Get him here as quickly as you can,' Dubb tells him. 'And don't wake the whole vessel.'

As the boy approaches midships, he sees Kama propped up, awake, against the hull just outside the Etruscan's barricade. He beckons him and points towards Dubb waiting at the tiller platform. The man nods, rouses those beside him and they gather themselves together in silence, and pad towards the stern. Men stir in the half-light.

He peers around the barricade into the Etruscan space. The priests are on their knees, counting stones in private meditation. How am I going to break into this and get Lord Hanno out? He takes a deep breath and steps forward into the holy arena.

A young priest sees him first. 'What? Out! Out!' he shouts, and springs up to grab him around the shoulders and swing him away.

'I come to bring you a message, Lord Hanno,' he says, as he plants himself in front of the still sleeping lord. He shakes the Etruscan off and kicks out at the man in front of him. 'A message from Dubb of Miletus,' he shouts, as he bends to the man's face.

His lordship opens his eyes, grunts with displeasure and turns away.

'Forgive me, my lord, you've got to come and speak to Dubb of Miletus. Alone. You must come to the tiller platform. Now!'

Hanno's eyes, bloodshot and lined, look back at him with incomprehension and a deep furrow drops between his eyes. 'It's not him and his stars again!' he says. 'Flaming Melqart, what is wrong with the man?!' He staggers to his feet.

By the time the lordling arrives at the tiller platform, the crew is murmuring discontent. News is leaking out.

'Your lordship,' says Dubb, voice low, 'I need to inform you that Kochab, our guiding star, has disappeared from the night sky. Which means we have no sure way of finding our way back home.'

'Is that what all this fuss is about?' says Hanno. 'That some stars have gone missing. How many times do I have to say it? As long as we are coasting, there is no need for us to worry about being lost!' His voice is loud and angry by the time he finishes.

'Lost!'

'Lost.' The word passes from mouth to mouth and there is a stampede to the tiller platform.

'Last night, Qart and I discovered that Kochab, our guiding star, is no longer in the night sky,' Dubb says to them all. 'We went out to look for it, but it was no longer there.'

Deep silence falls. Some men shift on their feet and clutch at the amulets at their necks and wrists.

The Libyans, Rusadirians, Nyptan and Tanu are all there.

'You mean we're at the mercy of the tides and weather,' says one man.

'Got to find our way out of this mess of a coastline without knowing where we're going!' says another.

Spots of rain begin to drop from the sky and splatter the deck. 'Oh no, not again!' comes the groan.

'We must return to the Great Sea as soon as we can,' says the navigator to Lord Hanno amidst the increasing din. 'While we remember a little of the seascape and location. If we do, we might just make it home again.'

The morning's downpour intensifies. The men, riled, take to their shelters.

'We've got to do something to convince him to turn round,' says Chares. 'Otherwise, we'll have a mutiny on our hands.'

The Enquiry – Day 12 – Part Two

'So, you stirred it all up, did you?' Lord Apsan sits up straight, eyes focussed on Dubb, feet planted squarely on the floor, water at his elbow. At last, he's getting to the bottom of this voyage. He'll be having something to say in the Senate report. 'Lord Hanno led an expedition on which there was a mutiny,' he repeats, with heavy emphasis on the "mutiny", and looks over at Tasii taking notes on his tablets. Monkey jugs and buffers, porcupine feeders and wire wool are lined up on a side table, arranged from tallest to shortest. He's not touched them at all for days, so hard he has come to concentrate on events on The Delphis.

'Well, it turned into a kind of mutiny, yes,' says Dubb.

'A "kind of a mutiny"?! What do you mean? You must surely know what a mutiny is,' he spits.

'Well, eventually Lord Hanno was forced to listen to us because the crew divided at that point. The Libyans joined us wanting to return immediately. The Rusadirians supported Lord Hanno. And we did then what we've done in such circumstances in the past. We decided that rather than directly oppose Lord Hanno, we would simply work as normal. We split ourselves into two; half of us helped him, the other half rested. That way, if he decided to go forward, we could at least slow him down.'

'A vessel like The Delphis needs a full crew to row. Without our cooperation he really couldn't get anywhere,' says the Hellene.

'Exactly what does that mean?!' he says, head whipping round to look at the man.

'That, at best, Hanno could only ever muster three quarters of the men,' says the floppy-haired one, and grins.

'So they couldn't get very far.'

The navigator, taking no part in this description, looks at him, triumphant.

'So, although Lord Hanno wanted to go on, it seems you agreed to comply only to suit yourselves and your own timetable,' he says, fists on his lap, opening and closing.

'If that is how you want to interpret it, my lord,' says the navigator, distain leaking from him at the line of questioning.

'It's not a question of interpretation,' he says, eyes wide. 'It's what you did! You undermined the authority of your leader!'

'On the contrary, at that point, there was nothing we could do except follow him. We didn't have the manpower to do otherwise. But neither did he! We had to work together to get anywhere.'

Lord Apsan's brow comes down in a deep frown. What's all this? Am I going to have to go into proportions of which crew rows at each station for every shift in order to understand precisely what happened?

'May I ask the witnesses a question or two, my lord,' says his slave under his breath.

'Try,' he says, voice low, 'or I'm going to have to close the session for the day. The navigator is enraging.'

'Just to clarify, for my records,' says Tasii to the witnesses, 'are you saying that after you discovered this guiding star, Kochab you call it, was missing, Lord Hanno nonetheless persuaded half the crew to continue the journey forwards? Even though he didn't know where you were going?'

'That is correct…' answers the navigator, looking at Lord Apsan. He pauses, seemingly unclear of who is in charge now.

'And Hanno's crew rowed without a break? No shifts amongst them?'

'Well, that's how it began. Pretty soon, they were all exhausted. When it was our turn, we did our work and left our other half sleeping as usual.'

'So you see, it wasn't a mutiny exactly,' says the Hellene. 'Just going slow.'

'What does Lord Hanno say about this, my lord?' asks the navigator, unexpectedly. He turns away from Tasii to ask his lordship directly. 'It seems you've heard nothing at all about this part of the voyage until now.

What did you discover when you cross-questioned him? Didn't he tell you there'd been this problem after Oyediran?'

'What I have found out, or not found out from Lord Hanno, is no concern of yours,' says his lordship.

'You could ask him, couldn't you?'

His stomach clenches. 'I will speak to Lord Hanno as and when I choose. That's it. Today's session has ended. Clear them out Tasii.'

As the witnesses troop out, he returns to his work table with a vengeance and plonks his bottom on the seat. I'm so sick of the navigator, his crew and this whole task. Why does this sort of job always fall to me?! His arm drops with such weight onto his worktable that a monkey vase over-balances, teeters, then falls and smashes to pieces on the terracotta floor.

The Heat, the Smell

Since the crew split in two back at the lagoons, there has been something of a change of regime on The Delphis. Lord Hanno has put himself in charge of the tiller, with Lord Bostar as his first mate. The Rusadirians fill all the other roles. 'Although everything has changed, it's all the same,' Chares had said a couple of days ago.

'Like rolling out a new sail only to discover the rats have been at it,' Rabs had added, and they'd both snorted with derision.

Dubb can only agree. All the worst aspects of the old regime have been represented to the crew as the way forward. Both aristocrats continue to chew their root, even in charge of the vessel. The Etruscans maintain their search for lightning and rattle their stones. The Rusadirians have escalated their complaints until the air rings with them.

'Where's the food? I'm half-starved!'

'These rowlocks are rubbish.'

The navigator is pleased to be free of it all, for the moment at least. He leans back against the mast after his shift at the bench and examines the lordlings as they manage the vessel. Lord Hanno's hold on the tiller is heavy, one palm only wrapped around the handle, wrist bent and fingers tight. The gods help him if we get into rough water, he thinks, and he absent-mindedly twirls his hands round on his wrists.

Bostar has the opposite problem. He has both hands at the handle yet doesn't hold it firmly enough. His thumbs and forefingers curl around the wood, palms open and free. Consequently, The Delphis is bumpy when she should be calm, erratic when she could be straight.

Dubb turns away and gives his head a small shake. The sigh comes unbidden from his belly. They really should know better these two.

'One, two, three and four,' goes his lordship, as he stamps his feet on the tiller platform. 'One, two, three and four!'

Now that Berek is resting, no one else knows how to carry the rowing tune. Ani, the priest, does his best. The Rusadirians at the oars seem to have trouble following him. Several pairs are out of sync, men rowing to the beat of their own tune.

Dubb's shoulders ache, and he lifts and lowers them, rolls his head around, then collapses back onto the fir behind him. It's been a long time since he did so much work at the oars. His hair is long and thick with sea water, and hangs like lank rope. He has it tied at the back to keep it out of the way of his elbows. The sail, strapped to the crossbar above him, is grey from wind and grime. Beyond it, the sky is a pale shade of lemon.

Rabs slides onto the deck beside him. 'Have you seen the haze?' he asks, voice urgent. 'It can't be more than late morning and we're running into this!'

Dubb frowns. What's up? He gets to his feet and they move to the topside. Chares joins them. All around, from zenith to where the horizon might be, there is a yellow glow. It seems to pulsate, radiating colour.

'The sky has got a lid on it,' he says, and takes a deep breath. Stuffy.

They stand in silence for a bit and ponder, only the beating of the oars stirs the air. Not even rain could make it through this atmosphere. The water beside them is a sheet of pewter. Dubb leans out to look at their following vessels, the dinghies stacked with coracles that they've been towing. They scarcely make a wake. His head turns the other way. Even the water at the prow seems thick. On the port side, the thin line of land, which keeps them tethered to safety, disappears in places. The deck itself feels contaminated by the vapour, rowing men growing fuzzy at the edges.

As if of one mind, one brain, the three men head for the bow. They gather Kama and his party on the way, and barge through the barricade, scattering Etruscans as they go. Ahead, Dubb can see only haze and, by now, the land to port has disappeared completely.

'What is it, Kama? Why the heavy atmosphere? Do you know?'

The black man shakes his head, eyes troubled. His skin is no longer shiny but cracked and dusty like the rest of them. 'There was a story, long ago, of a fire mountain down the coast from Ngap, though I've never had it confirmed and I've never seen it myself. Perhaps this is it?'

Fire mountain? he wonders. What's that?

'A volcano?' says Chares, alarm in his voice. As he speaks, there is a dull thud in the far distance. It ricochets through the mist and the water beneath them quivers.

The interpreter's head snaps round to face the sound. 'See what I mean. A mountain, which catches fire.'

Lord Hanno's counting stops. The men's rowing falters. Dubb turns to see his lordship thrust the tiller into Bostar's hands and start up to join them at the bow. The Rusadirians lift their oars out of the water as he passes and The Delphis slides to a halt on a metallic sea.

'Kama,' shouts the lordling harshly, at midships. 'Kama, come here!' He stops before the barricade and waits for the interpreter to join him. 'What is that noise?'

Dubb cannot hear the black man's reply. His head is faced away and the Etruscans start up their drones.

'Can you smell it?' says Chares nearby, and taps his finger on his nose. 'Sulphur!'

Dubb coughs as a cloud of the pungent stink rolls down his throat and into his eyes.

The thumps ahead in the distance have become persistent. He looks through the murk, eyes smarting. Try as he might, he can see nothing fiery to port or ahead. It must be some way off, he thinks.

From the gloom behind, Nyptan appears. She takes his arm. 'Husband, what was that?' she asks, voice thick with anxiety. 'Why did the earth tremble?' He hears the quiver in her voice, her other hand on her belly.

'We don't know for sure, but we think there is a volcano up ahead,' he says, and puts an arm around her. 'It will be alright. We will row away from here.'

'A volcano! Like the one in Sicily,' says Tanu, arriving to join them. There is a deep furrow between her brows.

'I don't know,' says Dubb. 'We think so.' He adds her to his encompassing arm.

Nyptan pulls at the leather thong around her neck. Great Laughing Dog pops up from between her breasts and she kisses his zigzag face.

'Protect us, protect us,' she whispers, and leans into Dubb. She and Tanu are so close to him, he can feel their breath.

There is a further pop in the distance, then several more. All heads face towards the noise in alarm. The sea shudders. Dubb looks over the side. On top of the water ripples meet, stop, stand on end, change direction and run chaotically towards and away from each other, spreading like sardines running from a shark. Fear crawls up the back of his neck and down his arms. 'Right, my dear women.' He turns them around, hands shaking. 'You must return to quarters,' he says, voice so controlled he could use it as a knife. 'The Delphis is about to turn around and get away from here.' He shepherds them for a few steps towards the stern before he sets off on his own at speed towards the tiller platform.

'Time to leave!' he says, as he passes through the oars and men. 'Prepare to turn!' He gets to the tiller platform to find the lords Hanno and Bostar in an argument about what to do, Kama glued to them by necessity, eyes wide and resentful.

'Right,' says Hanno. 'Time to set off again.' His foot goes down on the boards. 'One, two, three and four…'

'Wait,' says Dubb, and jumps up onto the platform beside Hanno. 'Where are we going?'

'To shore!' says Hanno, voice blustering. 'We are going to land.'

'To shore! Are you mad! No! We must return the way we came. Immediately!' He makes a grab for the tiller handle. Lord Hanno blocks the way. Sweat breaks out on his palms, and he feels a tremor begin at the base of his spine and work its way up until it reaches his neck. His head begins to wobble. What? Is this waster from Carthage going to row The Delphis into oblivion? Not if I can help it! He turns to midships to get help and it is as if his eyeballs immediately melt in the heat. Nothing of the dolphin at their prow is visible. The Etruscans have disappeared and each row of men between him and midships is thick with fumes. His nostrils are full of toxic air. His lips are tight, shoulders hunched. Fury rises in his belly and he launches himself at Lord Hanno, knocks him aside. 'Berek!' he shouts, with all the force he can bring to his voice. 'The rowing tune! I want the rowing tune!'

Berek leaps to his drum. Thrruuumm, beat, beat, beat. Thrruummmm…

* * *

It feels to Qart as though his face is on fire. People have been rushing past him for the past few minutes. Now he hears the rumpus at the tiller. He simply can't wait any more. He throws his oar aside and sets off towards the stern. He skirts round the heaving shoulders of his fellow oarsmen and launches himself towards the row. He meets Rabs coming the other way.

'Work together!' shouts the small man to everyone at the top of his lungs, as he passes. 'We're turning, turning!' He disappears over Qart's shoulder towards the bow.

The boy dodges the hawsers, skips past the lines of rowers and arrives at the platform to find Bostar sprawled in the leads, a Libyan on top of him. Hanno has his arms pinned behind his back, and Shadra and all his men pass him on the way back down the rows to replace the Rusadirians. Dubb is at the tiller, Chares beside him and both lean into the handle with all their strength.

He jumps onto the platform to Dubb. 'What do you want?' he says. It feels as if all the breath has been knocked out of him, the air thick with fumes. Scuffles break out at midships between the two crews. He can't see much of them through the yellow haze.

'Go to Nyptan and Tanu. Help them,' is all the answer he catches from the stream of words pouring from his master's mouth. 'Men,' Dubb continues without stopping, voice hollow in the air, 'oars to starboard, oars to starboard, turn! Berek, drums louder! Pull harder!'

Qart spins towards the women's quarters.

Nyptan is at the curtain, face aghast. 'What's happening?' she asks. 'Is there a mutiny?'

'No, no, missus,' says Qart. 'Just a bit of a rush to change crew.' He feels nervous. What can I say to "help" at a time like this? He looks around for something he can move, fix or hold.

'Dubb said we are turning for home,' she says. 'So what's gone wrong?'

'Hanno wanted to land and Dubb has just taken over from him at the tiller. There's been a scuffle or two, that's all.' She looks relieved. 'Can we think about something else?' He takes her arm and they move back into the sick bay.

'Are we going to sink?' says Tanu, the minute they enter. Her hair falls down over her face in dishevelled strands. 'Are we going to die?' She is upset.

'Not at all. Please, let's sit,' he says. He grabs at a globe of garlic which hangs from a bunch at the side and starts to peel it.

'Let's do some garlic!' He yanks hard at the green stalk.

The two women ignore him and start to pace about the small space. Their eyes scan the line where land should be. They're not fools. They know exactly what's going on.

'I can't really tell you what's happening to be truthful,' he says, and throws the garlic aside.

To port, in the near distance, there is an explosion which sounds a bit like a small arms store blowing up.

Nyptan's head jerks up and she swings around to look over the topside. The expression on her face changes to one long line of shock.

Qart follows her line of sight. His mouth drops open. Behind them to port, clouds of heavy air have cleared and settled for a moment to reveal a mountain twice the size of Etna towering above them, set back from the sea's edge. 'No!'

'Mummy?' says Tanu, voice high with alarm.

'Darling!' says Nyptan. The two fall into each other's arms.

Qart grips the topside so tightly his nails dig into the wood. Holy Melqart, he thinks, as a wave of fear flows through him from head to foot. Sweet Zeus, help us! Herakles, have mercy! He grabs at the two women and turns them back away from the sight.

'No, no, turn away. We mustn't look,' he says.

Nyptan's eyes tear up in panic. 'Let me go! I won't turn away. We've got to get to Dubb. He's got to get us out of here, faster, further!' She shakes off his hand and sets off towards the main deck, mantle flapping behind her.

'Please, missus,' he says, and tries to catch her. 'Stay here. My master asked me to help you, to be with you while he manages the vessel.' Oh, how I wish I knew what to do, he thinks, what to say, how to help.

***

Dubb puts up a hand to stop Nyptan just as a huge ball of orange flame explodes into the air behind her. It casts shadows on the clouds, irradiates the haze. It's as though Zeus himself has thrown a thunderbolt to Earth. Mighty Melqart, save us.

Tanu follows her mother. Both rush towards him, faces crumpled, mouths wide. His wife's mantle is clutched around her. Tanu leaps the thwarts like a gazelle. The weight of Nyptan's body catches him off balance.

She launches herself into his arms, hair flying into his mouth and her whole body shudders. He staggers backwards. Ash rains down. Mariners stop rowing and cover their heads with their arms. Berek's drum falters. Chares and Rabs are beside him. There, through the haze, they watch as the whole side of a mountain falls into the sea before them. Earth and rock collapse in long shards. The water into which it slides arcs high. The Delphis gives a deep shudder, from hull, through the boards to the top of the sail. The ocean surrounding them fizzes and pops.

'Qart?' he calls. 'Where are you?!'

'Here, Dubb, here. We're all here,' Qart says. Dubb clasps him around the shoulders.

The earth shakes, the sea slashes, the mountain, which was there before, has turned into molten rocks and noxious fumes. Above, somewhere, deafening detonations raise plumes of flame and soot into the air. Behind them, a line of fire marks the coast along which they have just travelled and the sea is sulfurous.

From lord to diviner, all on The Delphis call on the gods. They stand in appalled silence as a heat wave hits them, a giant club swung from the sky.

He gasps for breath. 'To oars, to oars,' he shouts, and continues to bellow until his voice gives out. Men spring to their benches, Berek raises his tune and The Delphis turns its prow away from the land to skid across a still shuddering sea. At their backs, the earth continues to blast, and the deck starts to buck and roil in a gathering wave.

Dubb sees the faces of the rowers before him change and he turns to look behind him as clouds of vapour hiss towards them, a seaborne serpent. It fizzes and switches course, this way and that, and swirls across the water to engulf them all. The men stop rowing, put their arms over their eyes and nose. Nyptan beside him gasps, bunches up her mantle to cover her mouth. Tanu shoves her veil across her nose. The snake overtakes them, tries to suck all the air from their bodies. The rising wave catches The Delphis as it would a twig, and drives her across the surface of the sea.

'Come, come to stern,' he shouts, and beckons and gives up on the tiller entirely. The men crowd with him at the back to keep the bow of The Delphis high in the water. Carried along, Melqart, Zeus, the gods, thinks Dubb, we are your creatures. Our fate lies in your hands! The bow threatens to plough into the sea ahead. The men make for the anchors, jump up and down, clutch onto the sides for fear of sliding forward to their deaths. Further and further into River Ocean they ride, one wave after the next carrying them they know not where. A Rusadirian slips overboard. A howl of fear rises from the belly of the crew. It wraps itself around the mast, rises to the heavens and stalls in the iridescent haze. Oh gods, we, your people, are your playthings. Do with us as you will! He and Nyptan, Tanu and Qart, cling tight to each other and the tiller handle. The lords and Etruscans link arms, interpreters brace themselves against the side and many of the crew bow their heads in prayer. Dubb closes his eyes and nestles his face at Nyptan's ear.

'I love you, my darling,' he says. 'I have loved you since the moment I first saw you. If this is to be our final moment, at least we have been together. There has been a you and me.' He cannot hear her reply, just the feel of her tears on his wrist and the weight of her body. They wait for the end to come: one vast boulder to hurl itself onto the vessel and sink them; the tidal wave, which will overturn them; the fumes, which will suffocate them; the heaving sea, which will pour down on them and suck them under.

Dubb thinks why? For what have I given my life to the sea? Why have I put myself and my dear ones into such dangers for the sake of understanding the sky? Hekataios would not want this. It would not be his will that we disappear from this Earth to the River Styx in this way. I have been deluded all my life in believing that knowledge about how the world works is important, a worthy task on which to spend my time and energy. Yet the Earth responds to me in this way. It spews its contempt on me, puts my life in danger and that of my loved ones. He takes a gulp of what appears to be freshening air. Or should I say it's the gods who are indifferent. They are the ones in charge. They are responsible for this. How I hate them, be they Hellene or from Carthage or even Lady Gula. He looks down at his wrist and the pathetic feather still attached there by its leather thong. What can it do, compared to this catastrophe? He looks over the topside. The water beneath them seems to be calming. He wishes with all his heart that he had not come on this journey, put himself at the mercy of a gold-crazed lordling and his foolish Etruscans. The air thins a little, the sea settles. Is it clearing? Are they out of danger? The deck levels, the bow drops down and the men look from one to the other. Are they saved?

Then he feels Nyptan falling from between his arms towards the deck. No, no. Things are getting better. She cannot collapse now. He drops his head to search for her. Her body has gone limp. The air that held her in his arms a moment ago is now vacant. He sees nothing but the top of her head and Tanu locked at her side.

What? he thinks. He drops to his knees to face her. Her wails overwhelm him. Her tunic is streaked with blood; pools of the bright red liquid congregate on the deck beneath her.

'Mummy!' cries Tanu. 'No, no. We can save it! We can save the baby.'

Nyptan lurches up onto all fours, head down, knees apart, tunic around her waist. She howls and groans and heaves as the child that is in her belly, his child, empties itself onto the boards of The Delphis in a broken lump.

* * *

She won't move. She won't be touched. She crouches above it, head down, arms tucked in, her blood seeping down through the boards of the platform to the goods below. Tanu arches over her, her body a comfort, her mouth near hers. Their howls reach for the heavens and their tears plumb the depths of the sea. The smell of the blood engulfs her and the warmth from the dead body seems to burn her face.

Where are you, my darling child? she thinks. Where is your head? Where are your feet? She shifts about above the body to look. Are you a boy? Are you a girl? Do you have two heads? Do you have more than four limbs? I must search you. Her hands shake as she shifts her weight back from her knees and elbows. Tanu lifts off her and a chunk of light appears on the dead baby. Together, they crouch over it, tears falling across their faces and down their hands to smear the blood away. There he lies, eyes closed as though asleep, lids translucent, tiny, perfectly formed, his fingers and toes wonders of the gods, a little tuft of dark hair on his head. You would have been like Dubb, she thinks, and lifts him to hold him to her breast. You would have grown up to be like him, my lovely boy. She kneels back on her haunches and raises the small form as high as her arms will lift him.

'Here, here you are. All of you,' she whispers, voice lost in the clamour all around. 'I give you my son, my darling, one-headed son.' She collapses down onto herself, all her strength gone.

* * *

Her pain and rage can be heard above Berek's drum. Dubb's hands shake as he stands above her, legs wide, to grip the tiller handle and drive The Delphis away to safety. Ahead, in the clear air, he can see a long, flat, purple plain. The men, shaken, have returned to their benches and picked up their oars. They fall into line with the rowing tune. The lords Hanno and Bostar huddle at the bow with the Etruscans. Kama and his interpreters sit at midships and keep an eye.

'Qart, Rabs, get Nyptan back to our private quarters,' he says, voice unsteady. A son, I have had a son! It feels as though his own legs will give out any minute. 'She needs to be private, not out here in public. Tell her I will come to her as soon as I can. Chares, I need you here with me.' Chares stands beside him, calm, solid, brow crinkled with concern. Dear child, my child, you have gone before you arrived. Even before I knew you, you disappeared. Gone to where? The ancestors? The Styx? To nowhere? I miss you, my son. His eyes fill with tears and, with a nudge, Chares moves in to take over the handle, and he sits down, heavy on the edge of the tiller platform, head in his hands, and cries.

A pair of feet stand in front of him. He looks up to find Lord Rath, imperious, an angry expression on his face.

'Your woman is responsible for the disaster of this journey,' he says. 'I knew the minute I saw her that she should not have come. She has brought the gods down on our heads!'

'He's right,' says Lord Hanno, who stands at the man's shoulder. 'She's the reason we've found nothing!'

'She has given birth to a two-headed baby. She should be punished!'

'Don't be ridiculous. She has given birth to a perfectly normal child,' says Dubb, and stands to his full height. 'You just make things up to suit yourselves.' He turns to step up to the tiller and take over from Chares. Shadra and Kama join him, shoulder to shoulder, leaving the lord surrounded by his own men.

'I demand to see the corpse,' says the Etruscan. 'There needs to be a public examination of it so we can see that you are not hiding anything.'

'What? Can't you be satisfied if I tell you that there is no double-headed child on this vessel? Must you humiliate my woman and myself with a public display?' Rage has risen up to replace the sadness and he is about to leap onto Lord Rath. He doesn't care whether his child has two heads or not. He will not go through such a demonstration.

'Dubb, stop!' says Rabs, and puts his small form between the navigator and diviner. 'Don't let them rile you.'

'I saw the baby born and I can assure you it did not have two heads,' says Kama, his words coming out crisply in Punic. He, too, stands directly in front of the Etruscan, fellow interpreters at his side. 'There is no such thing, in our country, in yours, or anywhere else.'

'I demand to see the child for myself,' says Rath, stubborn. He takes a step backwards into a circle of Rusadirians and Lord Hanno steps forwards.

'Lord Rath is right. We need to see it,' he says, and his shipboard friends agree. They are as eager as he is to find anyone other than themselves to blame for their encounter with the volcano.

Rabs and Kama hoist Nyptan on their shoulders and move her towards the women's private quarters. The men step back, away, as she passes. They touch their amulets.

'Melqart, have mercy. Save our healer,' they say.

* * *

'I'm here, Mummy, right beside you with the baby,' says Tanu, into her ear. Her face is streaked with tears, a bundle in her arms wrapped in her mantle. They lie Nyptan down, the curtain drops and they are alone.

'Birthwort,' she gets out, her throat cracked. 'Water. Fresh and sea.' Her head swims and her body rages, her insides heavy, bloated, bleeding.

'We need lettuce, onions, garlic…' Her lips continue to mouth words. She has no breath left to speak.

'Hush, Mummy, lie back,' says Tanu. 'I know what to do.'

Through lids she can scarcely hold open, she watches her daughter take a vial of birthwort from her medical bag, remove the stopper and add half of it to a beaker of water. With a quick swill, she mixes it, gathers bay and lavender and comes to kneel beside her. She raises her head up and holds it while she drinks it down. Bitter and grainy, the powder gathers at the back of her teeth.

'Slowly,' she says, finishes the beaker and falls back onto her pallet, eyes unable to stay open.

Tanu washes her private parts, her hands firm, warm and decisive. She rinses her whole body in fresh water and pulls a clean tunic over her head. She ties her hair back from her neck and settles Great Laughing Dog at her throat.

'Bring cloths and bowls,' she whispers. 'There will be a lot of afterbirth.'

Her breasts hum and nipples leak, her belly flops and her arms ache with longing for the little one as she drifts into sleep.

When she wakes, Dubb is beside her. He kneels, face haggard, eyes set deep into their sockets. She tries to lift her head to nestle into him. Her body won't do her bidding.

'Hush, my darling. Lie back,' he says, and puts his face close to hers. One arm circles her head, his other on her chest. 'You have slept a little Tanu tells me. I am glad.'

She has no strength to reply.

'I am sorry I could not come sooner. The Delphis is safe now. We have ridden out the danger.' She nods at him and swallows, and wonders what is coming next. His shoulders are too high on his frame, his face too tense to be coming simply to support her.

'I'm sorry to tell you that Lord Hanno and his Etruscans are demanding to see the body of the baby,' he says, and his hand tightens on hers, his chin lowers and his eyes are full of dread.

What? she thinks, and tries to understand exactly what he is saying. What is it they wish to do? Her head swims and she tries to sit up.

'No, no, you must rest. I can do it,' he says, and falters. 'We can do it.' Tanu's face appears over his shoulder.

Nyptan shakes her head violently on the pallet, hair sticky around her throat. 'No, no. I don't want the baby shown!' she says. 'He must be with me. I will bury him on land, not here at sea. Where is he? Where has he gone?' She tries to lift herself onto her elbows.

Tanu's hand is on her shoulder and there, beside her on the pallet, the baby lies, bright, clean and dead. Over his eyes, two flat shells give him an otherworldly look.

'Here, here,' she says, voice light, eyes heavy with anxiety.

Oh, say Nyptan's lips. She does not speak a word. She rolls over and runs her finger down the cheek of her dead child. Her nipples spurt and her womb expands.

'He is so perfect,' says her daughter, as the tears run.

'If you will allow us, Tanu and I can take the child and show him to the diviners. This will prove to them that he...' his voice falters, 'that you are not responsible for the disaster they say has come upon this voyage.

Lord Hanno agrees with them.' His voice is falling into his chest. She can hardly hear him. 'My darling, there is no alternative but to display the baby if we are to dismiss their superstitious nonsense.' She reads the last of these words through half-closed eyes, her lashes forming stripes across his face.

'Can't they see him at burial?' she manages to get out.

'They want a public exhibition now, today,' he says, head low with misery. 'You don't need to be there. We can be very quick.'

Lady Gula, I call on you. Lady Gula, where are you?' she screams, mouth emitting no sound.

'Tanu, give her something, anything, to bring her peace,' he says.

Tanu dashes her essential oil under her mother's nose until she closes her eyes and sinks to sleep.

* * *

Dubb walks to the tiller platform, the body of his son in his arms. The Etruscans stand in a row before it, the lords Hanno and Bostar to one side, the Rusadirians bunched between it and the mast. Heads bob sideways as they try to see what's happening up front. None of our friends are in this line-up, thinks Dubb, and he sees that they have gathered behind him: the Libyans, Qart and Rabs, outside the women's quarters, squatting, standing tall, all grim faced and quiet. The Delphis drifts southwards on the current, only Chares standing guard as ever at the tiller.

He forces his legs to take the step up, his arms to be strong. He crosses the scrubbed boards, the stain of her blood still clearly visible on them and, without waiting for words, or ceremony of any kind, he drops the mantle, and holds the pale and lifeless body up to the men. There, they can see, he thinks, his shoulders shuddering with the effort of keeping still.

'Look all your fill. Look! You can see. One head, one set of eyes, one nose, mouth, two arms, two legs, one body.' He raises him up to the crowd, to right and left, lifts and lowers his load, so that every man standing there has an opportunity to examine it. 'That's enough, you have seen.'

'And its little prick too,' says someone, and the men at the back laugh too quickly, uneasy at being dragged into such things.

Even as Dubb feels unable to keep on holding his son so high, he feels fury rising in him, at himself, the Etruscans, how this kind of stupidity could happen. He drops to his knees, drags the mantle from beneath his elbow and lays the baby down onto it to wrap it up once more. Tears of rage come to him. His jaw sets, head shakes, mouth in a straight line. This innocent, so perfectly formed, the outcome of my union with the woman of my life, now reduced to this, a showpiece for the diviners, the butt of jokes, a tool in the struggle for control of The Delphis. Qart is at his side, helps him wrap, helps him to his feet. Why, oh why, did I listen to Nyptan and let her come with me? he thinks, and steps back. If only I had refused to let her travel, this child would still be alive now.

From behind their curtain, Nyptan's howls rise skywards. Chares, standing upright at the tiller, bends down to puts an arm on his shoulder. Dubb falls sideways into his friend's shins and clings on to them for dear life, to hide his face, control his rage and obscure his helplessness from the eyes of their accusers. The Etruscans start to dance. In slow rhythm, they stamp on the boards, snake around and through the Rusadirians, and call on Nethuns, the God of the sea.

'We need a sacrifice, a pure sacrifice,' says Rath, and pauses in front of Lord Hanno. 'It is clear we have been lazy. We have not understood the will of the gods. This child's death, the volcano, our divisions - all demonstrate we have missed our way.'

Lord Hanno's head drops to his chest and he shuffles sideways to move out of the way of the high priest.

Rath turns to the Rusadirians. 'Let me tell you something important, a precedent, which will show us what to do next. In the years after Archias founded Syracuse, a sailor's wife from the nearby settlement of Casmenae gave birth to a two-headed child and an earthquake followed. Here, we have the same circumstances. An ill-fated birth and a natural catastrophe. What the ancients did then in Etruria was sacrifice and humble themselves. The discipline of the Etruscans said then, as it says now, that human blood must be offered to the gods to win back their favour.'

Dubb's eyes go wide and he sits bolt upright. He cannot believe what he is hearing. I have just shown the man, and this whole vessel, the perfectly formed body of my dead child. Isn't that a human sacrifice, if one is needed? Why does Rath not mourn such a tragedy instead of requiring another? His shoulders strain as he hauls himself to his feet.

He wipes his nose on his arm and takes two huge steps down onto the deck. He stands directly in front of Lord Rath.

'This child, my child, was not born with two heads,' he says, hand raised behind him to the lifeless bundle. 'As you well know. I have just demonstrated to you that the infant was completely normal until…' He falters '…until his spirit left him. How can you…'

Lord Rath's voice cuts across him. 'If we are to return to the safety of the Great Sea, the gods' ways must be followed. Human blood must be let.'

The gathered crew shuffles from foot to foot. Murmurs swell amongst it, which turn to mutters, until fear breaks out into the open.

'Not one of us.'

'Who are you talking about?'

'Stab yourself a chicken then. Or a sheep.'

'Who said that?!' Rath's head whips around and across the crowd. 'Do you see any chickens or sheep on board?' he says, his voice high and guarded. 'Go on, show me one and I will sacrifice it.' His Etruscan priests gather around him, and his hat stands tall.

Even Lord Hanno seems troubled. 'My lord, is this a good idea?' he says. 'We will have a true riot on our hands. Surely, we can find some other way to know the will of the gods.'

'Enough of this. Enough!' Dubb bellows, and leaps up onto the tiller platform. His voice rings out over the top of them all. He snatches his baby up. 'Is my child not good enough for you? Not pure enough? Not dead enough? Was there not sufficient blood?' He points to still stained boards at his feet.

'The gods do not like women's things,' says Lord Rath, and his priests nod their agreement.

'We need to find someone on shore,' comes a voice from the crowd.

'Yes, ashore!' responds the crew.

Kama and his men look shocked. Dubb puts a hand on his interpreter's shoulder.

'Very well,' says Lord Rath. 'There is nothing in the annuls, which describes the kind of blood that must be spilt, except that it be human.'

'So now,' says Lord Bostar, speaking to the Rusadirians, and taking the tiller handle from Chares, 'it's time for us to take over again! To oars, men. Let's get to shore and find a sacrifice!'

Dubb and Chares stand back with the others to watch as the Carthaginian lords take control of their vessel once again and turn the prow towards land.

The Enquiry - Day 13 – Part One

Stunned silence has fallen on the upstairs room of the official residence of the Commissioner for Trade in Gadir. Though the wind whips around outside, it feels like all the air has been sucked from the room. Breath from the witnesses seems laboured, the beating of Lord Apsan's heart like a drum.

'You mean Lord Hanno hasn't told you any of this? The volcano, the baby, the sacrifice, nothing?' the navigator says, voice incredulous. 'Nothing at all?!'

It seems to Lord Apsan that his stomach has been punched. A volcano! Human sacrifice! Can it really be true? He attempts to sit up straight.

'Or what happened afterwards?' adds the boy.

Tasii's stylus has stopped. His slave too looks winded.

'Lord Hanno has told me everything there is to know about this voyage,' he lies, voice weak. 'Didn't he, Tasii? We have everything written down on those tablets.' He waggles his finger in the direction of the piled up slates at his slave's side. Tasii nods, head up and down, too many times.

The navigator's eyes flick from one to the other. 'He's not been here, has he?! You haven't heard from him, let alone talked to him.' His brows arch with incredulity. 'He's missing, isn't he? I knew it!'

'Never you mind about him. He's no concern of yours,' says his lordship, brows down. Please, Mighty Melqart, someone find him! Let me question him before this lot find out. 'Tasii, more cinnamon oil when you're ready. This remedy is from you, madam, with many thanks.' He acknowledges Nyptan elaborately, with a hand, in the hope of making the navigator lose his train of thought. His slave moves to refill his beaker and he takes as much time as he can to slurp back the thick liquid. His head hurts with the thinking, and his gut churns. The point is, where can I go now with my questioning? If I say I want to know more about the volcano, it'll be obvious I've lied. That's true about the human sacrifice too. As for the two-headed baby! Well, the less I know about that the better, he shudders. Still, he thinks, as he beams at Nyptan, she might just crack under pressure, create a diversion, get me out of a hole.

The healer sits upright beside the navigator, back against the wall, a good deal healthier than when she first walked into this room. His lips form a small smile as he congratulates himself on how well he has looked after these prisoners and at his strategy for how to cope next.

'Madam,' he says abruptly. She turns her eyes to him though otherwise does not move. Should he congratulate her for what she has done for his health or attack her for something else? Well, it'll be a bit of both, he thinks, as he looks into her anxious eyes. 'The cinnamon oil really is spectacularly good.' She looks fed up. 'Your skills in healing are clearly outstanding.'

She purses her lips and looks away.

The next bit is not going to go down well, he thinks. But needs must. 'It is a surprise to me therefore that you gave birth to a deformed baby.'

There is an audible gasp in the room. That's got them all going, he thinks, and turns to look at Tasii, expecting to see a smile of triumph at his clever tactics. His slave looks at him aghast, mouth wide open.

'You recall,' says Tasii at speed, voice heavily moderated, 'that the healer here did not give birth to a two-headed child. That was what the Etruscans claimed had happened.'

'Well, with all due respect for your loss, madam,' he says, brisk and polite, as he turns to throw her what he hopes is a sympathetic look, 'that is only your side of the story. The Etruscans have been allies of Carthage for many, many seasons so, perhaps, in the midst of the crisis, you remembered the facts incorrectly. Isn't that so?' He examines her closely, and waits to see what happens.

Nyptan's face has gone stoney. Her hands clench, the knuckles white. Her daughter puts an arm around her.

Then her voice comes to him as if from the bottom of a well.

'My lord, I pity you,' she says, and shakes off her daughter's arm to look directly at him.

His stomach turns. No, no, he thinks, what have I done now? He puts a hand up to try to stop her speaking.

'How could you possibly know, my lord, what it feels like to lose a child?' Her voice grows stronger. 'What would you care about it? You and your slave live here in wealth and ease. You have little sickness around you, no women, no young people. You are completely alone. To bring new life into the world is a joy and a privilege, which I would not trade for any of your power or perfect isolation. As for the charge that my child, my son,' and here her voice cracks, 'had two heads, I will not deign to answer it. You have been told the story. You can choose to believe it from our mouths or take comfort from a lie. You know in your core that there can be no such thing as a two-headed child yet, if you choose to believe otherwise, there is nothing I can do. By all means enquire more from Lord Hanno, should you ever see him.' Her eyes are fiery. 'But do not use my lovely boy, my darling dead child, for your own purposes, to conceal the facts. I am finished with helping you.' She leans back against the wall, breathless, lifts her veil up from her shoulders and covers her face.

He is shocked at her ferocity, her lucidness. 'Alright, alright, madam, I can see I've made a mistake. Your child was not an augur of bad things to come. The fact remains that things went badly wrong on this voyage and I am trying to discover why.' His mind whirrs forwards to what he can do next to get control of the conversation.

'Lord Apsan, can I show you something?' says the navigator, half out of his seat, eyebrows up.

'Why not?' he says. 'Everyone else is having their say.' He sits back and tries not to seem too foolish. A small pool of self-pity congregates in the pit of his stomach. Anyone could say or do anything right now and I've got no control over it. Tears prick at the back of his eyes.

The navigator stands and goes to the side table with the cylinder on it. He lifts it, holds it to his nose and then stands tall. 'This star map is not the only thing of note to return to Gadir,' he says. 'I am not speaking about gold or treasure. There may well have been an abundance of that. If so, we know nothing about it. There were other things that came back with his lordship, which we know about. Did he mention skins for instance?' The navigator turns to look around the table, and on the shelves and the floor.

'Skins!' he gulps, voice faint. Now what? They haven't brought back the skin of a human, have they? He feels sick. Oh, how do I know anything? he thinks, and shakes his head. Perhaps I should have owned up and told them I don't know where Lord Hanno is, and be done with it. It'd be simpler that way. He tries to keep from gagging and examines the veins on the back of his hands.

'Another thing he didn't tell you about,' says the boy, voice going up an octave. 'Shame you've missed so much.'

'So, my lord, if I may summarise, the situation?' says the navigator. He stands at the centre of the room, completely in charge of the enquiry. 'You have spoken to us for days on end, heard every little twist and turn of our sad story, and prodded and poked and insulted us at every turn. My guess is that Lord Hanno is not in Gadir, but has absconded, and may never have been here at all. And he's certainly never been questioned by you.' The man scarcely pauses for breath. 'Which makes this whole enquiry a vindictive sham.'

The Hunt

Qart and Rabs stumble forward on the path. The Delphis and the burial of the baby are left far behind. Light faded the minute they left the open spaces of the shoreline and they are in an eerie half-world: looming trees, a thick canopy above and stagnant pools obscured amongst the vegetation.

'Flaming Melqart!' says the boy, roots and thorns jabbing his feet.

'Ow,' winces Rabs, as he hops in front of him. His knee jerks up with each footstep. 'The locals must have the skin of an elephant to cope with this.'

Qart hurries to keep up. Dubb has asked them to keep an eye on the hunting party, and let him know what is going on, but he and Rabs left The Delphis too long after Lord Hanno's party, and it's not clear they'll catch up with him. For this task, they have to miss the burial of the baby.

Qart is relieved to have something active to do, some task of his own, away from the tension on board. The memory of the child and the smell of the blood as it flooded the deck, is in his nostrils still and he swallows. I do love Nyptan, he thinks. And I love Tanu. I don't really understand them though, and their women's ways. He'd been shocked to see blood-stained rags hung up to dry in their private quarters one day. He didn't know what to say or where to look. He'd asked Dubb afterwards. His master had just said, 'Don't worry about it, boy. You'll find out soon enough.' So he's none the wiser. The baby's death was an even greater mystery. How can it be born dead? How can it look so whole and yet be without life? Why is Nyptan so upset? The echoes of her wailing fill his ears. Her pain makes him wobble inside, bringing back memories of his mother and all her suffering. He shakes his head and stomps on the forest floor. Ow! Ow! No, leave me out of women's things, he thinks, and steps more gingerly next time. I need something straightforward to do. I wouldn't know how to behave at a burial like that.

'To port bow! Quick!' Rabs stops dead to stare ahead and to the left. Qart runs into him from behind. 'Over there, on the hillside,' the small Carthaginian says, and Qart lifts his eyes past the gloom and out the other side to a clearing. There is Lord Hanno. He and his men fan out in a line; his lordship's commands carry through the undergrowth. 'They're not what you'd call stealthy hunters,' mutters Rabs, and looks about him. 'Not that I blame them in this undergrowth. Anyway, it'd be best if they make as much noise as possible and frighten everyone away!'

Qart nods. Much better they should fail at this, get back on The Delphis and go home. The path divides.

'You go this way and I'll go that,' Rabs says, voice low, and points to either end of the hunting party. 'If I need you, I'll call you like this.' He puts his fingers to his mouth and gives three short blasts through his lips. 'Only louder, of course. You're to come at once if you hear me do that, do you understand?' He looks directly at Qart, brown eyes for once serious. 'And if I want to let you know where I am, I'll do this.' He gives a single low whistle with a swoop at the end. 'Got it?' Qart nods. 'What about you?'

The boy lifts his hand, purses his mouth and the two settle on identical signals.

'Good luck, my friend,' says Rabs, and they clasp arms. 'Stay out of trouble. May Melqart guide our steps to safety.' In an instant, he has disappeared along the trail.

Qart suddenly feels very alone. He wants to call out "wait!" to Rabs, though doesn't. He knows he'd just get ridiculed. "Can't you even spend half an hour in the bush without needing someone to hold your hand?" he would say, before punching him on the shoulder and saying, "Oh come on then, young man, follow me." No, I won't call him back. I'll get on with the job Dubb has given me. I'll be strong and carry on. He hurries forwards on the trail and ignores the pain in his feet. I must catch up with them soon or whatever they are up to will be long over by the time I get there.

Thick vines take over from broken branches underfoot, making it easier to move. Birds bicker in the canopy. Monkeys call. Animals scuffle to right and left. The jungle drips with moisture. It falls from branches, runs down tree trunks in rivulets, leaves shine with it and leaf mould squelches beneath his feet. It's sweltering and the sky, when he can see it, is overcast. I wish I'd brought water with me.

When Dubb first told them to follow Lord Hanno's party and report back on it, Rabs had immediately said, 'So, you want us to be spies now?' Qart had been taken aback. He didn't think of himself as a spy, despite all the information he'd been collecting for Dubb about the Etruscans. What they knew of the constellations in their liver reading was useful for the navigator, helped him with his work and was something he himself needed to know for his future life. He was happy, too, to have found some way of pleasing his master. But since that day with the baby, he has come to hate the diviners even more, them and their rituals and demands. So, even if it is called spying, I don't really care, he thinks. They deserve it. They are every bit as bad as Lord Hanno if not worse. I don't want to help them or protect them. I want to undermine their work, stop them doing it. His hands are balled into a fist, his jaw is tight and his feet are getting hot as he stomps along the forest floor like a driven animal. I'd take off in The Delphis and leave them all behind if it was up to me, even if we did need them to row.

He stops dead, almost tripping over himself, as he finds that he has come upon the hunting party, crowded at the edge of a clearing. He drops to his knees immediately, hides himself behind the undergrowth and stays very still for a long time. Through the leaves he examines what is around him. To his left, arrayed in a wide arc, the band of crewmen hide themselves behind a layer of forest. Every one of them looks ahead. At what? He creeps forward on his knees and peers into the light. In the clearing in front of them a small group of stocky Ethiopians are gathered. The men sit back to smoke pipes or break wood into pieces to feed a fire. In the silence of the forest their voices make the leaves tremble; the crack of their wood bounces from trunk to trunk. Beyond them, under a lean-to, women bend and stretch around earthenware pots, babies tied to their backs. They bring food pots to the fire, even in this heat, he thinks, as the sweat pours from his brows to his eyes. He lifts his elbow and swipes it, and the pounding he can hear is the sound of his own heart. Where is Rabs? He examines each patch of greenery on the other side of the open space. Somewhere in there no doubt. He waits to hear his signal, ready to run to him.

Hanno, at the centre of his group, lifts a hand. 'Forward. Shhhhh,' he mouths, and the hunting party creeps towards the clearing, clubs raised. One of the party, a Rusadirian near Qart, trips over something and falls heavily onto the forest floor. The hunting party freezes, the undergrowth shudders and the noise ripples across the glade towards the Ethiopes. Qart's bottom lip goes between his front teeth and he holds his breath.

The local men lift their heads and look straight towards him at the noise. A barked instruction is issued to the women, who stop what they are doing and stare into the bush. Two of the Ethiopes take a few steps towards the edge of the glade. Others put down their pipes.

At that moment, Lord Hanno's arm goes up and from his mouth comes a strangled roar, 'Let's get them!'

The crew of The Delphis rushes the clearing. Before they can leap, barge and hurl their way upon their victims, spears and axes materialise from nowhere. What was, a moment ago, a small group of peacefully smoking men becomes a tribe of armed and angry warriors. Lined up at the clearing's edge, they are ready to cut down any intruders as they emerge from the bush.

Qart's eyes widen, the thudding of his heart reaches his ears and his eyes lose focus. He tries to whistle. Rabs, where are you?! His lips won't obey his instructions. Oh, they're going to be killed! They'll all die here and so will we. He begins to back away, bare feet catching on branches underfoot, grimacing with the pain of sharp roots. I've got to get Dubb, he thinks. I've got to report back. He'll know what to do. We'll get Kama and Berek and Chares. He turns and flees the scene behind him, hurling himself back along the track towards The Delphis.

* * *

Nyptan is on her haunches at the grave's edge. The earth is dark and rich and smells fertile. Good that he goes to the gods in a place like this, she thinks, and puts both hands into its damp fecundity to bring a handful of it to her nose. The land seems blessed. The earth falls between her fingers onto the child, laid crosswise, on her knees. She flicks it away and wipes the sweat from her forehead, a black residue smearing across her face. Beside her, a creek runs inland, edged by perfumed trees. Small animal tracks go into the forest. Behind her, the bay and The Delphis suffocate in the humidity. Gathered round her, a small group of men stand in silence, hands held in front of them, heads lowered.

Dubb lifts Lady Gula's makeshift shrine with one hand. 'Is this the best place?' he whispers, poised over the deep, small pit, ready and waiting to receive its precious load. 'At the head?'

She nods. She hasn't enough strength to speak. 'And Lady Gula…' she trails off. Not even her finger will point.

Tanu takes over, setting their goddess in reeds on top of the shrine, directing Chares and Shadra to manoeuvre the black-glazed burner into place beside the creek.

The babe is wrapped in rough, woven river grasses. It's all I can do for you, my love, Nyptan thinks, and flicks off a clod of earth, smooths out the wrinkles. Her mouth is dry. It is not a splendid suit fit for the gods, but all I can manage. She looks up to Tanu, who moves amongst the men with ease. Her hand goes to the baby's chest, so still, so hollow. My last precious moments with you, my darling, she thinks, and tries to swallow. His face is pale, veins blue above his lids, limbs stiff, mouth open. Your first, and last, call to me it seems, and the tears come, spill down her face and into her tattered tunic.

'There's very little perfume left, Mummy,' says Tanu, her voice light, at her side.

She lifts her eyes and looks into her daughter's. They are thread through with anxiety.

'Thank you, my darling,' she says, clasps her hands and her eyes fall into the pit. I don't care, she thinks. What does it matter whether Lady Gula has enough incense or not? My child is dead and even her perfume will not bring him back. 'Not to worry.' She swipes her cheeks dry with the sleeve of her tunic. 'Do your best.'

Tanu stands at the incense holder, a flint in her hand, beads of sweat on her brow. She strikes it and lights the perfume. It flares and flames and spits its heavy aroma around the glade. The men stand about, those who chose to disobey Lord Hanno's command that they go on the hunt.

In both hands, Nyptan lifts the babe to shoulder height. 'Lady Gula, I call on you to accept this child, to take him into the realm of the gods.' Her voice has come back. It rings around the clearing and startles the birds.

She tries to stand. Her legs won't support her. Dubb takes her under the arms and brings her to her feet. Together, they bring the child to the burner first, where they waft him in the aroma of their sweet lady. Next to the altar itself, the golden symbol, with its slashed face, shines up at her. 'Please accept this sacrifice as a token of our love, my lady,' she whispers. She and Dubb both bow. They turn and lower the body into the grave. Her hands feel light as he departs from her to the ground, her heart bereft, her nipples weeping. Berek plays a melancholic tune. Supported by Dubb, she watches as each man present comes to her, one by one, to bring comfort in their own way. Chares, Berek, the Libyan.

'May the spirit of your child rest in peace,' says Shadra.

'May Great Melqart bless his journey forwards.'

'The spirits protect him.'

They lay down their precious stones, feathers and shells. Kama and his interpreters also bring their tokens, small dolls wrapped in brightly coloured cloth, beads and iron.

'Kama,' she calls. 'Stay a minute.'

'Yes, missus.' His eyes are dark and wet.

'What is the name of this place?'

The interpreter puts his hand to his chest. 'I am not sure, my lady, but I think it is called the Horn of the South.'

Her face is as pale as the moon. The pit fills up in front of her. She takes her own clod of earth and drops it into the grave. Then, she herself falls to the ground, her whole body convulsed by shudders and sobs.

There is a shout from somewhere nearby. She raises her head to see Qart rush into the clearing. He comes to Dubb, then to Chares. She turns away. Who cares what he's here for? What does it matter? They can do whatever they want, these men, she thinks. They can sacrifice as many people as they like; they can die in droves of the fever. I don't care. I won't heal them any more. I'll let them die. I've had enough of them and their vanities, their strutting and their laws. She slumps, exhausted, by the graveside and her whole body longs for the touch, the smell, the weight of her child.

* * *

Qart rushes up. 'We need more men! You've got to come now,' he gabbles, out of breath.

Dubb turns and sees the boy as if for the first time, a wild-haired young man with wavy brows and bright eyes. Is he speaking to me? he wonders, and a frown comes across his face. Of course he is. He bends down to catch the words. The boy pulls at him with both hands.

'There's a fight going on in the forest. There's not enough of us,' he says.

Ah, thinks Dubb, I don't care. He disentangles his arm and pushes him away. 'Not me! Not now. Speak to Chares,' he says, and turns his back on him, turning back to Nyptan and the baby. The incense of the Lady Gula reclaims him, memories of her, of home, of Carthage, of the life that he and Nyptan and Tanu have had since they first got together at the edge of the Great Sea all those years ago pulsate through him in waves. What would my life have been without them? he thinks, and puts his own hands to the pit. He pushes clods of earth around, covers his own amulet with earth. What might this child have been? A healer, navigator or ship's boy? The glade rings with music as he lifts earth from the ground and smears it across his face. Why not join my son in the grave? he thinks. Go to the land of the spirits holding his hand.

After a time, he stirs. Berek has stopped. The wash of the creek, rustle of creatures in the bushes and the distant call of a monkey greet him in the present. He lifts his head to find Chares sitting on a tree branch nearby. The first mate seems to be waiting for him, calm and patient. Dubb clambers to his feet, parched. He takes a swig of water from a skin at his waist and, with a glance at the still prostrate women, steps across the clearing to speak to him.

'What's happened?' he says in a low voice. 'Where are all the men?'

'They've gone to help Lord Hanno,' says Chares, and glances at the women. 'Qart was sent to get more men. There's been a fracas in the jungle it seems.'

Why am I not surprised? he thinks, and realises that what he thought were bird calls are actually the whoops and yelps of the crew in the distance. 'What is it? A fight? Baal only knows what the fools are doing.' He feels weary to the bone and his head drips with sweat. 'What else did he say?' A pit has opened in his stomach and he must summon strength now to take on something new. Have I got to try and manage this fiasco too?

'Just that you are to come as soon as you can. Lord Hanno and the Etruscans have been attacked.'

He sits down heavily, beside Chares. 'Perhaps the gods will smile on The Delphis and these men will die along the way,' he says, and drinks still more water.

'We can only hope so,' says Chares. 'That would be the best solution of all.'

'Stay here with the women for the time being. When they're done, take them back to The Delphis and get them settled.'

The first mate nods. 'We'll be ready and waiting, ship shape, when you return. Be safe, my friend. May the gods go with you.'

Dubb stands, and takes a last look at his wife and daughter, before he turns into the forest to find the hunt.

I've got to get the sensible crew of The Delphis out of there, he thinks, as he tries to work out where in the forest the hunting party now is. He has walked some way along the track into it, and the whoops and yelps have stopped. All he can hear is dripping water. He swats at a mosquito on his back. Whatever the consequences for our journey home, we must separate from Lord Hanno and his Etruscans. Even if it means living in this land for the rest of our days. He pauses as the path in front of him diverges. Does that broken bracken mean the hunters passed this way? He searches the entrance to the paths for signs of recent movement. I wish Kama or his men were with me; they'd be able to help. His ears feel like they have grown to the size of a cabbage with listening, his jaw set and mouth a straight line across his face. I have to choose one path or the other, for right or for wrong. I can't stay here, and he sets out to the left. Perhaps I should have insisted we return after the volcano. But the eruption took us over. Or that the Etruscans drop demand for blood? What could I have done to control them? How can the death of a human possibly help us to find a way back home when the route is written in the stars? He shakes his shoulders to free the tension, rolls his head around on his neck. It feels as though a boulder is stuck in his throat. This whole voyage has been a lesson in failure. Failure to see the stars, failure to make Lord Hanno see sense, failure to control the diviners, failure to skipper The Delphis. Lagoons, islands, tides, currents, volcano and peoples - what use is it to know about them if we can't get home?

He hears a whistle, low with a swoop at the end, and stops dead. He knows that style. Rabs is about. He always uses it. I'm here. I've caught up with them. To his surprise, someone very close to him responds. He drops to his haunches and begins a systematic examination of the forest to his left. Who was that? Impossible to see. He scarcely breathes as he waits for them to move. Nothing. Still, there's no fighting going on. Good. I might be in time to stop it before it starts. There is a sudden rustle beside him and Dubb jumps as Qart springs out onto the path in front of him.

His heart pumps in his chest. 'There you are!' he smiles, and relief washes through him.

'Shhhhhh!' says the boy, finger to his lips. 'Quiet. They're over there.' He points behind him into thick darkness.

'What? Where? In there?' The jungle looks so dense it can't be possible to penetrate it. They head towards it, into tangled roots and vegetation. 'I thought you'd forgotten to look out for me,' he whispers. 'What's happening?'

'Lord Hanno raided a party of locals. They drove him back,' says Qart over his shoulder. 'They've disappeared. I came to get help. You were busy.'

'Never mind that,' Dubb says. 'Tell me about now.' He bends and twists to follow the boy through the undergrowth.

'They've found another group to fight. They've been watching them for ages, just behind that set of ferns.'

Dubb lifts his eyes from the forest floor. A great outcrop of bright green vegetation is partially obscured by hanging vines and twisted logs.

'Where's Rabs?'

'Over in that corner by the big trees,' says Qart. 'His whistle just told me so.' He points at what looks like a clearing. 'I haven't seen him since this morning.'

Dubb puts up a finger and pushes aside a hanging vine. A chill runs from the top of his skull to his toes. There, at the edge of a beaten down clearing, right in front of them, is a small group of dark heads. They chat amongst themselves and groom each other.

'Tsst! Tsst!' goes someone in the bush.

'That's Lord Hanno,' whispers Qart. 'He's lining people up ready to attack. They're all around us.'

Dubb looks into the intense green and can see no one. These poor bastards, he thinks. How can I warn them without being attacked myself? Perhaps I should skirt around them, get to Hanno and call the whole thing off. He sees a small child climb around the shoulders of its mother. His heart stops. But that is not a child. I've never seen a child like that. The face is squashed and pink; hair comes down thickly all over its body. Eyes bright, very close together, pale palms, brown skin. No, that's an animal!

'But they're not humans! They're animals!' he says to Qart, with sudden certainty.

'Shhhhhh,' says Qart, eyes on the prey.

'Qart, that's an animal out there!' repeats Dubb, persistent, and points. 'There's no need to be quiet! We need to make a noise!' He grabs the boy by the arm and stands up. 'We've got to stop this!'

'Really?' says Qart, and ducks his head under a branch to observe them. 'Hanno thinks they're just a different tribe from the last group he tried to massacre.'

Ignorant as ever, thinks Dubb, and his jaw sets. He thrashes in the undergrowth as violently as he can. This stupid lordling, this scion son of the House of Magonids of Carthage, I'm going to find him and tell him to stop. He should never set foot on an expedition again. Dubb is about to step out into the midst of the clearing when, with a great whoop and hullabaloo, the hairy creatures are surrounded by the sweaty bodies, raised clubs and screeching mouths of Lord Hanno's hunting party. Rath, the high priest, Bostar, the Rusadirians - they're all there, crashing from the undergrowth, Hanno following behind. They swing weapons high and low. There is a mighty eruption of activity from the hairy ones and they rise up, as one body, to protect themselves. A larger one stands forward, barks, mouth wide, teeth bare. Almost all the others go vertical, into the trees, climbing with a skill and expertise, which leaves Dubb's mouth open and the hunters stymied.

'What by the gods!' says Hanno, as he stares at the bums of the still climbing creatures.

'Let's go after them,' says a Rusadirian, and takes to a tree. Other men follow suit.

'Wait, wait! We've got to think about this,' says his lordship. 'Stop!' The men stall. 'Where are the nets?' He turns and looks back to the gang of men gathered around the edge of a glade.

There, Dubb sees, the hunters have collected nets, clubs, spears, pots, chains, everything they might want to capture a sacrifice. Kama and his interpreters are also there in a huddle. We've got to get out of here, he thinks, and turns to look for Qart. He's no longer there beside him. A frown comes down between his brows. Where has the lad gone? He needs to be careful. He turns around and searches for a tree to hide behind. He glances up to check that none of these extraordinary animals are perched high above him in the canopy. They're like humans but not, he thinks, and finds a trunk wide enough to protect him. Big, powerful tree climbers who, with one swat, could kill a man. He leans back against its bark, sweat pouring from his face and into his neck, and listens to the bloody battle between man and beast.

'Watch out, Dubb!' he hears Qart say, and he turns towards him just in time to see a huge, white-streaked animal launch itself directly at him. It lopes towards him sideways from the greenery, shoulders heavy, brow thick and haunches immense. He catches the rancorous smell of it as it swings its massive arm towards him. He ducks and swivels and dives into the undergrowth. The animal falls heavily against the tree, stunned. Dubb thrusts himself forward on his shoulders and drags himself away under thickets of ferns and branches. They lash his face, his mouth open, teeth clenched. Then, with a mighty effort, he brings his legs up to meet his torso, rolls onto his side and lies, panting, to play dead. The jungle rings with the thrashing, neighing and shrieking of men and animals. With breath held, he realises the fight is on the move, going beyond the ferns.

He focusses on catching every sound, every possible footstep on the forest floor. An insect's legs, a frog, but nothing: no heavy breathing, no pawing, nothing that might be a large animal waiting to pounce. Best of all, he can't hear a boy being attacked. He counts to a hundred and then whistles softly, a long, low note with a swoop at the end. No response. Both the animal and Qart have moved on. Holding himself rigid so as not to cause a single sound, he raises his head. A solid wall of green meets him, only a few waving fronds at the corner of his eye. He unravels himself to push them aside and looks into the tree tops. Nothing. He gets to his knees and searches the scene. In a pool of light well ahead of him, past the ferns, Qart and Rabs are together in a deeper glade. The trees beyond them are dappled green and above them hang the dark shapes of the hairy tree-borne creatures. They swing in pairs, babies on their backs. They are the females, thinks Dubb. It must have been a male that attacked me. He sets out to join Qart and Rabs.

By the time he arrives at the scene, berries, fruits, nuts and vegetation rain down on the hunting party below. One of the larger animals bounces on a branch until it cracks, then waits for it to drop onto the men below.

'Pissing animals,' someone shouts as men run for cover.

'There's no way to trap them. They keep moving.'

Hanno's voice rings out, commanding and harsh. 'We will get one of these smaller ones with the baby. You men.' He points to several of the crew. 'Climb up those trees. They're just like a mast. You over there,' he says, and shouts at another group, 'put the nets under here. We'll get one or other of them, or I'll die in the doing of it.'

'But they're not humans, mate,' says Rabs. His voice rings out sharp amongst the trees. 'Can't you see they're animals?' He grins at his lordship. The whole hunting party stops what they're doing and looks up to see him, shocked.

Lord Hanno looks around. His face falls. 'What?! Why are you here? Get back to The Delphis.'

'I agree with Rabs.' Dubb steps out into the open to join the small Carthaginian. No point in hiding from Lord Hanno now. Best to be as visible as possible. Give the animals the time to escape. Rabs and Qart look at him, surprised. He puts out his arm to greet them and notes the stillness in the hunting party, the focus they have become of everyone's attention. He deliberately speaks to be heard by all. 'You'll not be doing the gods any favours if you bring them an animal rather than a human' he says to Lord Hanno and those who watch them in the clearing. 'So best give up.'

Lords Rath and Ani regard him sourly. 'I don't care what you think,' Lord Hanno says, and turns back to his men. 'Well, what are you all looking at? Get back to the hunt. The success of this mission depends upon us finding a human to sacrifice!' He stomps off across the greenery to join Bostar and his men at the ropes. A new flurry of activity on the ground begins as men climb trees, rig up nets or bang the bottom of a cooking pot to corral the animals into submission.

Dubb feels a thud on the ground first, a great heavy step, which comes from behind and alerts him to danger. He jumps sideways out of the way. Next, comes the smell of a rancid armpit. Lastly, he sees the streak of animal as it drives past him on the path.

'Rabs, Qart…!' he shouts as the animal continues its charge. One of its shoulders is down, it leans forward like a battering ram. Its great head is held upright, its teeth bared. Its muscles sway and ripple and its skin shines white as it grabs at Rabs with both hands, catching him from behind. With a great swoop, he raises the Carthaginian high above his head. His arms continue their downward arc towards the nearest tree and he crashes the mariner's body against the trunk. Rabs's limbs float like lines of seaweed. The animal raises its face to the canopy and lets out a deafening roar of rage. With giant limbs, it pummels its victim against the wood.

Where is my club? thinks Dubb, panic at his throat. Why didn't I bring one? His eyes flash around the glade. Where is a branch? Or a stick? I can poke the animal's eyes out. He launches himself, full weight, against the massive body. Its fur is strong and slippery. He falls backwards, gets up and tries again. He is thrown aside.

The animal does not stop. It continues to lift Rabs, to hurl him against the trunk time and again until, for no apparent reason, it suddenly stops. It discards him, throws him into the undergrowth as if he was a piece of fruit, and storms off into the forest. Rabs whimpers as he lands, gasps for air and is still.

Dubb and Qart fall to the ruined body of their dear friend. They hold him in their arms and call to him. His eyes are open, his head at a strange angle, his breath a rasp.

Kama comes to their aid. His men tear their garments into strips for his wounds. They raise him to their shoulders and follow Qart as he leads the way back through the forest paths to the shore.

* * *

My friend, my special helper, my confidant, come back, thinks the boy, his mind a mass of panic and fear. Don't leave me alone. His arms sweat and his feet are numb to the forest floor. His mouth forms the words 'Nyptan will fix you' over and over.

As soon as he glimpses the shoreline, he flies forward. He launches the coracle and paddles to The Delphis with all his strength.

'Nyptan! Nyptan!'

Chares's head appears over the topside.

'Rabs! It's Rabs. We must save him!' The coracle bangs against the hull and he leaps up the ladder. 'Nyptan! Where's the missus?' he gasps, as Chares comes to midships with the healer by his side.

'What is it?' she asks, face lined with weeping, her tattered mantle flowing behind.

'Rabs, he's been attacked by a big animal, a huge animal, who threw him against a tree. He needs you.'

Nyptan looks over the topside. Dubb is at the shore line with another coracle. 'It might be better to look at him on land,' she says to Chares.

'Let's go! Tanu! Where's our bag?' she calls.

'Forget about your bag, missus. We need to drag him back from the gods. Now!'

'Qart, without my bag I can do little. We must try to be calm.' She puts both arms around him and draws him in. The smell of her skin, the touch of her hair and warmth of her comfort unhinge him. His eyes go hot, his throat tight. 'If he is as you say, he might have gone to the gods already, dear Qart. Life ends when the gods choose, not at our bidding,' she adds into his ear. Tanu arrives at her side, bag tight, fresh water. 'We will do our best for him, of course! Lady Gula may help him or she may decide that it is time for him to leave this world. And whether he stays or goes, his time here has been a blessing to us all.'

Sobs burst from him, uncontrolled. He turns his back on her. His friend's mocking voice rises in his ears. "Stay out of trouble!" But he didn't! He didn't take his own advice!

'I command you to be well,' he says out loud. 'Tell the gods, whoever they are, to leave you be.'

Nyptan pulls him back to her, wipes his nose on her mantle and takes a vial of lavender from a pouch at her waist. 'Here, have this.' She dabs it on his upper lip. She glances up and then gives him a gentle push towards Dubb, who has boarded now behind him. The perfume from the oil is powerful, the air cool against his cheek. The remedy fills his mind, makes it float. His vision swirls and he goes to his master, who takes him around the shoulders, leads him to a hawser near the tiller platform and sits him down.

'Stay here for a few minutes, lad,' says his master. 'You can watch. Our friend is not dead yet. There is still time and we will do our best.'

He looks up to see Kama winching the small Carthaginian up over the topside.

The women do everything they can for Rabs. In a fury of activity they put compress of lavender under his nose. They patch his wounds with onions and lettuce soaked in water. They light oil lamps and pray. Berek strums his favourite song. Still, his friend's breath remains laboured, his neck at an odd angle.

Deep silence descends on deck as the end comes. The man's eyes flash open momentarily and his fingers twitch. His chest rises in a rasp and never falls.

'He has gone,' whispers Nyptan. 'Dear Rabs, you have left us. Our lives are the worse for your passing.' She closes his lids.

The women fall into each other's arms and weep. Kama and his men bow deeply, palms to chest.

'Not us gods. Do not take us!' the crew howl, and hold their amulets up before their faces in sweaty palms.

Dubb steps forward and stands over the crumpled body. 'Rabs, you were our friend, one of life's brightest sparks: funny, true, faithful. I should never have allowed you to go on a hunt like that. Against such an animal you had no chance whatsoever.'

Tears roll down Qart's cheeks unchecked.

* * *

Hanno and his men return from the hunting trip at dawn. Dubb gets up from Nyptan's side as they turn over the topside. The ladder clacks as they come and they stink of roasted meat.

'There you are, old man,' says the lordling, and shoves something right into the navigator's face. 'We got one!'

Dubb pulls back. Chunks of flesh are still stuck to the dark and bloody skin of a hairy animal. The lordling's clothes and arms are caked in its blood, and his face shines with triumph and animal fat. 'And damn good they taste, too, those people,' he adds.

Rath and his priests arrive, hearts and livers cupped in their hands. They brandish them at the navigator.

Dubb recoils. 'I don't wish to know what you've done today.' He waves their trophies away, his face pinched and mouth askew. 'Keep them away from me and everyone here,' he orders. They shrug and turn away. 'Before you return to the bow though, I do need to inform you of one important thing. Thanks to your activities on the hunt The Delphis has, this day, lost one of the finest members of the crew we've ever had, Rabs the Carthaginian, our dear friend.'

* * *

Nyptan and Tanu use the last of their essential oil of lavender to massage Rabs's limbs. They dress his head and neck with balm, ground acacia root mixed with palm oil. Nyptan has asked for oil lamps at the four corners of his body, day and night, and Berek has taken on the task. When he's not refilling the lamps, he's at his aulis.

'It's hard to make him soft again, Mummy,' Tanu says, beside the body. Her hands are oily, eyes wet. 'I'm really sorry, Rabs.' She turns to him. 'I'm doing my best.'

'It can't be helped, darling,' says Nyptan, voice heavy. 'He was already partway to the gods by the time he arrived here. We must do what we can.'

Kama and his fellows have made a bower of sweet-smelling trees. 'We give this to you, our cheerful friend.' They place it on the bier at the tiller platform. 'May you rest in peace.' They add their own oils to the mix and light their own lamps.

When the time comes to pass Rabs into the water, the whole crew is assembled at midships, even the Rusadirians. Hanno has decided to say a few words. Nyptan closes her ears to them and looks out at the horizon. The body slides over the side and drops into the sea without a splash. She moves to the topside to watch it float away.

'Did we weigh him down enough?' she says, and looks anxiously at Dubb beside her. 'He's supposed to sink.'

He puts an arm around her. 'Let's wait and see. He should be alright.'

Slowly, Rabs revolves and dips, first his feet below the water, then his chest. Finally his wizened face goes under and his whole body swirls away on the current.

She turns back to the deck and the crew is silent. She steps her way through them towards her private quarters. Her neck goes stiff as she passes. It was time, long ago, for you to return to your wives and daughters, she thinks, your sons, and cities and civilisations. I am tired of all of you, your obstinacy and malice. I'm sick of being responsible for your welfare when you can't be bothered to look after yourselves. I despise you. She sees the calamity, which has come upon them marked on the face of each man she passes, even in the expression of that most mercenary of men, Lord Hanno, the Magonid prince of Carthage.

Heading for Home

It is a grey and olive dawn some time after Rabs went to the gods. The Delphis, still at anchor, drifts in bevies on a grey sea. The clatter of astronomy tablets breaks the silence. Dubb has his records out, for the first time in many months, and spread across the tiller platform. This lot should be the ones from before Lixus, he thinks, as he hauls the first armful from the hessian. He casts his eye over them. Yes. The writing is large, squandering space on the wax. He puts them down, then crawls forward on his hands and knees to slide them into the top left-hand corner of the beaten boards. He turns to grapple with more. These are Lixus to Ngap, the pastoral paradise markings smaller and more organised. He moves them to the top right. Down here, and he shunts backwards to the edge of the platform, I'll place the ones which record the voyage up to King Oyediran. He opens a fresh bag. Last of all is where we discovered that Kochab had gone. They'll be here, directly in front of the tiller handle. He empties the last hessian, gets off the platform and surveys his layout. There must be about fifty of them, many sand covered, all waiting to be analysed and catalogued. At his feet is the leather cylinder in which are his velum, stylus and ink.

His turns to scan the bodies towards the bow. 'Qart, are you ready?' he calls in a loud whisper. Now that Rabs is no more, the boy has gone to sleep with Kama and his fellow interpreters. A head pops up from their midst. He gets a nod and the boy stands, picks his way through the sleeping bodies, washes his face at the barrel and comes to Dubb's side to help.

'We've got to do the master documents once and for all,' he says. 'Even if the voyage isn't finished, we must make a good copy of our findings, finalise them and give them a time and a season. Who knows what will happen next and, if we don't have it summarised and written down up to the present, all these records could be lost. Hold this, will you?' He hands one side of the rolled up velum to Qart and pulls a section out. It springs back in his hands. We can make these maps into a testament to Rabs, he thinks, and tries to ignore the pit of sadness in his belly. They will be a perishable, friable stele to the journey we have taken and everything we encountered along the way. His jaws clench.

Hanno and the Etruscans, behind their barricade, sleep after yet another day of hunting and feasting. Nyptan and Tanu stir in their quarters. The rest of the crew, Chares included, remains dead to the world.

'Let's lay out a sheet at a time with weights on the corners,' he says, the velum rolled up in his hands like the insides of a shell.

'But these are in a mess,' says Qart, as he stands in front of the Kochab pile. 'What's happened to the numbering?'

The two begin to sort and replace the tablets across the width of the whole platform. They are very muddled, he thinks, as dawn breaks to the usual overcast day.

'Which batch do you want to start with?' says the boy.

'We should begin with the night we couldn't find Kochab and work backwards.' It all went especially wrong after that, he thinks, so best to get that grim finding down first in the records.

'Are you hungry, you two?' says Nyptan, coming from their private quarters. 'Do you want fish if I can find some?' She trails her hand across his shoulder as she passes and gives Qart a faint smile. She is suffering under all that calm exterior, he thinks, that courageous woman of mine.

He labels and numbers the velum. These, too, have got to make sense to anyone who comes across them for the first time. Qart mixes the ink and sharpens the styluses. Morning turns to afternoon and they've not made a single mark on even one animal skin. The heat picks up, sweltering, and the sleepy atmosphere has long evaporated under the crew's demands for food and entertainment. Lord Hanno and his men have gone ashore again, and a competitive game of dice has broken out between the interpreters and the Libyans.

'I had it!'

'No, I did!' They jostle and curse.

Good that the men are capable of enjoying themselves, he thinks. It's been so bad these last months and the journey home is going to be worse.

'Feed me a tablet at a time, will you? When I've finished with it, you must place it back exactly where it was originally, just in case I get confused and need to start again,' he says.

Qart is beside him, to pick up and replace, to keep the tablets under control. The navigator dips his stylus into the ink and lifts it, poised to start. I've never really solved the problem of how to draw the bowl of the heavens onto a flat surface though, he thinks. Or how I can link the measurements on one velum with those on the next. Or, for that matter, how to mark distances across the sky. There must be a way. Perhaps I should create a grid? His mind begins to swirl and pop. His knees are at his shoulders, his torso squashed between them as he places his first mark onto the skin. He writes with speed. Before I can think about it too much, or I'll never do it. 'Next!' he says, and the boy places a tablet at the top of his line of sight. He marks down the star pattern. 'And the next!' His fingers grow numb with writing, his armpits sweaty. They swig from beakers of water.

What if, instead of the heavens being round and the Earth flat, the heavens were round and the Earth was round too? That would explain why we've seemed to tilt as we've travelled from the Great Sea. A large sigh blows out through his mouth and his hair puffs.

Over the next days, the unrecorded tablets reduce and the velum piles up. As he struggles with grid lines and scales, and looks at what they saw with their own eyes when the sky was clear, he becomes ever more convinced that it's not just the bowl of heavens he's describing but the circle of the Earth. From time to time, they shift position on the boards. They shove a coil of hawsers over to rig up a writing bench.

In mid-afternoons, they take a break, walk around the deck a few times and nibble ship's biscuit. It takes them days to complete the task. By the evening of the fifth, the bulk of it is done, leaving only the arrangement in the cylinder to go and Dubb's conclusions. I need to come to them by myself, in the quiet, somewhere where what I've seen doesn't shock anyone.

'Qart, that's it! It's done! The tablets are complete. Go and get some food, find friends, play a game.'

The boy gives a huge sigh, stretches and is gone, to Kama, to food, to dice. Dubb stands at the topside and looks out towards the forest, the place in which Rabs died. The pit of his belly fills with sadness. Not even the achievement of the records can overcome the gloom. This is the site of my great shame, he thinks, the place where I could do nothing to save the life of my dear friend. He rubs his eyes and tries to remove the image of Rabs flung against the tree from the backs of his lids. It could also be a place of great discovery, the location where he first thought of something which had never crossed his mind before. Or the mind of anyone else. That the stars are round and the Earth is round. He shakes his head. Too complicated for me. I'll have to leave that for Hekataios to sort out.

'Kama,' he calls. The interpreter leaves his game to join them. 'Did you tell Nyptan that we are at the Horn of the South?' he asks. The man nods. 'What is it beyond here, the place we will end up at if we don't go home?' he says, and tries to keep the tremor from his voice.

'Mr Navigator, I have no name for anywhere beyond here. And even the Horn of the South is only approximate. As you know, none of us have ever been this far from home on the sea before. And we know nothing of what places are called. You need to speak to the locals to find out, though I'm not sure you'd get much of a welcome from them after all that's happened. Call it anything you like for the time being.' The man smiles, a good, open, kind smile, and Dubb clasps him around the shoulders and they hug.

'Go back to your game.' The man nods and turns back to his crew. 'Play something for me' he adds. 'I've got to keep going.'

I will dedicate these records to Rabs, he thinks, our friend and shipmate whose humour and willingness is sorely missed. Hekataios will understand. He'll like it. He blinks repeatedly, scarcely able to keep himself awake after all the concentrated effort of recent days. But will Nyptan? he wonders. She might like the star map to be a tribute to our son.

He turns to find Nyptan, Tanu and Shadra at the door of their quarters with garlic bulbs. He lifts his head to his wife, and she comes and puts her arms around him, rests her head.

'What is it?' she asks. She is warm and smells of bay. Deep circles under her eyes and a coarsening of her skin show that hard times are taking their toll. There are grey strands in her hair. Underneath her tattered tunic most of her body is a skeleton, the rest a stretched wreck where the baby was. By the gods, what have I done to you and our lovely daughter? he thinks.

Tanu watches them from the curtain, ready to come at any moment.

Nyptan seems to read his mind. 'I would rather be nowhere else in the world than here just now,' she says. 'Despite it all. Even after everything that's happened. The deranged lords, the arrogant Etruscans, the privations, the death of our son.' Here, her voice goes so soft that he must bend forwards and put his ear to her mouth in order to hear her. 'In spite of it all, I still want to stand by your side, and die with you if it comes to that. My life did not begin until you came along. It will end when you go. I never want to be away from you.' She leans into him and sighs deeply.

Tears fizz at the corner of his eyes though never come. Too much sorrow, too many disasters. I am a cracked, old stick about to break, little except a brain on legs. Yet she, my woman, supposedly the weaker of us two, is the one who's holding us up.

'What do you think? Should I dedicate our star maps to Rabs?' he says, 'or would you like it to be named after our son?'

A small frown inserts itself between Nyptan's eyes. 'No, not our son. Don't name it after our son.' She pushes off him. 'It's these men, this lordling, Lord Hanno, who will claim credit for this voyage, if we ever get back. And I don't want my, our son,' she falters, 'ever to be linked with him. He and his cronies have done enough damage already.'

He nods. I agree with her, he thinks, and gathers her to him again. Lord Hanno has a lot to answer for. He will certainly crow about this voyage if we return. He will trumpet his achievement all over the Great Sea and beyond.

'It was only an idea,' he says. 'No need to do it.' He takes her by the hand. 'So let's write a memorial to Rabs on the records together, shall we?' He leads her over to the tiller platform and they drop onto their haunches by the velums. "For Rabs of Carthage", he writes, careful not to blot on the top of the document, and she bends over to put her finger in the ink and add her signature.

* * *

He smells the change first. The heady odour of vegetation and the rich tang of lagoons gives way to a fresh, open smell of wide horizons and tossing waves. It is just a glimmer at the start, a tiny flash of hope riding on the breeze.

His eyebrows raise and his head turns towards the sun, now on the way to its watery grave for the day. He swivels to look towards midships. Chares is climbing to his feet, nose in the breeze, eyes at the horizon. Shadra, Berek and the others also sense the change. His eyes drift around to a distant blanket of cloud, where it coagulates in clumps. One star appears, too small, too isolated, to identify. He raises his chin to Chares, Chares nods to Berek and the musician moves towards his drum and lifts his sticks to start the rowing tune. Hanno emerges from behind the barricade and starts to rouse the crew.

'Up, up,' says the navigator, heart light. 'There's a breeze on the way!'

The drum rolls, the Libyans take to the benches, the Rusadirians to the sail and, before the wind proper comes, The Delphis is underway, oar and sail together. There is no discussion about their direction. No appetite to carry on forward. Not even Lord Hanno wants to continue his search for gold. Dubb leans on the tiller handle and turns The Delphis homewards.

As they leave the Horn of the South behind, the clouds clear and Dubb gets a complete picture of the whole evening sky. The strongest pattern he sees first is Orion, not high above him as it should be but tipped sideways and low down in mid sky. It is like taking the first gulp of a strong drink, a hit followed by the slow burn. There is no Kochab or Big Bear and certainly no Melqart. Instead, there are hundreds of new patterns to be explored.

'Chares, grab this,' he says, and steps aside to let the first mate take the tiller handle. 'Make sure you don't lose sight of land and keep going as long as we can in the dark. Qart!' He goes to his astronomy bag, takes an empty tablet from the pile and, together, man and boy move to the stern among the leads. 'Scribble down any new shape you can see. If you do the right of Orion, I'll do the left. There's a completely new half of the sky! Shapes and stars I've never seen before.'

From time to time, as they continue their journey back along the coast, Dubb looks at the sky behind them and wonders why The Delphis never slid sideways off the Earth as he would have predicted. Or worse, dropped from its edge into a cauldron of fire. No, he thinks, as they row their way home, it looks as if we could keep going around the ocean, perhaps forever. From the evidence of my eyes, there is no end to the circle of the heavens or the Earth beneath.

The Enquiry – Day 13 – Part Two

Lord Apsan's nail clacks on the delicate surface of the cylinder and breaks the silence. It has brightened outside. Sunshine slants into the upstairs room of his official residence and they are coming to an end, please, Mighty Melqart, of this enquiry.

'So that's the story of this object,' he says. Despite himself, he has stopped everything to listen to these witnesses. Duck terracottas and baby porcupines lie, unattended, beside him. How have they lived to tell this tale? That eruption. That animal! Tasii, too, has downed tools. His stylus lies beside his folded hands on the table, eyes wide in disbelief. This will never do, he thinks, and stands, noisy and abrupt, to walk about. The table wobbles. The witnesses could tell me anything now and I'd believe them. He moves his lower jaw from side to side, tight from clenching his teeth, and goes to stand directly in front of Tasii.

'Give me a quick massage' he says tersely. His slave stands, takes his master by the arm and turns him round. He stands on tip toe and presses his knuckles into his scrawny back. He moves up to his neck and across the blades. That feels good, he thinks, and catches at Tasii's hand with his chin as it reaches his collar bone. Time for a bit of an unwind. 'Adyat!' he yells from his standing position. The witnesses jump in shock. Gatit, his bodyguard, sticks his head around the door jam.

'Your lordship?'

'Get Adyat for me.' His bodyguard's heavy feet thump downstairs towards the kitchen. 'I need a drink,' he says to the room. No one is interested.

The navigator sits by the window, velums spread open on his lap. The other witnesses cluster round. The boy holds down one edge of the documents so they won't roll up, the Hellene the other. The woman's mantle twists in her hands, floppy-hair's eyes are damp and you could cut the concentration with a knife.

He shrugs Tasii off and goes to the navigator, stands over him for a moment to see if he can make out the writing on the records. He needs a proper look. Elbowing his way around, he bends forward, arms wide and snatches the whole pile from the navigator's lap.

'Please, my lord!' says the man, and slaps his hands down on the now vacant space where the documents lay. 'They're precious!'

'So you keep saying.' He lifts them high above his head to fly them across to a table on the other side of the room. With speed, Tasii shunts his stacked tablets aside as the velum, intact, make it to him without a single one sliding out of place. 'There!' he says, as they land together with a thump. 'Do you think I can't handle precious things? Look around you. Delicate objects everywhere.' His eyes float past his terracottas and on to the Egyptian amphora.

The navigator's lips are pursed, resentment in his eyes.

'Well, what's wrong with this?!' he says, and gives them a caress. 'Still dissatisfied?'

Tasii gets to work smoothing them out.

'Mi lord,' says Adyat, up from downstairs, face a dirty mess, as usual.

'Wine is what I need. And now. Lots of it. Fresh water for the witnesses. You will have a bit of a break,' he says to them. 'Please return to your benches.' They do not move. He feels expansive. They will sit down and drink. He will relax with wine. He will look over the records and, as a result, the real intentions behind the expedition will be revealed. It will all fall into place and I can halt the enquiry forthwith.

'So sit down.' He sweeps his hand towards the bench. Still, they remain in a clump around the navigator. He sighs. Not this again. 'You will have to return to the wall,' he says, slow and deliberate, 'or I will call security and I don't just mean Gatit.' Now that they are better, this group could take it into their heads to abscond with the records at any moment. Best get security in any case. 'Gatit!' His bodyguard emerges from the lintel.

'Send a runner for Shipit Eli. Bring him here to the corridor and tell him to wait outside.'

The witnesses, sullen, return to their wall.

He sits at the records and casts his eyes over the top one. He puts a finger to the velum pile and flicks through them. I can't understand a thing, he thinks, and the weight of a boulder lands on his stomach. He pulls one of them out and peers closely at it. Blobs and lines, indecipherable squiggles. 'If I need your help understanding what is written here,' he says, too brightly, 'I will call on you. You see, I am being very careful.'

He beckons to Tasii and they move the rolled records to a different table in better light. He sips at his beaker of wine. They put weights at the corners and he looks at them this way up and then, from a different position, that way around. He frowns as he examines the lines of ink on their surfaces, the splotches and water marks. At an empty page, he stops. 'What are these? Why are they empty?' he says sharply.

'Empty, my lord?' says the navigator. 'What are you talking about?' He is being as stubborn as ever.

'These pages here,' he says, and holds them up, pinched between finger and thumb, so that the man can see them across the room.

He shrugs. 'How can I tell, my lord? I can't see what they are. You wanted to examine them. So look.'

'Anyone else?' he says. 'Why are these blank?'

There is silence.

'Oh, Mighty Melqart, alright,' he explodes. 'Two of you, just two, can come up here to help me. But I want no arguments, you understand, no obfuscation.' The navigator and the boy get to their feet and join him.

'They're empty, my lord.' The navigator looks over his shoulder. 'Because, as you will see from this,' and his arm comes forward to point at a small square of writing in the corner under his elbow, 'these were days when there was no sun, no stars, nothing to report.' The man stands tall and stays ranged above him with a good dose of arrogance, 'In any case, it's no wonder you can't follow it. You have the whole stack sideways. Turn it the right way round.'

Lord Apsan feels his neck go back in shock. How dare he speak to me like this?! I am the official around here; he's a mere seaman, a man who never misses an opportunity to undermine my authority or demean me. His outrage boils. Yet I don't understand what I'm looking at and he does. So I've got to let him alone, however infuriating he becomes.

He clamps his lips closed as the man leans forward to lever his two hands under the stack.

'Qart, take that side. Put them to face his lordship.'

The boy slips in beside Tasii on the other side of the table and shunts sideways. Crablike, they manoeuvre the pile around the table. When they've done, they stand back and look at the documents, reverence on their faces.

'Well, enough of all this carefulness. I need to know what's in them,' Lord Apsan says. 'Explain them to me. The gaps go on for document after document. Why? There must have been a lot of days when there was no sun, stars or observations.'

There is a scarcely audible sigh from the man at his side. 'That is what we have been trying to say to you, my lord,' answers the navigator, voice thin. 'We did not know our location.'

'Are you telling me you spent this much time not knowing where you were?' He flicks through the empty sheets. 'It must be whole sailing seasons.' He rifles through a few more and sees short, clipped words at the top of each. Sometimes they expand to state what the navigator has seen that day. "Lightning in the afternoon", it says. "Arrived at King Oyediran", "Anchor ashore approximately four moons". At other times, there is just a day, a season and a time.

'How could you tell there were moons if you couldn't see the sky?' he demands, and peers at the man beside him.

'You see that symbol there?' the navigator says, and points to a short squiggle dashed onto the velum. 'That means "approximately" in Miletus. We don't know how you would write it in Carthage.' The man turns to gives the boy a quick look.

The boy shakes his head.

'Might I be allowed to take these records to Hekataios, my lord?' the navigator says, unexpectedly. His head is down, voice quiet.

A laugh pops out of Lord Apsan's mouth and into the room like the bark of a dog. It rattles the documents. Perhaps it's the wine. Perhaps it's because he's generally feeling better. Or even because he's finally getting somewhere with the enquiry. The navigator's tone is so pathetic, so lost. 'Oh, you and your wretched records,' he says, and chuckles. 'Anyone would think your life depended on them.'

'Someone has lost their life through them, my lord, and we nearly lost ours.' The man's voice is entirely devoid of sarcasm, arrogance or even irritation and there is a note of desolation in it.

'These observations of the sky, taken by us at great personal cost, could tell us how the world works.'

His eyebrows come down across his forehead like a plank. How the world works? He shakes his head. This is the kind of stupid speculation the Hellenes are famous for. Not satisfied with creating elaborate systems of gods, demi-gods, speaking Minotaurs and what-have-yous, they now appear to be starting on stories about the workings of the world! As if it operates independently of men. His eyes flick to the navigator's face. No, he's not being clever or snide. He is making a completely genuine statement. 'What is there to know?' he blurts. 'There's living, making money, dying and any pleasure you can get in between. That's all, isn't it?' He lifts his beaker. 'Good health.'

The navigator's hands open and close at his side. 'Perhaps not all, my lord, not everything.'

'Well, whatever your Academy in Miletus might do with this information, some merchant would pay a fortune for documents like these. They're an open invitation to squeeze through the Pillars of Herakles, as you call them, set off down the coast and take all our trade. I haven't been here protecting that waterway from the likes of you for all these decades just to hand it all over in a set of velum. So, no, you may not take these records to your Hekataios.'

Tasiioonos stirs beside him. 'May I ask a question of the witnesses, my lord?'

He inclines his head and sits back to enjoy what might happen next.

'How did you get back to the Great Sea?'

The navigator is sunk in silence; the rest look into their laps. Only the Hellene seems alive.

'Well, come on,' says Lord Apsan briskly. 'Excellent question. Are you going to answer the question or not? Someone, anyone?'

The Hellene opens his mouth and then pauses. He looks along the line of witnesses. As no one else appears to want to speak, he continues, 'We rowed mostly, close to the shore. The wind wasn't strong enough to help us. We fished, found water, rationed ourselves. We got lost. Local people helped us. Various groups crewed us, in a kind of relay.'

'Turns out there were a lot of people who lived along that coast,' says the boy.

'We'd been too far out at sea to meet them before,' says the floppy-haired man, joining in.

Tasii's hands are a miracle of motion. He scratches away at the wax. Lord Apsan's eyes flash in admiration. Such an accomplished man, my slave, he thinks.

'So what happened with the divisions on board?' says his beloved. 'Did they get worse?'

'There wasn't much division after the Horn. Things were so bad, we had no choice but to work together.'

'Most of us were sick with fever. Nyptan and Tanu saved us, didn't you?' says the Hellene, and leans forward in the line to look at them. They stir, lift their chins and say nothing.

'The main problem was the current,' he adds.

'The same current, which had whisked us away down the coast, became a major problem on the way back.'

'We lost a lot of men, through fever, exhaustion. We only ever just had enough to row.'

'The worst of it is what happened when we got back to King Oye-diran's kingdom,' says the Hellene. 'Lord Hanno and his Etruscan friends just disappeared.'

'Disappeared? What do you mean?' he intervenes. He looks sharply at the navigator, whose head is down. 'You there, Navigator. Time for you to play your part and answer questions.'

'I don't know how,' says the Hellene, carrying on.

'He might have paid the king off,' says the boy. 'With some of that gold we never saw!'

'By the time we got to Lixus,' adds the Hellene, 'Hanno had been and gone weeks before. The governor said he'd just taken his penteconters and rowed away. We got restocked there; he gave us crew men and put us in one of his regular convoys to Gadir. That's how we arrived.' The man sits back, satisfied he has told the story to the end.

'What happened to your tablets and all the raw material for these records?' asks Tasii, ever the secretary.

Good question, thinks Lord Apsan. 'You, Navigator, you must answer this one,' he says, and tries to reach the man with his foot to kick him into action.

The navigator raises his head. 'I have not seen them since Ngap. Perhaps Hanno took them? Perhaps they are lost. No one could take this from me, though,' he says, and lifts his finger to the empty cylinder, 'except you.'

Lord Apsan feels something unusual happening around the back of his neck. It is getting warm. The heat increases and rises up the back of his head. Once at the top, it drops forward, down past his eyes and into his cheeks. He puts a hand to his chin. Hot. It's shame, he thinks. I am ashamed. Of harrying these people, belittling them, scorning their evidence, doubting them. After all they have been through. He clears his throat and Tasii looks up, curious.

The navigator continues, 'I have slept on these records, hugged them, carried, protected and nursed them as if they were my own child.' He pauses and swallows. 'Now you, the official representative of one of the most powerful cities in the world, denies them to us, us who have spent more than five seasons collecting them, suffering danger and death. You, a comfortable bureaucrat living off the fat of the land here in Gadir, would humiliate us and destroy our evidence.' The man's head is rigid on his neck, back straight, mouth turned down at the corners. 'How can you live with yourself and know what you have done?'

'Perhaps we can come to an arrangement,' he says without thinking. 'Perhaps you could take a copy.' And then he feels appalled. His throat goes dry and he turns to look at Tasii, eye's wide. The Senate in Carthage would crucify me if they knew I had suggested this. He sucks hard at his bottom lip.

'…very good idea, my lord…' comes Tasii's voice through the roar of anxiety, which engulfs him. He feels dizzy. His slave's hands drop lightly onto his shoulders. He feels his body at his back, warm, his voice soft by his ear in solace. '…we have to be very quiet about it…' He puts his hands into Tasii's, feels his comfort and strength. I don't care what any of them here knows about us, he thinks. Let them speculate as they might.

The whole room lifts. It is like a tiny explosion. The navigator and the boy are on their feet. 'We can do a copy. We can do it very quickly. No one will know, except us. We can start now!'

'Shall I clear space, sir?' the woman says to Tasii. 'Might we work here?'

'Yes, go on, get on with it as fast as possible,' Lord Apsan mumbles, 'before I change my mind.' He stands up and feels compelled to walk out. 'Tasiioonos here will help you. He'll get you vellum. I do not wish to know about it. I do not wish to be involved.' At the door, he turns to face them. 'You must understand this. If I am ever asked whether or not I gave you permission to do this, I will deny it. I will say you stole them. Should this ever get out, I will give testimony which will put you to death. Do you understand?'

'One thing more, my lord, just one,' says the navigator, who rushes across the room to stand in front of him. 'Can you send a message to my master in Miletus to tell them we are safe?'

Oh, by the gods, will this never end, this man and his demands?! 'Yes, why not?' he says. 'I've already gone too far.' And he crashes through the door into their private quarters.

Tasiioonos drafts a message to be sent from Gadir, the Carthaginian outpost at one end of the Great Sea, to Hekataios of Miletus, at its other.

"Lord Apsan Azrupal Nimiran, Commissioner for Trade for the Senate in Carthage, informs you that The Delphis, navigator Dubb of Miletus, has arrived in Gadir from its voyage to the Horn of the South."

An Unwelcome Guest

Winter turns to spring. Grey skies lighten to pale lemon and life at the residence has returned to its regular routine. Lord Apsan sent off his report in time for the Senate's Spring Plenum. He has received no response to it as yet. It's been a shocking year for transport, so he hopes his runner got across the water. Strong easterlies have battered the coast; the current through the Strait of Calpe is vicious and only the urgent, brave or foolish venture out. Gargoris, the Street Cleaner, reports to him that donkey trails up into the hills are quagmires and mines have been flooded. Trade is sluggish or even stationary. Gadir's docks are rammed with vessels waiting to leave the minute the wind changes.

Downstairs, before the dregs of a fire, he and Tasii box up factory ware in preparation for sale.

'How many do the temple people want?' he asks. The Temple of Melqart at the strait is always a good place to make a killing. So the stock there has to be plentiful. Once the sailing season gets underway, amulets fly off the stalls, seamen anxious to placate the gods before they launch themselves into the unknown. Funeral ware must be available, discreetly of course, especially in a season like this one. Once the weather turns, they can concentrate on shifting the more upmarket items: the monkeys, porcupines and duck speciality wares for sale to wealthy settlements like Nora, Motya and Tharros.

'They want none,' says Tasii, voice muffled, head down in a box.

'What?' He stops his packing, a frown on his face. 'What do you mean, "none"? Come out of that box!'

'The temple wants nothing. Arish, the high priest, refuses to let us supply anything. He's decided, it seems, that we are too much competition for their factory. So their order is nil. Our figures will be down.' He pulls a face.

'How can he? What a nerve! We've been supplying sailors with spiritual comfort at his temple for years. Doesn't he make enough money from his own trade to share a bit out?'

Tasii shrugs and his head goes down into the packing case again.

'The wealth that that man accumulates by scaring the living daylights out of sailors beggars belief. I've never come across a richer temple.'

'Isn't that just what we do?' says Tasii, head up again, 'scare people?' He closes his box and heaves it towards the door. 'Make sales from people afraid they'll never get home again?'

'We do not! Relative to him, we sell very few. We don't conduct religious ceremonies designed to frighten men out of their wits and offer them amulets for sale a minute later. And anyway, our funeral jars are essential equipment. How else can you carry your dead around, get them back to Carthage to bury them, for instance or wherever. That doesn't exploit them; it helps them. And our goods offer comfort to those left behind when a man goes to his final journey. Providing high quality goods to adorn the graves of a loved one brings succour. So, no, I don't think we are the same as Arish at all.' He sticks a shipping label on the final box on his work table and stands up to stretch. 'Anyway, time for lunch.'

Since his gastric problems disappeared, with that woman's help, Lord Apsan has had the hunger of a horse. Not that he wishes to eat one, which seems to have become Tasii's approach to all ailments. The healer installed a cat in the yard, under the strictest orders from him that it was never to come anywhere near his private rooms. 'I'll wring its neck with my bare hands if it appears,' he'd said to her when she pointed out that the simplest and most hygienic route to health was to simply get an animal, which would take care of the rats. Now he was eating everything: bread, peppers, stew and even a few vegetables.

Tasii has recently been away for a couple of days. The botched message in Tartessic, and Gargoris's reports of the mining community, made him want to get back in touch with his family up in the hills after all these years. So he'd taken his life into his hands and gone up to visit them.

'Such poor circumstances they live in,' he'd said when he got back. Which made Lord Apsan happy. At least he's not going to leave me and live back home! he'd thought.

The security network up there appears to be muscular enough. Gargoris has ploughed his way through mud, flood and rain to climb the mountains, cross the ridges and establish proper connections across the trails. Wherever Hanno got to at the end of the sailing season, he'd been holed up there somewhere. Sooner or later, a red rag message will arrive at his door and the man will be discovered.

His ongoing anxiety is what the Senate will make of his conclusions about Lord Hanno. Will they take exception to the critical nature of his remarks? He did word them all carefully of course. "...not what you might expect from...", "...most unusual circumstances...", "...surprisingly no immediate evidence of treasure...".

This last could be very damaging. If the senators expected him to provide them with a financial reckoning of everything Hanno found on his voyage to the Horn of the South, they will be disappointed. Which could mean no retirement for him to Carthage. The worst possible outcome would be if Hanno's family gets vengeful for his failure to give a less than ringing endorsement to their favoured son. In which case, if the Magonid faction get their way, it could be death. He starts to bite the inside of his mouth. Should that happen, maybe Tasii will be there to pop his ashes into his Egyptian vase and weep for him a little. He does hope so. He shudders and decides not to think about it any more.

The goat and tomato tastes delicious. He is most of the way through it when he hears Gatit's voice, alarmed, at the outside door.

'I will ask if he can see you now,' he says. 'Stay there!' A moment later, his bodyguard knocks at the door. 'One of your security men is outside, your lordship. I did say you couldn't see him. He says it's urgent.'

'Who is it?' he says crossly, and wipes his hands on a cloth. 'I saw Gargoris only yesterday and the rest of them ought to be down the coast doing their job!' He pushes his stew out of the way and stands to greet the man now coming in. He has long hair, long earrings and an aristocratic look.

'I am Lord Hanno, Magonid son of Carthage,' he says. 'Am I speaking to Apsan Azrupal Nimiran?'

Lord Apsan's eyes go wide. For the first time in his life, he does not know what to say. He gulps, and stutters, 'Please, your lordship, be seated.' He shoos Tasii off the nearest chair to invite the lordling to sit down. He gulps for air, feeling as though he has been punched in the gut. 'To what do I owe the pleasure of...'

'I am here to lodge a complaint,' says the man, who remains on his feet, angry. 'You have been writing a report to the Senate about my voyage to the Horn of the South without speaking to me.'

Lord Apsan's mouth is open wide and his mind whirrs. Who told him that?! Tasii looks aghast.

'I have been travelling up country on business for many moons,' says the man. 'Now that I have returned to this hole, I did not expect to discover that the top bureaucrat of our state of Carthage, our very own Commissioner for Trade, has sent a document to Carthage without taking my evidence. I hope that you have not done it yet. If so, there will be consequences.'

'Stop a minute, your lordship, please.' His hand goes up. 'Have you eaten? Have you slept? Can I bring you warmed wine? You are cold and worn out. My slave here,' he goes on, emphasising his formal relationship with his secretary and dearest, 'will bring you the best refreshments this humble household can offer: stew, wine. Would you like to visit the bathhouse?' He can feel himself gabbling but can't seem to stop. As long as it is his voice dominating the room, he can hold back disaster. What is the man doing here? How has he just turned up like this when we have been scouring the country for months?!

Tasii swipes at some of the evidence of their domestic life on his way out the door: two beakers and two bowls. Lord Apsan sees the panic in his slave's eyes. He, himself, moves to stand in front of the open curtain. Beyond it, on the pallet, lay two pillows still indented by two heads, side by side.

Lord Hanno appears oblivious of all this. 'I want nothing other than to have my say on the matter of the Horn of the South,' he says. 'I do not wish to stay in these, your very humble headquarters, a moment longer than necessary.' He lifts his chin, disdainful. 'I certainly don't want to eat, drink or bathe here. I will set off for Carthage by land the moment I have given you my version of events and I shall pick up a vessel when the wind changes. In the unfortunate event that you have already sent your report to Carthage, then you will rescind it forthwith and send another. I will have my side of the story heard.'

'What makes you think, my lord, that my report is anything other than wholly complimentary about your part in the expedition?' he says.

What a catastrophe, he thinks. I have written an official report saying that the man has gone missing then, less than one moon later, he turns up on my own doorstep demanding to give evidence. 'Of course, I am only too happy to add your views, but there is nothing in it you need to be concerned about.'

'So, you have sent it off?' says the lordling. 'Where is it? I demand to see it.' He pounds his fist on the table.

'We don't have a copy of it, my lord,' he lies, and tries to keep his eyes from straying to the top shelf where he knows the duplicate rests. 'I can tell you its conclusions, though. Here, here's the slave with refreshment.' He looks at Tasii, who has returned with food and wine. 'Please sit and I will inform you. Thank you, slave, that will be all.' Tasii steps out of the room backwards.

'No, it is I who will do the informing. The whole of Byrsa Hill will learn of your incompetence when I get back there. We will start the process of rewriting it now. Where is your scribe? Bring him back, so he can take notes.'

And so, for the next days, he listens to Lord Hanno, Magonid son of Carthage, tell about his deeds as the heroic leader of an expedition to the Horn of the South, the settlements he founded, privations he suffered, animals he fought off and the triumph of his navigation. Even when lost, he found the way home. As trophies, he brings with him gold dust and rare animal skins, which he plans to have hung on the wall of the great temple to Ball-Hammon on Byrsa Hill.

Burning questions, which Lord Apsan cannot bring himself to ask, are "Where were you when I was searching for you all that time?" and "Where is the gold hidden?"

On a Hillside

It is a yellow and blue spring day. Mimosas cast their golden blossom across the hillside and the sun is warm on her back. Nyptan and Tanu sit on a large, flat rock overlooking the iridescent expanse of water, which is the Pillars of Herakles. Or Strait of Calpe, as I have learned to call it, thinks Nyptan, and she picks up a large sprig of rosemary and puts it to her nose. The huge base of Herakles's boot is clear in the distance on this side. On the other, a mound of grey marks the landscape. Ethiope, she thinks, land of sorrow.

'Much as I learnt while we were away, it's so very good to be home, isn't it, darling?' she says, and cups her hands around a frond of lavender. 'Or nearly home.' Tanu nods, a string in her mouth, which she uses to tie up a small, hessian bag. Nyptan leans across and holds the herb out for her daughter to smell. 'Hmmm. Don't you just love to go to sleep to this!'

On the slab between them lies a collection of grasses, berries, bark, beetles and grubs. Stacked to one side are vials, containers and beakers. She feels more cheerful than she has for many months. My insides, if not the rest of me, have healed after the baby's birth. I have food in my belly, my skin is clean from fresh water, we have new tunics, mantles without holes and my hair is braided. She puts her hand out to feel the thick plait, which runs around her head like a crown.

Up the hill, the men are at the fire and the grog. A snatch of one of their endless rounds rolls down the incline on the breeze.

'I dream of a girl with golden hair, golden hair, golden hair. Her eyes were fine and her face was fair...' Most of them are out of tune.

'Oh, that song!' says Tanu, finished with her tying, and she shoves the sack aside and looks around, exasperated. 'I'm so sick of it! Why this golden-haired girl, anyway? She must look very peculiar.'

Nyptan laughs. 'Yes, pale. Very pale.'

'Hey, you two. Food is on the way.' It is Dubb's voice and he strides down the hill towards them, a big smile on his face. He is a happy man, my husband, thinks Nyptan, and she can feel her face glow. At last, at last, you are smiling on us, Lady Gula, and she nudges at her breasts to feel Great Laughing Dog snug between them. Thank you for this moment, this day.

'The new crew are set and ready, The Delphis loaded,' he says, and plonks himself between them and examines their haul of medicaments. 'The men are mostly from here, waiting to get back home. Only one day to wait before the sailing season begins!' He raises both his hands in the air in celebration. 'Hurray!'

His hair is still short, though growing out, his body leaner, eyes more deeply set. Yet he is still the man for me, she thinks, and whisks the rosemary under his nose. Especially after Ethiope.

He rolls his eyes. 'Hmmmmm, that's good.'

'When will we set out?' says Tanu? 'Do we have to wait for a tide?'

'No tides in this part of the world, dear one,' says Dubb, and gives her arm a light cuff. 'The sailing is all different from now till we get through those waters outside Miletus. We do, of course, need to wait for wind. So we could leave tomorrow, or the next day, or the day after that.' He laughs.

'We have presents for the men. For our men, I mean really,' says Nyptan with emphasis. 'We'd like to give them out sometime today before everything gets too raucous. Is that possible?'

'I don't see why not. Shall I get them now? It'd be a good time, before lunch. I can't promise anything for what will happen after that.'

Chares leads the way. He is half the weight of his former self, his head completely bald, face lined. The expression on it, as ever, is consistent, kind, calm, precise, totally trustworthy. Berek and Qart are next, the musician's ankle scarred but otherwise healed, Qart with a small set of drums from Kama slung around his shoulders. Dubb comes last.

He carries an amphora and drinking bowl, and places them on the rock amongst the herbs. They settle down.

'Time for a little celebration of our own.' Dubb begins to pour the wine. 'We have survived, survived against the greatest of odds and will soon be home. May Great Melqart show us his face; may he stand upright! And all eyes are on Kochab, our guiding star,' he declaims, slurps, and passes the beaker on.

When everyone has had their say, and the beaker arrives back at Nyptan, she gives a nod to Tanu. Her daughter lifts the hessian bag from her side and starts to untie the string.

'Tanu and I have decided that, to mark the end of our voyage to the Horn of the South and the beginning of our last leg home, we would like to give each of you a present to celebrate the occasion.'

Tanu pulls the first tiny object from the bag and hands it to Nyptan.

'This is for you, Chares. The marks on it represent constancy and love.' She hands him a terracotta bead with brightly coloured shapes embossed round it.

'There's a leather string here somewhere,' Tanu adds, and rummages in the bag. 'Please, wear it however you like: your neck, your wrist, wherever. We have feathers here too.'

The man is taken back, surprised. 'Thank you, Nyptan. I don't know what to say.'

'This one for you, Berek, with a twig attached that looks like an aulis,' says Nyptan, and passes it to the musician.

'If you say so,' he says, and squints at the shape through one eye. He grins and gives a little bow. 'Thank you.'

'And now there's this one' says Tanu, and looks at her, enquiringly. 'Shall I do it?'

She nods and her daughter fishes in the bag and places a red and blue bead at the centre of the rock. It is emblazoned with barnacle-like shapes on the side and raised dots to embellish.

'This one is for Rabs,' says Nyptan, and looks down at it, bright and cheerful on the granite. 'Our dear departed friend.' The men around her go silent. 'Come now. Don't be afraid. Who shall I give it to? You, Chares? You, Qart?' No one replies. 'Qart, wouldn't you like Rabs's amulet? You can wear it, or hang it on The Delphis or whatever you like.'

She looks at Tanu and raises her brows. He daughter gives her head a little shake. 'There's one for everyone, so no need to take it if you don't want to. Here, Dubb, this is yours. And this one's for you, Qart.' They arrange more beads on the stone.

Qart puts out his hand. 'I'll have it,' he says and takes the one for Rabs. The look on his face is obscured by the light behind his head. 'Thank you.'

The very last token to come out of the bag is a tiny one. It is bright green and gold, no bigger than the tip of her finger. It sits in her palm like a tiny sea snail. On it, you can make out curly hair, eyes, a nose and mouth.

'And this one, this little one, is for our baby,' says Nyptan, 'may Lady Gula protect and guard him.' She turns to Dubb at her side, and smiles.

'This one's mine,' says Dubb, and he snatches it up to add to the one already tied around his wrist. 'I will remember him; I will carry him.'

'We all will,' says Chares.

Dubb raises the bowl high above his head. 'To the departed.'

'To the departed,' they respond, sombre, and the wine goes slowly round the circle again.

* * *

The red and blue amulet is in Qart's hand as he steps down through the rocks on the hillside to get away from everyone for a minute and think. He crushes wildflowers as he walks. There is a gap in the pit of his stomach, a Rabs-sized hole, which this amulet will do nothing to fill. Yet it has cracked open his sorrow again when he thought he had sealed it all up. He brushes through box brush and rosemary to find a place out of sight of the others, and throws himself down on the turf. He lifts the bead to his lips. You, my dear friend, how you would have loved to be here today. How much I want you here today. He rolls the barnacle shape around between his thumb and forefinger and wonders at the bright colours. 'You go this way and I'll go that,' Rabs had said the day before he was broken by the animal. Qart shapes his mouth into a whistle and lets out a single, long, low call with a swoop at the end. Heat rises from the hillside beside him. He whistles again, following it with three short blasts. 'I want to know where you are,' he whispers. 'Come back.' All he hears in response are the curlews, a breeze and distant singing. Tears roll down his cheeks into his tunic.

Dubb's hand is on his shoulder then, his master right at his side. 'Here, let me put it on for you,' says the navigator, and sits down beside him to tie the amulet around his wrist. 'Rabs is with us in spirit, you know,' says Dubb, and lifts the edge of his mantle to dry the boy's eyes. 'Rabs and our baby, they are both with us in spirit.' He lifts his wrists to show off the tiny blue and gold one attached to his larger one, linked by a feather.

The crew of The Delphis stay on the hillside late into the day, eating, singing, drinking. Back-to-back, they lean on each other and watch as the sun drops down into River Ocean and the blazing heavens appear.

Historical Note

The story of Hanno, the Navigator, is found in fragments of Greek manuscripts scattered in libraries and monasteries across Europe. If you group these remnants together, they tell the tale of an extraordinary voyage which, it is claimed, took Hanno from Carthage, out through the Straits of Gibraltar and down the coast of West Africa. Exactly how far south the expedition went is a matter of much speculation, as is its date. If true, it is the first recorded contact between Europe and West Africa over two thousand years before the Portuguese showed up there in 1400 CE.

Hanno himself, they say, led the Carthaginian expedition. He was a merchant prince of the city state at a time when it far surpassed the commercial power and maritime reach of ancient Greece. The Roman Republic would be founded hundreds of years in the future. Christ and Muhammed were still to come.

The accounts say that the prince recorded his exploits by carving them onto the walls of the great temple to Baal Hammon on Byrsa Hill, the city's aristocratic, religious and administrative centre. There they stayed until the place was utterly destroyed by Rome in 146 BCE.

The veracity of the voyage must have seemed incredible to people even at the time because Hanno accompanied his written testimony with extra proof. Near to his carving, he had animal skins hammered onto the temple walls. He had brought them, he said, from a place at the farthest reaches of the known world, a place he called the Horn of the South. Greek records say that these skins, too, remained in place until ancient Carthage was destroyed by Rome. The authenticity of the skins is in doubt. The animals, so the translations say, were called "gorillas", the first time the species was heard of in Europe, also many thousands of years before modern times.

In *By the Horn of the South,* I have chosen to believe such an extraordinary voyage took place, though I have expanded its historical context to include the wider spirit of enquiry which was taking place across the eastern Mediterranean around then. Setting it, as I do, at the end of the sixth century BCE, enables me to explore the Miletian philosophers' first steps towards establishing what we know today as "scientific method", that is, applying observation to natural phenomenon rather than ascribing them to the gods, demi-gods or other forces from a spirit world.

Even so, my work is primarily an adventure story. How might it have been possible for sailors and their vessels to ride the wind and strong currents, negotiate unknown cultures and strange animals, survive volcano and privation, lose their way and still return home to tell the tale?

Another book of mine, featuring the same characters, describes a voyage taken a few years earlier. It is to a place which was not so geographically remote though, I would argue, just as dangerous and frightening. It is called *By the Pillars of Herakles.*